DAUGHTER OF DOOM

Daughter of Doom

By **JEAN-CLAUDE VAN RIJCKEGHEM**

Translated from the Dutch by
KRISTEN GEHRMAN

LQ
LEVINE QUERIDO

MONTCLAIR | AMSTERDAM | HOBOKEN

This is an Em Querido Book
Published by Levine Querido

LQ
LEVINE QUERIDO

www.levinequerido.com • info@levinequerido.com

Levine Querido is distributed by Chronicle Books, LLC

Originally published as *Onheilsdochter* by Querido
Text copyright © 2022 by Jean-Claude van Rijckeghem
Translation copyright © 2025 by Kristen Gehrman

All rights reserved.
Library of Congress Control Number: 2024942371
ISBN 978-1-64614-503-4
Printed and bound in China

Published in June 2025
First Printing

The publisher gratefully acknowledges the support of the
Dutch Foundation for Literature.

Nederlands letterenfonds
dutch foundation
for literature

For Willy,
who set me on the trail of our Danish ancestors.

*For the Vikings, who you proved yourself to be,
rather than your outward shell,
really does seem to have counted for something.
We all have a hamr, a shape, but it is the hugr,
the mind or soul, that counts more.*

—Neil Price, Children of Ash and Elm: A History of the Vikings

PART 1

MIMIR'S STOOL

1

"BEHOLD, JORMUNDGANDR!" Kveldulf the Norwegian roars. The old man wields the wooden head in front of the boys as if he had chopped it off the sea monster himself. Its maw is open, and its neck is covered with scales. This must be what he looks like—the great Jormundgandr, a sea serpent so long he can wrap his body around the entire flat world and hold it together by biting the end of his tail.

"When the Parisians saw this head on the bow of our ship, they shook like rabbits," Kveldulf declares. That was more than thirty years ago, back when Kveldulf had hardly any fuzz on his chin, just like the boys he's training today. The aspiring warriors stare at the monster's head with bored looks on their faces. They've seen the grimy, mossy thing before. The wood is full of wormholes, a tooth is missing, and the right eye is nothing but a dark hole. That head's not going to scare anybody these days.

"Whoever has the monster's head in their possession at sunset will be a prince of the solstice!" Kveldulf roars.

Now that gets the boys' attention. They shout and beat

their willow shields with sticks. Every one of them wants to be a prince of the solstice. They team up in groups of two or three and accept the challenge: to not only find the wooden head but also keep the others from running off with it. They are allowed to use whatever means necessary to claim their prize, and tonight the mothers will be there to lay cold cloths on their bruises and rub their wounds with honey. The winners will be bursting with pride, for when their fathers return at the end of the summer, they will see the monster's head hanging over their house from the sea.

The sun has passed its highest point when Kveldulf walks onto the beach with the wooden head under his arm. Then, the boys watch their spear master disappear into the dunes to hide it. He's gone for what seems like an eternity. The boys fidget nervously with the hammers of Thor that hang from the leather cords around their necks. Eventually, some sit down; others sprawl out in the sand. After a while, they start bickering. Finally, the old Norwegian returns from the dunes and the boys gather their sticks and shields. The time has come. This is their first chance to make a name for themselves—to show that they have what it takes to be a warrior.

Kveldulf blows the goat's horn, and the boys race across the wide beach toward the dunes. Their shrieks are louder than the gulls'. Before they even reach the dunes, they're yanking at one another's clothes, tripping their opponents, and tackling each other to the ground. Troels is the first victim of the day. He trips over his own weapon—a long stick with the name Wolf Tooth carved into it—and falls face-first into the wet sand. He stands up, pulls the stick from his belt, and tosses it away. Then he walks off the beach, his pants soaking wet. Meanwhile, the other boys have disappeared into the dunes. Troels hears sticks clattering and boys shouting, but he doesn't look back. His younger brother, Little Sten, runs over to find out what's wrong. They are going to capture the head of the sea serpent together, aren't they?

"I crushed my shoulder," Troels wails dramatically.

"We're not giving up, are we?" cries Sten. He's only eight, and he's so disappointed that his eyes glisten with tears.

But if there is one person in Mimir's Stool who is not cut out to be a warrior, it's Troels. Like the other boys, he follows Kveldulf's warrior lessons on Wednesdays. The old Norwegian often selects two boys to pick teams. Troels is always chosen last. No one wants him on their team. Troels is a pretty big guy, but he's clumsy and as nearsighted as a chicken. On more than one occasion, he has mistaken one of his teammates for an enemy and given him a blow to the head. The name Troels means "Thor's spear," but the day Troels actually hits a doe with a spear is the day that lobsters grow wings. Troels is fifteen and already knows that his father, Toke the Helmsman, has his doubts about taking him to sea next summer. *You wouldn't scare a seagull*, Toke has said to him. But if Troels captures the head of the sea serpent today, things will be different. His father will be proud. He'll give him a piece of chopped silver and most certainly take him on an adventure next summer.

"What are we going to do, brother?" Little Sten demands impatiently.

Without a word, Troels walks toward the shipyard. Sten chases after him, waving a stick to scare off imaginary attackers. Down at the shipyard, they run into their sister, Yrsa, in the boathouse. She and three other women are stitching a sail.

"So, Troelsie, you got the head yet?" Yrsa asks without looking up.

"I have a plan," he says mysteriously.

"You always have a plan," Yrsa replies as she ties a knot in the wool.

"Come with me to father's tree," he says.

"Why would I want to go there?" she asks.

"I'll give you a coin if you come, sister."

Finally, she looks up at him.

"Your dirham, you mean?" she asks.

Troels can spend hours looking at the Arabic characters engraved into the silver coin. They're all so enchanting, as if they were made by elves. He would hate to part with it, but still, he nods. The sea monster's head is worth more to him than that coin.

The sun is low in the sky when Yrsa enters the forest and finds her brothers sitting in the shade of the giant, sacred tree that doesn't lose its leaves in winter. Sunlight seeps through the thick foliage and dances around the boys.

"What are you two lobster-heads up to?" Yrsa asks.

"Finally, you're here. It's about time. It's almost sunset!" Troels grumbles.

Little Sten takes hold of his big sister's hand and gives it a squeeze. He feels safe with her. She used to comfort him when he was afraid of the dark or the older boys.

Troels has never been completely comfortable with his sister. She's a scrappy fighter and has wrestled him to the ground more than once.

"So tell me, hero, why did I have to come out here?"

"Because I'm going to be a prince of the solstice," Troels says with exaggerated confidence, as if Thor had lent him his hammer himself.

"What?"

"See that big, gray thing high up in the tree, sister? That's a bees' nest!"

Troels points to the top of the tree, but, being as nearsighted as he is, he has no idea where the nest actually is.

"I saw it first," Sten exclaims.

"So, here's what we're going to do: we're going to climb the tree, remove the nest, and put it in this bag," says Troels as he holds up the oldest, crustiest leather bag Yrsa has ever seen.

"Then we sneak into the dunes where Njall and his cousins are hiding with the snake head," Sten shouts with enthusiasm. Njall and his cousins are the top dogs of the warriors-in-training. Yrsa isn't the least bit surprised that they already captured the monster's head.

"We toss the bag with the bees' nest down in front of them," says Troels. "They'll panic and scatter. Then we snatch the wooden head, run away, and hide until sundown. After dark, we'll reappear and be princes of the solstice."

Sten points up and says, "You can see the nest pretty good from here."

Yrsa can just barely make out the bulbous gray form hidden in the leaves, way up at the top of the tree. Her neck hurts from looking up.

"I tried to climb up there myself," Sten says. "But I couldn't do it. I'm too little. My arms are too short."

Yrsa can't believe her ears.

"You could've broken your neck!" she exclaims. "The dumbest squirrel in the forest wouldn't try to climb all the way up there."

"Come on, you're exaggerating," Troels says. He stands next to Yrsa and Sten and looks up, as if he's hoping that the power of their collective stare will be enough to bring down the nest.

"What about you?" Yrsa asks Troels.

"I crushed my shoulder this morning. One of the boys rammed into me, and I fell down on it hard," Troels says indignantly, as if he can't believe that Yrsa would dare to ask him such a question.

"You're a real nincompoop, you know that?" Yrsa sneers.

"He'll give you his dirham if you climb the tree," Sten reminds her.

"Is this what I left my work for? I'm going back!" Yrsa turns and walks away.

"You'll be a princess of the solstice," Troels shouts after her.

Yrsa shrugs. "That competition is for boys, and they need me in the boathouse."

"Right, because otherwise all the sails will fall apart," Troels scoffs.

Yrsa whips around. She wants to whack Troels right in his crushed shoulder. But her brother is already backing away. Troels grins because he knows that Yrsa isn't quick enough to catch him. She was born with a crooked foot and walks with a limp.

"Come on, sis, help us," Sten begs. "Or would you rather see Njall become a prince of the solstice?"

"What do I care?" Yrsa retorts.

"The head will bring us glory," says Little Sten.

"And I might be able to go with Father to sea," Troels adds.

Yrsa looks up at the tree again. Its height is dizzying. But Sten isn't wrong. It would bring them glory. The head would command respect. It would make an impression. It would show the world that luck is on their side and the gods are looking down on them with favor. Yrsa thinks of her boyfriend, Nokki. The two of them were kissing in the dunes just a few weeks ago. Now he's with the men at sea, and it'll be months before he is back in Mimir's Stool. She can already imagine it: him asking her if she was the one who helped Sten and Troels capture the head. The mere thought of it makes her warm inside.

"Fine," Yrsa says. "I'll do it."

Sten and Troels are already celebrating their victory. They're going to be princes of the solstice, kings of Mimir's Stool. They slap each other on the shoulder.

Yrsa lays her hand on the trunk of the old tree. She

knows it well. She's been leaving streaks of butter on it for years as an offering for the elf, so that the álfar would protect her village.

"Make sure you don't fall," says Troels. "Father would chop our heads off."

"That'll hardly make a difference in your case," Yrsa snorts.

Sten hands her the old bag. It's made of seal leather. There is a hole in the bottom the size of a fist.

"Is this really the best bag you could find, Troelsie?"

"Don't worry, sis. It's not like the nest is going to fall out."

"But the bees will," Yrsa snaps.

"Stop complaining; it'll be fine," Troels says.

Yrsa puts her good foot on a branch and pushes herself up the tree. She has to be careful on her bad foot. The muscles are stiff, and it hurts to put weight on it for long. But fortunately, the tree is old and gnarled, with plenty of knots to hold on to. Her arms are long enough to pull herself up, and her legs are strong enough to clamp around the branches. The leaves rustle all around her. As she gets closer to the top, the bees start buzzing around her. They're big and fat, and surprised to see a girl so high up in their tree. She glances down, but quickly realizes she shouldn't. She's so high that the boys look like mice standing among the moss and roots below. If she were to fall now, she would break every bone in her body on those roots. The hairs on the back of her neck stand up. *No*, she thinks. *I have to have faith in the tree elf. He won't let me fall.* She climbs until she feels the cold wind on her back and the smell of the sea tickles her nose. She's never seen her village from high up before: five houses in a circle, the oblong structures like stranded ships turned upside down. Their round, thatched roofs rest on beams, and the sides are made of clay, peat, and wood. The outer walls are whitewashed, and they shine like silver in the twilight. She holds two fingers out in front of her eyes, and the houses disappear behind them. How strange it is to think that her whole village can fit behind two fingers. She pulls herself up to the nest. It's darker than it looked from the ground and humming like a wild animal. Bees crawl in and out of its cavity. She touches the side of it with her palm. It feels warm and pulses gently, as if it were the beating heart of the tree. The bees dance before her eyes in a swarm of black and yellow. Their legs wiggle beneath their bodies. It's now or never. She slides her wrist through the strap on the leather bag and opens it. She grabs hold of a thick branch; she can't quite wrap her fingers around it, but she has just enough grip to stay steady. This should work. She nudges the nest with her bad foot, and she can feel the heat of it through her shoe. Ever so slowly, it lets go of the trunk, moaning and creaking. A few bees clamber out. Then, suddenly, it breaks away completely, leaving behind a streak of honey. A second later it falls into the open leather sack with a thud. The sudden weight in the bag causes Yrsa to lose her balance. Her hand slips off the branch and she slams into the trunk.

The blow knocks the air out of her lungs. She clamps her arms around the trunk to keep herself from falling. Her fingers cling to the bark; she even tries to bite it with her teeth, pressing all her weight into the trunk of the tree. But her feet can't catch their grip. *Don't let me fall, tree elf, don't let me fall. Come on, I've brought you an offering every day. If you let me fall, there'll be no more of that. No more bread crumbs, no more smears of fat, no more chicken blood.* She scrapes along the bark with her good foot in search of a knot. Maybe—the thought flashes through her mind—she was wrong to disturb the bees in the first place. Why on earth did she listen to Troels? He can't even carve the runes. Why didn't she just go back to the boathouse? How could she have been so stupid? But right now, she has to remain calm, as calm as a flatfish in the sand. She inches her fingers down—slowly, little by little. She feels the pins in her work dress scrape against the bark. A sharp branch stabs her in the gut. She feels the nail on her left index finger tear off as she clings to a tiny crevice in the trunk. She bites her lip against the pain. *Don't let me fall!* Finally, her left foot lands on a branch. She lowers herself a little more, and she's got it! A good, thick, strong branch. She's saved. For a moment, she can breathe again. She even smiles. Wait until Nokki hears about this!

But then come the bees.

The first one buzzes in front of her eyes. Then it rams into her forehead as if it believes that its own head is harder than hers. She swats it away, but then she sees more bees flying out of the hole at the bottom of the bag. She can feel them creeping up her bare calves. Any second now, her entire backside will be covered with bee stings. Suddenly, somebody screams. She looks down and sees Troels running away. There, standing in front of Little Sten, are Njall and his two cousins. Njall parades his spear and shield as if he were the grandson of Odin himself. His cousin Birger has the body of a bear and the brain of a clam. His other cousin, Egill, is tall and gangly. He squints his eyes into white slits, trying to look as crafty as thirty foxes combined. Sten, who's small but brave, holds his stick and shield at the ready, but as the three boys move closer he drops everything. He tries to climb the tree, but Birger pulls him down by his shirt and hurls him against the ground. Then he places his foot between Sten's shoulder blades and presses him down into the sand.

"Stop flailing or I'll have to hurt you," Birger threatens as he presses all his weight onto Sten's spine. The little boy groans.

Egill sets the sea monster's head down in the grass and sits on it. He chews on a piece of straw as if the sun's already down and he's enjoying his new title.

Njall leans back and shouts up the tree, "How's it going up there, Yrsa?"

Yrsa doesn't respond. The bees are nestling in her hair. One of them is perched on her eyelid. She swats it away and almost loses her balance. Then she feels a sting. Then another one. And another one. She hears Njall laughing. When she feels a bee crawling up her nose, she lets out a wail and tosses the bag away. The entire nest rolls out. It slides down a branch and slips through the dark green foliage. Njall roars with laughter as the buzzing nest sails through the air in a wide arc and lands with a dull thud right on Birger's head.

But his laughter doesn't last long. He can't believe his eyes. The nest is stuck on Birger's head like a helmet.

Everyone falls silent. Then Birger lets out a scream so loud that it must have been heard in Odin's palace on Asgard. The boy staggers backward and rips the gray mass off his head like a wild man, trying to wipe away the honeycombs. His hands turn yellow and sticky. He can't get the combs off his fingers. He runs toward the beach followed by a swarm of bees. Njall can't seem to figure out what's just happened. Egill just stands there with his mouth hanging open as Birger howls his way to the sea. Neither Njall nor Egill runs after him to help.

Njall's eyes search for Yrsa among the leaves, but she has no intention of coming down from the tree. Not before sunset at least. The tree elf is taking care of her. So far, he hasn't let her down. She'll bring him extra offerings for a month. A herring on a skewer, even.

"You did that on purpose!" Njall shouts.

"You bet I did!" Yrsa hollers back. "And if you don't shut up, I'll throw a nest on your head too."

Njall spits on the ground. "Why don't you come down here?"

Sten, meanwhile, has stumbled to his feet and is trying to get away.

"Behind you, Njall," Egill cries.

Njall catches up to the boy and trips him. Then he kicks Sten in the belly and again between his legs. One. Two. Three kicks.

"Stop it!" Yrsa yells.

Sten is just lying there curled up in the grass. He can barely move, he's so stunned by the pain.

"Then come down here, cripple," Njall roars. His voice cracks with anger.

Yrsa clambers down the tree, carefully lowering herself from one branch to the next. She doesn't dare jump. She could break her good foot, and then she'd never be able to lean on it again. As soon as she hits the ground, Njall shoves her against the tree. Yrsa yanks at his long hair with all her might, and Njall grabs her by the throat.

"Let go," he sputters.

Yrsa lets go of his hair. Njall's fingers slacken around her throat, but he keeps her clamped against the tree. His breath stinks of beer. Then, he licks her face.

"You like that, cripple?" he asks.

She pounds at his arms, but he's not deterred. He's as strong as the surf.

"I can do whatever I want with you. You're nothing but the daughter of a slave."

"My mother was not a slave," Yrsa says.

Njall squeezes her breasts.

"Get your hands off me! I'll tell Nokki," she cries. "He'll beat you to a pulp."

Yrsa could've kicked herself. Why can't she keep her big mouth shut? No one knows that she and Nokki are together.

"Why would you go whining to my brother?" Njall demands.

She doesn't answer. He pulls up her dress and slides his hand down her thigh.

"You know," he says, "We should get to know each other

better. You're going to be married off soon, and you should have a little experience first."

"I'd rather kiss a seal," Yrsa hisses.

Just then, Njall feels a sting in his cheek. He flinches and takes a step back. A few bees are buzzing around his head. He swats at them, trying to shield his eyes. Yrsa could run away. Now's her chance. She could just let it drop, and go back to the boathouse to tie knots in the new sail. That would be the smart thing to do. But she's furious. Njall kicked her little brother in the groin. And he had his filthy hands all over her. She's hot with rage. Soon, Njall is no longer paying any attention to her. He's too busy swatting away the bees. It's now or never. With a raucous cry, she pounces on him before he even knows what's happening. Njall falls backward with Yrsa on top of him, crushing the air out of his lungs. She rams her elbow into his chest. Before he can grab her, she rolls off him and jumps to her feet so fast that she almost falls over. Then, she moves toward Sten.

"Come on. Get up!"

She pulls her brother off the ground. He cries.

"We're done here, Njall," Egill says, taking the mossy snake's head under his arm.

Njall whimpers, his face contorted with pain as he struggles to his feet.

"Yrsa!" a voice calls behind them.

Troels comes running up to the tree, followed by Kveldulf. The old Norwegian gasps as he struggles to catch his breath. His necklace of wolf claws clatters.

"Snitch," Egill snarls at Troels.

"I'm not done with you, cripple," Njall hisses. "I'll drag you out to sea and push you underwater, you'll see."

Yrsa feels her hatred for Njall surge like the wind in a storm. "You have no honor, Njall son of Naefr. If you ever enter Odin's Hall, it'll be as nothing more than a piece of shit that fell out of a wild boar's ass."

Njall is shocked by the weight of the insult. Even Kveldulf the Norwegian is stunned, and so are her two numbskull brothers. Egill just stands there chuckling like a two-headed troll. Njall is furious.

Even Yrsa is startled by her own words. Her cheeks turn red as fire.

"Apologize," Kveldulf commands.

"Why should I?" says Yrsa.

The old Norwegian is still trying to catch his breath.

"Apologize, girl. Take back the insult. Words like that bring nothing but misery."

Yrsa says nothing. Njall can apologize first for grabbing her breasts, licking her face, and running his hand down her thigh. The storm still rages in her body. She can't remember ever being this furious.

"Girl, are you deaf or just foolish?" Kveldulf roars. She flinches at the booming sound of his voice, the spit spewing from his lips, the scars writhing across his face like snakes. For a moment, she hesitates. If she doesn't apologize, everyone in the village will hear how she attacked Njall's honor—how she gutted him from the inside out with her tongue. A good Danish girl doesn't do that, especially to the captain's son. Blood demands blood.

"I can't hear you, slave daughter," Njall sneers triumphantly. At that, she stiffens.

"Bite your tongue, boy," the spear master barks.

Kveldulf has explained to the boys during their training that they mustn't listen to their blood, that anger will make their heads spin. The boys all nodded, but of course they didn't listen.

Njall's face goes as pale as worm on a fishhook. His shoulder is turned inward. Yrsa is pretty sure she broke one of his ribs. He's no warrior, just a braggart with a stick. What's he going to do with that practice spear of his? Does that mollusk brain think he's going to hurt her? Her father is the helmsman of Mimir's Stool, a hero with silver armbands. Njall is all bark and no bite. The thought makes her eyes twinkle.

No, Yrsa thinks. She's not going to apologize.

"What are you waiting for, cripple?" Njall barks.

Yrsa turns to Njall. Slowly. Very slowly, like a ship on a choppy sea. She pronounces her words as if they were made of gold, each one carefully weighed on a scale. "Njall son of Naefr, prince of the solstice, I promise to ask you for forgiveness."

Njall lowers his spear a little. Kveldulf looks relieved.

"I will ask you for forgiveness," Yrsa continues, "on the day the crabs walk straight and the geese carve the runes."

Njall can't believe his ears.

At that, Yrsa turns to her brothers. "Come on, lobster-heads, we're going home."

Njall is at a total loss for words. He glances at Kveldulf.

Why doesn't the old man say anything? Is he going to let this girl piss on his honor like that?

But Kveldulf sits down. He's getting too old for midsummer's day. Let the youngsters run and shout, he thinks. They'll never heed his advice. He might as well teach the seagulls to do tricks.

Yrsa's bad foot is hurting from the climb and the scuffle. For a moment, she thinks of leaning on Troels's shoulder but decides not to. She will not appear weak while Njall can still see her. She hobbles back to the village, followed by her brothers. If anyone has made a name for themselves today, it's her. Wait until Nokki hears about this. He'll beam with pride, she's sure of it. The thought makes her smile. She feels the warmth of the last sunlight on her cheeks as a red evening glow settles over the horizon.

2

IN LATE MARCH, three months before the bees' nest incident, Yrsa's life took a strange turn. In the course of one rainy day, she became engaged to the jeweler's son and had her first kiss with her cousin Nokki.

The jeweler and his son Ljufr had ridden on horseback to Mimir's Stool at the invitation of Yrsa's grandmother, Gudrun. The steam rose from their shoulders as they burst into the front room of the house. They removed their dripping cloaks and sat down on a couple of small stools. Gudrun laid a plank across two wooden trestles to make a table and handed them each a cup of hot fish soup. Yrsa stood in the light of the doorway so the men could get a good look at her. Right away, she could tell that Ljufr wasn't pleased with what he saw. He sat there gawking at her crooked shoulders and bad foot. His face looked like it was about to implode.

"Look how beautiful my granddaughter is in that dress!" Grandma Gudrun exclaimed. She didn't seem to notice the boy's disappointment.

Yrsa wore a purple dress with gold embroidery that was

usually buried at the bottom of her trunk; she only wore it during the winter festivities. She had twisted her reddish-brown hair into two braids, and hanging from her neck was a leather cord with nine orange beads and a bronze amulet with the goddess Frigg etched into it. But the young man wasn't interested in her dress, necklace, or braids. His eyes were glued to her foot. Yrsa had already snuck a look at him as he climbed off his horse and was greeted by Grandma Gudrun and the other people in the village. "He looks like a troll," Troels said. "Thick eyes, little chin, big forehead. He really suits you." Yrsa tried to slap him, but he ducked out of the way.

Gudrun told her not to be nervous about the engagement. Eligible young women from good Danish families were hard to come by these days, and Yrsa was the daughter of a respectable Danish seafarer.

"Yrsa daughter of Toke is an excellent match for your son," Gudrun told the jeweler. "I take it you know of her father's reputation?"

The jeweler nodded, but Yrsa saw the disappointment in his eyes. The man scratched his beard as if he were seriously considering her as a bride for his son. Gudrun poured him some mead, and he thanked her with a polite nod.

Yrsa's grandmother had a distinguished air about her. The gold pins in her white hair and the bands on her wrists testified to the importance of the men in her life, but also to her own adventurous existence. She was old—at least fifty winters—and had a crooked back, bony hands, and sunken cheeks. She spoke in a soft, almost fragile tone. Sten said there were cracks in her voice.

"They can marry after the winter, on a beautiful Thursday," Gudrun said, "so that they may enjoy Thor's protection."

"Did your granddaughter break her foot in an accident or was she born that way?" the jeweler asked, staring deep into his cup as if the mead interested him more than the answer to the question.

"I was born this way, sir," Yrsa said before her grandmother could answer.

Yrsa could tell her grandmother was annoyed. Gudrun would've most certainly lied and claimed that Yrsa had fallen from a tree as a child and that her bones hadn't healed properly. But she didn't want her grandmother leading Ljufr and his father on. The boy would never forgive her if he found out. For the record, Yrsa didn't think Ljufr looked like a troll at all. He had thick, long dark hair and one of his teeth was black. Enough to get by, she thought. If she had to get married by the end of summer, maybe he wasn't such a bad choice.

"With all due respect, Gudrun," the jeweler said, "if your granddaughter has children, there is a very good chance they will also come out of her belly crippled. And what if she has a boy? With a twisted foot like hers, he may never make it on a ship. A limp like that is surely a bad omen."

The room fell quiet. Yrsa looked at the ground.

"You must understand, Gudrun," the man continued. "How can I promise my son, who will one day take over my successful business in Odin's Hill, to a woman with a bad foot? He can't even dance with her around a tree. No matter how much gold and amber he gives her, she will always be crooked."

Ljufr flashed his black tooth in Yrsa's direction. The smile held nothing but disdain, and the message was clear: *If you think I'm going to marry you, crippled girl from the coast, then you're as foolish as the giants in Jotunnheim. I'm going to marry a beautiful woman with two straight legs, not some lame, hobbling creature like you.*

Yrsa clenched her fists in fury.

"Yrsa is a sailmaker. She's sturdy and fertile," Gudrun said in a soft voice, so soft that the jeweler and his son had to lean in to hear her.

"She will bear healthy children. She will bring honor to your son. You have my word that I won't make a fuss about the bride price," Gudrun said. "The wool of fifty sheep will do."

Yrsa knew that the wool of fifty sheep was quite a lot, but the jeweler didn't flinch. He just shook his head.

"You should have told me about this girl's unfortunate foot," the man said. "It would have spared us the trip. You know, Gudrun, people come from all over Denmark to visit my gold smithy."

"Our gold smithy, Father," his son corrected.

Yrsa had heard enough. She didn't want to move inland anyway, she thought. She wanted to stay in her village on the bay. And she certainly wasn't about to share a bed with some snooty jeweler's son in the soggy marshes around Odin's Hill.

"I'll have you know that I recently forged a silver necklace for my brother-in-law—the sea king, Lord Rikiwulf."

The jeweler pronounced the name as if it was a threat.

"My son Toke once saved the sea king's life," Gudrun said. "Lord Rikiwulf would be delighted to learn that your son is marrying his daughter."

"I'm not so sure about that," the jeweler snapped. "If the sea king learns that my son is marrying a girl who was born crippled, he might start buying his jewelry elsewhere. People will think my shop is shrouded in doom."

"My granddaughter doesn't bring doom," Gudrun mused aloud. "She has been with us for fifteen summers, and in all that time the men have always returned from their journeys west unharmed. She helps weave the sails, and not a single sail of hers has torn yet."

"I'm sorry. We don't have much use for a sail weaver in the hinterland," the jeweler concluded. He downed his mead and slammed the mug on the table. As far as he was concerned, the meeting was over. His son was already getting up from his stool.

"Wait a minute," Gudrun said as she fingered the gold bishop's ring in her necklace. Fiddling with that ring always had an effect on people. The jeweler and his son knew full well that Yrsa's grandmother was a legend. Like everyone in Jutland, they had heard her story on a chilly winter evening around the fire—how she became known as "Gudrun the Torch." Many summers ago, when she was only seventeen, she had stood before the walls of Paris, splattered from head to toe in the blood of Frankish warriors. She had wriggled the ring off the finger of a dead bishop who, the story goes, had run into the tip of her long knife several times.

"We are as good as neighbors," Grandma Gudrun said, sounding aggrieved. Suddenly, her back seemed straighter and her voice was steady.

"These are uncertain times. We've all heard about the Danish and Norwegian warlords who are raiding villages and burning down unguarded settlements. My sons Naefr and Toke have always protected Odin's Hill. They consider you their friend. No Danish warrior would dream of plundering your village. Surely, my dear jeweler, you can do something to repay them for their friendship."

Ljufr looked at his father. Yrsa could tell that her grandmother's comment had made him uneasy.

"With all due respect, Gudrun, I *am* paying for that friendship," the jeweler replied irritably. "I give your sons a substantial amount of silver every winter."

"Now, don't get all wound up," Grandma Gudrun said. "All I'm asking for is a favor. A small gesture. Your son for my granddaughter. Don't you have plenty of sons? And it must be a comfort to know that your village is so well protected."

The jeweler scratched his beard. He should never have accepted Gudrun's invitation in the first place. He should've known better than to bring his son to this sandy village of east coast savages. And how dare she threaten him when she knew perfectly well that the sea king was his brother-in-law! Nevertheless, the jeweler was afraid of Gudrun's sons, just like everyone else.

"Wouldn't Yrsa be bored in the hinterland? She's a child

of the sea, isn't she?" the jeweler asked, but there wasn't much fighting spirit left in his words.

He wasn't wrong about that, Yrsa thought. She was a child of the sea. She had no interest in lakes and swamps. She could feel a cramp forming in her bad foot. She wanted nothing more than to get away from this table and out of this room.

"Yrsa will fulfill all the duties of a good Danish woman. She'll look after your son's house, keep his bed warm, nurse your grandchildren, and assign work to the slaves," Gudrun said.

The jeweler fell silent. Ljufr's eyes filled with despair.

"All right. But for the wool of twenty sheep," the jeweler finally said.

"Father," Ljufr sputtered. His voice trembled with disbelief.

"Twenty-five," Gudrun said, extending her bony hand. The bangles on her wrist clattered.

"I'm not marrying that cripple," Ljufr said. "Not on my life."

His father gave him a hard slap, and Ljufr fell silent. He sniffed away his rising tears.

"Twenty-five," the jeweler confirmed, shaking Gudrun's hand.

"Next winter you will be married, granddaughter," Gudrun said.

"I am honored," Yrsa said politely, and nodded to the jeweler. Ljufr didn't even dare to look at her. His father gave him a sharp kick.

"I, too, am honored, Yrsa daughter of Toke," Ljufr stammered reluctantly, and stood up from his stool. He was barely taller than she was. *I can handle him*, Yrsa thought. *I'll wrestle him to the ground if he gets mean. I'll knock that black tooth right out of his mouth!* Ljufr shook her hand without looking her in the eye. Yrsa took a good look at his face from up close and decided that maybe he did look like a troll after all.

"They're waiting for me in the boathouse," Yrsa said. "I will see you soon."

She hobbled through the rain as the jeweler and his son watched her from behind.

Yrsa sat down on a bench in the boathouse. Rain drummed on the roof. She massaged her bad foot, which ached from standing in the same position for so long. She wanted to forget about the jeweler and his son, but the other weavers were eager to know how the meeting had gone. Had they agreed on a bride price? Had the boy kissed her? But Yrsa was in no mood to answer their silly questions. She immediately set to work braiding a leather rope, and they had their answer. Yrsa had expected the boy to like her. She had washed her hair this morning and smeared her eyelids with paint. She had hoped he would be honored to take her as his fiancée. She'd thought he would be impressed to hear that she was the youngest sailmaker in the village. She had woken up with a strong feeling that today would be a good day, and Yrsa's premonitions were rarely wrong.

"You'll have the most beautiful jewelry in all Jutland," one of the sailmakers chimed in after a while.

"Gold and amber," another woman said. "Even the goddess Freya will be jealous of you."

"Freya? I highly doubt it!"

Finally, the women left her alone and returned to their work. The sail was almost ready. It was stretched out in a wooden framework under the roof of the boathouse. For months, Yrsa and the three other women had braided, sewn, and knotted the wool. Then they'd rubbed the thick weave with fish oil, seal fat, and tar so that it was as strong as leather and could withstand the wind and rain. The smell of fish oil was embedded in Yrsa's hair, and her fingertips were black with tar. In the yard next to the boathouse, logs were being split with axes, and nails and clamps were being pounded into boards. Despite the noise, Yrsa managed to relax. She liked the smell of the boiling tree tar that the boys used to seal the gaps between the planks.

"So, I hear you're engaged," somebody called out ahead of her. Yrsa looked up and saw Nokki and Sporr. The boys were as inseparable as Odin's two ravens. Nokki worked in the yard sawing logs into planks and also happened to be the son of her uncle, Captain Naefr. Sporr did the more delicate work. He carved and painted waves, fish, and ravens on the stern of the longship. Nokki and Sporr were both sixteen, and they were going on their first Viking voyage that summer.

"Engaged to a boy from the hinterland, no less," Nokki said. He flashed her a wide smile, the kind of smile that, as the mothers liked to say, could melt all the ice in the North. If you asked the eligible peasant daughters from the hinterland if they knew Nokki from Mimir's Stool, they would all burst into giggles. They made regular trips to the village by the bay just to catch a glimpse of him. One time, Yrsa caught him in the hay with another girl, and she couldn't help but feel jealous. Whenever Nokki stopped to chat with her in the boathouse, she felt heat rising from the roots of her hair. But on that particular day, the day she got engaged to that miserable troll, she didn't feel the least bit of warmth at the sight of Nokki standing in front of her.

"It's true, I'm engaged. You missed your chance, Nokki," Yrsa blurted out. Sporr sputtered under his breath.

"I think Nokki is scared of you," Sporr said.

Everyone in the village knew Yrsa's reputation. Last summer, a boy started a rumor that Yrsa couldn't kiss because her mouth was as crooked as her right foot. The next day, Yrsa grabbed him in a chokehold and pushed him down into a cesspit so he could taste the sludge with his own worthless lips. The boy tried to defend himself and broke two of her teeth. But she didn't care. The humiliation he suffered was worth two broken teeth to her. It took three mothers to pull him out of that pit.

"Oh, you don't have to be afraid of me, Nokki," Yrsa said, feeling her cheeks grow hot anyway.

"What's the bride price?" Sporr asked.

"The wool of twenty-five sheep."

"Ouch, that's too much for me," Nokki said, shaking his head. Yrsa could hear the mockery in his voice. No, Nokki wasn't afraid of her.

"Then get lost. Go hack a tree trunk," she barked.

"C'mon, let's go," Sporr said, pulling Nokki with him. The two boys walked to the yard, Nokki with his hammer carelessly slung over his shoulder and Sporr with his chisel dangling from his belt. The rain had stopped.

Yrsa saw the sail weavers on the other side of the sail eyeing her suspiciously. Her head was boiling. She didn't know whether it was from anger or shame or both.

That night, a heavy fog rolled in. It must have been the breath of the frost giants because it was a greasy, slimy mist from the North. The villagers stayed indoors and sat around the fire trenches in the middle of their houses. Despite the cold, Yrsa went out for a while to make her offerings. She couldn't neglect the elves. Elves cannot be seen or heard, but they're always there. They live in the rocks and trees and watch over the village, crops, animals, and people. That night, she left drops of chicken blood by the oldest trees at the edge of the forest and smeared butter on the rocks around the village. She was in a hurry to get back to the fire as soon as possible so she could curl up under a thick fur and warm the soles of her feet by the flames. The mist was so cold it burned her lungs. She made a wide circle around the village and ended at the Great Dune. She loved this place. From a distance, the giant dune looked like a crooked old man. The young dunes near the village were nomads. In a single winter, they could be blown dozens of yards to the south, always subject to the whims of wind. But the Great Dune, dense with bushes and beach grass, remained firmly in place. It protected the village from the spring tides in the winter, which was why

Yrsa always brought food for the dune elf, even on the coldest winter nights. She dug a hole in the sand, tossed in a fish head, and buried it. Then she rubbed her hands in the stiff grass. Her ears tingled with cold. She wanted to go home.

"You know you're probably the only person around here who makes offerings to a dune," said a voice behind her.

Yrsa whipped around and landed on her bad foot, causing her to lose balance. She stumbled to the ground and immediately scrambled back to her feet.

"You scared me, Nokki," Yrsa said.

Nokki son of Naefr emerged from the fog like a dead person reentering the world of the living. His brown hair hung to his shoulders, and his eyes twinkled as he smiled. He had a small goatee that was no more than a patch of stubble on his chin. He seemed happy that he'd caught her off guard.

"What are you doing sneaking up on a girl in the fog," Yrsa demanded, trying to sound as casual as possible, but she felt her heart beating faster and faster.

Nokki stroked his chin emphatically, as if trying to make the hairs grow longer. Something inside Yrsa wanted to count those little hairs one by one.

"How did you like your fiancé?" Nokki asked. "I personally thought he looked like a troll."

"No, he doesn't," Yrsa said with feigned indignation. "His father makes the most beautiful jewelry in all of Denmark, and one day Ljufr will design pieces especially for me."

"'The most beautiful jewelry in all of Denmark,'" Nokki mocked.

"Ljufr is rich and really quite handsome," Yrsa said, but the way she said it made it sound like she was overcompensating for the fact that he was actually poor and ugly.

"'Rich and really quite handsome,'" Nokki mimicked.

"You're mocking me, Nokki. Grandma Gudrun says that only numbskulls repeat what other people say."

"Grandma Gudrun is always right," Nokki said.

Yrsa was silent. *Then kiss me, you idiot,* she wanted to shout. *Can't you see that I've spent the last two summers trying to impress you with every stitch I make, every knot I tie, every bit of wool I clench between my teeth?* But Nokki didn't move. He just stared into the fog as if there were something out there to see.

"Ljufr is madly in love with me," Yrsa sighed, as if she could barely keep track of all the boys who were madly in love with her.

"You're only fifteen summers old," Nokki said. "I thought Gudrun would wait until you were sixteen."

"Our village needs wool," Yrsa replied. "How else are we going to make our sails and cloaks?"

"That's true," Nokki said. "But if you leave, the village will lose a good sailmaker."

Yrsa swelled with pride.

"Strange how quickly things change," Nokki murmured. "Here I am leaving in a few days, and you're getting married after the summer. I thought things would stay the way they were a little bit longer."

"Well, what can you do about it?" Yrsa replied with a shrug.

Nokki exhaled a cloud of breath into the icy air. Then, all

of a sudden, he took a step forward and kissed her. He did it quickly, as if Yrsa were a wild animal that could bolt away at any moment and disappear forever. But she didn't mind. She kissed him back, so violently that their teeth clashed. She wrestled him to the ground, and he let her overpower him. She pushed him onto his back in the sand and leaned over him, then gently nibbled at his lip and ear. He laughed. She laughed. She didn't care that the frost giants were blowing their dirty, cold breath over Denmark, or that their noses were wet with snot. She kissed him softly, their tongues briefly touching. She wasn't even shivering anymore. Her insides, her hugr, were glowing like logs in the fire. In the end, it turned out to be a pretty good day after all.

Her premonitions were almost always right.

When she got home, everyone was asleep. The long room with beds on either side of the fire trench was dark. The fire still smoldered in the pit. Her head itched with sand, but she didn't comb it out. She wanted to wake up with sand on her pillow. There were exactly twenty-seven hairs in Nokki's goatee. She had counted them herself. They didn't even prickle against her face—that's how soft they were.

"Where were you?" Gudrun snapped. Yrsa almost jumped out of her dress.

"With the elves," she stammered.

Yrsa could only see the whites of Gudrun's eyes staring at her from the shadows.

"Whoever he is, girl, put him out of your mind," Gudrun whispered.

Then her grandmother lay back down. Yrsa undressed and placed her clothes at her feet. Then she crawled under the blankets and pelts. She couldn't help but chuckle. She wanted to laugh out loud. Freya, the goddess of love, must have been jealous of her that day.

Yrsa and Nokki didn't tell anyone about their secret meetings on the Great Dune, but they continued to see each other until the day in April when Nokki went to sea with the men.

3

YRSA PRESSED HER HAND against the stone on the beach along with all the other women, children, and elderly. The old rock was as high as a house, as wide as a man, and as flat as a pancake on the top. It has always been there, all the way back to the time of their ancestors. The villagers believe it was placed there by the giant Mimir at the dawn of time, before the worlds were formed and the gods had just been born. Mimir was roaming the mortal world in search of the source of wisdom. In Jutland, the giant passed a beautiful bay and decided it was time for a rest. He scraped the massive rock flat with his rough, callused hands and placed it upright at the edge of the beach. Then he took a seat. It was the perfect spot for Mimir to rest his legs and muse over his colossal existence with a view of the bay and the sea beyond. For him, the massive stone was no higher than a stool, which is why it's still called Mimir's Stool today.

The stone connects the people of the bay with their ancestors. By laying their hands on it, they're asking the ancestors to call on the gods to save the ship from peril and protect their sixteen-year-old sons going to sea for the first time. After all, they were only boys. Wearing thick cloaks of tightly woven wool and padded helmets, they paraded across the wet sand wielding their swords and spears. They called out to their mothers to say goodbye and promised to take care of themselves and keep their warm helmets on at sea. The women huddled together and talked about how it was only two or three summers ago that their sons had little hands and high-pitched voices. And now there they were standing among the sailors, grown men like giant trees with full beards, green tattoos, and bands on their arms. That day, the boys would embark on the whaling road. They weren't children anymore.

Yrsa's father, Toke the Helmsman, was in good spirits that day. He burst into thunderous laughter at even the silliest joke. He hugged his wife and patted Troels and Sten on the head and told them to listen to their mother. Then he turned to his daughter, who was standing alone by the tall stone. The men didn't want her anywhere near the ship with her crooked foot. She wasn't even allowed on the beach that day.

"Don't forget the elves, Yrsa," Toke said, though he knew she wouldn't—she made offerings to them every day.

"I won't, Father," Yrsa replied.

Toke stood there, gazing at his daughter. His little sailmaker had grown up.

"Keep an eye on your brothers, will you?" Toke added. He kissed Yrsa on the forehead and walked down the beach toward the surf. It was almost high tide. The men trudged through the shallow water, tossed their leather shoes on board, and arranged themselves on either side of the longship so they could lift the giant vessel made of oak, ash, and beech wood. The little boys of the village kicked off their shoes and ran out to help. Maybe next summer or the summer after that, when they were old enough, they would be allowed to join the men. The children whooped and cheered when the ship started to float, as if it were all thanks to their efforts. One by one, the men climbed aboard and took their positions on the benches in their wet pants. They dropped the oars in the water and rowed the ship out into the bay. The sea roared. The waves splashed. Yrsa was already headed toward the Great Dune.

It wasn't long before the women and children were running past her. From the Great Dune, they waved and called after the ship, which was already past the surf by then. The men stopped rowing and the ship bobbed in the swell. It was time to hoist the yard. From the dune, Yrsa could hear the men groaning as the crossbeam scraped its way up the mast. It moved so slowly that it made her nervous. They tilted the yard to one side until it reached its horizontal position. Then they slowly unraveled the sail. It was Yrsa's sail. She had worked on it for months. For a moment, it danced in the wind—flapping, rolling, refusing to be caught. *Come on, catch the wind*, Yrsa thought. *Catch it.* But the sail wasn't cooperating. It brushed off the gusts like a sailor. *Don't be afraid. Your threads are tight, your knots will hold.* When the sail finally caught the wind, it swelled like a tidal wave, as Yrsa would later boast, and the longship jerked forward. With forty men on board and fully loaded with wool, water, amber, and food, the ship was heavy in the water. But the sail pulled it through the waves as if it were carrying nothing but feathers. Yrsa's sail—strong, supple, indestructible. It gave the ship its speed. It would surely last a lifetime. Yrsa cheered. "Look at my sail!" she shouted at the seagulls. "Look!"

Everyone watched as the *Huginn* sailed north. It grew smaller and smaller on the open sea. On land, the people clung to their amulets, their hammers of Thor, and their metal plates bearing the face of Odin. Some clutched raven skulls or wolf's teeth in their fingers. Yrsa held her amulet of Frigg. She could only hope that the gods would protect the men now that the ship was at the mercy of Rán, the goddess of the sea.

Twelve geese flapped warily across the bay. They, too, were headed north, in the same direction as the ship. Everyone was relieved. The geese were a good omen. Everything was going to be all right. The women finally went back to the village. There was work to be done. The girls rolled down the dune and ran after their mothers. The boys, both big and small, kept an eye on the *Huginn* as if it was their job. Yrsa's little brother Sten hung back for a while, trying to hide his tears.

"Father is coming back," Yrsa said. "Our ship is named after Odin's raven. You know that Huginn the raven always returns to his master."

"Do you think Odin ever gets scared?" Sten sniffed. "I mean, does he ever worry about his ravens? That they might not find their way back to the world of the gods?"

"Probably," Yrsa replied. "But Huginn and Muninn

always find their way home. They're the only ones who can deliver Odin the news of the day. You'll see. Father will be back by the time the nuts are falling from the trees."

And Nokki too, she thought. That very morning, in the stables, he had cut a lock of her hair and tucked it in his coat. She had kissed him slowly and gently on the lips. Yrsa wiped the tears from Sten's cheeks. The little boy clenched his fists and took a deep breath, puffing up his little chest. Then he rejoined the bigger boys. Only after the ship had slipped behind the horizon did Yrsa also head back down to the village. The only person left gazing out to sea was the young slave, Stink Breath.

Toke the Helmsman had bought the slave for ten pieces of silver at a Danish market two summers ago. When the boy arrived in the village, dirty from the boat trip and dressed in rags, he didn't exactly smell like lavender. Yrsa's mother cut his hair short with the wool scissors. He came from a warm country with long summers, a land of grapes and olives. He was smaller than the boys in the village and stood out because of his brown skin, dark eyes, long eyelashes, and short black hair. The boys decided to call him Stink Breath. He called himself Mikel, but the boys said that was no name for a thrall, so Stink Breath it was. He worked in the stables, milking the cows and goats and collecting eggs from the chickens. He kept the stalls clean and slept with the animals. Every day, he brought a wooden bucket of cow's milk, and Yrsa was always the first to get a cup. Sometimes, he told Yrsa that he dreamed of having a sword and going down the whaling road with the men. Like most of the boys in the village and the hinterland, he too wanted to be a seaman. He also wanted a beard, long hair, and a green tattoo. He seemed to forget it was that same bunch of hairy savages from the North who had kidnapped him two summers earlier. Despite all that he'd been through, Stink Breath still dreamed of becoming a Dane and going home a rich man. He would see his land of grapes and olives again and tell his mother and brothers about the day he first set foot on a longship and rowed away with the men. How they visited the markets on the shores of the Western Sea and sold their cargo of woolen cloaks, amber, and skins. Or how he had rowed up a river with the men after hearing about an unfortified farm where the harvest was still drying in the attic or a monastery where the silver was waiting to be plundered. Stink Breath could only dream of it. Yrsa was sure her father would release him one day and take him to sea, perhaps in a few summers. She told him to be patient. But Stink Breath couldn't wait.

When they were done celebrating the ship's departure, the village boys came to the stables. They were shaky on their legs, their stomachs churning with beer. They told Stink Breath that there was a test for slaves who wanted to become sailors. If he passed, they would put in a good word for him with their fathers. Then, he could learn to fight with a shield and a spear, and when the long winter was over and summer came again, he could join them on the *Huginn*. He would no longer be enslaved, and they would stop calling him Stink Breath. They swore on the little hammers hanging around their necks, so Stink Breath could be sure they were telling the truth. Only dimwits and sheep-heads would be stupid enough to break a promise on the hammer of Thor and provoke the wrath of the gods.

Stink Breath followed the boys to the beach. They pointed to a long sandbank out in the water. It was known as Heath Ridge because it was covered in scraggly heather bushes. There's nothing out there except seagulls hunting crabs, dunlins rooting in the sand, and, when the weather's nice, seals basking in the sun. But it's a dangerous place. If you try to walk out to the ridge from the beach, you'll immediately feel the force of the icy water around your ankles trying to drag you out to sea. At low tide, the sea gets especially wild out there. The water swirls and foams around the sandbank. It's as if there's a monster living under the sand that flashes the spiny ridges on its back. The mothers of Mimir's Stool have told their children for generations that anyone who tries to swim out there will be sucked down by the monster. It will drag you down to the depths and swallow you alive, and you'll never be seen or heard from again.

"The test," the boys told Stink Breath, "works like this: you go out and sit on Heath Ridge and wait for high tide to pass. When the water starts to recede, you swim to the beach against the current. If you make it back, you'll be stronger than the sea and become one of us. If you fail, you'll remain a slave. You'll be Stink Breath for the rest of your life."

When Yrsa came to the stable that evening with a bowl of bread and cheese, she was surprised to find Stink Breath gone. The cow's udders were swollen, and the goats looked as if they knew where the boy was but had no intention of telling her. Yrsa sat down on the stool to milk the cow herself. Her bucket was already half full when Revna, the fisherman's daughter, wandered into the barn. She had brought a basket of herring and was surprised to see Yrsa on the stool. Revna was Stink Breath's sweetheart, and she also happened to be one of the prettiest girls in the village. The boys from Mimir's Stool were jealous that Revna, with her fiery hair and round hips, would rather roll around in the hay with the stable slave than with them. The beautiful Revna didn't even notice the other boys. Every day she rowed a sloop into the bay to pull up lobster baskets, then distributed her catch around the village. She would walk past the boys with her nose in the air as if she were the reason the gods hoisted the sun into a horse-drawn cart every morning and sent the ball of flame across the sky.

"I don't know where he is," Yrsa said.

She stood tall and kept her chin up as she talked to Revna. After all, she was the daughter of a seafarer, with precious beads in her necklace. She wouldn't be caught dead in the hay with a stable slave.

"Do you think the ship has passed Skagen by now?" Revna asked. Cape Skagen is at the tip of Jutland where the two seas collide; many a ship has been lost in its rough waters.

"Most likely," Yrsa said. "The winds were in their favor."

Just then, they heard a startled bird flutter into the sky, and a boy came running toward the barn. It was Sten. His shoes crunched on the wood chips between the houses. He burst through the door and fell to his knees in front of Yrsa, completely out of breath. His eyes were wide as oysters.

"What's wrong?" Yrsa asked.

Her little brother wanted to say something, but he couldn't find the words.

"Did an elf steal your voice, kid?" Revna laughed.

"Heath Ridge," he blurted out finally. "The monster swallowed Stink Breath."

Revna stared at the boy. For a moment, she was speechless.

Yrsa raced outside and called for help. One by one, the mothers emerged from the houses, the heavy doors creaking behind them. One came running with an ax in hand, ready to bash in the skull of a forest troll.

Sten breathlessly explained that the boys had challenged Stink Breath to swim from Heath Ridge to the beach. That he had thought the boy would succeed. After all, Stink Breath was a good swimmer. He made it halfway before he ran into trouble. Before Sten could finish, Revna was already running to the beach. Night was falling, and one mother took a torch with her. There might still be time! Quick! They hurried down the ox road to the shore. Yrsa knew she could not keep up with the women. She went inside and picked up the polished wooden rod near the door. It had been part of a loom but was discarded by the sailmakers because it was made of soft pine and not of hard beech. Yrsa hobbled along the dirt path behind them, following the light of the torch and pushing her weight onto the rod with every step. The wind tugged at the prickly dune bushes along the path. An animal rustled in the brush. A bird flapped its wings. At the end of the road, Mimir's stone stood guard in the moonlight. Yrsa felt a sense of doom sliding down her back like ice.

By the time she reached the stone, the women were already on the wet sand, scanning the surf. They called out, but there was no answer, only the squawking of the gulls. Maybe Stink Breath had made it, she thought, maybe he really was a good swimmer and had managed to escape the whirlpools. But there was no sight of a head or arms in the waves. Revna ran to her skiff in the sand. The mothers and Yrsa helped her push it into the surf. A wave hit Yrsa dead on, soaking her from the waist down. The water was ice cold. They all jumped into the boat, grabbed the oars, and started rowing. The skiff cut through the churning waves. Foam splashed across the bow. Revna sat in the front, scanning the sea and shouting, "Mikel, Mikel!"

Yrsa, Revna, and the mothers stood upright in the boat as it bobbed up and down in the swell. There was no one left on Heath Ridge. They searched the dark water in the moonlight, but there was no one to be found and no voice calling for help, just the roar of the waves and the laughing of the gulls. All hope was lost. Yrsa touched Frigg's head on her necklace. Two other women clasped their amulets as well. Someone spat into the water to ward off evil. Revna wailed and banged her fists on the side of the boat. The mothers called on the gods in Asgard. The high beings of the heavens were trying to tell them something. The gods sent them warnings, signs. A clear sky, a thunderstorm, a cat with a mouse between its teeth, whales on the horizon, a flock of starlings perched in a tree—they were all signs from the gods. That morning, everyone had been so excited to see the twelve geese flying north. They were a good omen, as was the osprey that Yrsa's father had seen the day he met his wife, Signe. The bird had plucked a salmon from the sea right before his very eyes. At first, her father hadn't given it much thought, but later, when it turned out that Signe was as fertile as a field in summer, he was certain that the gods had given him a sign. It's not always easy to know a good omen when you see one. You can never be completely sure, and most of the time you only recognize it in hindsight. But bad omens are easy to spot. Everyone recognizes those immediately.

The sea roared as the women pulled the boat back onto dry land. Revna walked into the dunes to her fisherman's cottage, utterly defeated. The cottage was so covered in sand that from a distance it looked more like a dune with a door in it. Yrsa sat down by Mimir's stone. Her arms were sore from rowing, and her bad foot throbbed from running. She gazed out at the sea, and it occurred to her that never again would Stink Breath hand her a cup of milk, never again would he tell her about his dream of going to sea. He was only fifteen, the same age as Yrsa. The thought that someone her own age had died was unsettling. But not as unsettling as the omen itself.

The night after the men went to sea, a boy drowned. There was no omen worse than that.

4

ON MIDSUMMER'S NIGHT, the day of the bees' nest incident, Njall hangs the sea monster's head on a hook above the doorway to his house. He may call himself a prince of the solstice, but his chest throbs with pain with every step he takes. He wants to break something, kick a hole in the wall, file a complaint with his ancestors in Odin's Hall. Word has spread—not only through the five houses in the village, but also to the farms in the hinterland. Everyone has heard about poor Birger, who got a bees' nest stuck on his head and threw himself into the sea screaming. And about the helmsman's daughter with the crooked foot who broke one of Njall's ribs and gave him a verbal lashing. Even the slaves in their drafty shacks are talking about it.

In the helmsman's house, an enslaved woman known as Bulging Calves looks for the red bumps on Yrsa's legs. She has poor eyesight, but she still manages to find the stingers in Yrsa's skin and pinch them out. Yrsa lifts her skirt for Bulging Calves, who finds a bee still wriggling around with its stinger planted in Yrsa's butt cheek.

"You've got a bee in your behind," Bulging Calves giggles. Troels is gawking at them from his chair.

"Go find something else to gawk at, boy, and shut your mouth," Grandma Gudrun snarls.

Troels snorts indignantly, as if he weren't looking at Yrsa's bare behind at all, but simply gazing at the decorations in the wooden beams that have been there for years.

Bulging Calves gently pries the insect loose with her broken nails. The stinger slides out of Yrsa's skin and the bee flies up through one of the three holes in the roof, free to go on buzzing and making honey.

"Its stinger didn't break! Can you believe it? Fortune must smile on that bee," the woman says.

"Thanks, Bulging Calves," Yrsa mutters.

The woman smiles, but then she starts coughing. Yrsa can hear her lungs wheezing as if they've sprung a leak. Fortune has not smiled on Bulging Calves.

When Bulging Calves was brought to the village as a young woman, she was wearing a skirt that stopped at the knee, exposing her lower legs. So the men started calling her Bulging Calves, and the name caught on. She started out as a weaver, but when her eyesight deteriorated and she could barely see the wool threads anymore, Grandma Gudrun took her in as a house slave. She helps with the cooking and cares for the children and the elderly. She is even allowed to sleep in the house. Still, she prefers to sleep in the weaving hut against the side of the house. There, she's the oldest and looks after the younger slaves like a mother hen. The younger women look up to her. Gudrun hands Bulging Calves a pan of roasted seal meat and places five flatbreads on top. The girl thanks the old woman and walks out with the food.

It's dark in the house. The only light comes from the fire in the middle, which is surrounded by stones so the sparks won't fall on the animal skins. Yrsa hands a bowl of seal meat to Troels. Two cats prowl around his stool and jump into his lap. They rub their bodies against him and huddle together, purring affectionately. When Troels looks away for a split second, they knock a few chunks of meat out of his bowl, scramble to the ground, and gobble up their catch. Sten sits alone playing knucklebones and occasionally takes a bite of meat. A cat tries to sneak up to his bowl but Sten, quick as a fish, whacks it away with his stick.

Toke's wife, Signe, walks into the house with a sigh. She kicks off her shoes in the front yard and holds her pregnant belly with two hands, as if the child could fall out at any moment. There's a dark look on her face. She's always irritable when she's pregnant. Her last three children were so weak that they didn't make it to their second birthdays. It was the fever, always the fever.

Signe sits down on a stool by the fire in the middle of the long room. She looks sour, as if she's just bitten into a rotten oyster. Then she proclaims to the whole room, "Birger's face is so swollen that his own mother doesn't recognize him. He has a high fever and is delirious in bed. Poor thing."

Yrsa gnaws on the tough seal meat and says nothing.

Signe hikes up her long dress a little, slides her feet into the warm ashes of the fire trench, and continues, "Word has it that a couple of little snotnoses called Njall 'swine shit' or something like that and then ran off like lightning. Now his honor has been tarnished."

"Serves him right," Sten says.

Yrsa chuckles, which annoys Signe.

"Njall doesn't have any honor yet to tarnish," Grandma Gudrun snickers. She's sitting in the shadows a few feet from the fire, sharpening her long knife, her sax, as if her warrior days aren't over yet.

"They're not children anymore, Gudrun," Signe snaps. "Yrsa has struck Njall on the inside—his hugr—where it really hurts."

"He put his hand down my skirt," Yrsa protests.

"He kicked me in the nuts," Sten pipes in. "That really hurt!"

"Njall was asking for it," Yrsa says as she massages her ankle. Her bad foot is still throbbing from the ordeal in the tree.

"Yeah, we were right to spoil his victory," says Troels.

"What do you mean, *we?*" Sten says as he tosses the knucklebones. "You ran away and left me behind."

"I had a bad shoulder," Troels retorts. "I couldn't even use my spear."

"You've never hit anything with that stick," Yrsa snarls.

Sten bursts into laughter.

"And you owe me a dirham," Yrsa adds.

Troels growls.

"Yrsa shouldn't have interfered," Signe snaps in exasperation. "Tomorrow you're to stay away from the shipyard."

Yrsa can't believe her ears.

"Don't look at me like that, Yrsa. You refuse to apologize. So Njall doesn't want you in the shipyard, and neither does the shipmaster," Signe says.

"But I still have to stitch the leather straps into the sail," Yrsa laments.

"They'll find someone else to do that," Signe replies.

"I've been working on the sails for two summers!"

Signe shrugs. "It's your own fault."

"What else is she supposed to do with that crooked foot of hers?" Troels snarls.

"Shut up, fish breath," Yrsa hisses.

"She can clean the nets," Signe suggests.

"What?" Yrsa sputters. "No way! That's so unfair! Njall tarnished my honor too, you know."

Now it's Signe's turn to burst into laughter. Troels laughs too—as if his sister has honor!

"He called me the daughter of a slave," Yrsa says.

At that, Signe stops laughing. Her eyes dart to Grandma Gudrun in the shadows. The old woman stops sharpening her knife. In that soft, calculating voice of hers, she mutters, "You're not the daughter of a slave. He's not allowed to call you that."

Yrsa knew her mother was a merchant's daughter from Frisia; of course Njall shouldn't call Yrsa the daughter of a slave. When Yrsa's father arrived in Dorestad on the *Huginn* to sell wool and amber, he fell in love with Cara the Frisian. He offered her a piece of amber. She put the translucent orange stone on a leather strap around her neck and said she would happily kiss him if he removed the bread crumbs from his beard first. Toke combed his beard like an idiot, and that's how Cara ended up in Mimir's Stool, all the way on the east coast of Jutland, the Danish peninsula of forests, dunes, and lakes. That's how Cara became a Dane. This is the story that Toke told his daughter. This is what Yrsa knew about her mother. But Grandma Gudrun just said that Njall was not allowed to call her the daughter of a slave, as if someone had forbidden him to do so.

"Your mother was a free woman," Gudrun insists, but her tone is anything but sincere, as if the words came straight from Loki, the god of a thousand lies.

Signe stands up and rubs her pregnant belly. She offers no confirmation that her stepdaughter is indeed a Dane. Instead, she grabs a log and tosses it into the fire.

"Why are you so quiet?" Yrsa demands.

"What do you think, girl?" Signe retorts. "That your mother came here for love?"

Her voice is as cold as the boulders on the beach.

"Enough, Signe," Gudrun hisses irritably from the shadows.

Signe shrugs and says, "I'm in my own house, Gudrun. I can say what I want. I can't help it that Njall shot his mouth off."

Yrsa feels a shiver roll down her spine. Sten drops the knucklebones and looks back at his big sister. Suddenly,

Troels is more alert as well. A log cracks in the flames. Sparks spring into the air like glowing fleas. Then Signe says, "Your mother came here as an ambátt, a female slave. When Toke came back from his first Viking trek, he brought her with him. She was a scrawny thing, skinny as a stockfish. You were there, Gudrun."

Gudrun stabs the tip of her warrior knife into the floor. "Yes, I was there," she growls.

Yrsa can hardly believe what she's hearing. Cara the Frisian. Her mother from a distant shore. A slave.

"Did Toke buy my mother?" she asks.

"For a pound of silver," says Gudrun.

A pound of silver, Yrsa thinks. *That's a lot for a slave girl.*

Gudrun comes closer. The gold in her hair glistens in the firelight. Her hands and face are speckled from the sun.

"Toke bought your mother in Denmark," Gudrun explains, "at the slave market in Hedeby, from his cousin, Harald son of Karl. The girl was dressed in rags. When she arrived here, I gave her a dress to wear and fed her until her ribs disappeared and the color returned to her face. I cut her hair short, as we do with every slave. The men called her Paddle because she was so skinny. She was difficult, always muttering that she belonged to no one. That she'd been kidnapped. I sent her to the weaving hut. That's the best way to teach someone their place. One winter in the weaving hut and they'll stop squawking, all right."

"And then? What happened after that?" Yrsa asks.

Gudrun shrugs and pokes at the fire as if she's trying to decide how much she wants to tell her granddaughter. For a moment, no one says a word. The cat on Troels's lap purrs loudly.

"Toke couldn't take his eyes off that young thing," Gudrun says. "He was only seventeen at the time and had a big mouth. But he hardly dared to say a word to that Frisian girl. The men all joked about it. They said Toke was up to his ears in love. But the girl never batted an eyelid at him."

"She lured him into her nets," Signe sputtered.

"Paddle walked to the beach every evening, pulled the scarf off her head, and washed the wool out of her hair," Gudrun continues. "Toke made it clear to the other men of the clan that the Frisian girl was his and they better keep their hands to themselves. Cara didn't work in the weaving hut for long. Toke took her in as a house slave. She knew how to season meat and could cook a good fish. She would make a fish soup with carrots, goat's milk, and nettles—a recipe from Frisia."

"That sounds delicious," Troels said.

"There was nothing special about her fish soup," Signe barks jealously.

"And then what happened?" Yrsa demands impatiently.

"Toke told us to call her Cara from then on. Not Paddle. Signe was pregnant at the time, but he wanted Cara as his second wife. Like a cock among the hens," Gudrun chuckled.

"She bewitched him," Signe snaps. "What do I care if they were fooling around in the hay? But then he had to go marching around the village with her on his shield to show everyone that he wanted to marry her. He went too far. It was as if Toke had fallen on his head and had his brains pecked out by the gulls. Why did he have to humiliate me like that!"

Then Signe purses her lips. All this talk about Cara is like rubbing salt in an old wound. She pours some milk into an earthen cup and accidentally spills it. She curses and sets the cup in the warm ashes by the fire.

Yrsa stares at Signe. Most of the people in the village are in awe of her. She is tall and beautiful and can stay underwater for an exceptionally long time. Rumor has it that on the full moon she runs down the beach naked and dives into the sea. Then, she's gone for hours. Every now and then a head will appear above the waves. But it's not Signe. It's the head of a seal. The only witnesses to this transformation have been sailors and drunks, but Signe is a good swimmer, and she taught Yrsa how to move with the sea.

"Toke's ancestors must have been ashamed and complained to Odin in the Valhöll," Signe says.

"Come on, Mother, it's not like the Allfather doesn't have other things on his mind," says Troels. "Such as the day of the wolf. Or the eternal winter. Or Ragnarok, like a seeress predicted long ago."

Oh for the love of Odin, groans Yrsa inwardly. Troels is obsessed with the end of the worlds. Every conversation with him—whether it's about plucking a chicken or how to win at King's Table—somehow ends with the downfall of the gods.

But Signe won't let herself be distracted. "The mothers started talking. How could a great helmsman from Mimir's Stool be out of his mind for a slave from Frisia, that land where the gods go to piss? Taking a Frisian girl as a second wife would bring nothing but doom. A silk dress wasn't going to change that."

"Did Toke really buy her a silk dress?" Yrsa asks.

"Red silk," Gudrun recalls.

"A scarecrow in a red silk dress is still a scarecrow," Signe sighs. She dips her finger into the milk to check if it's warm yet.

"Signe even tried to poison Cara," Gudrun says.

"You're exaggerating," Signe replies. "It was a mash of rotten oysters and red elfin saddle mushrooms. Nothing more."

"Well, that mash left her vomiting and burning with fever for three days," Gudrun retorts. "When she came around, she was thinner than ever. Only her belly was a little swollen. I think you were already in it."

"Is that true?" Yrsa asks.

"It was just a test," Signe says, soundly a little embarrassed. "If that scrawny Frisian wanted to survive here in the North, she was going to need a stronger stomach."

Yrsa stares at Signe. Strong stomach, her foot! Signe is as jealous as a dog and more spiteful than Loki, who wouldn't give the other gods so much as a boiled crab leg.

"In the end, Toke didn't marry her," Signe says. "I talked him out of it. But he did treat Cara like his second wife. She was allowed to grow her hair, a sign to everyone that she was no longer a slave. She and I were pregnant at the same time. Me with Troels. She with you, Yrsa."

"Cara died shortly after Yrsa was born," Grandma Gudrun says. "She lost too much blood during labor. Troels had already been born by then. Signe took both of you at the breast. She nursed you as if you were her own child."

As if I were her own child, Yrsa repeats in her mind.

"There's nothing more to tell," Signe says.

Silence falls over the house.

Then Troels asks, "So, was her fish soup really that good?"

"One more word about that fish soup, and you'll be sleeping outside," Signe snarls.

Troels lowers his head and says nothing more. He searches for the cat in his lap, but it's gone.

Signe takes her cup from the warm ashes and blows on the steaming milk.

"Be grateful for what you have," she says to Yrsa. "Toke and I have taken you in as our daughter. You're lucky, you know. So stop egging Njall on. He's the captain's son. You don't want him telling people that you're the bastard daughter of a house slave and her master. You don't want him calling you a half-slave."

"If the jeweler from Odin's Hill gets wind of that, the marriage is off. No one will want to marry you anymore," says Gudrun.

"Then the village can forget about the wool of twenty-five sheep," says Signe.

"I'll make sure Njall keeps his mouth shut," Gudrun growls.

"I am the daughter of Toke. I'm as Danish as anyone," Yrsa says. Her voice trembles with indignation. She looks around. Her eyes seek confirmation, but Signe and Gudrun don't respond.

"Yrsa is my sister," says Little Sten.

"She's your half-sister, and she's half Danish," Troels sneers.

"She's still my sister," Sten cries. He stands up and throws his arms around Yrsa's shoulders. She feels his nose against her ear.

"Your mother's name was Paddle," Signe says.

And for the second time that day, Yrsa feels the anger welling up inside her like a gust on the beach.

"So, if I understood all this correctly, Signe, you were Toke's second choice."

Signe throws the cup of milk at Yrsa's head. The hot liquid burns her nose and cheeks. Sten jumps backward.

"Hey!" Yrsa screams.

"You'll be picking nets for the rest of the summer!" Signe roars.

Later, when the damper is on the fire and everyone is lying side by side on the beds, Yrsa walks out in her wool coat. The surf hums faintly in the distance. How is she supposed to sleep with such a storm raging inside? She folds her arms over her cloak against the cold. She spots Bulging Calves sitting in front of the fire outside the weaving hut. Yrsa hobbles over to her.

"I could hear you yelling all the way out here," Bulging Calves says.

"Was my mother beautiful?" Yrsa asks as she takes a seat beside her.

"Beautiful and proud," Bulging Calves replies.

Yrsa thinks Bulging Calves must have been beautiful herself once too.

Bulging Calves starts coughing. It's a deep, guttural cough that lasts for fifteen seconds. Thick, bloody mucus runs down the corners of her mouth. The woman may not live to next summer. If she dies, her body will be abandoned in the forest, prey to wolves, crows, and beetles.

"Cara chose your name," she whispers.

Yrsa is surprised. She had always assumed that her father had chosen her name: Yrsa, "the Wild One."

"I can still picture her," Bulging Calves says. "She wasn't that much older than you are right now. A sassy little thing. She wasn't afraid to show her teeth when she had to. Just like you did today against Njall. Your name suits you, you know."

With that, the storm in Yrsa's body subsides.

5

IT'S SEPTEMBER. The ship left four months ago, and Yrsa has been engaged for five months. In all that time, she hasn't seen the jeweler from Odin's Hill once. Summer is almost over. It's the time of year for making cheeses, salting butter, and gathering hay for winter. Every morning, Yrsa helps Revna clean the fish nets, which are braided with seal leather. The sand is warm and soft around Yrsa's bad foot. She buries it in the sand whenever she has the chance. The nets rustle and drip and smell of the world beneath the waves, of shells, salt, and algae. Yrsa picks out the clumps of seagrass, crabs, and dead fish tangled in the weave. She tosses the carcasses into the sand at her feet. The second she's gone, the giant gulls will swoop down for a bite of crab or perch. For now, the greasy birds watch her with one hungry eye, while their other eye—the watchful eye—remains fixed on the rest of the flock.

"You're getting pretty good at cleaning nets," says Grandma Gudrun in a tone dripping with mockery. Occasionally, Gudrun comes out to help. She sits down beside them, her bones creaking like a ship in a storm. It's a strange sight—Gudrun with her golden hairpins, elegant dress, and fancy necklace sitting on the beach, as if she wants to show the goddess of the sea that she has achieved a life of reputation and fame. She claims to enjoy cleaning the nets because it allows her to gaze out at the sea. She can't get enough of it.

"Njall is still waiting for an apology," Gudrun says.

Yrsa doesn't respond.

"Who knows, maybe she'll be Njall's sister-in-law one day," Revna teases.

Yrsa feels her cheeks burn red. *Put a cork in it, Revna!* One morning, while they were picking nets, Yrsa told the fisherman's daughter about how she and Nokki had kissed in the dunes. Revna swore never to tell a soul.

"Njall's sister-in-law? What makes you say that?" Gudrun asks.

"She and Nokki have a thing," chuckles Revna.

"Nokki is her cousin," Gudrun corrects her.

"Haven't you heard, Gudrun? Yrsa is madly in love with him," Revna exclaims. Then she bursts into laughter, her red braid dancing back and forth on her shoulders.

"Is that so, Yrsa?" Gudrun asks. "Then why am I going out of my way to find you a good husband?"

Yrsa doesn't answer.

"As soon as your father gets back we will send you to Odin's Hill. You'll be married before the snow falls," Gudrun says as she rips a mussel from its broken shell with her teeth.

"Thanks a lot, Revna," Yrsa snaps.

Revna looks mortified. Yrsa jerks the net closer to her.

She focuses all her energy on extracting the crabs, slugs, and slime from the wet, smelly heap in her lap.

"I already feel sorry for that jeweler of yours," Grandma Gudrun says. "He's getting a bride who spends her days thinking about someone else."

"I'm only fifteen." Yrsa scowls. "You could've waited a year, you know."

"I wanted to marry you off last year. I knew that sooner or later word would get out that your mother was a slave."

Revna looks at Yrsa, her eyes wide.

"Your mother was a slave?" Revna asks.

"You just worry about your nets, Revna," says Gudrun. "It's none of your concern."

The old woman strokes the bishop's ring on her necklace, something she only does when she's afraid—Yrsa knows that. It has something to do with Cara.

"I can understand that your father fell in love with a slave. It happens," Revna cackles. "Just look at me. I was crazy about Mikel."

"Why don't you shut your trap, girl?" Gudrun snarls.

"How dare you insult me, you old squid," Revna retorts.

"Who are you calling an old squid?" Gudrun shouts. "I went to sea with the warriors. I was out hunting whales when I was your age. I fought with spear and shield. I captured slaves and sold them myself."

"Yeah, back when clams had teeth," Yrsa says, yawning widely, and that really makes Gudrun mad.

"You'll be married as soon as your father returns," Gudrun snaps. She pulls a small crab out of the nets and tosses it to the gulls. The birds flap and screech, pecking at one another as they scramble for the snack.

Yrsa says nothing. She secretly hopes she can persuade her father not to send her to Odin's Hill. She hopes Nokki will return from his first trip with some gold or silver, a bounty worth more than the wool of twenty-five sheep. But the engagement to Ljufr is already a done deal. Gudrun and the jeweler shook on it.

A gust of wind blows down the beach. Yrsa shivers. Gudrun stands up, walks over to the fire in the sand, and stokes it.

"Don't worry," Revna whispers. "Nokki won't turn his back on you when he hears that your mother was a slave. He'll just shrug and say that your mother could've been a goat for all he cares."

That makes Yrsa smile. Revna giggles.

"What's so funny?" Gudrun demands as she sits back down at her nets.

"Nothing," Yrsa says, and the two girls burst out laughing. Gudrun groans in exasperation.

If I pick this clam out of the net, Yrsa thinks, *and then count to one hundred, then look up at that exact moment, then—and only then—will I see a tiny dot appear on the horizon. I'll stand up and stretch my neck to get a better look, and yes, that tiny dot will still be there: the mast of the ship bringing Nokki home, the sail of the* Huginn. But when she counts to a hundred and turns her eyes toward the sea, there's nothing there. The water is empty. There's not a speck on the horizon. The men have been at sea for more than four months now. The apples have been harvested.

The nuts have been gathered. The summer is almost over. The days of snow and ice will soon be upon them. Yrsa gazes out at the sea, as if she might be able to raise her father's ship out of the water by sheer willpower. The wind cuts through her nostrils. She tastes the snot on her lips. The high, narrow stone of Mimir doesn't offer much shelter.

Yrsa lets the fishing net slide off her lap and goes to warm her hands by the fire. She pulls up her dress and petticoat and feels the warmth against her legs.

Revna joins her by the fire, and she too warms her legs. Gudrun looks up from her nets annoyed, as if the fire belongs to her and no one else. She takes a handful of herbs from a leather pouch and tosses them into the flames. The fire crackles, releasing a cloud of smoke. Revna jumps back, but Yrsa isn't quick enough. She feels the hot smoke seep into her mouth and nose. It fills her head, her throat, and her lungs, burning inside her. She grows dizzy. Tiny flames appear on her dress, but she doesn't notice. Revna pats them away with her bare hands. Yrsa staggers. For a moment, she thinks Gudrun has poisoned her with the herbs. She loses her balance and grabs Revna by the wrists. She falls. No, she sinks. Not into the sand, not into the sea, but into the girl herself. All of a sudden, she sees Revna's cottage, like a dune with a door in it. Revna runs out toward the village—Yrsa can hear the gravel crunching under her feet. She hurries into the stable. Stink Breath is waiting for her inside. He smiles at her. Yrsa feels his kisses on her neck and her cheeks. It all seems so real. Then suddenly, a wave washes it all away, and she sinks deeper. She sees Revna lying in a rowboat, on her stomach, one arm slung over the edge. The hems of her sleeves are scorched. At the front of the boat are nine lobsters. One of the females with eggs under her tail is trying to climb over the side, but she loses her grip on the slippery wood and tumbles back into the boat. In the distance, the god of thunder rumbles. Yrsa feels the girl's heart grind to a halt. Her blood stops flowing. Her brain stops thinking. Yrsa sinks even deeper. Her heartbeat slows, her blood slows, her brain shrinks like a shrimp in hot soup.

Someone slaps her on the cheek, and only then is Yrsa jerked back to consciousness. Only then does she let go of Revna's wrists. She gasps for air as if she was being held underwater. Her heart gallops in her throat. Her ears ring. She just felt Revna die.

Revna rubs her aching wrists. They're streaked with blood where Yrsa's nails punctured her flesh.

"What was that all about?" asks Grandma Gudrun.

Yrsa doesn't answer. She tries to breathe calmly. In and out. In and out.

"You were convulsing," Gudrun says. "I thought you were dying."

"I was inside of you, Revna."

"What?"

"Don't go to your lobster traps. It's going to storm."

Grandma Gudrun and Revna gape at Yrsa as if she'd just sprung a set of gills.

Then Revna gazes up at the deep blue sky. There's not a cloud in sight. "No storm today," she says.

"There will be," Yrsa says. "Don't go out to sea. I saw you dead, struck by lightning in your boat. You were lying on your stomach. There were nine lobsters in your boat."

"You were dreaming," Gudrun says. "It's because of the herbs I threw into the fire. You inhaled all that smoke."

"No, I really saw it."

Revna isn't sure what to believe. She felt Yrsa's iron grip on her wrists and saw the terror in her body.

"You're as pale as an oyster, girl," Gudrun says, worried. "Go inside before you get sick. We'll finish the nets."

Yrsa staggers past the high stone of Mimir and heads down the ox path.

"Hey, Yrsa, are you all right?" a woman at the edge of the village calls. She's hanging herring on a rack to dry, high enough so the cats can't reach them. Yrsa doesn't answer. She feels nauseated. She walks into the dune bushes and vomits. She spews all the milk, fish, and nuts she ate that morning into the sand. Everything inside her comes out. She feels her heart thumping in her throat, as if it's trying to escape her body. Yrsa spits out the last of her saliva. Then she sinks down into the sand. All she wants to do is lie there. Lie down and sleep and forget. She can smell her vomit in the bushes. A bird scurries away. The last things she sees are the orange berries in the bushes. The same shade of orange as the beads on her necklace, she thinks. Then she falls into a ravine of sleep.

She's awakened by a cold snout on her skin. The dog looks like a cross between a sheep and a wolf. He's only got one eye, which is why Yrsa calls him Odin, because the Allfather has one eye too. His fur is so long and thick that you could hide half of your possessions in it. Any rat that's stupid enough to bite him in the throat will find itself lost in that tangle of hair and become easy prey. His ferocious jaws hold more teeth than you can count—fangs that will clamp down on an animal and refuse to let go, incisors that can break a bone, and molars that can tear skin and flesh to shreds. Sometimes, the fleas drive him so crazy that he bites somebody in the calves. Then he gets mud flung at his head and hides out for the rest of the day. The dog likes to follow Yrsa on her walks, especially when she spreads dashes of butter and leftover food for the elves. When she's not looking, he laps it up. Odin takes what he can get—he's not one to pass up a bite for the elves.

Yrsa's head spins as she tries to stand up. For a second, she thinks she's going to pass out again. She wonders how long she's been lying here in the bushes. Hours, it seems. The ground is dry and the sky is clear. There's no thunderstorm coming, she thinks. But it all seemed so real. She felt everything she saw. It must have been a dream. It was all Gudrun's fault. She threw those nasty herbs into the fire. Yrsa clambers to her feet. Odin walks off ahead of her toward the village. His tail swishes like a broom, as if he's clearing the way.

At the end of the afternoon, after the work in the shipyard and the weaving huts is done, after all the fires have been lit, Revna pushes her skiff out into the surf. At first, she was hesitant to go out to sea, but Gudrun told her to stop being ridiculous. Revna had seen it for herself: Yrsa had inhaled the smoke, passed out, and slipped into some kind of dream. Nothing more than that. Revna paddles through the tide until she reaches the edge of the open sea. There's a wooden float bobbing in the water. She pulls up the chain and slowly lifts a braided basket from the water: her lobster trap. Water sloshes out. The basket is teeming with lobsters. Big ones. What a catch! She sticks her arm through the round opening and extracts the sputtering creatures one by one. She works carefully, patiently, so they can't pinch her fingers with their claws. She drops a couple of dead bass into the basket as bait and tosses it back into the water, hoping for an equally good catch the next day. Then she starts transferring the creatures into her seal leather bag. She counts them. There are nine. Nine! A cold breeze ripples through the air. She looks up. The sea doesn't look so friendly anymore. Whitecaps have formed on the waves. The wind slaps her face, as if it's trying to call her to attention. From the east, grim clouds pass over the hills as if they're being chased by Thor himself. She hears the clouds rumble and remembers Yrsa's warning. Fear shivers down her spine like a ball of ice. "Nonsense," she murmurs. The daughter of a helmsman couldn't have possibly seen her fate. Only old women with white hair could do that. Women with ravens and tall staffs. Seeresses. Witches.

Still, Revna touches the shark's teeth and the tiny hammer around her neck. She grabs the oars and rows. It's low tide, which means she has to paddle against the current. She lets the lobsters crawl over her feet. The clouds move like a dark blanket across the sky. She rows hard. She thinks of Stink Breath, of his kisses on her neck, of his body against hers, of his death at Heath Ridge. She manages to overtake the waves, cutting through the surf. She can smell the wood fires from the five longhouses in the village. Ten more strokes, and she'll hear the sound of sand crunching under her boat. Nine more. Eight.

Then lightning flashes, and for a split second the world goes white as milk. Thunder cracks. One of the oars slides into the water. The tide washes the boat onto the beach.

Sten is the first one to spot the skiff. He finds Revna lying on her stomach with her arm slung over the edge. The boy shouts for help. Pretty soon, the entire village is standing around the boat. The lobsters snap their claws at the approaching hands, as if they're trying to protect their captain. No one dares to touch the fisherman's daughter. What if the fire of Thor is still in her body? People cling to the hammers, plates, teeth, and bones hanging around their necks. Some even spit on the ground to ward off evil.

No one wants the lobsters. They're tossed back into the sea. Everyone on the beach is whispering the same thing: "Yrsa saw this coming."

6

TWO WOMEN COLLECTING mussels at low tide heard from a passing longboat that the *Huginn* was in Ribe, on the west coast of Denmark, and that the men might be home tomorrow. Everyone heads to the beach to welcome the ship. Sixteen women from farms in the hinterland travel to the village to greet their husbands, who had joined the men at sea. Three goats are slaughtered. Fifteen salmon are rolled in salt and dill and buried in the ground to marinate. But that afternoon, a violent storm rolls in, darkening the sky and nearly blowing the women off the beach. Only Signe remains at the lookout, sheltered by Mimir's stone, but the men don't return that night.

The next morning, the storm has passed, and the sea is as empty as a shell on the beach. There's no sign of the *Huginn*, not even a speck on the horizon. Everyone is worried; no one knows what to do. The women from the hinterland linger around the village. They don't want to go back to their farms without their husbands. When Signe, exhausted from the night watch, comes down for a bite of salmon, it takes a while for anyone to remember where they buried the fish. After a few mouthfuls of the salty, oily fish, she regains her strength.

But the ship doesn't turn up that day either. Fear is written all over everyone's faces. They can't help but recall all the bad omens: the boy who drowned the day the ship left, and then his beloved, the fisherman's daughter of all people, struck dead by lightning. All they can do is spit in the sand to ward off evil.

Little Sten hangs mackerel over the fire trench in the long room. Gudrun lights the fire to smoke them. Yrsa sits on her cot. She tries not to think about the ship that's supposed to bring her father and Nokki home. Odin the dog has been bitten by a rat. Yrsa cleans the wound and rubs honey over the raw flesh where the skin has been torn away.

"You're wasting good honey on that half-wild beast," says a voice in front of her. Yrsa looks up, startled. Standing before her is Kveldulf the Norwegian.

"Odin is a good rat catcher. He deserves care," she says.

The dog gnaws at his paw through his impenetrable fur, sending clumps of hair flying.

Kveldulf sits down on the clothes chest at the foot of Yrsa's bed. Rarely has Yrsa seen the old Norwegian up close. She does her best not to look away from the scars on his face. Every winter, when the cold seeps in through the walls and everyone gathers around the fire, Kveldulf tells the tale of his infamous battle in Brittany. The more he drinks, the more enemies he pounded to death on that fateful day. But he didn't leave the battlefield unscathed. His face was in tatters, like a curtain clawed to shreds by a cat. An old Breton granny had sewn the strips of skin back together. Either she did it with a fat knitting needle or she was half blind, because the scars on Kveldulf's face are like ropes of wild flesh. Young children cry at the sight of him, and women avert their eyes so they don't have to look.

Yrsa doesn't understand why he's here.

"You predicted Revna's death," Kveldulf says.

"It wasn't my fault," Yrsa says. "I didn't wish her dead."

"Of course not," he says, his voice gentle.

Meanwhile, nine women have entered the house. The smoke is slow to escape through the holes in the roof, giving them the appearance of ghosts in the mist. They remind Yrsa of the nine daughters of Rán and Aegir who the waves are named after. It takes her a moment to realize they're the women from the hinterland.

"What's going on?" asks Signe, who has just come stumbling into her house. Her eyes are red with fatigue. Sand clings to the hem of her dress.

One of the women points to Kveldulf. "He says your daughter is having visions."

"We need Yrsa," Kveldulf says.

"And why is that?" Signe demands.

"Let him speak," says Gudrun.

Signe sighs. Why does her mother-in-law always have to contradict her? Signe looks at Yrsa as if this is all her fault.

"The boys tell me this isn't the first time you've had a vision," Kveldulf says. "That you've predicted things before, like when it was going to snow or when a merchant was coming."

"Well, that's not that hard to guess," Yrsa says.

"At the beginning of summer, your grandmother's scissors were missing," Kveldulf continues. "You knew exactly where she'd dropped them."

"That was a coincidence," Yrsa whispers.

"She also had a dream about a whale," Little Sten pipes up suddenly. "She dreamed that the bay would turn red with whale blood, and two days later the fishermen caught a whale."

Yrsa is puzzled. She had completely forgotten about that dream.

"So, you've had visions before?" Kveldulf asks.

"This time I was inside her," Yrsa explains. "In Revna."

Astonishment ripples across the scars on Kveldulf's face.

"But that was just this once."

Yrsa had seen a seeress at work once. She'd tossed bones carved with runes on the ground, and based on the order in which they landed, she could predict the future. She was old and wise.

"Only a völva can predict a person's fate," Signe says.

Everyone holds their breath. The word had been said: völva. A woman with a staff. A seeress. A witch.

"Only an experienced völva can know what the Norns have decided," Signe repeats.

Signe often speaks of the Norns, the three weavers who live under the roots of Yggdrasil, the world tree. It is they who decide on matters of life and death. Every decision a Dane makes in life has already been made for them by the Norns. They weave people's destinies into tapestries just as

Yrsa sews patterns into sails. The Norns aren't so different from the fickle old ladies who shuffle through the village arm in arm, except they can be mercurial and cruel. Maybe it's because their calluses itch or because their noses are always running from hay fever, or because one of them has just eaten the last piece of licorice root and the other two are cranky about it, but when the Norns are in a foul mood, you'll commit blunder after blunder. You'll find yourself tangled up in woes and wonder why you keep making the wrong decision. The Norns delight in weaving all kinds of misery into people's lives. It helps them forget about their own. They can't wait to watch fate fall on their victims like an oak tree on a drunken lumberjack's head. The Norns have even determined the fate of the gods. Odin, the father of the gods, knows exactly how he will die on the day of Ragnarok. The monster wolf Fenrir will swallow up the sun and plunge the world into darkness. Then he will pounce on Odin and devour him—skin, hair, beard, and all. Not even Odin, the most powerful of all the gods, can resist his fate. There's nothing he can do to keep his worlds from perishing or protect himself from ending up in the belly of the great wolf. The destiny of every Dane is knotted into their navel at birth. And the only one who can see that destiny is a seeress, a woman with a staff. A völva.

"If Yrsa is a seeress, I would know about it," Signe exclaims. "That girl can't predict anything. She doesn't even know when the fish is done. She lets everything burn. Just the other day I asked her to stew some black beans, and—"

"Signe," Kveldulf interrupts, "I didn't come here to listen

to how your daughter stews beans. The men of Mimir's Stool should've been home two days ago. Every house in the village and farm in the hinterland has a father, son, or husband on the *Huginn*. Including you."

Signe nods so violently that her earrings clatter. She grips the white shark tooth on her necklace.

"All the women with men at sea have made offerings to the sacred trees, and to the goddess of the sea. There's nothing more they can do," Kveldulf says.

Rán, the goddess of the sea, likes blood sacrifices, so the women cut open their hands and let the blood drip into the waves. Some even threw gold into the sea. If there's one thing Rán loves more than blood, it's gold.

"Yrsa, we want to know whether the men are coming back," Kveldulf continues. "And if something has happened to them, we want to know that too."

Yrsa grasps the amulet around her neck, the face of Frigg, Odin's wife who spins the clouds on a spinning wheel in her lap. The goddess who gives advice.

"I can't help you," Yrsa says. "I wouldn't know how."

The women grumble. They don't believe her. Hadn't she predicted the death of that poor fisherman's daughter?

"It was because of the herbs," Grandma Gudrun says.

Everyone looks at Gudrun. The gold sparkles in her white hair.

"It was because of the dried herbs I threw into the fire," she explains. "A mixture of nightshade, wolf cherry, dried fly agaric, and some other stuff. I like to toss them into the fire on cold days to ease the pain in my knees and shoulders. They make me feel like I'm floating."

"What do you mean? They make you drunk?" asks one of the visitors.

"Yes, kind of like that. I just sniff a little of it. But Yrsa inhaled all the smoke at once. Her heart started racing, and she couldn't stand straight. She was delirious. She was having delusions."

The room falls silent. Yrsa hears someone coughing in the smoke.

"I still have some of it," Gudrun says casually. "If you want, I could throw some into the fire. Then you can see for yourself."

"But it almost killed me, Grandma," Yrsa says. "I felt my heart stop."

"Oh, you're exaggerating. My heart stops sometimes too, but it doesn't kill me. You're always complaining, granddaughter. Even your monthly bleeding makes you whine. Think of your forefathers, those great adventurers who explored the high seas. They never complained."

"They didn't bleed every month either," Yrsa mutters.

"Show your forefathers some respect," Gudrun hisses, as if they might walk in at any moment and start mingling among the women.

Kveldulf rubs his hand down his ghastly face.

"I think you want to know what's happened to your father too, Yrsa," he says.

Deep down, Yrsa knows that her father—that oak of a man—is all right. It's Nokki she's worried about. She dreamed about him last night and heard him screaming. Did something happen to him? Could Gudrun's putrid herbs help her see that? She can feel the women's eyes burning into her skin. They just want to know if their men are alive.

Yrsa stands up from her cot. She steps toward the fire trench, into the ring of light and warmth in the middle of the house. Gudrun staggers toward her. All eyes are on the old woman, and she beams—the vain old net picker. People whisper that she once found a golden apple in a field, an apple that had fallen from the empty sky. Such golden apples only grow on Asgard and are the food of the gods. The apples give eternal life and some women believe that Gudrun, old as she is, ate the apple whole and cannot die. Gudrun tosses a handful of herbs into the fire. They crackle and curl. Sparks fly. Everyone takes a step back. Yrsa bends over the flames. She closes her eyes. Her cheeks glow. The smoke burns in her nose and throat. It smells of dog piss, and all of a sudden her head feels heavy, as if someone has filled it with water. She staggers dizzily. Her thoughts seem to trip over one another. She tries to think of the sea. The *Huginn*. Her father at the helm. Nokki at the oar. But everything turns black.

"I can't see anything," she says.

Yrsa feels the milk churning in her stomach. Kveldulf comes closer. His breath smells like a rotten clam.

"Concentrate," he says. "These people are desperate."

Yrsa stumbles. She grabs Kveldulf's arms to keep her balance. Her nails dig into his skin. The mothers murmur in amazement.

Yrsa doesn't hear them. She's sinking. Not into the sea,

not into the sand, but into Kveldulf. Waves wash over her body. Suddenly, she sees Kveldulf bashing his saber into the enemy; he's surrounded by six men and dripping with blood and mud. This must be the day that made him great, the day he got his scars. Then she's struck by another wave and sinks deeper. A young woman stands before Kveldulf. She has sharp features and black hair. Yrsa feels the woman's fingers on his skin. They are soft and cold. She dabs Kveldulf's scars with ointment. Then a wave washes it all away. Yrsa sinks even deeper. She sees a sky full of stars and a trail in the snow. A trail made by skis. Kveldulf follows it. He's on skis too, and propelling himself forward with a wooden stick to gain speed. He looks back at a man following him. Yrsa can see the breath rising from his lips. He stops at the shore of a frozen lake. He looks out in the middle, at a hole in the ice. There are two skis bobbing in the black water. But beyond the hole are footprints. The person Kveldulf is following has fallen through the ice and climbed out again. They must have continued across the ice to the other side of the lake. Kveldulf doesn't dare step out onto the ice. He'll have to go around the lake. He hurries. He skis like a man possessed. Yrsa feels the falling snow sting her face. Across the lake, Kveldulf picks up the trail again. He follows it. Suddenly, he slows down. There, in front of him, is a naked woman on her knees, curled into a ball. Her back is blue. Frozen. Her black hair is stiff on her neck. It's the woman who tended to Kveldulf's wounds. Her clothes are bunched up and wedged between her chest, arms, and knees. That's all Yrsa can see. The scene is washed away by another wave, and Yrsa sinks deeper. She feels Kveldulf's pain. A stabbing pain in his chest. She smells fish. Live fish, salty, from the depths of the sea. Kveldulf is lying on his back surrounded by eels. Hands trembling, he searches for something among the writhing creatures. The eels gnaw at his fingers with their tiny teeth. He writhes back and forth as the fear of death grips his body. His breath is trapped like a fishbone in his throat. At last, he finds what he's looking for—his sword. He clutches the leather hilt, feels the wood and iron in his hand, and is reassured. Yrsa has just seen Kveldulf's death, just as she saw Revna's. She feels her heartbeat slow down to a halt with his. Her brain stops thinking.

Yrsa feels a hot slap on her cheek. Signe stands in front of her. She's completely beside herself, shaking Yrsa desperately. She screams, but Yrsa doesn't hear her. Suddenly her ears pop, and she gasps for air. But all she breathes in is more smoke.

"Make room, give her some space!" shouts Signe.

Yrsa slumps to the floor. She breathes heavily, like a fish on dry land. Her ears are ringing. Her heart is pounding in her throat, and for a moment she's afraid it will bounce out of her mouth and run away. No one says a word. The women clench their amulets in their fists. Their faces are as white as the inside of an oyster. Yrsa sits up and leans against the side of her cot.

"Have you seen the men?" Kveldulf asks.

Yrsa doesn't answer. She stares at the warrior whose body she has just been inside.

"Is the *Huginn* coming?" he demands.

"Surely you can see that she's out of breath," Signe protests.

Yrsa hasn't seen the ship, but somehow she's certain that her father is still alive.

"The men are coming back," Yrsa bluffs, though she has no idea if this is really true.

Kveldulf stands up and shouts that the ship is coming. Cheers erupt. The boys wriggle between their mothers' legs, stepping on people's toes and pushing their way out of the house. Yrsa hears the door slam. The boys want to be the first to reach the fire pits so they can light them. They'll spend the whole night on the beach to make sure the fires don't go out.

Yrsa's nails have left imprints on Kveldulf's wrists. He bends over her and asks, "What exactly did you see?"

"I saw your death," she whispers.

The Norwegian stares at her. His face turns as gray as the ashes in the fire. For a second, Yrsa is afraid that the knots of wild flesh in his face will loosen, the scars will unravel, and his whole head will fall apart.

"My death? When? This winter?"

"I don't know. You were surrounded by fish. Eels. They were still alive."

"Eels," the old warrior repeats. This girl predicted the fisherman's daughter's death the day it happened. How long did he have left? Days? Weeks? Or longer? Kveldulf springs up from the stool as if he's just scorched his hindquarters on it. He has to go. He has to get out of this cursed house.

"Kveldulf?"

He whips his scarred face in her direction. His eyes plead, begging her for more time. One more winter, one more summer, and then another winter. But he knows he cannot change the fate that the Norns have woven into his navel. Only a fool would think such a thing.

Yrsa wants to ask him about the woman she saw in the snow, but there's so much despair in his eyes that she doesn't dare.

"I'm sorry," she says.

Kveldulf makes his way through the smoky house like a ship cutting through the surf. There's hardly anyone left inside. The entire village has left for the beach. Signe groans at the marks on the floor. She opens the front door to let out the smoke. The fire crackles wildly.

"Are you okay?" she asks.

With that, Yrsa vomits on the floor.

Signe and Bulging Calves carry Yrsa to bed and lay her head on a pillow stuffed with dune grass. Yrsa feels them drape a fur pelt over her body, but her mind is already far away, in the depths of slumber.

That night, she doesn't even hear the men coming home.

7

WHEN YRSA WAKES UP, there's a cat lying at her feet, all curled up, as round as a silver coin. A wisp of smoke floats above the fire pit. It's going to be a beautiful day. She can see the blue, cloudless sky through one of the holes in the roof. Sten is sitting by the fire. He waves three sheets of parchment in the air.

"Look! They've got Latin letters and little paintings on them. Father brought them," he squeals.

"They're back? And Nokki?" Yrsa blurts out.

"Yeah, I think so," says Sten.

Yrsa smiles. Why did she let all those nightmares and bad omens get to her? The ship is back. The men are home. Yrsa runs outside and races to the latrine behind the house. As she crouches over the wooden bench and swats away the flies, all she can think about is Nokki. She still needs to brush her hair, wash her armpits, paint her eyelids, put on her finest dress and rings, and, of course, her necklace with orange beads and the amulet of Frigg. There's so much to do. She can't wait to see Nokki, count the twenty-seven hairs on his beard, and kiss him until she has no feeling left in her lips. She laughs out loud as she wipes herself with a couple of dead leaves. She leaps off the latrine and skips—no, *runs*— back to the house, bursting inside.

Her father is waiting in the front room of the house, his chest hard as a rock. He opens his arms and Yrsa throws herself into his embrace. She feels his armbands pressing into her back—bands of silver, a testament to his travels, his name, his reputation. The most beautiful one was forged by the jeweler from Odin's Hill, whose son Yrsa is still betrothed to. It's in the shape of the sea serpent Jormundgandr biting his own tail. She takes a step back and gazes at her father. He flashes her a boyish smile—to him, life is a game. His eyelids are tattooed with thick, dark lines, making his gray eyes look larger and fuller. He smells of lavender and is wearing a new, clean shirt. He's even combed his hair and beard.

"You've grown again, girl," he says.

Yrsa is dying to ask about Nokki, but she holds back. When the time is right, she will tell her father that she has no intention of marrying the jeweler's son, and that she wants to marry Nokki instead. Nokki, Nokki, Nokki, and no one else.

"The mothers were very worried," she says.

Toke rubs the raven tattoo on his neck. He always does that when he's not sure what to say. Odin's ravens are never lost for words. Yrsa has always loved listening to her father, the way he talks about the sacred trees as if they're old friends and never tires of telling stories about his adventures at sea.

"Sit down, daughter," he says. He points to the stool in

the front room. Yrsa takes a seat. She thinks about her chest of belongings at the foot of her bed. At the bottom is her purple dress. She will wear it today and paint her eyelids in a matching shade of purple. Then, she'll rub her teeth with salt until they sparkle. She needs to get ready now. Right now.

"Everything went well on the voyage," Toke whispers. "We sold our wool, amber, and fur pelts at the markets in Diepe and Havn. Then we met up with the Duke of Brittany and helped him scare off the Franks at the border. On the way back, we docked at Walacria, where we learned that the palisade around a monastery near Ganda had collapsed, leaving the place completely undefended. The grain harvest was just sitting in a barn. The Count of Ganda and his men had been called south to help their king settle a spat, so we plundered the monastery's grain, took a bunch of shiny cups and bowls and a few slaves. It couldn't have been easier."

Yrsa hears what he's saying, but isn't really listening. The Viking voyages are always the same, except when the captains decide to form a fleet and attack their target as one giant pagan army. But that doesn't happen very often. Nokki will tell her all about it later. She wonders whether he thought about her while he was out on the whaling road. His smile flashes through her mind. She can't help but glow as her father rattles on. She scratches her head. Soon her hair will be full of sand from rolling around with Nokki.

"Last week, we docked in Ribe," Toke continues.

"Really?" Yrsa asks in an attempt to sound interested, but she can barely sit still on her stool.

"Yes, that's where we sold the slaves. They were young

and strong, so they brought in quite a bit. We sold all but one: a girl, a nun from Ganda."

Yrsa is impatient. Why is her father going on about slaves and nuns?

"After we left Ribe, we ran into a storm," he says. "We lost some of our oars, the ship was creaking, and the yard was swept away in the wind. Then we lost our sail. The gods were furious with us."

Now he has Yrsa's attention. How could the *Huginn* lose her sail?

"I was afraid the storm would pound the nails right out of the ship," Toke says. "That the planks would be ripped apart and the *Huginn* would collapse like an old raft. We battened down the oars and the men remained seated on their benches, pressing their shoulders against the ship's sides and their feet under the oars. We clutched our hammers of Thor. The storm goddess held us in her grip the entire night. We threw all the gold we had into the sea to calm her. But nothing helped. Rán is as greedy as they come."

"Don't say that," Yrsa scolds, afraid the goddess of the sea might hear them. She feels a knot in her stomach. Something's wrong, she can feel it. Something involving Nokki, perhaps.

"Naefr said it was the nun's fault. He wanted us to throw her into the sea."

Yrsa looks up in surprise. No one contradicts Naefr's orders. The men are afraid of their captain.

"The nun was down in the belly of the ship the entire time with her hands clenched together, praying to her god. Naefr kept saying that the goddess of the sea was furious because we had a nun on board. He shouted that we should've sold her in Ribe. That we had to throw her into the sea immediately. I said that Rán likes gold and Danish blood, not Christian nuns. She has no use for them. But Naefr told me to shut up. The nun had to go overboard, he said. He dragged Sporr to his feet and ordered him to toss the girl into the sea. Sporr trembled like a newborn lamb as he stepped away from the side of the ship. He went down and pulled the nun out from between the sacks of grain and carried her onto the deck. She tried to grab the ropes around the barrels, but eventually she had to let go. He dragged her to the foredeck by her black robes to toss her overboard."

The poor girl, Yrsa thinks. *No one deserves to die like that.*

"The nun flailed around like a seal. She wriggled out of her robes, and Sporr was left standing on the bow with the black rag in his hands. The nun remained on her knees in her white linen shirt and cap, like a ghost. She was soaked to the bone, but she kept her hands clenched in prayer. All of a sudden, the bow cut through the foam head of a wave, tipping the ship forward and down. We plunged down the back of the wave, and everyone held on to whatever we could. Sporr lost his balance on the bow, and a second later he was gone. I didn't even see him go overboard. The girl was still there, praying on the deck in her soaked undershirt."

Toke sighs and takes a moment to gather his thoughts.

"When the men realized Sporr was gone," he continues, "they all stood up and looked over the edge of the ship. But it was so dark. We couldn't see a thing. Nokki hung over the edge, thrashing wildly with his arms, as if he might catch Sporr in the water. The men pulled him away from the edge and forced him to sit. They tried to calm him down. The nun was hiding among the sacks of grain. She hadn't held on to anything. We didn't understand how she wasn't thrown overboard."

"Sporr," Yrsa whispers. "He... wasn't even seventeen winters."

Sporr drowned at sea, one of the cruelest forms of death. Since he didn't die in battle, he will never be one of Odin's chosen ones. He will never enter the realm of the gods. He will never take his seat in the Valhöll at the long table of his ancestors, the great men of Mimir's Stool. He will never drink Odin's honey wine or feast on one of his boars. He will never see the walls of spears and the roof of shields. Instead, he will go to the dark world of Niflheim, to spend eternity roaming in the fog with the shadows of the dead.

"Soon, the storm was over," Toke continues. "Nobody touched the nun. She stayed down with the barrels with her hands clenched together. We all thought the same thing: it must have been the nun's god who knocked Sporr overboard and saved her life."

"What god?"

"You know, that skinny corpse on the cross. Maybe that god is more powerful than we think."

"And you were still on the high seas?" Yrsa asks.

"There was no land in sight. We had no idea where we were. Nokki didn't know what to do with his misery. He was as furious as Odin. He blamed me for bad steering, shouted that the men should've stopped Sporr, that Naefr should've never told him to toss the girl into the sea in the middle of a storm. He was ready to throw himself into the waves and dive down to the sea floor to battle Rán himself. We had no choice but to tie him up. That boy was out of control."

"Sporr and Nokki were like Odin's two ravens," Yrsa says.

Toke nods. They both fall silent for a moment.

"Luckily, it was a clear night," Toke says then. "The stars showed us the way home."

Yrsa wipes the tears from her cheeks.

"What's wrong?"

"I feel sorry. For Nokki."

"Nokki?"

Yrsa feels herself turning as red as a cooked crab. She wonders if Toke remembers the day he saw her walking down the Great Dune with Nokki. He asked them what they were doing up there.

"Hunting rabbits," Nokki had said, raising his bow in the air. But there was no dead rabbit hanging from his belt.

"He's got terrible aim," Yrsa chuckled as she brushed the sand from her cheek. "His eyes are almost as bad as Troels's."

"The wind wasn't right," Nokki hissed.

Toke just shook his head and thought nothing more of it.

"Are you and Nokki close or something?"

"Just as friends," she says. "But still."

Signe walks past them into the long room. She squeezes Toke's shoulders as if she still can't believe he's home again.

She even strokes Yrsa's hair. She's always nicer to Yrsa when her father is home.

That afternoon Yrsa walks out of the house in her finest dress with her beads around her neck. She walks down the path to Nokki's house. Njall, Birger, and Egill are standing at the door. She can tell by the look on Njall's face that they've heard about Sporr's death. Above their door hangs the sea serpent's head, its eye eaten away by worms, making it look more like a skull.

"Is Nokki here?" Yrsa asks as calmly as possible. The boys look at her in surprise.

"What do you want with Nokki?" Njall snorts.

"To talk to him," Yrsa replies.

And comfort him, she wants to add. Run her fingers through his hair. Count the hairs on his chin. Feel the warmth of his hands and...

"Why would he want to talk to you?" Njall demands.

"Go away," says Egill.

"I'm sorry about Sporr," Yrsa says softly.

For a moment, Njall's face softens. For a split second, he looks like the little boy he used to be, the little boy who searched for shells in the sand with Troels. But then his eyes turn stone cold again.

"Leave us alone, cripple," he hisses.

His words cut deep. Birger grins.

Yrsa limps away. She can hear them whispering behind her back, but she's glad she can't hear what they're saying.

8

WHEN YRSA WAS A LITTLE GIRL, Toke would let her climb on his back. She'd rest her head on his shoulder as he carried her into the forest. He would point out the sacred trees that were older than time itself, the same ones their grandparents had known: the elm, the ash, the oak, and the evergreen at the edge of the forest. Together they would spread their arms as wide as they could to embrace the forest giants together. Often, their four open arms weren't long enough to fit around the tree. Yrsa would wail helplessly when she couldn't reach her father's outstretched fingers. She would ask him to squeeze the trunk with all his might so that their fingers could touch. Toke would growl and squeeze hard. But then he'd burst out laughing. "You're not trying hard enough," little Yrsa would cry, and he would laugh even harder.

Today, they place offerings at the feet of the sacred giants. The elves who live in the trees, stones, and dunes have protected the village in Toke's absence. He's grateful. He walks slowly so Yrsa can keep up. She uses the rod for balance because her father likes to go into the forest, where the ground is hard and uneven.

"The mothers tell me you have the gift of sight," Toke says.

Yrsa shrugs.

"What have you seen? The Norns at their spinning wheel?"

"No, I saw someone's fate—Revna, the fisherman's daughter. I saw scenes from her life—nothing special. I saw her kissing the stable slave. But maybe I imagined it."

"But you also saw her death, exactly as it happened."

"Yes."

Her father gently strokes the silver hammer of Thor around his neck.

"And Kveldulf the Norwegian?"

Yrsa recalls the dying Kveldulf: the pain in his chest, the rattle of death in his throat, the stopping of his heart. She had felt it all.

"He will die on a winter night among the eels," she says.

"The spear master is an old man," Toke says after a moment.

Yrsa is silent. Once again, she sees the slimy eels biting at Kveldulf's fingers.

"Word of your gift is going to spread," Toke says. "When the people from our village go to the markets in the hinterland, they won't be able to keep their mouths shut. All of Denmark will hear about it. Your value as a bride will double."

"Double?" says Yrsa. "That'll make Grandma happy. Then she can sell me for the wool of fifty sheep."

But Toke isn't listening. He starts pacing back and forth, as if he's being struck by one idea after the other, as if the tide is rolling in inside his head. Then he points at his daughter. He seems to want to say something but can't find his words.

"Forget that jeweler from Odin's Hill," he says. "He doesn't have enough wool or jewels to buy you. A seeress, one with a true eye, is worth a whole herd of cattle. Maybe one of the great lords of Denmark will take you for a wife."

Toke is as restless as a shoal of herring. He's so wound up that you'd think he'd found a magic ring from the gods—the kind that makes you rich or invisible.

"Don't be silly," Yrsa says, but she loves hearing him brag about her like that. A seeress! Is that the fate that the Norns tied into Yrsa's navel at her birth? They must have chosen her lot in life on a good day, a sunny day, a happy day with no hay fever or toothaches, when there was plenty of licorice root to go around.

"Believe me," Toke says, waving his arms in the air, "a nobleman would love nothing more than to have a seeress as a wife, his own personal völva to whisper words of advice into his ear. He'd feel as strong as Odin. And I'm talking about a real nobleman here. Not one of those half-wits who claims to be a distant second cousin of some king but turns out to be dumber than a troll."

"Stop it, Father," Yrsa says. "No nobleman would want me. As soon as he sees my foot, he'll run in the opposite direction."

This puts a damper on Toke's enthusiasm, but Yrsa doesn't want a nobleman, anyway. She wants Nokki.

"And besides, there are lots of seeresses in Denmark," Yrsa says.

"More than fleas on a dog," Toke admits. "And the last völva who came to our village was completely useless. She predicted a great catch on the full moon, lots of apples in the summer, and the death of a couple of children that winter. My big toe could have predicted all that."

Toke lets out a thunderous laugh that startles the birds.

"What did you do? Did you chase her out of the village?"

"Are you crazy? I paid her in silver. You never know. I don't want a völva putting some kind of secret curse on me."

"I'm not a seeress, Father," Yrsa mutters. "I didn't really see your ship coming back. I just said that to appease Kveldulf."

"But you said it, and the whole village heard you."

"I don't want to marry a nobleman. Or the jeweler's son. Please, call off the engagement. Let me stay here and work on the sails," Yrsa says.

Toke looks at his daughter and grins from ear to ear. "Gudrun told me you're in love. She didn't say with whom, but I have my suspicions."

Yrsa lowers her head. She can feel her cheeks turning bright red.

"Is it Njall?" asks Toke.

"Njall?!" Yrsa almost spits out the name.

"I heard you called Njall a piece of swine shit. That you really chewed him out."

"I did."

"So?"

"So what?"

"Well, it wouldn't be the first time that words of hate were actually words of love. I'm right, aren't I?" Toke gloats at his own intuition.

"Trust me, there's no way I'm in love with that jellyfish. You know he said my mother was a slave?" Yrsa says.

The smile disappears from Toke's face.

"Was Cara the Frisian a slave?" Yrsa asks.

Toke flinches at the sound of her name. He looks around, avoiding his daughter's gaze.

"If she was, that would make me half-slave," Yrsa says.

"You're a Dane," Toke snaps.

"But you bought Cara in Hedeby? From your cousin Harald?"

He sighs and scratches the raven tattoo on his neck. He scans the forest like a rabbit looking for a hole to jump into.

"Father?"

Finally, he says, "I saw her with that iron ring around her neck. She had big eyes. I couldn't look away."

"Really?"

"I paid twenty pieces of silver for her," Toke says. "My cousin Harald is a swindler, you know, a swindler and a thief and—"

"And then what did you do?" Yrsa interrupts. "Did you take her as a bed slave?"

Yrsa hurls the words at him like stones. Toke is stunned. His daughter has never spoken to him like this before.

"She loved me," Toke says. "And she loved life here. The sea. The people. When she became pregnant, I swore that I would always take care of you."

Yrsa waits for him to continue, but he says nothing more.

"You're not explaining this very well," Yrsa says.

"What do you want me to say?" Toke asks, annoyed. "She died after you were born. She came down with a fever, and it was all over. There's not much to tell you about Cara. She was with us for a short time. One summer and one winter. Everyone has forgotten her."

"You, too, then?"

He shrugs. Yrsa knows that the memory of people fades after they're gone. It's hard to remember a whole person. You remember words, the color of their clothes, the shape of their tattoos. Yrsa can barely recall Stink Breath's face, and he's hardly been gone one summer.

"What did you do with her? After she died, I mean?"

"We took her to the death ship," Toke murmurs.

"The death ship. Really?" Yrsa asks suspiciously.

"I considered her my wife," says Toke. "I dressed her in silk and laid her on a funeral pyre. Afterward, I scattered her ashes in the ship."

A wave of relief washes over Yrsa. So her mother's body hadn't been abandoned in the forest to be eaten by wolves, beetles, and crows.

"Do I look like her?" Yrsa asks.

"You're as stubborn as she was," says Toke. "And she loved you."

"How do you know that? She died right after I was born," says Yrsa.

"She was so sure that she was going to have a daughter. She said she would love you more than the gods," he says.

Toke and Yrsa follow the ox road out of the village until they reach the death ship at the edge of the forest. It's a dry, grassy field lined with stones forming the outline of a longship. It's here where the ashes of Yrsa's ancestors have all been scattered, including Cara's. In many ways, a human life is like a ship: birth is the bow rising out of the water like a knife, and death is the stern returning to the depths. In between, on the wide deck with the rowers and cargo, is life. Sometimes you have the wind in your sail, and you can pull in the oars and relax. And sometimes you have to row like mad, against the current and into the storm. The passing of a ship is like the passing of a life. When it's gone, only waves and ripples remain. And then nothing. Nothing is left of Cara either. And as Toke said, it doesn't matter.

Yrsa climbs on her father's back and wraps her arms around his neck.

"You're heavy," he groans, but he carries her like he used to. She rests her head on his shoulder. Her father: the seaman, the hero, the warrior. When they get back to the village, she carefully slides to the ground. The wood shavings on the path between the houses crunch under their shoes. They have a strong, oaky scent. The boys from the shipyard must have just scattered them today. The path is so soft that she feels almost no pressure on her bad foot.

"So, are you going to call off my engagement then?" Yrsa asks.

"I'll talk to Gudrun about it," Toke promises.

Yrsa smiles. She feels hopeful again. Toke will persuade her grandmother to let her stay in Mimir's Stool, where she'll be close to Nokki. Everything will be all right.

"I have a task for you," Toke says, motioning for her to follow him inside.

Toke and Yrsa walk through the house to the long room with the fire trench and beds on either side. Toke points to the far wall on the other end of the house. There, in the shadows, is a young woman sitting on the floor with her back against a beam. She's wearing a gray habit made of stiff cloth and a leather belt around her waist. She wears a dirty white veil, wrapped so tightly that you can't see a single hair on her head. Her ears are fully covered as well. All you can see is her face peeking out.

"That's the nun," Toke whispers. "I need you to look after her."

"Why?"

"The men are too scared to do it," says Toke. "Nobody dared to touch her after Sporr went overboard."

As soon as Yrsa hears the name Sporr, she remembers Nokki. Her thoughts ignite like a flame. She wants to see him. To comfort him. To hold him. Why hasn't he come looking for her?

"Are you listening?" Toke asks.

"What kind of slave is she going to be?" Yrsa asks.

"She's not a slave; she's a hostage. Her grandfather is the king of the Franks, which makes her a descendant of Charlemagne," Toke says. Then, he calls over to her, "Hey you, nun."

The filthy, pitiful-looking thing perks up. She stands up and walks toward them. Her face is dotted with pimples. She's at least a head and a half shorter than Yrsa, but she looks at them as if she's twice her size. Her eyes are dark and sharp as a spear.

"Don't call me 'nun,' you heathen," she says in broken Danish. "My name is Sister Job."

9

IT DOESN'T TAKE LONG for Job to realize that the young woman standing before her is the helmsman's daughter. She's built like her father—sturdy and angular. Her fingers are swollen and red from working outside, and her auburn hair is pulled back in a loose ponytail. In Ganda, on the River Scheldt, where Sister Job is from, you would never see hair like that. There, young women cover their heads, especially if they are married. There's also something wrong with the girl's shoulders, Job notices. They're crooked. When Yrsa takes two steps forward to shoo a cat away from a bucket of milk, the nun notices her leaning on the outer edge of her right foot. She has a way of navigating the narrow passages in the house, touching a beam, a rafter, or a clothes chest to keep her balance and stay clear of the fire. She must have been practicing those movements all her life.

"Job? Isn't that a man's name?" Yrsa asks.

"Job is a saint in the Bible," Job replies. "He lived a long time ago, before Moses fled from Egypt."

Yrsa has no idea who Moses is, or why he fled from some place called Egypt.

"God was testing his faith," Job explains. "He lost all his land and money. His children died, and he became ill. But he continued to trust the Lord. His faith was as strong as the mountains. I'm like him. That's why I chose his name and—"

"So, what's your real name?" Yrsa demands.

"No one calls me by my birth name anymore."

"You speak pretty good Danish."

"My mother and I had a Danish stable hand," she explains. "He taught me some Danish words. But that was a long time ago, before we entered the convent."

Yrsa looks the girl up and down. Her bare feet and ankles are covered with scabs from old wounds.

"You need shoes," Yrsa says.

Just then, Signe walks in. "You better watch out," she mutters as Yrsa opens her wardrobe and rummages around for a pair of shoes. "Christians are always trying to win you over to their god. Those nuns have all kinds of tricks up their sleeves. They'll fill your head with ridiculous stories so that you forget your own gods."

Job eyes Signe suspiciously. She's spent most of the day sleeping with her back against the cold wall. She just can't get used to this long, dark house with its thick wooden beams intricately carved with waves and shells. The ceiling is lower than that of a chapel, but it bulges outward as if there's so much life inside the house that the roof has started to expand. Spears are hammered against the front door as if the house is supposed to defend itself against intruders. On the wall hang dried flowers and shields emblazoned with raven heads. Fish hang on ropes over the fire to dry.

So far, Job has managed to distinguish the inhabitants of the house: the heavily pregnant Signe, who threw her arms around the helmsman's neck as soon as the ship was pulled onto the beach; their eldest son, Troels, who's constantly trying to pull off her tight white cap; and Little Sten, who mutters happily to himself as he plays out the stories in his head. The one who worries her most is Gudrun, with her strict, sharp mouth. She may be old, but her teeth haven't rotted away yet and her white hair is thick and full. She carries a long knife on her belt and is quick as a cat. When Job asked for some milk, Gudrun snapped at her and said that she still hadn't decided whether they were even going to let her live.

Yrsa returns with a pair of shoes and says, "Put these on."

Job holds the shoes upside down. She wants to make sure there are no nails in them. You never know with these heathens. She puts them on and ties the laces. They're lined with fur and very warm, quite comfortable actually, but she has no intention of thanking the daughter of her captors.

"Seal leather and rabbit fur," Yrsa says.

Job looks into the helmsman's daughter's eyes. They're the lightest eyes she's ever seen. Reverend Mother Philip told her she should never trust a person with light eyes. When you look into a pair of light blue eyes, you see your own reflection, and you'll be inclined to trust that person without questioning their true intentions. People with light eyes can deceive you without you even realizing it.

The helmsman's daughter beckons her to follow, and Job walks with her to the corner of the house, where there's a little mound of peat covered in furs. It's Sten's corner. Yrsa points to three sheets of parchment tacked on the wall.

"Can you read these?" she asks.

"Those are pages from a Bible," says Job. "Where's the rest of the book?"

"My father used it to make a fire," Yrsa says. "He gets cold easily."

Little Sten laughs. Job feels the anger boiling up in her body and says, "A Bible takes years to make."

Yrsa's surprised at how loud her voice is for a woman of such small stature.

"Did he burn your monastery to the ground?" Yrsa asks.

Job says a quick prayer at the thought. Then, she shakes her head.

"Well, you're lucky," Yrsa says. Job reaches for her necklace, but it's no longer there.

"I want my cross," says Job. "It's made of gold."

"I'm sure the blacksmith has melted it down already. He'll make a pin out of it."

Job glares at her.

"He's been known to roast monks in his oven too," Yrsa says.

Job can't believe her ears. For a moment, she thinks of St. Sebastian, who was pierced with arrows and spears by the Romans.

Little Sten starts to giggle, and then he barrels over with laughter. Yrsa starts laughing too; she was just joking. Troels gives Job's white veil a good tug, revealing a head of dark, greasy, spiky hair.

"My father doesn't burn down monasteries," Yrsa says. "Your king makes that up so the Franks will hate us. Come on, just tell me—what's written on that parchment?"

"What does it matter? It's all a joke to you anyway," Job growls.

"I don't understand why we're taking you hostage," Yrsa says. "Your clothes are tattered and you smell like manure. No one around here would pay much for a mutt like you."

Job's fingers twitch. She tucks her hands into her wide sleeves. She doesn't want them to see how scared and angry she really is.

"What's on that parchment?" Yrsa repeats.

Job looks at the three sheets. She recognizes them. She helped make the pages. She was in charge of the colors. A monk had taught her how to make and mix colors, and they used her paint for the drawings on all 258 pages of the Bible. They were beautiful pages—the words of the prophets and apostles immortalized by the hands of two scribes. The illustrations of the capital letters that opened each sentence were so beautiful they brought tears to her eyes. These three pages were all that remained of the Bible she had worked on for more than two years. The rest had been trampled and burned by these pagan fire worshippers. How dare they treat the Holy Word of God this way!

"Can you even read Latin?" Yrsa asks. "I'm starting to doubt it."

Job takes the sheets of parchment. The text is about the feast of Pentecost, when the Holy Spirit reminds the apostles of the words of Christ and says that their faith should burn like a holy fire within them. These pages are a sign that she mustn't bow to these primitive savages. Courage burns inside her like a holy flame. The Lord is testing her, just as He tested Job in the Bible. The Lord is testing her out of love. Now it's up to her to show Him that she's worthy of His love.

Job clenches her trembling fingers into fists and looks down at the passage in front of her. She remembers the priests in Ganda, who often ranted against the Northmen during mass.

"'From the Gentiles of the North, deliver us Lord,'" she quotes. "'May their ships fall from the edges of the Earth and perish. May black locusts destroy their crops and starlings peck their fruit trees bare. Send them the ten plagues of Egypt, Lord, and then another twelve plagues after those. May their women contract scabies, and their children contract smallpox. May their men bleed from their mouths and ears. And when one of these demons from the North lays on his deathbed, Lord, please take Your time. Prolong his agony and make him beg and groan for Your grace. But do not grant it. Throw him into the hottest caverns of hell, where the red-hot floor will burn the soles of his feet and where the starving dogs of Satan will tear the flesh from his bones, day after day, week after week, until the end of time.'"

Yrsa watches Sister Job gasp for breath. She'd rattled off the whole thing in that booming voice of hers. Yrsa grasps her amulet of Frigg. Did the nun just put a curse on her?

"Is that all?" shouts Gudrun from the front room. Her many jewels twinkle as she walks over to Sten's corner. Her eyes are black with fury.

"Amen," says Job.

Gudrun smacks her with a belt. And then again. Job weaves her fingers together in a prayer.

"Stop it, Grandma," Yrsa says. "Father doesn't want us to beat her."

"Don't believe a word of that Bible talk, Yrsa," Gudrun spits. "So, how much are you worth, nun?"

Job looks at her, confused.

"You claim to be the daughter of a count and the granddaughter of a king," Gudrun says. "But for all we know, you're the daughter of some poor nobleman who has nothing more than his honor and the clothes on his back."

"King Charles the Bald is my grandfather. And he is the grandson of Charlemagne," Job declares, her voice swelling with pride. Gudrun grins.

"How much will your father pay to get you back in one piece?" asks Gudrun.

Job doesn't answer.

"I would say at least a hundred pounds of silver," Gudrun declares.

"That's a fortune," Job says.

"To us, it certainly is," Gudrun replies. "But to your grandfather the king, it's nothing. Can you write?"

Job nods.

"Fine, I'll dictate the letter and you write it down."

"I'll need parchment."

"Parchment," repeats Gudrun, not quite sure what to make of it.

"Yes," says Job. "A piece of tanned hide for me to write on."

"We know what parchment is, girl," says Gudrun. "And we have ink. I bought it myself at the market in Hedeby. I thought it might come in handy one day."

Gudrun shoots a gloating look at Sten's little corner and plucks the three Bible pages from the wall. "Here's your parchment."

"Those sheets have already been written on!"

"And Father gave them to me!" Sten says indignantly.

"Your father will bring you some more. We've got a whole damn Bible here if you're stupid enough to want it," says Gudrun. "Well, nun, can you do anything with that?"

"I'd have to sand off the ink and paint," says Job. "But it's a mortal sin. It's the word of God."

"My granddaughter will help you," says Gudrun, handing Yrsa the sheets. Yrsa has to admit, the Latin letters *are* beautiful. There is not a splotch or smudge to speak of. But most beautiful of all are the colorful flowers and animals painted around them.

"It's calfskin," says Job. "The best parchment there is. Feel it."

Yrsa glides her fingers over the cool leather.

"And look at that letter!" Yrsa says.

She points to the capital J resting on the back of a donkey.

"The J is for Jesus. He arrived in Jerusalem on a donkey," Job explains. "Jerusalem is the center of the world."

"That's what you think," Yrsa says. "The center of Midgard is here in the North. With us."

Job shakes her head at Yrsa's ignorance. As if the center of the world could be anywhere but Jerusalem! That's why all the altars in all the churches in Francia and beyond are built to face the Holy Land.

"The monk who made this painting probably spent days or even weeks on it. First, he formed the letter in lead pencil and then painted it in with ink," Job says. "The monks use brushes with no more than five hairs and apply the ink in teeny tiny dots, like the footprints of an ant. There's almost a month's work in those three pages."

"It sounds a bit like making a sail," Yrsa says.

"A sail?" Job asks, perturbed. Does this Danish philistine really think that making a sacred masterpiece is comparable to tying a smelly piece of cloth on a stick?

"Sand it off!" Yrsa commands.

That afternoon, Job scrapes the ink off the parchment with a sponge stone. She watches as the letters and paintings slowly disappear. The ink leaves behind a faint, dark film on the leather. Then Job takes the jar of ink and stirs it with a quill. She lays down the parchment on a piece of wood. Gudrun watches over her shoulder as she dictates the letter, nodding occasionally, as if she can read Latin. The letters curl like earthworms as the tip of the quill scratches across the calfskin. Troels and Sten come over to watch as Job fills each page with words that no one in the village understands.

"So that's Latin?" asks Signe, who has just walked in carrying a basket full of mushrooms.

"The language of civilization," murmurs Job.

"But not the language of the gods," says Yrsa. "They write in runes. Those signs have magical power."

Job sighs. Runes! She's seen those rudimentary characters. They were carved into the walls of the ship that brought her here. She even saw one of the men carving them with his knife. He worked from top to bottom, which made sense—it would be hard to carve from bottom to top with a knife. Job asked him what the runes meant, and he said, "Halfdan rowed here."

Finally, Job puts down the quill and presses the cork back on the inkwell. Her hands are black with ink splatters. Just then, Toke walks in and asks what the letter says.

"It says you want a hundred pounds of silver before the thaw," Gudrun explains. "The silver will be weighed in Hedeby, on a Danish scale. Then, we will bring them the nun."

"Sounds good to me," says Toke. "And does it say that she will meet a bitter end if we fail to collect this ransom?"

"It most certainly does," Gudrun says. "I told her to write that we are bloodthirsty monsters who wipe their asses with the Ten Commandments."

"What are the Ten Commandments?" Yrsa asks.

"I'll explain it later," says Gudrun. "Give us your armband, son, so we can seal the letter."

Toke pries the silver armband of Jormundgandr from his upper arm and hands it to Gudrun. She runs her fingers around it. It's a masterfully forged piece of silver—a snake biting its tail.

"Beautiful, isn't it?" says Toke.

Job shrugs. No, she says to herself. There's nothing beautiful about an armband made of silver stolen from monasteries. Gudrun takes the candle and drips hot wax onto the folded parchment. Then she presses the head of the snake into it.

"The snake will protect the letter," Gudrun assures Job.

Later, Job follows Yrsa outside. They walk across the path to the barn that's built against the house. Signe has sent them out to collect eggs for dinner. It's not quite dark yet, but the moon is already out. The sight of it gives Job courage. It's shiny and full, reminding her of the silver plate that the priest uses to serve Holy Communion. She crouches down and digs around in the wood chips on the path.

"What are you doing?" Yrsa asks.

Job picks up two long, narrow chips. She lays them on top of each other crosswise and binds them with a string. Then, she turns and shows her creation to Yrsa. She's about to ask for a strip of leather to tie it around her neck when she stops with a gasp. There, behind Yrsa, is a giant wolfhound.

"Behind you," she whispers in fright. Yrsa turns and smiles.

"Oh, that's Odin," Yrsa says. "How's that wound of yours, you little furball?"

The beast whimpers. Yrsa crouches down and examines the dog's paw. The animal leers at Job with his one eye and sniffs at her long habit.

"His name is Odin?" asks Job uncertainly.

"I call him that because he has one eye."

"So your god is half blind?"

"No, Odin already sees everything. He gave up his left eye in exchange for a cup of water from the well of wisdom."

"Jesus doesn't need a well, and he's all-knowing."

"Odin is not," says Yrsa. "But he gets wiser every day. He even raises people who have been hanged from the dead, just for a moment, so they can tell him their secrets. Then he shuts their eyes forever. He is the father of all, the creator of the nine worlds."

"Nine?"

"Yes. We are in the middle world, Midgard. The gods live in the upper world, Asgard; the dead in the lower world, Niflheim; the giants in Jotunnheim. The stars are sparks from the fire world, Muspelheim, and—"

"There's no such thing as nine worlds," Job says emphatically. "There is heaven and there is earth. That's it. Odin is nothing but a child's tale."

"You better watch what you say," Yrsa says. "Odin can hear you. Sometimes he turns himself into an osprey and flies across the human world. Sometimes he wanders through Midgard disguised as one of us. That's why they call him the Wanderer. And he can get incredibly angry. Then, they call him the Screamer or the Savage. He has at least two hundred names."

"My god is just called God."

"That's easy."

"He sees everything and knows everything. He loves me."

"Well, nobody loves you here, Job," Yrsa snaps.

When Yrsa opens the barn door, they're struck by the sour smell of hay, manure, and animals. It's dark inside, but full of life. The goats, cows, and pigs all look up in surprise. Odin the dog wanders into the barn and starts sniffing around. A chicken flutters up from her perch.

Job looks back at the forest in the distance, a dark wall of trees. She could make a run for it right now. The girl would never catch her with that bad foot.

"There are wolves and trolls in those woods, you know. And they're far more vicious than we are," Yrsa says, as if she can read Job's mind. "They'll eat you alive—skin, hair, and all. You wouldn't be the first person to disappear without a trace, but who knows, we might find some of your fingers with all the bone marrow sucked out of them. Trolls love the marrow of young women."

"Have you ever seen one of these trolls?"

"No, but believe me, they're there. They have red hair and their bodies are as dark as dirt."

Job makes two signs of the cross.

"And even if you manage to avoid the trolls and the wolves, you'll get lost or drown. Beyond the forest are swamps and lakes so wide that you can't even see across them. And in the winter, it's twice as treacherous."

"Why?" asks Job.

"It gets so cold that that skinny, naked god of yours would freeze to death in a second," Yrsa says as she plucks a few eggs out of the hay and hands them to Job.

"Here, take these," she says.

But Job doesn't respond. She stares at the open barn door, where three young men are standing, watching them. Two of them enter. The third stays by the door.

"What do you want, Njall?" Yrsa asks, clutching the seven eggs in her hands. Job hears the agitation in her voice.

Njall looks at Job and says, "Get out of here, Yrsa. She's the one we want."

Then he draws his sword.

10

EGILL FORGED THE SWORD especially for Njall. He works in the blacksmith's shop, where he mostly makes nails and clamps for ships, but this summer, he made his first sword. He worked on it for weeks, forging seven pieces of iron, pounding them down with a hammer, putting them all back into the fire, and pounding them down again. He even worked a ring that Njall received from his father into the hilt. The blacksmith told him the weapon was too heavy at the tip and too light at the hilt, making it out of balance. But Njall thinks it's magnificent. He coats it with fish oil every night so he can pull it out of his scabbard in one smooth motion. He even gave it a name, which he etched into the blade in runes.

"I call my sword Vengeance," Njall says to Yrsa and Job. "Vengeance for Sporr."

Yrsa reads the jagged runes cut into the blade—if she didn't know any better, she'd say they were carved by a five-year-old. She tries to make eye contact with Egill and Birger, but Njall's cousins avoid her gaze.

"Come here, nun!" Njall shouts, but Job hides behind

Yrsa, clasping her new wooden cross. The last streaks of daylight seep into the barn through the chinks in the wood.

"My cousin is dead, and it's her fault," Njall says.

"Your cousin fell overboard," Yrsa says.

"I've come to avenge him," Njall declares.

"You always hated Sporr," says Yrsa.

Njall is surprised. He doesn't know that Nokki told her that he'd been jealous of Sporr because Nokki spent more time with him. Whenever Nokki and Sporr went fishing or hunting, Njall wasn't allowed to go with them.

But Yrsa suspects that it's not Sporr's death that Njall is upset about. It's his father. She has heard the rumors.

Naefr has barely said a word to Njall since he returned home. He hasn't even looked at Njall's new sword. He hasn't said a word about the sea serpent's head hanging over the door. Not once did he stop and give Njall a pat on the back. And he was a prince of the solstice, for Odin's sake! Meanwhile, the men were all grumbling the same thing: it was the nun and her god who'd killed Sporr. It's her fault that Naefr is so distant.

"The nun is being held hostage," Yrsa says. "She's worth a lot of silver."

"If your father believes that, he's a fool!" Njall shouts. Yrsa takes a step back.

"The nun is under my father's protection," Yrsa says as confidently as possible. "If you so much as touch her, Toke will chop you to pieces. Or better yet, he'll castrate you."

Egill, the stupid one, can't help but laugh.

"If there's anything down there to castrate, that is," Yrsa says. Egill roars with laughter.

"Shut up, Egill," Njall snarls. "And you, cripple, step aside." Yrsa doesn't budge.

"Get on with it," Birger squeaks at the door. "I hear voices outside."

"That nun should've died at sea. Not Sporr," Njall declares.

"Jesus protected me," Job says from behind Yrsa's shoulder. "And He will protect me here, as well."

Yrsa groans. Why can't she just keep her mouth shut? She'll only provoke him.

"Your god is dead!" cries Njall. "He's nothing but a corpse on a cross."

"Jesus is alive," Job says, grinning, as if she knows something he doesn't. The grin makes the three boys pause. How can she smile in the face of death?

"Go home, Njall," Yrsa says.

At that, Egill lunges forward and grabs Yrsa by the wrists. He tries to press her against the wall of the barn, but she swings her arms down and yanks her wrists free. She cracks the seven eggs in her hands against his ears, and they splatter down his face. Egill, with his head dripping in eggshells and slime, doesn't dare to slap her. She is the helmsman's daughter, after all. Then, he feels Yrsa's fist ram into his stomach. For a moment, he hesitates. Spear master Kveldulf has never taught them what a warrior should do when his hair and cheeks are covered in egg yolk and a girl is pounding him in the ribs. But Egill knows Yrsa's weak point. He kicks her bad foot out from under her, and she immediately loses her balance and topples sideways, landing among the chickens. Then, he throws himself on her and pushes her arms against the ground. The chickens cluck indignantly, feathers flying. Odin the dog is wound up from all the tussling and flapping. The pig grunts, the goats bleat, and the cows moo as loudly as they do on the first day they're let out to pasture after a long winter.

Njall raises his sword with both hands. The nun just stands there in the middle of the barn, as stiff as a dried stockfish, with the wooden cross between her narrow fingers. She murmurs prayers that Njall doesn't understand. She murmurs the words so fast that they seem to fall from her lips like crumbs from a table.

"Hurry up!" Birger hollers from the door.

Njall hesitates. Why isn't the nun begging for mercy? Why isn't she crying and screaming? That would make this a lot easier.

"What are you waiting for?" Egill shouts through all the barking and cackling and mooing.

Yrsa squirms under Egill like a wild animal. She scratches and bites. Egill groans as she shoves her knee into his groin. He struggles to keep her against the ground.

"Is she cursing me?" Njall asks.

"That god of hers has no power here," Egill cries. "Cut her down."

Njall raises the sword above his head, arms trembling. He has to. He has to show his cousins that he's a man.

Suddenly, the hairy wolfhound springs in front of the nun.

Njall's raised sword reminds the dog of the old days, when he was just a pup and the boys chased after him in the dunes with sticks. How they beat him and jabbed him wherever they could. That's how he lost an eye, and if he hadn't taken cover under the low dune bushes, they would've killed him. After that, the pup hid in the bushes and wasn't seen for a long time. He fed on mice and rabbits and waited for the pain to subside. When he finally emerged from the bushes months later, he had grown into a giant, hairy beast. No boy ever thought of going after him with a stick again. But even now, whenever someone holds a stick—or a sword—in the air, the dog springs into action.

Odin growls menacingly.

"Get out of here, you beast!" shouts Njall, swinging his sword at the dog. The animal leaps aside and bares his teeth, the teeth of his ancestors, the wolves of Denmark. Njall swings the sword down at the dog. The blunt edge of the weapon gets tangled in the mass of hair on the animal's back. Njall, groaning in frustration, yanks it out, pulling entire tufts of dog hair with it. The dog howls.

"Someone's coming!" Birger cries.

Shoes crunch on the path outside. Through a crack in the barn door, Njall sees Birger make a run for it. Clearly, whoever is out there is about to enter. But all it will take is one swing of the sword. One well-aimed blow to the neck, and it'll be over. That's what Kveldulf taught them in their lessons. Njall raises the weapon one last time, but it's too late. He feels Odin's teeth sink into his wrist like a trap around a deer's leg. He drops the sword and screams with every ounce of hugr inside him.

Just then, Toke appears in the doorway.

"Down, dog!" roars the helmsman. Odin immediately releases Njall's wrist and takes shelter under a cow's udder.

Then Toke sees his daughter lying in the hay with Egill on top of her. The boy immediately jumps to his feet. His hair is full of eggs and his face is scratched from Yrsa's nails. Blood streams from his left ear. Yrsa has bitten off a piece of it. Egill raises his hands in the air as if he can explain exactly what he was doing on top of Toke's daughter in the hay. But before he can even say a word, Toke shoves him, and he falls among the goats.

Job stops praying. She can't stop staring at Egill's bloody head.

Toke turns to Njall. "What do you think you're doing?" he barks.

Njall doesn't answer. He looks at the ground, clutching his maimed wrist, and lifts his weapon. His sword hand trembles as he struggles to lift it high enough to push the tip down into his scabbard. Njall turns to Toke and says, "If you touch me again, or even insult me like your daughter just did, I'll call for a duel on a bull skin."

"Get a grip, boy," Toke says. "I understand that you're grieving the loss of your cousin. He was a good boy."

"He wasn't a boy," Njall says. "He was a man, like me."

Njall brushes against Toke's shoulder as he walks out of the barn.

Toke goes after him.

"Wait a second," Yrsa hears her father say.

Egill stumbles past her. He keeps his hand pressed against his ear. Blood seeps through his fingers.

"Kick my foot again and I'll castrate you, you troll," Yrsa says.

Yrsa watches Job tuck a lock of hair back into her habit and pull down her wide sleeves to cover her arms. She doesn't understand how Job remained so calm through the whole ordeal. Is she really that brave? Or is she a little thick between the ears?

Odin scampers over to Job and licks her fingers. That mangy, smelly furball never licks anyone's fingers except Yrsa's.

"You humiliated Njall. He will not be happy about it," Yrsa says. She can't help admiring the little woman.

"I put my trust in God," Job replies. "And I'm not afraid of death. This life is temporary. The next life is eternal. The Lord will reward me in heaven."

Yrsa shakes her head. The girl is out of her mind.

11

IN THE FOLLOWING DAYS, Egill and Njall do not leave their house. Egill has a huge bandage around his head and Njall's hand has swollen to twice its size. Tiny as the hooded sister may be, she has beaten two princes of the solstice and sent them home crying for their mothers. At least, that is how the story spreads. The men avoid Job now, stepping out of her way and occasionally touching their amulets. The women are curious. They repeatedly ask her what exactly happened in that barn and if Yrsa had a hand in it. Sister Job proudly states that Jesus intervened on her behalf and that the Danes can expect more of His interventions. It irritates the women more than it scares them. Moreover, they don't like the way Job shakes her head or scoffs while they are offering a sheep's head to Odin. Some say the nun needs to be taught a lesson in respect. The slaves, on the other hand, have taken an immediate liking to Job. They invite her into their damp, shabby weaving hut and she helps them pick apart the sheep's wool. Some of the fibers are so thin that Job can barely grasp them with her fingers. She can even taste them in her mouth and feel them in her lungs. She can't believe she's breathing the fibers in. The other slaves tell her she will be fine once she coughs them out. The slaves cough all the time, even when they're not working on the wool.

"You will not remain slaves," Job assures the slave women. "Pray to God, trust in Him, and one day your people will leave this place of enslavement. God will help you like He helped Moses. He made the seas part for Moses."

"Did that really happen?" Bulging Calves asks, tugging at the raw wool on the loom. She weaves it very tightly to keep out the wind and rain.

"It is the absolute truth. It is in the Good Book," Job says.

"If the seas could part, the Danes would know about it," Yrsa says, coming into the weaving hut.

Sister Job bristles at the blasphemy, but Yrsa doesn't give her a chance to speak. "Come along, it is bathing day."

"I have no need for bathing, thank you very much," Job says.

But the slaves get up and follow Yrsa outside. They line up behind the Danish women and take the path toward the sea. Job walks out of the hut and wonders if she should follow them, when she notices Yrsa looking back at the house with the sea-snake head. These past days, Job has often seen Yrsa near the racks with drying herring, watching that house. Waiting for someone to come out, it seems.

"Come on," Yrsa says, and walks down the ox road through the dunes. The line of women has already gone far ahead.

"Bathing is something that we do indoors," Job says.

"Indoors?" Yrsa repeats, surprised.

"Well, I suppose we could bathe in the creeks around Ganda, but no one does that. My convent is perched on a hill, you see. We overlook the River Scheldt, but there are lots of small creeks too. Flowers grow on their shores in all shapes and colors. From high on the hill, you can see the creeks in the landscape glistening in the sunlight like threads of silver. It is a beautiful sight."

"Sounds awfully wet," Yrsa says.

"The monks call it 'the flooded land' because the water overflows its banks and submerges the meadows and fields. The earth is wet, soggy, and—"

Suddenly Job stops talking. They have arrived on the shore and all the women are throwing off their clothes on the dry sand.

"What are they doing?" Job asks with a tremor in her voice.

"Bathing," Yrsa says, undoing the decorative pins that hold up her dress. Job's mouth drops when she sees the women walk naked across the wet sand and into the surf. She hears their cries as they hit the icy water. Job crosses her arms in front of her habit. She's never taken off her clothes in front of anyone before.

"What are you standing there for?" says Yrsa. "Take that off."

"At the convent, we wash without taking off our habits. That's just how we do things," says Job as she walks onto the wet sand toward the basket with bars of soap. She takes the soap in her hands, turns it around in a bit of water, and starts rubbing her legs with it.

"What are you doing?" asks Gudrun, who wears her jewelry even in the sea.

"Bathing!" shouts Job.

The women all laugh. Two mothers approach her. Their feet splash in the surf.

"Don't touch me! Yrsa, help me!" Job shouts, but the women have already grabbed her. They pull off her habit, then her white petticoat, and finally the cap on her head.

"Look, she's bald!" shouts one of the women.

They stare at the bald spot on the crown of Job's head: a perfect little circle called a tonsure, a sign of her devotion to God. The hair around it is short, dark, and greasy.

"Doesn't your hair grow there anymore?" asks Gudrun.

Job is as naked as Christ on the cross. She clutches her arms in front of her chest, shivering, and not just from the cold.

"Cat got your tongue, nun?" asks Gudrun.

"That spot on my head is where I was touched by God's finger," she bluffs.

The women step back. One of them touches her amulet.

"Bible talk," says Gudrun. She takes Job by the wrist and pulls her into the waves. The women cheer Gudrun on.

"Not so deep," shrieks Job, and the women hoot. They grab Job under her armpits and around her ankles and hurl her into the waves. Her head goes under, and she bobs back to the surface. The women are buckled over with laughter, having forgotten all about her strange god who touches women with his finger. Only the slaves do not laugh. They've probably been through the same ordeal. Freezing and terrified, Job screams with misery. She tries to stand up, but a wave splashes over her head, and she falls forward.

"The water is toxic, it's toxic!" she shrieks as she gags on the salty foam.

Job runs back toward the shore but slams right into Signe, her pregnant belly as heavy as a loaded ship.

"Don't forget to wash your face," Signe says. "Seawater works wonders against pustules, you know."

There is more laughter. Signe pushes Job back toward the waves.

"That's enough, Mother," says Yrsa. Her voice startles Signe somewhat. Yrsa helps the young woman up and leads her to the wet sand. The women whistle and mock Job's cowardice. How can anyone be so afraid of the sea?

Later, the women pull their dresses back over their heads and fasten the shoulder straps to their chests with pins. Then, they huddle around the fire in the sand. The slaves walk back to warm themselves in their hut. Job walks up to Mimir's rock, faces east, and makes the sign of the cross. She opens the leather bag on her belt and takes out a book. The parchment creaks as she opens it.

"Again? How many times do you have to pray?" Yrsa asks.

"Seven times a day. These are my afternoon prayers. Please don't disturb me."

Job turns angrily back to her prayer book and spits out her prayers. Yrsa doesn't understand a word of the Latin gibberish, and walks on toward the village. When she arrives,

Bulging Calves calls her over. She's standing next to a cart by the weaving hut. Yrsa walks toward her and looks inside the cart. Inside are bales of wool. "The wool of twenty-five sheep," Bulging Calves says.

Yrsa is so surprised that she accidentally leans on her bad foot and almost loses her balance. Her dowry has arrived. She's been bought by the jeweler. Apparently, Gudrun has had the final word on her marriage.

After dinner, Yrsa collects the leftovers in a wicker basket. Toke hands her a piece of meat and licks his fingers. Sten and Troels give her their leftover cheese. Only Job has cleaned her plate and has nothing for the basket. Yrsa heads outside, and Job follows her. She doesn't like being alone with the rest of Yrsa's family—especially Gudrun.

The moon is three-quarters full. Yrsa smears a streak of butter on a rock.

"An offering for the álfar," she explains. "They watch over us and heal us when we're sick."

"Is that so?"

"But if you don't take care of them, if you forget about them, they'll make sure the harvest fails or that you get sick. They live in stones. And trees."

"And I suppose these elves talk to one another?" Job asks, barely hiding her scorn.

"Oh yes, elves are chatterboxes."

Job kisses the wooden cross around her neck and murmurs a Hail Mary. She asks God to shine his light on these wandering, ignorant fire worshippers.

All of a sudden, Yrsa stops, and Job bumps into her from behind. She's watching a boy walk out of the village toward the shipyard. She can't take her eyes off of him.

"Go back to the house," she says.

"What are you going to do?" asks Job.

"Go back, nun!" she hisses.

Job walks toward the village. Yrsa hurries to the shipyard.

12

MOONLIGHT STREAMS ACROSS Nokki's face. He's standing in a corner of the boathouse, fidgeting nervously like someone who can't find a place to pee. Yrsa just stands there, her head held high. She will not go to him. She has no intention of throwing herself at his feet. What does he think? That he can come back from his stupid Viking voyage and just ignore her? He's been home for a whole week! Meanwhile, she's been stuck listening to the Bible blah-di-blah of a nun who refuses to take a bath and endlessly complains that her eyes and throat and arms and toes hurt from working in the weaving hut.

Nokki sees Yrsa standing there, but he refuses to make eye contact.

"What is it, Nokki?" she asks finally. "Why are you avoiding me like this?"

She makes sure that he hears the pride in her voice. She is the daughter of Toke the Helmsman and Cara the Frisian, the woman who refused to be subjugated by the Danes and wore a dress of red silk. Yrsa crosses her arms in front of her chest to protect her hugr, even though she knows it's not enough. Nokki says nothing.

"Whatever happened on that voyage doesn't matter now," Yrsa says. "You're home now, Nokki."

"Home?" he asks.

The resentment in his voice surprises her.

"Is this my home then?" Nokki barks. "This hole? This nest of savages?"

"Nokki?" Yrsa asks. "Why didn't you come to me? Is it because Njall told you I'm the daughter of a slave?"

"What?" he asks, surprised.

"Oh, so that's not the reason then." Yrsa is relieved, almost excited. Then it must be her engagement. That's the only other thing it could be. Nokki is sad because he knows he's going to lose her to the jeweler's son.

"I told my father I don't want to marry Ljufr from Odin's Hill. He can get lost. I want to marry a boy from the village."

"What do you mean someone from the village?" he asks, confused.

"Did you get any silver on your voyage?" Yrsa asks, but she already hears the doubt in her voice. "Enough for a dowry?"

Nokki doesn't answer, so she continues.

"If you have silver, we can persuade Gudrun to send the wool back to the jeweler."

Nokki shakes his head.

"But if you have nothing, we'll just run away. As long as we're together."

Still, Nokki says nothing. He paces through the boathouse. His leather shoes shuffle on the wooden floor.

"We kissed a few times in the dunes," Nokki says without meeting her gaze. "That doesn't mean we have to get married."

So this is it, Yrsa realizes. It's all over. She can feel it in her hugr; it's bleeding. It must be her crooked foot. Nokki son of Naefr doesn't want to marry a girl with a deformity like hers. No matter what she does, even if she covers herself in amber and gold, she will always be crooked. Nokki is no better than the jeweler's son from Odin's Hill who stared at her so disdainfully, or the boy she wrestled into the cesspit when he puckered his lips at her. She feels the anger boiling up inside her.

"I climbed that stupid tree for you, you asshole!" Yrsa screams. "I knocked that bees' nest on Birger's head for you. I broke Njall's rib for you. I wanted to impress you. So you would say, 'Look what my girl can do.'"

Finally, Nokki looks at her. And she sees it—his thoughts are somewhere else.

He remembers how she wrestled him into the sand. Their teeth clashing. How they laughed. Yrsa would be his if he wanted her to be. But he doesn't want her. He wants some girl in Brittany with dark eyes and dimples in her cheeks. Wembrit was her name. She brought the Danes bread, cheese, and roasted sardines every day when they were there. And the whole time, she couldn't take her eyes off Nokki. One day, he followed her down a windy path between the boulders. She leaped from cliff to cliff as if the elves were pushing her along. Finally, he found her waiting for him at the end of the path, where the waves crashed into the rocks. He wanted to bring Wembrit back to Denmark with him, but she refused. She loved Brittany too much. He joked that he would just have to carry her away with him then, but she was startled. The next day she disappeared without a trace. Every evening he walked down the path between the cliffs and called her name. But only the seagulls answered.

One evening, Naefr asked him if Wembrit had left him for a real man. Naefr was slurring his words, completely drunk, and none of the Danes around the fire laughed at his joke. Then Sporr told Naefr to look in his own pants to see if he was really a man. Naefr staggered to his feet and charged at Sporr. One of the men tripped him. He fell into the sand and stayed there all night, snoring like a forest troll. The men hoped Naefr wouldn't remember the insult the next day. But later, during the storm, when the ship's planks were creaking and the waves were as high as the dunes, Naefr demanded that Sporr—and no one else—toss the nun overboard. When Nokki got up to help Sporr, Naefr grabbed him by the shoulders and pushed him back onto the bench. He held him down until the storm knocked Sporr off the ship.

"My father killed Sporr," Nokki says to Yrsa.

"What? I thought the storm killed him."

Nokki looks away.

"Surely, Naefr couldn't have known that Sporr would fall overboard," Yrsa says. "My father says you almost jumped ship yourself, that you wanted to battle the goddess of the sea."

"Leave me alone," says Nokki.

Is he grieving the loss of his friend? If that's it, then she wants to be the one to comfort him, to gaze out at the sea with him, put her arm around his shoulder, every day if she has to, until his sadness rolls out with the tide.

"What are you still doing here, Yrsa?" Nokki shouts. "You're getting on my nerves."

They both stand there in silence for a moment. The surf rumbles. The seagulls squawk.

"Then why did you come to me in the fog if you didn't love me?" Yrsa finally asks.

"You came to me," Nokki says. "You always loved me. When I asked you how the sail was coming along, your face would turn bright red and you could barely speak. Didn't you hear the guys in the yard laughing at you?"

Yrsa hears what he's saying, but she's not listening. She doesn't want to listen.

"You're better off with that jeweler's son. He'll love you. I won't."

His words cut her hugr to shreds.

"You know I don't want him," Yrsa sputters.

"We have nothing to want," Nokki sighs. "We have to accept things the way they are."

"I'm the dangerous one, you know!" she yells.

Her voice trembles with excitement, which makes Nokki laugh.

Yrsa throws herself at him with a scream. She bangs her fists on his head like a madwoman so that he has no choice but to take her in his arms, if only to absorb her blows, if only to grab her wrists and push her to the ground. If only to lie on top of her so that she can feel his cheek against hers one last time, so she can smell his hair and feel his warm breath on her skin. Nokki pins her down against the floorboards. His nose is bleeding. One of his eyes is red. He keeps his hand flat on her chest so she can't get up.

Still, she wants nothing more than to kiss him.

"Yes, you are the dangerous one," he says.

Then he stands up, walks out of the boathouse, and is swallowed up by the night.

Yrsa just lies there. All she can hear is the pounding of the surf. It's as if all her strength has left her body and is seeping into the floorboards. Finally, she clambers to her feet and hobbles away. Her legs feel heavy. It hurts to walk. The tide rolls in across the beach. She listens to the roar of the waves. The wind whips the foam from their crests. Yrsa pulls the woolen cloak over her head, drops it in the dry sand, and walks into the sea. Her dress is instantly soaked in the water. Soon, she is in up to her chest. She gasps for breath as her body takes in the cold. She feels the current pulling at her legs and ankles like a hungry animal. She swims out into the deep, where Stink Breath disappeared underwater, where he was pulled down by the monster. It was low tide then. It's high tide now and less treacherous, but still the water swirls. She plows through the current, the waves snapping at one another like dogs. Her dress is heavy. Her arms are tired. But finally, she feels the sand beneath her feet again. She's reached the sandbank. She stumbles up Heath Ridge and drops to the ground like an exhausted sea creature. Then she curls up in the sand and catches her breath. She smells the wet heather, seaweed, and empty crab carcasses. Around the overgrown sandbank, the sea growls and churns. She shivers in her wet clothes. The tide has engulfed the entire beach. Soon, it will start to recede, and she'll be trapped by the retreating water. Then, she won't make it back. She has to get up now and swim to the beach, or one day the mothers will tell their children that the sea monster swallowed the helmsman's daughter.

But what does it matter? She's not going to be the wife of Nokki son of Naefr, the boy with the ice-melting smile and twenty-seven hairs on his chin. She has to marry Ljufr the troll. This is the fate the Norns have chosen for her.

"Get up," she says to herself, but she can't. She hears the seagulls screeching overhead and looks up at the stars, sparks from the world of fire. She doesn't want to leave this spot. She doesn't want to forget Nokki. She has never been so tired.

Then, she hears a voice above the roar of the surf. There's someone splashing through the water in her direction. It's Job. Yrsa can tell by her white cap. For a moment, she can't believe her eyes. She almost has to laugh. Then she realizes that the nun is coming for her. She's wading out to Heath Ridge. Yrsa straightens up and looks at the beach. The tide has turned. Any moment now, Job will lose her footing and be swept out to sea. "Go back!" Yrsa shouts.

A wave splashes against Job. She falls over, but finds her footing again.

"Go back!" Yrsa shouts over the rumble of the waves. But Job is as deaf as the fish. *Odin, give that nun your wisdom! She's going to drown, and the village can kiss their hundred pounds of silver goodbye.*

Yrsa takes off her wet dress and wades into the water. Only then does Job stop. She waits. Yrsa is standing waist-deep and feels the current pulling her out to sea. The freezing wind gnaws at her bare back and shoulders. For a moment, she's not sure if she should dive in. There's no way she'll make it, she thinks, but then she gathers her courage. After all, it was her stepmother Signe, the woman who can transform into a seal, who taught her to swim. She taught her how every move counts, and how to use the current to her advantage. Yrsa hurls herself into the water. At first, she's sucked down by the current. She doesn't fight it; she lets herself be carried away, dodging the whirlpools. Only when she feels the current weakening does she start battling her way through the water. She swims in a wide arc toward the beach. It's a long way, but she'll make it. She's sure of it.

A little while later, Yrsa is sitting next to Job on the dry sand. She pulls her knees into her chest so her woolen cloak hangs over them like a tent and buries her feet in the sand. She's shivering. Her body just can't get warm.

"What were you doing out there? Was it that boy? Are you upset about him?" Job asks.

Yrsa can't believe the nun is bringing up Nokki now.

"Did you overhear us in the boathouse, or something?"

"I heard everything."

Everything! How dare she? Yrsa wrings the water out of her hair.

"Why did you come after me?" Yrsa asks.

"I had a feeling you were going to do something stupid."

Yrsa doesn't answer.

Finally, she says, "Come on, let's go back before we catch cold."

Yrsa walks ahead of Job into the house. Everyone is asleep. A bright orange log is still smoldering in the fire trench. Yrsa crouches down in front of it. She pulls up her cloak and lets the heat caress her legs. Beside her, Job steals a bit of warmth for herself.

"Have you ever loved anyone?" asks Yrsa, looking into the fire.

"You mean, except for Jesus?"

Yrsa rolls her eyes. "Yes, except for him."

"Well, the sisters of course. Especially Sister Mark. We arrived at the convent around the same time. I was ten, she was eleven."

"Mark?"

"All the sisters have men's names from the Bible. Mark and I are the youngest. The oldest is Sister John. She claims to be as old as Sarah in the Bible, which would be over a hundred. But I don't believe her. And my m—I mean, the Reverend Mother is called Philip."

Yrsa stabs the ashes. A flame pops up. She puts her bad foot close to the flame to soothe the muscles in her ankles.

"I'm sorry, I'm just babbling," Job says.

"No, it's fine. You can babble."

Job nods emphatically. For a moment, they listen to the wood cracking in the fire.

"Do you love your gods?" Job asks.

"Well, I don't know," Yrsa ponders. "I love Frigg. The rest are fickle. They look down on us from Asgard. We are their playthings. We amuse them. But I respect them. The world is their creation, after all."

Sister Job says nothing, not wanting to contradict Yrsa's words. Not now.

"Look," Yrsa says, pointing to the night sky, which is visible through the hole in the ceiling.

"The sky is the skull of the frost giant Ymir," Yrsa says. "It was Odin who killed him. The giant's blood created the sea, and his flesh became the earth. The mountains grew from Ymir's bones and the trees used to be his hair. Our world was once the body of a giant."

Job doesn't say a word. She keeps staring at the night sky.

"Thanks for coming for me," Yrsa says.

Job smiles, for the first time, it seems. It's a nice smile.

"Goodnight, nun," Yrsa says.

"Goodnight, heathen."

13

EVERY NIGHT, Job falls asleep at Yrsa's side. She's gotten used to the way the Danes smell—a mixture of fish and seaweed. Sometimes, just before she wakes up, she imagines that she's back at the convent. But as soon as she hears the snoring of the men, she remembers that she's far from home and surrounded by fire worshippers.

She wakes up early every day, just in time for morning prayer. Her fingers are stiff because she sleeps with them tightly folded in prayer, one finger over another. She starts by making five signs of the cross. Then, she pulls a woolen cloak over her habit. It's a gray Danish cloak eaten away by moths, but it keeps her warm and dry. She walks outside. The sharpness of the cold takes her breath away. She heads to the tall stone that looks like an altar and prays with her back to the sea. Somehow that stone makes her feel connected to her eleven sisters back home. They, too, must be praying and thinking of her right now. She reads aloud from her psalmbook in a voice loud enough for twelve. Still, she can barely hear herself over the crashing of the waves and the squawking of the gulls.

She imagines that the words she recites in Mimir's Stool are being answered by her eleven sisters in Ganda. She sits there, tiny in the shadow of the tall stone. Job misses the sound of the bells that mark the passing of each day. She misses entering the chapel with her sisters. The rustling of their habits. The creaking of their joints as they kneel on the floor. The murmur of prayers. The waft of smoldering incense. In that chapel, she felt as safe as a child in her mother's womb.

But praying at the stone gives her courage. She can't give up. She has to find a way to flee this place, just as Moses fled from Egypt.

One morning, on her way to the weaving hut after her prayers, she sees Njall standing outside his house, peeing in the grass. She immediately averts her gaze, but she's too late. He sees her and runs after her. She feels his hand on her neck. He pulls her back and whispers, "I'm coming for you, nun. If we don't get an answer from your father before the thaw, you're mine."

Then he pushes her away from him. Job runs back to Yrsa's house. Everyone is still asleep. She sits down by the fire pit, clasps her trembling hands so hard her fingers turn white, and mutters a prayer. The cats slither between her legs, but she ignores their hungry cries. Only after the seventh "Hail Mary, full of grace..." do her hands stop trembling. She tosses a few twigs and a bunch of hay into the ashes and strikes the flint. Sparks fall into the hay and quickly catch fire. Then she adds a few more twigs on top and watches them curl and disappear into the flame. Finally, she adds a log, which crackles in the flames. Job kisses the wooden cross around her neck, the same one she kisses at least a hundred times a day. She can't take a sip of milk before muttering a prayer of thanksgiving and kissing the cross. It is God who feeds her, not the cow in the barn.

In October, the women head inland to trade smoked fish, cheese, and seal leather for barley and rye to bake bread and brew beer. The slaves gather wood and peat, weave baskets, dig manure pits, harvest honey, and repair fences. One horse, two cows, four goats, six pigs, and thirty-two chickens are slaughtered during those weeks because they cannot be fed in the coming winter. Tables are laid out and the smell of roasting meat fills the five village houses for days. The men put on their most ornate clothes, adorn themselves with gold, and braid their beards. They pass around a polished silver bowl so they can see themselves in its reflection. The women paint one another's eyelids, cheeks, and necks to make themselves as beautiful as Freya, the goddess of love.

Job's jaw drops when she sees the paint on Yrsa's eyelids.

"'I have considered all the works under the sun, and behold, all is vanity, and vexation of the spirit,'" she mutters.

Yrsa looks at her, confused.

"Ecclesiastes, chapter one verse fourteen."

"What?"

"Never mind," Job says, but she can't resist a peek out the open door at the Danes parading through their gray, sodden village as if they were members of the king's court.

"You're the granddaughter of a king. You must have fine clothes and jewelry too?" Yrsa asks.

"Yes, but I gave all that up," Job replies, "and I've never regretted it for a second."

Job chops a few pieces of smoked pork and adds them to the frying pan with some onions. The pan sizzles.

Grandma Gudrun gets up from her stool and walks over to the skillet. She plucks a piece of pork from the pan.

"It's not ready yet," Job says.

Gudrun holds up her hand, and Job braces for a slap. Gudrun tosses the meat into her mouth. It must be piping hot, but the old woman doesn't seem to notice. She saunters into the front room and adjusts the gold pins in her white hair. Only when she's completely satisfied with her appearance does she exit the house.

"Gudrun the Torch is as vain as Freya," Yrsa says.

"Why do they call her Gudrun the Torch?" Job asks.

"As a young woman she followed her husband Leif to Paris on the Great Rampage. She was the same age as we are now."

Job makes the sign of the cross and mutters, "Lord have mercy."

Yrsa rolls her eyes.

"They took more captives than you could count: monks and noblemen who were good for a ransom and thousands of slaves to sell in the markets. But then three Danish warriors fell ill. Their bodies were covered with dark sores the size of chicken eggs. They started speaking in gibberish. A monk said it was St. Germanus who had made the men sick. Gudrun and Leif, young as they were, grabbed their warrior knives and demanded to know where the bastard was hiding. The monk told them that Germanus could be found in the same place he'd been for over three hundred years: under the floor of his monastery church. Boy, did Gudrun and Leif laugh when they heard that! As if Odin's warriors were supposed to be afraid of a pile of dried-up bones under some old church tiles. But all three men died that night. Their bodies were covered in the black from their oozing sores. The next day eight more warriors got sick, and the day after that, fifteen. Gudrun helped drag the corpses onto the wood pile. Then she set the wood on fire. To appease St. Germanus, the Danes released the hostages and returned the plundered gold and silver to the monks. But nothing helped. More than half of the Danish seamen got sick and died. Leif succumbed to the dark sores as well. He was only sixteen. It was his first voyage. Gudrun had to lift him onto the pile herself. She kissed his pus-covered face before shoving her torch into the wood."

"Didn't she get sick herself?" Job asks.

"She never even coughed. She's been called Gudrun the Torch ever since."

Job tosses some chopped turnips into the frying pan and adds a bit of water. The pan sizzles and smokes. Then she says, "It was St. Germanus who took revenge on the pagans."

Her eyes glow with pride, as if the story of Germanus taking revenge on the pagans came straight from the Bible itself.

"Gudrun believed it was Germanus's fault too," Yrsa says.

"So she pried open the church floor, picked out his bones, and threw them into the fire as well."

"Lord have mercy!" Job cries in shock. Yrsa grins and hands Job the bowl of chopped mushrooms.

"Poor Germanus," Job sighs, tossing the mushrooms into the stew. Yrsa hands Job the parsley and nettles they picked that morning. She throws everything into the simmering pot and stirs it.

"Soon, you can add some salt and milk, and it'll be ready."

"It smells good," says Troels. "Must be a meal of the gods."

"There are no gods," sighs Job.

Yrsa winks. It smells so good that she wouldn't be surprised if Thor or Odin came walking through that door to ask for some. What would Job say then? The door creaks open.

"It smells delicious in here!" Toke bellows as he enters the house.

"Monastery food," Yrsa says, and Job smiles again.

"No letter from Ganda yet," says Toke.

"It will come," says Job.

That night, the first snow falls. The flakes swirl into the house through the holes in the roof and hiss as they hit the fire.

A few days later, the village is covered in a blanket of white snow, speckled black by the ash from the smoke holes. Icicles hang from the thatched roofs. The cold penetrates the walls and creeps under everyone's cloaks and furs. The wind cuts their noses. The fire burns day and night. Yrsa goes out to the barn to milk the cow. The animal's udder is bursting. Beside her, the chickens peck around in the frozen dirt. Suddenly, she hears the crunching of footsteps outside in the snow. Kveldulf the Norwegian enters the barn. He didn't expect to find her milking the cow and is stunned for a moment. Thick clouds of breath rise from his mouth. He reaches for the hammer of Thor around his neck.

"Have you come for a cup of milk?" Yrsa asks.

Kveldulf nods reluctantly. Yrsa releases the udders, takes a cup, and scoops some milk out of the bucket. Kveldulf downs the milk in one gulp, as if he's been at sea for a month.

"Don't worry so much," Yrsa says. "I don't know exactly what I saw when I was holding your wrists. I'm not a völva."

Yrsa takes hold of the udders again. She doesn't want to see the fear in Kveldulf's scarred face.

"You saw that I will die this winter, didn't you?" he asks.

"I don't know if it's this winter. And it was a dream," she says. "It doesn't mean anything."

Kveldulf wipes the drops of milk from his mustache. His hand is trembling. He doesn't believe her.

Then Yrsa remembers something. "In the dream, I saw the day of your battle, when your face was hanging in tatters. How many men were you up against?"

Kveldulf hesitates for a moment.

"I counted five, maybe six," Yrsa says.

A smile stretches across his scarred face.

"There was only one," Kveldulf says. "It was man on man. I've always exaggerated the story a bit."

"See!" Yrsa exclaims. "The dream means nothing."

Kveldulf sighs, exhaling a cloud of relief.

"I'm not going to die," he says aloud.

"You will, someday," Yrsa says, and Kveldulf laughs so loudly it startles the animals. Yrsa pulls on the teats and milk splashes into the bucket. Kveldulf observes her for a moment. Then, he dusts the snow off his cloak as if he were brushing away his dark thoughts.

"You know," he says, "I always appreciated your mother."

The udders slip through her fingers. She looks up in surprise.

"She was a good woman," Kveldulf says.

Her mother. Lately, whenever Yrsa thinks of her, she sees a woman with a leather strap around her neck for sale at the slave market in Hedeby.

"You mean she was worth the twenty pieces of silver he paid for her?" Yrsa snaps, her voice as sharp as Gudrun's knife.

"No, that's not what I meant. I loved her."

The old Norwegian avoids Yrsa's gaze and nods at least five times to show that he's serious, that he really did care for her mother.

"Love in what way? Was she your bed slave too?" Yrsa asks coldly.

"No, not like that," says Kveldulf. "Not at all."

He picks at the fur on the back of a cow.

"She took care of me," he says. "She was the only one who didn't find me hideous."

The old man pulls up the collar of his cloak and turns toward the door.

"Kveldulf?" Yrsa asks.

"I better be off. It's getting dark," he says, as if the trolls and wolves were about to come creeping out of the forest.

"Is that it?" Yrsa asks. She throws up her arms and the milk splatters. *Come on, tell me more, you old bear. Give me an explanation. Something.*

"She was fiery, your mother. A real piece of flint," he says.

With that, he heads toward the door, watching his step so as not to disturb the chickens. Outside, he's swallowed into a swirling cloud of snow, and the door slams shut behind him. The cow kicks impatiently at the ground.

Yrsa has to stop and count to fifty before she can continue milking. Her thoughts churn like roaring waves in her mind. She recalls her vision of Kveldulf: the woman with the sharp features and black hair. The woman who combed his hair and tended to his scars. The woman she saw in Kveldulf's memory must have been Cara the Frisian. Cara, her mother—she was the one who was fleeing the village. She tried to cross the frozen lake on skis and fell through the ice. Kveldulf and another man found her later that night crouched on her knees in the snow, all curled up. She was naked and blue and dead. In her arms was a gray bundle of clothes. There's only one reason she would take off her clothes in the freezing cold like that: to save her child. The child who had fallen into the water and was already half frozen to death. First, she took off her cloak of raw wool, then her dress. She wrapped the child in the dress and then in the cloak. She held the infant in that cocoon of silk and wool and pressed it against her belly so it couldn't wriggle free or fall out of her arms and die. The cold must have drilled into every pore of her bare skin. Her muscles must have been paralyzed, the tears frozen in her eyes. The child must have cried and squirmed and gasped for air, but it couldn't budge. It was wedged between her arms, knees, and belly. With her last strength, she saved her child's life. Kveldulf must have found her. He must have wriggled the ball of wool and silk from her arms. At first, he must have thought that the child had suffocated or frozen to death. But it hadn't. It was alive.

That child was Yrsa.

14

EACH MORNING is colder than the last. The days are so short that they're almost nonexistent. The horse that pulls the sun across the sky in its cart doesn't have far to travel. At sunset, its mane catches fire and slowly dies out, turning the sky bright red. When darkness falls, everyone goes inside. Sten and Troels have set up a giant spruce in the back of the house, far away from the fire. The top of the tree scrapes the ceiling. The children decorate it with colorful ribbons and dance around it shouting "Jól"—a plea to the gods to end the winter in Midgard. Job wants to tell them that God, her god, is the one who brings the summer, but she bites her tongue. Other members of the household, both men and women, busy themselves with weaving and embroidery. It's the season of gift making. Toke slides off one of his silver armbands and chops it into pieces with his hammer and chisel. He gives a piece to Troels and Yrsa because they are both turning sixteen this winter. Little Sten weighs their pieces of silver in his hands. He says he wants to be sixteen soon too. The blacksmith's fire burns nonstop during the dark season. He melts down iron, bronze, silver, and gold to make jewelry and amulets. The ticking of his hammer can be heard all day and into the night. Yrsa asks him to make two ornamental pins out of the silver her father gave her. She'll use them to hold up her dress. That way she'll have something to pay with if she ever needs it.

On the fifth day of Jól, Yngvarr the Storyteller arrives in Mimir's Stool. Wearing expensive clothes and amber earrings, he travels on his sleigh through Jutland, where he's received like a king. Even his horse gets an extra scoop of oats in the stable. They say that the best storytellers of the North have drunk a whole cup of Odin's mead, whereas the bad ones have only tasted a few drops. Yngvarr must have had two cups. All the inhabitants of Mimir's Stool, even the slaves, gather in Toke's long room to listen to Yngvarr's stories. They sit close together, sniveling and coughing. There's fried fish for everyone, and Job can't get enough of it. She licks the bones and leaves nothing for the cats, who are going half crazy from the smell. Kveldulf the Norwegian enters the front room and kicks the snow off his shoes. Yrsa heads over to him. Ever since their conversation in the stable, she can't get him out of her mind. She's been having doubts about her vision. Her mother died of fever. That's what everyone always told her. Cara couldn't have possibly gone out on a winter night on skis, could she? She couldn't have been that stupid.

Kveldulf smiles when he sees her. His eyes look glassy. He's as drunk as the giant Aegir, the inventor of beer.

"I didn't tell you everything I saw in that vision," Yrsa says.

Kveldulf frowns. "Bah, it was only a dream," he says, slurring his words.

"Yes, of course, but I saw you in the snow too."

"It was only a dream, my girl." He laughs drunkenly.

"I saw you with a woman who was frozen to death."

At that, Kveldulf instantly sobers up. The knots in his face twitch with bewilderment.

"She was naked. Her clothes were balled up against her belly."

"Enough!" he shouts. His fingers reach for the little hammer around his neck.

"Was it my mother?" Yrsa whispers, grabbing his wrists. She wants to crawl back into his head. She wants to sink into him again, but Kveldulf yanks himself free and pushes her away. She falls down on the dirt floor.

"Leave me alone, you child of doom!" he shouts, loud enough for everyone in the long room to hear, and storms out the door.

The room falls silent. For a moment, it's as still as the bottom of the sea. Yrsa pulls herself to her feet and feels one hundred eyes burning into her skin. She brushes the dust off her dress.

"What was that all about?" Signe asks.

"He's drunk," Yrsa replies evasively.

She pushes through the crowd gathered around the fire and joins Job in the corner. Job places a blanket of fur on her lap. Then, Yngvarr the Storyteller stands up and everyone cheers.

* * *

Yngvarr speaks in beautiful sentences, and Job tries not to listen. Mother Philip would say that only foolishness can come from the mouths of fools. But when Yngvarr tells of the day that Thor's hammer was stolen by a frost giant from Jotunnheim, Job clings to his every word. The frost giant's name was Thrym, and he would only return the hammer to the gods if Freya, the goddess of love, agreed to become his wife. The gods were furious, but Thor had a plan. He transformed himself into a woman, doused himself in fragrant perfume, and donned Freya's finest dress and necklace. Then, he traveled to Jotunnheim, kissed the giant on the lips, and declared that she, the goddess of love, would become his wife. That night, Thrym was the merriest giant in all of Jotunnheim. But as he watched his future wife devour three barrels of ale and an entire ox, he became suspicious. But Thor, transformed into Freya, managed to reassure him. She explained that she was very excited to be in the company of such a colossal being as himself. With that, the giant's heart was filled with passion. He embraced the goddess in the middle of the banquet hall. All the giants stomped on the floor in delight. Then, Thor brought up the small matter of the dowry, and a servant placed the hammer in his lap. With that, Thor stood up, raised the hammer over his head, and bashed the frost giant's head in. Freya's wedding dress was splattered with blood, bone chips, and brains. Afterward, Thor beat a few dozen more giants to death and returned to Asgard. The dress was washed, but the blood, ale, and ox fat stains wouldn't come out.

When Yngvarr finishes the story, everyone claps. Even Job cheers, until she realizes what she's doing and quickly makes three signs of the cross. But Yrsa has hardly heard a word of it. She's just sitting there, brooding. She's visited the death ship every day since her conversation with Kveldulf in the barn. Sometimes, she stays there for hours, as if she hopes that her mother will rise up from the stones and tell her exactly how she died.

"How could Thor turn himself into a woman?" Job asks Yrsa.

It takes Yrsa a moment to return to reality.

"There are gods, and even some people, who can change their appearance, their hamr, when they want to," Yrsa says finally.

"That's ridiculous."

"No, it's not. I'm a Dane, and you are a nun. But one day, both of us could be someone else. Signe can change into a seal, for example."

Job looks over at Signe in surprise. She is leaning against Toke, who has his big hand on her bulging belly. There's nothing seal-like about her at all.

"Nonsense," says Job.

"Some men can turn into wolves," says Yrsa. "Our bodies are merely shells that we can shed at any time."

"When I hear your stories, I can't help but notice that your gods do everything wrong. They're entirely ungodlike," says Job.

"Of course they make mistakes. They're just like us. They're born, they whine, they shit, and they die."

"Then they are idols. There is only one God; He is immortal and omniscient, and He most certainly doesn't shit."

"But when you ask your god questions, does he answer?"

"Of course He does. He tells me everything. He is the light unto my path."

"No one tells me anything around here," Yrsa mutters. "I'm always in the dark."

The whole village of Mimir's Stool is packed into her house, which has become clouded with smoke. She looks for Kveldulf, but she doesn't see him. Toke calls for another story.

"You haven't eaten anything yet," Job says as she passes Yrsa a bowl of roasted eel.

Suddenly, it hits her. Yrsa stands up.

"What's wrong?" Job asks.

Yngvarr takes a slog of mead and announces the next story: the one about Frigg and her son, poor Baldr.

"Silence!" Yrsa yells.

"What is it, daughter?" shouts Toke, exasperated.

"Kveldulf is gone," she says.

Most of the men are too drunk to understand what she's saying, but the boys head for the door, and a moment later she hears them shouting.

Outside, Kveldulf is lying on the ground covered in eels. He seems to have tripped over a basket of fish in the dark. His lifeless fingers are wrapped around the hilt of his sword. The eels slither down his neck and arms like snakes. Yrsa wonders if the valkyrie, Odin's corpse collectors, will believe that Kveldulf died in battle so that he can go to the Valhöll and take his seat at the table of his ancestors. She wonders if, in his last moments, he thought of Cara the Frisian, the woman who rubbed his scars with ointment. Her fingertips were so soft on his skin. Yrsa felt them herself.

15

THE DAYS GET LONGER, but the snow and cold remain. Birds build nests in bare trees, and Signe finally goes into labor. Yrsa helps with the delivery. She draws runes on Signe's palms and swollen belly with charcoal to protect her and the child. Then, she and Signe clutch their amulets and ask Frigg for help. Signe groans and curses as she pushes the child out of her womb. Yrsa gently wakes it up. It's a girl. A living girl. A strong girl. She washes the child and wraps it in cloths and a wolf pelt. Gudrun takes the newborn into her arms, and for a moment Signe looks startled.

"Give her to me," Signe says. Her cheeks are covered with tiny cracks where the veins have burst.

Gudrun ignores her and walks out with the child as if she were a trophy.

"Follow her," Signe says.

Yrsa follows Gudrun outside. The men are standing around the fire, and Gudrun shows them the little wolf. She shouts that she has another granddaughter. The men touch their hammers of Thor and ask the god of lightning to protect the child. Then Gudrun passes the newborn to Yrsa, who stands there by the fire for a moment and feels the child wiggling in her arms.

When she closes her eyes, she no longer hears the voices of the men. She sees a young woman walking silently through the village. Even the wood chips don't crunch under her feet. She looks like a younger version of Signe, and around her shoulders is a wolf pelt.

"Watch out, Yrsa," Toke says.

Yrsa opens her eyes and feels dizzy. She almost falls, but Toke steadies her.

"Careful with my daughter," he says.

"I'm fine now," Yrsa mutters, hurrying back inside with the little one.

Signe is relieved and nuzzles the swaddled child against her breast. She tries to nurse her, but the child won't take the breast. Signe holds her finger to the baby's lips. Yrsa washes the blood from Signe's legs and hands her a cup of warm fatty milk.

"Will you stay with me?" Signe asks. Yrsa nods. She has helped her stepmother through three deliveries, and each time she asked her to stay with her and her newborn child.

"The girl will live," Yrsa says.

Signe looks up at Yrsa. Her eyes fill with tears. Three of her children didn't make it through their second winter. Only Troels and Sten managed to survive. Yrsa has never seen her cry—not even over the deaths of her own children. She just cursed the gods, kicked the baskets of fish, and chased all of the cats out of the house.

"Are you sure?" Signe asks.

"She's strong," Yrsa says. "I'm sure of that."

Signe trembles with emotion. Suddenly, she feels the little one trying to suck on her finger. She puts the child to her breast and sniffs away her tears.

Yrsa has never witnessed Signe in such a vulnerable state. She decides that now is the time to ask her the question that has been burning inside her for weeks. "Did Cara really die of fever?"

Signe looks up.

"What?"

"You always told me that my mother died of fever. But is that true?" Yrsa asks.

Signe stares at her stepdaughter without flinching. She doesn't nod or shake her head.

Suddenly, the door bursts open.

"I have a daughter!" shouts Toke as he swings into the house.

He sits down with his back to the fire.

"She's strong," Signe says. "She will live."

"We'll call her Ulfhild," says Toke. "She's a wolf and a fighter."

Her father roars with laughter. Yrsa searches for Signe's gaze, but she takes Toke by the arm and urges him to sit down beside her. He caresses her long blond hair.

The next day, Yrsa's father sits at the head of the table. All the men and women of the village have gathered to drink to the birth of little Ulfhild. There's so much laughter and shouting that the cats have fled the house. Gudrun is as drunk as Aegir and wearing every piece of jewelry she owns. She walks crooked under the weight, and every inch of her body seems to sparkle. Toke slaughtered a goat and put the animal's head on a stick as an offering. He thanks Odin for his newborn daughter as if the Alvader had birthed her himself.

Njall is there too, and when Job walks by, he pulls her onto his lap. She wriggles free from his grip and almost falls into the fire pit.

Yrsa hears the sound of her father's thunderous, drunken laughter again. His booming voice pounds in her ears. *He has to stop*, Yrsa thinks. *Stop!* Her body shakes. Her teeth grind. She feels Job's cold hand on hers.

"You're trembling," Job says.

"Hit me hard if you have to," Yrsa says.

"What?"

Yrsa gets up and walks over to Gudrun's corner of the house. She opens her clothes chest. On top of her dresses is the leather pouch containing the nightshade, wolf cherry, and dried mushrooms. She grabs it and makes her way over to the fire. As soon as she's close enough, she tosses the entire thing into the flames. A moment later, the herbs begin to burn. The house is so smoky that no one notices the cloud rising from the pit. Yrsa inhales deeply. The smoke burns in her nose and throat. She tries not to think about the breathlessness, nausea, and fatigue that will soon follow.

Her father is sitting on a stool, playing King's Table with Troels, who's grinning like Thor because he's beating his father at his own game. Yrsa wants to go sit with them, but suddenly the whole house tilts like a ship on a choppy sea.

"What did you do?" asks Job.

"To my father," Yrsa stammers. "Help me to my father."

Job offers her an arm for support.

"A little too much beer there, Yrsa?" someone calls out.

"What's wrong with you?" Toke chuckles as he sees her hobbling toward him. Yrsa falls to her knees in front of him and hits the game board, flipping it over.

The whalebone pawns roll across the floor.

"No!" cries Troels. He won't be winning tonight.

Then Yrsa grabs her father by the wrists and sinks into his body. She sees Cara with her tanned skin and black hair. She's lying in this very house, exhausted from childbirth, on the verge of sleep. Her eyelids fall shut, but she holds the infant to her chest. Toke attempts to gently pry the child from her arms, but Cara jolts awake. She cries out. Her face is riddled with fatigue, but her eyes are red and wild. She clings to the child with all her might. She's holding a knife. Toke backs away. Then, a wave washes it all away. Yrsa sinks deeper. Toke and Kveldulf are staring at Cara in the snow. Her body is completely blue. She's on her knees with the bundle of wool clamped between her belly and thighs. In front of her are runes carved into the ice: *your oath*. And again, a wave washes the scene away. Yrsa sinks even deeper. Her father is sitting on a dock. The water sloshes against the shore. Fishhooks tinkle in the wind. His heart beats slowly. He tries to breathe in and out, but he can't. His nostrils and windpipe are blocked. He's dying, Yrsa realizes. She feels her throat closing too. Like her father, she is a fish gasping for air on dry land.

The sharp slap on her cheek returns her to her senses. She gasps for air and breathes in until her lungs are completely full. Her heart is jumping like a trapped herring. It was Job who pulled her away and slapped her.

Toke rubs his wrists where Yrsa dug her nails into his skin. Troels, with the game board still on his knees, stares at her with his jaw dropped.

"What's with you, sis?" he calls out.

Toke clambers up from his stool, unsteady from drinking.

"What did you see, daughter?"

Everything, she thinks. Why hadn't it ever occurred to her before? A child with a crooked foot is useless, entirely unfit to be a warrior or a sailor or a farmer. Just another mouth to feed in the winter. What father wants a girl with a crooked foot? It's a terrible omen. But Cara pressed the child to her breast. She refused to give the baby up. Toke must have tried to explain to her that the child was better off dead, that they should throw it into the sea as a sacrifice to Rán. That way, it would at least be good for something. They could make another child, he and Cara. A child with two good feet. A better child.

As if the bundle in Cara's arms were nothing but a deformed kitten. Cara must have begged. She must have cried herself raw into those sheets, her body still wet with blood. She must have managed to persuade Toke to let her keep the child for one night so she could feel it, smell it, feed it. And then, that night, Cara, still exhausted from childbirth, must have fled with the newborn on skis. Toke and Kveldulf found her hours later, frozen in the snow. The cold wasn't survivable that night, yet the infant, wrapped in its mother's clothes, had managed to live.

Yrsa leans on Job and stands as tall as she can. Almost as tall as her father. She straightens her shoulders. For a moment, it's as if her foot is no longer crooked.

"What was your oath, Father?" she demands.

He shakes his head back and forth, his joints wobbly from the liquor.

"Your oath to Cara?" she repeats.

Cara could've only meant one thing by those runes in the snow: Toke had promised her that he would take care of the child. An oath he swore and broke. The runes in the snow are a powerful curse: a dying woman who, at the gates of the kingdom of the dead, condemns her husband for breaking his promise. The gods will not forget a thing like that.

All the color drains from Toke's face. Troels stares at his sister with the game pawns in his hands.

"Did you really scatter Cara's ashes among your ancestors on the death ship?" Yrsa demands, but she already knows the answer. No one dares to say a word.

"No, you didn't, did you? You left her there like a slave in the snow. You left Cara for the wolves."

"That's enough, girl!" Naefr cries.

Yrsa doesn't listen. "Why didn't you leave me for the wolves too?"

Toke spits into the fire to ward off evil and stutters, "You must have been lying in the snow for hours in that cloak. You should've been dead. But the gods interfered. They kept you alive."

"So you didn't dare to kill me," Yrsa murmurs.

She looks away from the man she has always loved. Her hero of the whaling road. The great helmsman who carried her on his back when she was a child. The big, strong man who made her world feel safe.

"I saw you dead, Toke son of Thorsen," Yrsa declares. "On a dock by a river."

"Enough!" Toke roars.

Then Yrsa vomits on the game board and falls into a deep ravine of sleep.

16

YRSA CLEANS the fishing nets on the beach. She's all alone, except for the seagulls squawking overhead. Everyone in the village is avoiding her. The other day, Njall bumped into her on the path between the houses, and she fell over. He didn't stop or look back at her. The two women who saw it happen didn't even help her up.

Signe doesn't want Yrsa around her anymore. And she certainly doesn't want her help with little Ulfhild—as if she's afraid she'll make the child sick or something. Worst of all is her father. Toke acts as if she no longer exists, as if he regrets not leaving her in the snow on that frigid night. Troels and Sten are confused. Her brothers have always looked up to her. As punishment, Yrsa is forced to sleep in the barn with the animals. She feels like a slave in her own village and wonders how long the banishment will last. But no matter what, she will not apologize to her father. Never!

Job is allowed to sleep in the house for now, but there still hasn't been any news from Ganda. The village has run out of food supplies. The chickens have all but stopped laying eggs. The cows and goats have less milk, the nuts are all gone, and no one dares to eat from the moldy grain anymore. The other day, Troels asked if there was any cheese left and Signe told him to eat the chunks between his toes. They can still catch fish on days when the sea isn't too wild. But there's hardly enough to feed the whole village. The winter has taken its toll on Gudrun. She's as thin as a sapling, hardly gets out of bed, and spends most of the day languishing under her furs. Everyone is irritable. They lash out at the slaves and slap them. Sometimes the men fight.

Yrsa shakes two shrimp out of the net. She snaps off their heads and eats them raw. Maybe picking nets isn't so bad after all. She sucks a sea snail out of its shell alive. Then she throws the rest of the snails, fish, and shellfish into a wooden bucket along with the pieces of seaweed.

Suddenly, she hears someone shouting her name and sees Little Sten running toward her. He leaps over the boulders around Mimir's stone and plops down in the sand beside her, gasping for air.

"Your fiancé is here," he says excitedly. "With his father and some nobleman with lots of gold around his neck. Signe thinks they've come to call off the engagement."

Yrsa pulls another crab out of the nets and tosses it to the gulls. They squawk and peck at each other furiously as they all dive after it at once.

"That's good news, isn't it?"

Yrsa shrugs.

"You didn't want to marry that troll anyway, right?" asks Sten.

Yrsa throws down the nets. She stands up and wipes the sea slime off her work dress. Then she rubs her hands clean in the sand.

"I don't know if Father even wants me here anymore," Yrsa says.

"You should come back and sleep in the house," Sten says, his voice quivering. Then he tosses his arms around her waist and presses his nose into her belly.

"Don't," she says. "You're going to smell like fish."

"I don't care," sniffs Sten.

Yrsa and Little Sten walk back along the path through the dune bushes. Yrsa carries the bucket, and Sten holds her other hand. It's hard for the little boy to walk as slowly as she does. Every so often, something will occur to him and he'll leap forward, swinging his arms in the air. It's all part of some grand adventure playing out in his mind.

In the village, Yrsa counts ten horses and seven men with beards, broad shoulders, and tattoos on their arms. In their hands are swords and spears. They look grim, as if they're expecting trouble. Standing in front of Yrsa's house are the jeweler and his son, Ljufr. Her fiancé. Beside them is a giant man with a polar bear skin draped over his shoulders. That must be Rikiwulf, Yrsa thinks. She's heard of him—a nobleman who, at the age of sixteen and armed with nothing but a spear, single-handedly slaughtered a polar bear. People say that, even to this day, his enemies tremble at the sight of that white fur around his shoulders. Only an idiot would dare to cross a man who went head-to-head with a beast of the High North. A man like that deserves the reverence of Odin himself. When he shows up at your door, you take him in, feed him, and maybe even offer him a bed slave. But other than slaying a polar bear, Rikiwulf hasn't achieved much fame. He calls himself a sea king and the captain of his fleet, but he has yet to plunder a village. Nevertheless, the boys in the village can't help but stare at him in awe. The bear's giant claws rattle as he walks. Yrsa hobbles along the path through the village with the bucket in her hand. She sees him eyeing her foot. He has long dark hair, a beard in two braids, and thick lines tattooed by his eyes.

"So, that's the girl my nephew is supposed to marry," Rikiwulf says.

"I don't want her," Ljufr grumbles.

"My mother negotiated the engagement, sir," Toke explains. "My brother and I weren't there."

"Where is this mother of yours?"

"In bed with fever. She probably won't make it to the end of the winter."

A little while later, the visitors are seated around the table in the front room. Signe serves them a bowl of fish soup with boiled shrimp. Toke and Naefr sit there side by side looking sullen. Unlike the nobleman's escort, they are not armed. Rikiwulf's arrival caught them by surprise. Njall, Troels, and Nokki watch nervously from a bench near the oven. Only Sten is oblivious to any harm or threat. He spots Yrsa's bucket and rummages through it, looking for a live shrimp or snail to eat.

"I understand why you'd want to send such an unfortunate girl out of your village," says Rikiwulf.

"Gudrun said the men of Mimir's Stool would stop offering my village protection if I refused the engagement," the jeweler says. "It was a threat."

"Ah, Gudrun is old. Her mind gets foggy sometimes," says Toke.

"I will not be threatened," the jeweler snarls, his voice trembling with disdain. The nobleman is clearly disturbed by his tone.

"Toke is the best helmsman there is," Rikiwulf declares. "When we sail our fleet around Cape Skagen, I, for one, am grateful that he is up there leading the way with his ship. And Captain Naefr is a hero of Jutland. One day, there will be sagas told about him."

Naefr and Toke nod, looking a little less annoyed. The jeweler seems to have lost his nerve. Rikiwulf calls Yrsa over. She stands up as tall as she can and approaches the men, trying to keep her shoulders straight. She passes the oven where the boys are sitting and feels her whole head heat up at the sight of Nokki. He looks at her for a moment, and she can't help but notice the hairs on his chin. The boy she kissed in the sand.

"Are you sure you don't want her, boy?" Rikiwulf asks. "This girl comes from a long line of renowned Danish seamen."

Rikiwulf is doing everything he can to remain in Toke's

good graces. He doesn't want any problems with two notorious seafarers like Toke and Naefr.

"You know, my boy," Rikiwulf laughs, "you can have two wives, like I do. It has its advantages. But you do have to feed them."

"I don't want her, sir," Ljufr declares, spitting out the words. *How dare he say that in front of Nokki*, Yrsa thinks. She clenches her fists. Njall chuckles, which only encourages the jeweler's son. Suddenly, he seems an inch or two taller.

"She's crippled, she's ugly, and her mother was a slave," Ljufr shouts.

Before she realizes what she's doing, Yrsa grabs the wooden bucket on the floor and dumps the whole thing—sand, snails, fish, seaweed, and at least seven shrimp—on Ljuhf's head. The jeweler's son screams, and she bangs the bucket against his head once more just for good measure. He falls off his chair.

"I don't want you either, you filthy troll!" she yells, loud enough for even the gods to hear.

Nokki pulls Yrsa back. He has his arms around her waist, which only makes her want to smash the bucket into the boy's head again.

The jeweler is furious, and Ljufr is squealing like a pig kicked out of its favorite mud puddle. Rikiwulf roars with laughter. He hasn't had this much fun all winter. Toke and Naefr are cracking up too. Even Nokki laughs, which makes Yrsa's heart leap with joy.

For a moment, it seems as if all is forgiven.

"You're a feisty one, all right," chuckles the self-proclaimed sea king. "But you'll never land yourself a husband that way. Who would pay a dowry for you?"

The answer comes from the other room.

"My granddaughter is worth a warship," Gudrun says.

Only then do the visitors become aware of Gudrun's presence. She's sitting in the shadows between the beds. All you can see is her jewelry. The rings on her fingers and the chain around her neck sparkle in the firelight; the pins in her hair glisten.

"My granddaughter is the best seeress in Jutland," the old woman declares as she stands up and approaches the men. She clamps her bony hand on Yrsa's shoulder. At first, Yrsa is stunned by the gesture, but then she beams with pride, if only to impress the boys.

Rikiwulf looks at his hosts. Toke nods, reassuring him that his mother hasn't lost her mind. Gudrun is incredibly thin. Her cheeks are sunken and her lips are covered in fever blisters. Her clothes hang loose on her body, and her tinkling bracelets threaten to slip off her wrists. She leans heavily on Yrsa and struggles to stay on her feet.

"Gudrun the Torch." The nobleman grins. "Your sons tell me that you are preparing for your journey to the underworld."

"The underworld can wait," Gudrun mutters. Her voice is as raw as an open wound; her hands tremble with fever.

"Are you sure Yrsa is a seeress? Surely such a trait is hereditary?" Rikiwulf asks suspiciously. "Was her mother a seeress too?"

"No, no one taught me," Yrsa says. "It's a gift that the Norns tied into my navel."

"You remember that then, do you girl?" Rikiwulf asks. Yrsa glares back at him, her eyes indignant. The nobleman makes no effort to hide his disdain. He might as well spit on her feet.

"Get up, girl," Gudrun says. Yrsa stands, leaning on the rod.

"Is that your staff, seeress?" Rikiwulf asks, chuckling.

"I don't know whether you want to make a real name for yourself as your forefathers did," Gudrun sneers with venom in her voice, "but suppose, my lord, that one day you have the courage to lead a fleet to Paris. Not only would Yrsa be able to advise you on your journey, she'd terrify the men of Paris. She can curse them."

"Paris? What do I want in Paris?" Rikiwulf replies, sounding about as eager as the embers of a dying fire.

"Where do you think the King of Francia keeps his silver?" Gudrun asks without waiting for the answer. "In the monasteries of Paris! Every single one of them is bursting with treasure. The Parisians used to have a saint to protect them, but I threw his bones into the river."

Rikiwulf slurps his fish soup loudly. The only reason he came to Mimir's Stool today was to get the jeweler to shut up about his son's engagement to a cripple. The nobleman had no desire to come here at all, to this nest of sea-foaming savages with their stupid rock. He had brought his best warriors just to protect himself. But now the old squid has all but called him a coward, a sea king afraid to walk between his own dunes. How dare she suggest that he—unlike his legendary ancestors, whose stories are still recounted on frosty winter nights—had yet to truly prove himself. That his only claim to fame is a moth-eaten polar bear skin. Everything about this village annoys him, and most of all that crooked girl who brought him here in the first place.

"Gudrun, that girl is far too young to be a völva," Rikiwulf snarls.

"I have an herbal mixture," Gudrun says. "If I throw it into the fire and Yrsa breathes in the smoke, she can see everything. Past and future."

"What is that? Nightshade? That stuff would make even the dead see things," Rikiwulf snorts. "A true seeress doesn't need quackery like that. A völva doesn't have to inhale some special smoke to see into the future."

Gudrun stands there weakly with the bag of herbs in her trembling hand. The jeweler nods as if his brother-in-law has just spoken an undeniable truth. Yrsa hears someone chuckling—it's Nokki. Is he mocking her?

"Ask me whatever you want to know, sir," Yrsa says.

The challenging tone in her voice surprises Rikiwulf.

"Ask her when winter ends, my lord," says a warrior, stomping his feet.

"Winter will last at least two more weeks," Yrsa replies. But she immediately feels stupid. Everyone can see that winter is almost over. The birds have been chirping nonstop in the trees to remind the gods to bring the thaw.

"Is that nun really a descendant of Charlemagne?" Naefr asks suddenly.

"Yes, and her ransom will be weighed on the scales of Hedeby," Yrsa lies. "I've seen it in a vision."

Rikiwulf laughs arrogantly, but it sounds forced. This conversation is making him feel uneasy. He's afraid of her.

"Give me your wrists, my lord," Yrsa says. "And I will tell you what I see."

Rikiwulf falls silent. He doesn't want to extend his arms to the girl, but everyone is watching: his warriors at the door, Naefr and Toke on their stools, the jeweler and his son, and even that old wench clinging to Yrsa's shoulder.

After a moment, Rikiwulf sighs. "All right then," he says. "Tell me what you see, and then we will know for sure whether you are a true seeress or just some silly crippled girl who should've been sacrificed to the gods."

Yrsa can tell her father is startled by the nobleman's words, and she realizes that Rikiwulf means them. The way he talks, you'd think he's got the finest sail in Jutland and drinks ale with the gods. He's mocking her, the daughter of a savage and a slave. She should've kept her mouth shut. She should've stepped back into the shadows instead of trying to prove herself.

Yrsa approaches the sea king, and Sten motions for Gudrun to sit beside him on the bench. Rikiwulf pulls up his sleeves. His arms are tattooed with runes. Yrsa places her fingers on his wrists. Someone spits into his mug of ale to ward off evil. Yrsa closes her eyes. She presses her fingers into his wrists. She can feel his heartbeat, the pulsing of his blood. She searches for a way inside, to his hugr. She hears the wood crackling in the fire. Whispers. She can hear her own breath, but she doesn't sink into the dark sea. It's not working.

"Our little seeress is very quiet," Rikiwulf says.

Yrsa hears Njall snickering. *I can't dive into this man,* Yrsa realizes. *I need the herbs.*

"Enough," the nobleman says, trying to shake her hands off his wrists. But then, as soon as he lets his guard down, his insides open up. Yrsa feels herself sinking. She sees a polar bear—a massive beast surrounded by reindeer hunters. The bear hits the head of one of the hunters with its paw. Blood spews into the air. The other hunters pounce on the animal with their spears. It growls and barks and howls until it finally collapses. The four hunters bury their friend in the snow, strip off the animal's fur, and pass it to Rikiwulf. He runs his fingers over the pelt and pulls three pieces of silver from his belt.

Then Yrsa falls to the ground. When she opens her eyes the nobleman is standing over her, rubbing his wrists. Her nails have left deep marks in his skin.

"Bitch," he hisses, but she pushes herself up and hobbles toward him.

"That fur of yours," she whispers into his ear so only he can hear. "You bought it from the reindeer hunters in Norway. You paid three silver pieces for it."

Rikiwulf stares at her in astonishment.

"I think we're done here, brother-in-law," the jeweler says, banging his cup down on the table.

Naefr and Toke stand up as well. The sooner the nobleman and his warriors leave the village, the better. But

Rikiwulf can't take his eyes off Yrsa. Suddenly, he draws his sword and places it on the table. It is a beautiful thing, a weapon for a king. On the blade, engraved in runes, is the name Conqueror.

"Touch the tip of the sword, Yrsa daughter of Toke," the nobleman says.

Yrsa feels the cold steel between her fingers. It smells of seal oil.

"You shall be my third wife," Rikiwulf says. "And my völva."

Yrsa sees the indignation in Njall's face, the pride in her father's eyes, and the gold sparkling in Gudrun's hair. She feels Troels's excitement and Sten's confusion. She catches Nokki's gaze. He slowly shakes his head. *Don't do it*, he seems to say. *Don't.*

And that's exactly why Yrsa does it.

"I will marry you and become your seeress," she says.

The nobleman nods. The two warriors at the door grin. Sten has tears in his eyes.

Then Gudrun staggers closer and sits down on a stool across from Rikiwulf. She reeks of fever and bedstraw. "There's still the matter of the bride price," she says.

That night the men laugh and drink as if they were being served by Odin's virgins in the Valhöll. They roar and shout and argue like a wild band of brothers. They don't even notice the women going out. Yrsa, Job, five young slave girls, and three sailors' daughters walk down the path between the houses. They head for the dunes, where they'll be safe from the drunken warriors. They take shelter at the old fisherman's house. The man has grown skinny and weak since the death of his granddaughter Revna. The women sit in a circle around the fire. There's no hole in the ceiling, and the whole house stinks of goat. The smoke struggles to seep out through the cracks in the thatched roof. The girls and women huddle together, eating the mussels the old fisherman has boiled. The sand crunches between their teeth.

"I don't know if I'll survive here in Mimir's Stool without you," Job says. She presses her psalm book against her chest as if it will protect her.

"But your ransom will come, won't it?" Yrsa replies.

Job shrugs.

"It's coming, right?"

"Yes, I'm sure it's on its way," Job mutters, and quickly changes the subject. "What did you see when you were holding his wrists?"

"That he's been lying about that stupid polar bear fur his whole life," Yrsa whispers.

"And you still want to marry him?"

"Maybe he won't be so bad," Yrsa replies.

"Maybe all the crabs will come out of the sea tomorrow and throw themselves into the pot," Job retorts.

"You're starting to sound like a Dane." Yrsa chuckles.

"No, I'm not," Job replies indignantly.

Yrsa shrugs. Better to be with the nobleman than the jeweler's son in Odin's Hill—or to stay here and be treated like a slave in her own village. Rikiwulf will give her wealth and power. She will return to Mimir's Stool a rich woman.

Nokki will curse the day he rejected her. It will be her revenge.

"You know that man will throw you overboard as soon as he no longer needs you," Job mutters.

For a moment, Yrsa thinks she's talking about Nokki.

"You, on the other hand, will never get rid of that sea king," Job says.

She flips nervously through her book of psalms, searching for a prayer to comfort herself with. The parchment rustles under her fingers.

"What's in that book, anyway?" Crane Legs asks.

"Songs," Job says. "Some are meant to be spoken, some are meant to be sung."

"Will you sing something for us?" one of the younger girls asks.

Job sings "Kyrie eleison" and silence falls over the women. The nun's voice is as clear as a cloudless day, as pure as water from the well of wisdom. No one in Jutland can sing like that. They're astonished to hear such a strong, high voice come out of such a scrawny girl. The sound hits Yrsa right in her hugr. She can't take her eyes off the nun. Her pimples have disappeared since she's started scrubbing her face with seawater each week. But her arms are so thin. Gudrun said those little arms would snap like twigs at the first frost, but so far, they haven't. How can such a fragile being survive in this savage world?

Sister Job ends her song with a long high note and nothing more. No one in the fisherman's house dares to sniff or cough.

Yrsa wipes away a tear with her sleeve.

"'Kyrie eleison' means 'God, have mercy on us,'" Job says finally.

"I'll say!" cries a voice in the shivering cold, and a few of the girls laugh.

"Sing some more, nun," someone says.

That night, Job sings one psalm after another, and the women ask her to sing the "Kyrie eleison" three times.

It's still dark when Job wakes up among the women in the dune house. She walks outside barefoot. The stars twinkle overhead. There's not a cloud in the sky. Foam sizzles on the waves and the air smells of sea grass. The wind whips through her habit, but it's not so cold anymore. She's seized by a burning desire to say the morning prayers. She's been neglecting them lately. The cold, the fatigue, and the smoke-filled evenings have made it hard for her to focus. But singing last night gave her new energy. She puts on her shoes and places the white linen cap neatly on her head. Then, she pulls her habit over her head and wraps herself in the old wool cloak.

She heads out. As she walks through the village, she hears the sound of dripping all around her. The ice is brown and slushy, as if it's rotting away. She walks down the ox road until she reaches Mimir's stone, where she recites her first prayer of the day. She sits down among the large rocks that the men use to weight their ships when there's no cargo in the hold. Then she takes out the prayer book from her leather bag and opens it to the page where she last left her bookmark. Behind her she hears the roaring of the waves and the screeching of the gulls. One by one, the stars disappear as she recites the morning prayer. When she finally stands up again, the sky has taken on a grayish hue, and dawn is about to break.

When she turns around, she lets out a scream. There, standing on the beach like a pagan monster from the depths of the sea, is Njall. And hanging from his belt is his sword, Vengeance.

17

YRSA YAWNS, still groggy from the night before. She looks around, surprised to find herself in the dune house. Then, she remembers what happened the day before. How, for the first time in her life, she swore an oath at sword point, and to a nobleman who's spent his whole life lying about his one and only feat. How could she be so foolish, she thinks. Now she has to spend her life with an arrogant impostor who thinks he owns the seas. She has to become his seeress and his wife. But then she remembers the dejected look on Nokki's face as he shook his head. *Too bad for you*, she thinks. *You didn't want me. You broke my heart. I'll show you. I'll return to this village as a noblewoman, dressed in furs and draped with gold.*

Hunger gnaws at her belly. She digs around in the cooking pot, but all that's left are cold clam shells. Everything is gone. Yrsa searches for Job among the sleeping women, but she's not there. She must be out praying by the stone, Yrsa thinks. Suddenly, she feels nauseated. A knot forms in her stomach, and she has to lean on both hands to catch her breath. It's the hunger, she thinks. Just the hunger. It's not doom.

* * *

Yrsa wipes the sand off her dress, pulls the woolen cloak over her head, and picks up her walking rod. It's still half dark outside. Blood rushes to her cheeks as she breathes in the cold. She walks through the village. The ice on the rooftops is melting. The whole world is dripping. No one is up yet. Why does that silly nun have to pray at such an ungodly hour? That woman is stubborn as hell. Yrsa walks toward her house. When she gets there, she'll light the fire and warm up, she thinks. The nun will turn up eventually. But she can't shake the dark feeling eating at her stomach.

Yrsa doesn't enter the house. Instead, she walks up the ox road, the dune bushes around her rustling in the wind. She walks as fast as she can, punching the rod into the ground. Her shoes are wet from the puddles in the sand. She tells herself there's nothing to worry about, that in a few moments, she'll run into Job on the path or spot her silhouette in the distance by the stone. But at the end of the path, there's no one out there. Her body pulses with dread. The sound of the waves is deafening. It's high tide. The waves on the gray sea simmer with foam. She scans the dark beach but it's hard to see anything in the early morning light. But then she sees it. The sword sticking out of the sand, and a little farther up, in the shadows, she notices something moving. Her breath falters. Job is lying on the sand, trapped under Njall's thrusting body. The nun struggles and screams. For a moment, Yrsa is stunned. Then, the words leap out of her mouth: "Get off of her! Get off!"

But Njall doesn't hear her. Yrsa can't shout loud enough.

Her voice is drowned out by the crashing of the waves. For a second, she's petrified. Then, she feels the tears welling up in her eyes. She drops the rod and pulls the sword out of the sand. The name Vengeance glistens on the blade. It's so heavy that Yrsa puts her weight on her bad foot and almost loses her balance. Her ankle winces in pain, but she remains on her feet. She walks up the beach, raises the sword with both hands, and holds it to Njall's neck.

"Get off her!" Yrsa roars.

Njall turns his head, his face wild and ragged. He is leaning on Job with his hand on her chest. Her white linen cap has been ripped off her head. Her face is covered in mucus and blood and tears. In her hands, she grips the wooden cross. "Hail Mary full of grace, the Lord is with thee..." she whispers over and over again. She doesn't even notice that Yrsa is there.

"Step back, you scum!" Yrsa shouts. "Before I smash your face in."

"I'm done here anyway," he says.

Njall pushes himself upright and takes a step backward. He rolls his shoulders one by one as if he's just lifted something very heavy. Yrsa averts her eyes so she doesn't have to look at his penis. Her arms begin to cramp. She wonders how long she'll be able to hold the unwieldy weapon in the air.

"No ransom has come," Njall declares. "So this little nun here is no longer a hostage but a slave. My slave."

Njall buttons his pants and picks up his belt. Job just keeps muttering, "Hail Mary full of grace, the Lord is with thee..."

"What are you going to do with my sword, cripple?" Njall sneers.

Yrsa pokes the tip into his chest. He flinches and takes a step backward.

"Ouch!" he cries.

"I'll stab you, you rotten piece of fish," Yrsa hisses.

"It's not the tip that's sharp, you imbecile, it's the side." Njall grins.

"Shut up!" shouts Yrsa. But she can't hold it up any longer. The iron is too heavy. The muscles in her arms throb in pain.

She lowers the weapon for a moment, and as soon as she does, Njall grabs her by the wrist and twists her arm onto her back. Pain shoots through her shoulder. She drops the sword into the sand. Njall pushes Yrsa's arm farther up her back. An inch more and it will rip out of the socket. Yrsa whimpers in pain. Then, she twists herself downward and yanks her wrist free. She tries to scramble to her feet, but Njall grabs her by the cloak, pulls her toward him, and rams his knee between her legs. Pain surges through her lower abdomen. His left hand clutches her throat. She pounds at his arms and claws at his cheeks with her nails, but he squeezes his fingers tighter and tighter, gripping her throat with all his strength.

"How dare you insult me, cripple. How dare you point a weapon at me. You—"

"Unhand her, you heathen!" shouts Job.

She stands behind Njall with the strings of her leather pouch clenched in her fist. Inside the pouch is her book of psalms.

Njall is shocked. What does this woman think? That she's going to knock his head off with her little book? That she can take on Odin's chosen one? He'll hack her to pieces and throw her to the gulls. In his brief moment of distraction, Yrsa seizes her chance. She tosses sand into his eyes and bites one of his fingers. He screams and lets go of her. Then he smashes his fist into her face and gropes around for his sword. Head down, he doesn't see Job approaching.

She swings the leather pouch with all her might and bashes it into Njall's temple. It hits him with a dull thud. Njall stumbles backward from the blow. He growls and roars like a ravenous animal.

Then he sees his sword lying there, the blade reflecting the dying moonlight. He leaps for it. This time, he won't hesitate. He'll thrust its sharp blade straight into the nun's neck. All he has to do is grab the hilt. He reaches for it but misses.

Yrsa sees the surprise on his face.

Njall reaches for the hilt again, but again he misses. Njall bends over his sword like a fool, completely baffled.

Yrsa is shocked. Is there magic in that book of psalms? Is it some kind of secret weapon? Is the nun's god hiding in the parchment?

Then, Job turns the pouch upside down. Out falls a chunk of rock.

Njall reaches for the hilt a third time, but his fingers claw into the dry sand. He can't pick it up. He whimpers, almost cries. Then he stumbles toward the sea, looks down at his wet feet, puzzled, and walks back to the ox road toward the village. But before he reaches the road, he collapses.

Yrsa walks over to him, pulls him up by his collar, tries to make him sit up. She calls out his name. But he doesn't answer. His eyes shine like white pebbles. A massive bump swells up on the side of his head, where he was struck by the rock. Blood seeps from his ear.

"Njall, Njall!" she shouts.

She puts her ear to his mouth. He's still breathing. But as soon as she lets go of him, he topples over like a shot rabbit.

"He won't sit up," Yrsa tells Job. "He can't."

Yrsa pulls him toward Mimir's stone and tries to shoulder him upright against it. She lays her hands on the rock. *If the ancestors ever want to help out a bit, now would be the time*, Yrsa thinks. She takes a handful of ice from the ground and rubs it on his cheeks and neck.

"Come on, wake up, Njall," she growls. "It was just a little rock."

Njall's back leans against the stone, but his head hangs on his chest.

"Njall? Njall?" Yrsa shouts. No response. She shakes him.

"Why won't you wake up, you spineless squid?" she shouts, but his head just hangs there.

Job has disappeared into the semi-darkness. Then Yrsa spots the white of her cap in the surf. She's wading in the shallow water, her habit and woolen cloak pulled up to her waist. She wants the sea to wash away Njall's filth like it washed away her pustules. She wants the icy water to numb the pain in her lower body. Up ahead, Yrsa sees the village karve bobbing on the waves. The light cargo ship is waiting for the women to take it to market in the summer.

Job emerges from the water and drops the habit over her wet legs. She searches for the cross on her chest and wraps her fingers around it tightly.

"I need to wake Njall up," Yrsa says.

"He won't wake up again," says Job.

"Of course he will. It's just a bump."

But it's not just a bump. There's also a stream of blood running from his ear to his neck. On top of that, he's completely lifeless. You'd almost think he was asleep.

"It was Jesus who punished him."

For a second, Yrsa expects the skinny corpse on the cross to step out from behind Mimir's stone and say, "Yes, it was me."

"Jesus led my hand," she said. "It wasn't me."

"Sure, he did!" shouts Yrsa angrily. "You're the one who smashed a boulder against his stupid clam head! Jesus had nothing to do with it. Nothing at all."

Job stares at Yrsa. Her whole body trembles.

"You're right. It's my fault," she says. "All my fault." She falls to her knees.

"Naefr will be furious," Yrsa sighs. "Everyone will be."

"I don't care about Naefr!" cries Job. "It's God who will never forgive me for this. I've committed a mortal sin."

"Your god is not your biggest problem right now," Yrsa says.

"I have lost my reward in heaven!" Job cries. "I must confess."

"What?"

"Please, you have to take me to a priest."

"To a priest?" Yrsa says. "Why not to Odin in Asgard? You need to get out of here, now. Go south. Don't stop. Keep running until you find a church or a priest."

Yrsa knows that Job won't make it very far. She doesn't know the region and is sure to get lost in the landscape where everything looks the same. She won't be the first foreigner to end up walking in circles. And even if she does find the road south, she'll be spotted by every farmer from here to the border of West Francia. A nun on the run will stand out like Thor in a wedding dress. Any Dane who sees her will know she's a slave on the run. Some peasant or shepherd will surely capture her and beat her half to death and lock her up until the men of Mimir's Stool come fetch her. Job doesn't stand a chance. She's as good as dead.

"Take me to a priest," she repeats.

"Who cares about a priest!" Yrsa shouts. "The whole village will want your blood."

"Help me," says Job desperately. "Take me home. My father is rich. My grandfather is even richer. I'll make sure you get that silver. Every last pound. Just for you."

"I swore an oath yesterday!" Yrsa cries.

"Yeah, to a liar," Job exclaims. She gazes frantically at the dunes. There's nowhere she can hide, and it's still too dark to find her way. Everything hurts. She can still feel Njall on top of her, inside her. His weight. His brutal thrusts. He's stolen her purity. He's taken everything from her. She grips the cross around her neck and looks east, searching for the sunrise. She longs to feel the warmth of the sun's rays on her skin. This may very well be the last day of her life, she realizes. She prays aloud. She begs forgiveness for her pride, her anger, the murder she's just committed. She should've shown humility. She shouldn't have put that stone in the pouch. She should have accepted her fate like Job in the Bible. She pounds her fists against her chest, hard and incessantly.

Yrsa walks up the dune so she can see the village. The scraggly bushes rustle and bend in the northerly wind. All is quiet. There's no smoke rising from the roofs yet. No one seems to be awake. Just then, she sees a door slowly open. Out walks her little half-brother, Sten. He pees against the white wall of the house. He's the first one awake in the village. Then, he walks to the barn with his stick. On the way, he waves it in the air to fend off invisible attackers, another adventure playing out in his mind. He picks up a bucket and heads into the barn to milk the goats. Odin the dog scurries out and shakes the hay out of his fur. Then, all is quiet again. What should she do?

Yrsa touches her amulet of Frigg. Her eyes burn. "Tell me what to do, Frigg. Give me your advice." Soon, everyone will be awake. They will find Njall. The village will be up in arms. Women will cry. Men will scream. "Blood for blood," they'll roar. Naefr will demand revenge for his son's death, and his wrath will be as deep as the sea. All the silver of Midgard wouldn't be enough to quench his thirst for vengeance and spare Job's life. But the nun's death won't be enough. Naefr will also want revenge on her, Yrsa, the girl who protected his son's killer, who insulted his son's honor, the girl with the crooked foot whom Toke should've thrown into the sea at birth. Naefr will tell Rikiwulf that he won't get his seeress, that she must be punished for the doom she's brought upon them.

Suddenly, Yrsa feels sick. Her stomach churns with fear. She can no longer lean on her crooked foot. She sits down and massages her ankle. She looks around her, at the wind in the bushes and the seagulls in the dark sky, searching for a sign. Something. Above the forest, a soft morning glow appears. It's the burning mane of the horse, ready to draw the sun across the sky. Drops of the animal's sweat are already clinging to the grass, as they do every morning.

"Stop that horse," she murmurs. "Give me some time, Frigg. Tell me what to do."

The morning glow lingers over the forest. There's still time. Just a little. Toke might not let Naefr kill her. Perhaps she can leave with the nobleman after all. That way, she won't have to break her oath. But Job will never make it. They'll slit her throat and leave her corpse in the forest as a feast for the wolves, gulls, and beetles. That's how they dispose of all the slaves. That's how they disposed of her mother, who fled in the dead of winter to save her deformed child. Her proud mother. Cara the Frisian.

Yrsa pushes herself upright, grits her teeth against the throbbing pain in her bad foot, and hobbles to the beach.

This must be some evil plan of the Norns. They're probably roaring with laughter under the roots of some tree right now. They must have tied this moment into her navel at birth. And they already know what Yrsa daughter of Toke will decide. Yrsa didn't interrupt Njall's rape only to see Job's head chopped off by Naefr. She has no choice but to break her oath. The gods will just have to turn a blind eye.

Yrsa finds Job by the stone. She's still deep in prayer.

"Come on, we're leaving," Yrsa says. "We'll take the whaling road."

Job looks up at her, her eyes wide and terrified.

"What do you mean? Surely not by sea?"

Yrsa gazes up at the stone, and suddenly she realizes for the first time that, for the men of Mimir's Stool, the stone isn't just the end of the road, it's also the beginning.

18

YRSA WADES THROUGH THE SURF. Job follows her. The icy waves splash against her chest, knocking the wind out of her. She carries their woolen cloaks and Njall's sword above her head.

She hears barking. She looks back and sees Odin the dog standing at the water's edge. The beast is yapping his throat raw. Other dogs come running and make even more noise. At any moment now, someone will run to the beach to see whether the dogs have captured a seal.

Job can just barely keep her chin above the water. In front of Yrsa, the karve dances on the surf. The stern bobs up and down, as if the boat is urging Yrsa to think twice about what she's doing, as if it wants her to know that this plan of hers is incredibly stupid.

Yrsa tosses the cloaks on board first, then the sword. The hull knocks hard against her, as if the vessel doesn't want to be stolen. She waits for the stern to drop down after a wave, and then she leaps onto the side of the ship and grabs hold of the edge. She bobs up and down for a moment until she can swing her arm and then her good leg aboard. Then she flops onto the deck with a thud.

Job is knocked away from the boat by a wave and sucked into a whirl of sand and salt. Her thick habit and petticoat are soaked and hang from her body like lead. She looks like a robed piece of wreckage. She struggles to find her footing in the shallow water. Everything about her trembles and drips. Her lips are blue. She clutches the wooden cross around her neck. Yrsa hangs over the edge of the ship and extends an oar. "Here, take this!" she shouts.

Odin jumps over the waves to show Job the way. The tiny nun moves forward with great strides, cleaving through the foaming water with her arms to cut the waves. She leaps toward the end of the oar and clamps her fingers around it. Yrsa pulls her toward the ship. Once she's within reach, Yrsa grabs the hood of Job's habit and drops the oar into the water so she can pull her up with two hands. Job grabs the edge of the vessel, and Yrsa gives her one last pull with all her strength and the two young women fall on top of each other on the deck of the ship, soaked, panting, and shaking.

"On your feet!" Yrsa shouts. They scramble upright. The ship bobs up, and Job immediately falls back onto the deck. Only then does Job notice that the belly of the ship has been filled with at least a hundred stones to weigh it down. Without the rocks, the light vessel would be battered by the surf.

Yrsa glances back toward land. Smoke is rising from the houses.

"We have to row," Yrsa says.

"I can't row," says Job, her teeth chattering.

"Either you row or you die," Yrsa roars. She unties the three remaining oars on the stern.

"I'll cut the anchor rope. Once we're loose, the surf will push us toward the beach. We have to row out to the open sea. Fast and hard."

Job has never held an oar in her life. She lifts the long thing with both arms. Yrsa drags Njall's sword behind her. The tip scrapes the deck. Then she lays it on the line that runs from a hole in the right side of the boat to the anchor. She puts her foot on the rope.

"Odin is drowning!" Job cries.

The dog paddles in the surf, howling desperately.

"Leave him," Yrsa cries. "It's high tide. The current will carry him back to the beach."

"He wants to come with us!" Job cries.

Yrsa is about ready to throw Job overboard. She knows the girl is an animal lover. She has to stop and pet every cat that rubs hungrily against her legs, and she's always trying to comb Odin's impossibly matted fur.

"Are you crazy? Odin is just a mangy ratcatcher," Yrsa says.

With that, she starts cutting into the leather rope with the sharp edge of the sword. She can hear the dog clawing desperately at the hull. On the beach, the other dogs bark wildly in support of their one-eyed companion.

"Look at him, he's exhausted. The poor thing," says Job.

This is madness, Yrsa thinks. Loving animals is for children, lunatics, and graybeards.

"Haven't you ever wondered how the dog lost his eye?" cries Job.

"What?"

"What if he's the real Odin in disguise?"

Yrsa stops sawing at the rope.

"Those gods of yours can change shape, can't they? What if it's *him*?"

"You don't believe in my gods," Yrsa says.

"But you do. And maybe he really is Odin, and he wants to help us!" cries Job.

Yrsa's never thought of that before. What if the nun is right? What if that smelly, one-eyed hairball really is Odin, the great Alvader who glides between worlds on his eight-legged stallion? The wanderer who passes unnoticed among the people of Midgard? The Screamer who shifts shape like changing a shirt? What if Job is right?

Yrsa drops the sword on the deck and looks overboard. The dog is paddling around in panic. He tries to bark, but swallows water instead. Before she even realizes what she's doing, Yrsa bends over the edge of the boat with Job at her side. Together, they try to grab the dog as the ship bobs up and down. Odin can barely keep his head above the water. Job grabs him by the fur on his neck and Yrsa by the tail. Odin howls as they pull him on board. Once on deck, the animal vomits profusely, shakes the sea out of his fur, and licks his tail.

Yrsa returns to the sword. She raises it high above her head and screams as she swings it down on the leather rope. To her surprise, she slices right through it. The rope swings into the sea, and the boat, dislodged from the anchor, spins in the surf. If the cargo hold hadn't been weighed down with rocks, it would have toppled over.

Waves splash over the side of the vessel. Yrsa sticks her oar into the water and uses it to keep the bow perpendicular to the waves. Job tries to row, but her oar doesn't hit the water. She tumbles backward on a bench, and it falls into the sea.

"Easy there!" Yrsa shouts.

Job takes the last of the four oars on deck.

"Now, row with me!" Yrsa shouts.

Job stands on the right and Yrsa on the left. Together they pull on their oars, and this time Job's oar cuts through the water.

"Follow my lead!" Yrsa shouts.

Job pulls the oar toward herself as Yrsa does. The tide is pushing them back to the beach, but with every stroke they manage to pull forward. The karve is bigger than an ordinary skiff and designed for four rowers, two in the front and two in the back. It's backbreaking work with just two, but with every stroke they propel the vessel a little farther away from the beach, away from Mimir's stone and the five houses of Mimir's Stool.

With each stroke, Yrsa slips farther and farther away from her world. Away from her afternoons in the shipyard, away from her lunches sitting on a log with the other women, from drinking fish soup with chunks of herring in it, from summer fruits drenched in creamy, sour milk. She's leaving the only home she has ever known, where she spent her childhood, her sixteen summers by the bay. The one place in the world where everyone knows her name. She's rowing away from her entire clan, her uncles, aunts, cousins, brothers, from the place where she fell in love with Nokki, the boy who didn't love her back. In Mimir's Stool, she was Yrsa, the helmsman's daughter.

Job murmurs Hail Marys. Odin runs to the bow and barks, his tongue hanging out of his mouth. They're almost out of the bay. On their right, they pass Heath Ridge. Herring gulls, petrels, and kola geese watch the ship from the sandbar.

"Come on!" Yrsa calls to Job. "We're almost there!"

The karve reaches the edge of the bay, where the waves cross with the open sea. The ship lurches and sways in the raging currents. They press on, and finally, with Heath Ridge behind them, they're out of the surf.

"Okay, you can stop now," Yrsa says.

Job drops the oar on the deck. "I can't feel my arms anymore!"

"Take the tiller!" Yrsa cries.

"The what?"

"That long stick to starboard."

"Where?"

"Starboard is to the right, that's where you steer the boat! Keep the bow pointed toward the open sea."

Yrsa turns to the ropes around the packed sail. It's hard work; her fingers are stiff from the cold.

"Keep it straight on the waves!" she shouts.

The sail rope is tied in a tight knot and appears to be

frozen. The knot reminds her of her father's fist. When she was a little girl, her father used to challenge her to untie the fingers of his clenched fist one by one. She would tug at them with all her might, but she never managed to pry one loose, not one. Her father got a good laugh out of it.

Yrsa blows on her cold fingers. She has to untie that knot.

Job holds the tiller, and the ship remains perpendicular to the waves. The sea foams and thrashes before her eyes.

"What if we fall off the edge?" cries Job.

"What?"

"On the horizon," she gasps. "There's a waterfall at the edge. We'll plunge into the abyss."

"Oh, come on!" Yrsa cries.

"It's true," says Job. "The sea is full of monsters. It says so in the Bible. It's a wilderness of dark, slimy creatures, a maw of a thousand teeth. All things evil slip beneath the surface of the water. The farther you go into the sea, the bigger the monsters get. And somewhere out there is the great sea dragon, the Leviathan. He will swallow us alive, like he swallowed Jonah."

"It's not monsters we should be worried about, it's Rán and her daughters!" shouts Yrsa as she wriggles and prods at the knot.

"The sea goddess has daughters?" asks Job.

"Rán's husband's name is Aegir, but he's not a god," Yrsa explains, panting. "He's a giant who drinks a few tons of beer a day. Sometimes Rán gets so mad at him that she unleashes a storm. That's why we have to offer her a sacrifice."

"If the goddess of the sea is a woman," says Job, "perhaps she'll be kind to us. Do we have anything to offer her?"

She makes two signs of the cross, as if she wants to apologize to her Jesus for even thinking such a thing.

"Yes, there is one thing," Yrsa says as the knot finally comes loose. She picks up Njall's sword, Vengeance, the work of a novice with a gold ring sloppily forged in the middle.

"Take my offering, Rán!" Yrsa cries, and hurls the weapon into the waves. The dog barks, and for a second Yrsa is afraid the stupid beast will jump in after it.

The winds are against them. They need a south wind to push them around the cape of Skagen so they can sail up the Western Sea toward Francia. The north wind will blow them south, to the heart of Jutland.

Now for the hardest part. Yrsa twists the sail rope around her wrists and hoists the yard with the sail hanging from it. The rope runs through a block and tackle, a pulley system with two wheels to lighten the load, but it's still incredibly arduous work. Normally, it takes two strong women to hoist the sail of the karve. She pulls on the rope with all her weight. The yard inches upward, but it's still too heavy. The rope shoots out of her hands, and the yard falls down on the deck.

"There are people on the beach!" shouts Job.

Yrsa looks back and sees Toke running across the sand. Her knees go limp; she's paralyzed with panic.

"Why did you drop the sail?" Job demands.

Yrsa touches the bronze amulet around her neck. "Help

me, Frigg," she murmurs. She swallows her fear and takes hold of the rope again. "Help me pull," she says.

"What about the tiller?"

"Get over here!"

Little by little, Yrsa and Job hoist the yard together. The boat shakes and sways back and forth, turning in a semicircle. Odin barks at the wind. The dogs on the beach bark back as the ship dances on the waves.

"Just a little more!" Yrsa cries, and at last the yard is high enough. She ties the sail rope around a spar, then pushes up the end of the yard. The long beam tips down until it's horizontal with the mast. The sail, which bears the crest of a raven, falls into place and flaps in the wind. But the boat is still turning. The bow is now pointed toward the beach.

"We're heading straight for Heath Ridge!" Yrsa shouts.

Job practically throws herself on the tiller. Whatever happens, they can't hit that sandbank.

"Yrsa, come back!" Toke shouts. He runs into the water, splashing through the surf.

"Turn the ship!" Yrsa cries. "The wind is coming from the north, so the bow has to point south."

More people are running down the beach. Job can hear them shouting. She doesn't dare to look. The mast sways back and forth.

Yrsa needs to grab hold of the two ropes hanging from the right and left corners of the sail. Only with those two ropes in her hands can they catch the wind. She pulls one rope through a rigging block on the deck, but the other dangles overboard. She leans over the edge and reaches for it, but it swings out of her reach.

"Don't do it!" she hears her father yell, but she doesn't dare to look. If she catches sight of his big brown eyes under those tattooed eyelids, she'll lose her courage. Her muscles will go limp as a dead fish.

A wave pounds against the side of the ship, drenching her in icy water. The ship sways, and the rope—praise the gods!—swings toward her. She grabs it and twists it around her wrist, but the whole maneuver causes her to lose her balance, and she falls to the deck. Pain ripples through her shoulder. She crawls back to the block and tackle and feeds the rope through the wheels. Then she pulls it tight, and the pulleys allow her to tighten the sail. She scrambles upright and looks at the beach. A crowd of dogs and people has gathered at the waterline.

Her father swims toward the ship. His mighty arms slash through the waves. His long hair and beard are dark in the water. He's barely twenty yards away. Or is it less? A little farther and he'll be able to grab hold of the side of the ship. Yrsa's eyes fill with tears. There are so many reasons to hate Toke, but there are so many reasons to love him too. The sail flaps in the wind. The ship creaks. Toke dives under a wave and surfaces a few feet from the bow. A high wave splashes over the edge of the ship, and it tilts dangerously to starboard.

"We're sinking! We're going to capsize!" cries Job.

But Yrsa is now standing in the middle of the deck. She twists the soft ropes around her wrists. They're made of linen and hemp, so they don't cut into her fingers or wrists. She helped braid them herself. Yrsa pulls the sail ropes toward her until they're tight. The block and tackle spring up from the deck. The sail bulges. Finally, they've caught the wind. The ropes dig into her wrists. She lets herself hang there for a moment and rests the heel of her good foot on the deck. The karve lurches forward. The small freighter is not as fast as a longship, but it quickly picks up speed.

Yrsa looks back. There, where the boat was rocking back and forth just a moment ago, is Toke's head sticking out of the water like a hairy seal. He curses, screams, and wails. She watches him grow smaller and smaller. Soon, her father is nothing more than a speck in the foaming sea.

Yrsa turns toward the horizon, to the water passing under the bow as the ship heads south. The dog races back and forth, barking at the gulls. His broom of a tail slaps against the side of the ship, and his thick coat flaps in the wind.

"We're going too fast!" Job cries.

"Can you give it a rest!" shouts Yrsa. Sinking. Capsizing. Sailing too fast. It's always something with that nun. Yrsa holds the ropes.

To the right, they sail past the dunes. There, on top of the Great Dune, are Troels and Little Sten, the half-brothers she grew up with, the two rascals who made her help them capture the sea serpent's head. Troels, who's not cut out to be a warrior and too nearsighted to throw a spear. Little Sten, who's always playing out some kind of fantasy in his mind, who always comes to her for a hug when he has a bad dream. The boys watch as she sails away, and she can't help but imagine Troels squinting to make out her silhouette on the deck of the ship, Sten wiping his face with the back of his hand, and the tears that must be rolling down his cheeks. But she can't even wave goodbye. She can't let go of the ropes. Later, when the wind dies down a bit, she'll tie them down one by one with Job's help.

Yrsa keeps looking back at her brothers until the muscles in her neck wince with pain. Her eyes burn. The last thing she sees is Little Sten, raising his hand in farewell.

Then, Yrsa turns her eyes to the whaling road before them.

PART 2

GANDA

19

NOKKI CARRIES HIS BROTHER HOME and stays with him. There's very little of Njall left in his limp body: a bump on his temple, a dark spot under his skin, some blood from his ear. Nothing more.

"He'll wake up again soon," Naefr insists. Still, he wraps Njall's fingers around the handle of an ax, just to be on the safe side. Nokki presses his ear against his brother's chest. He can hear his heart. The beating sounds far away, as if it's coming from somewhere deep inside his body. Nokki places a piece of ice wrapped in cloth on his bump and says, "Remember, brother, the day Kveldulf the Norwegian told us how he got the wolf claws on his necklace?"

Njall doesn't respond. His face is frozen. But his chest continues to rise and fall ever so slightly. So Nokki continues, "One night, on the full moon, Kveldulf was walking through the forest, and suddenly he found himself face-to-face with a giant wolf. Kveldulf took his ax, and when the animal pounced on him, he sliced its left front paw. The wolf ran away howling, leaving behind two bloody claws on the path. The next morning, Kveldulf saw the master carpenter with a bandage around his left hand. The man told him that he had chopped off two of his fingers the night before. Kveldulf asked how he—a master of the chisel and hammer—could've done such a clumsy thing. Too much to drink, murmured the carpenter. Kveldulf didn't believe him. Do you remember what Kveldulf said to us, brother? He said, 'Feel the claws.' And you touched the two wolf claws around his neck. Then Kveldulf said, 'Those are the fingers of a master carpenter.' You immediately pulled your hand away. Your face was white as snow. We all laughed about it later."

Nokki crushes down the ice with his fingers. The dark spot on Njall's face keeps getting bigger and bigger.

Njall wheezes as his lungs struggle for air. Nokki pushes his mouth open so he can breathe better. He doesn't want to think about that chilly winter night when Njall bragged about Stink Breath's death and how he would take the nun as his bed slave and make Yrsa pay for insulting him. People would call him Njall the Cruel, he boasted. No, Nokki preferred to think back on the good times.

"And remember that day we went walking through the dunes and got caught in a thunderstorm? We were so little back then, and terrified. We held hands in the pouring rain until the crackling thunder stopped."

Njall's breathing gives way to a long, protracted growl. Nokki talks about their father's sailing lessons, about the mounds of sand they shoveled as the tide rolled in. Soon, the low growl falters in Njall's throat, and Nokki frantically searches for another happy memory to tell.

But it's all over. Njall's chest has stopped moving.

Nokki calls in the men. They all reach for their amulets when they see that Njall has died with his fingers around an ax. The valkyrie will come to Midgard to collect him.

Naefr stares at the corpse of his second son. He can't believe it. How could those two girls have slain this giant of a young man? That little nun couldn't have possibly done it on her own. This has to be the work of that crippled niece of his—the daughter of his own half-brother.

"Yrsa always was dangerous," Nokki mutters.

"What?" shouts Naefr.

"Nothing, Father," Nokki says. He thinks back on that night in the boathouse when Yrsa launched herself at him in tears. She was overwhelmed with despair, yet he still struggled to wrestle her to the ground.

"This is all Toke's fault," Naefr grunts. Then, he grabs his spear and runs out of the house. Nokki and the men chase after him, urging him to calm down.

Naefr saunters along the path between the houses. "Helmsman!" he roars, brandishing his spear. Toke is standing by a fire pit with Rikiwulf's men when he sees Naefr approaching.

"You did this!" Naefr roars. "We should've sold that nun when we had the chance. A great-great-granddaughter of Charlemagne! Like rotten shrimp she is! All the monasteries in West and East Francia are filled with the great-great-granddaughters of that dog!"

"Calm down, Father," Nokki says. "He's your brother."

"Half-brother!" Naefr roars. "You should've left that daughter of yours to the wolves!"

He raises his right arm, ready to throw the spear. Someone tosses Toke a shield. He catches it as Naefr takes his aim. The iron tip of the spear smashes through the shield, just above Toke's arm. Unscathed, he drops it and pulls out the weapon.

"Hand me a sword!" Naefr shouts, but the men don't budge.

"Enough!" Gudrun roars. She stands in the doorway of the house. The sound of her voice drains Naefr of all his strength. Her face is still the color of death, but her voice is much stronger than it was yesterday, and her warrior knife has returned to her belt. Only the women are not surprised. They believe Gudrun cannot die.

"You'll get your revenge," she says.

Naefr hangs his head like a child.

Gudrun washes Njall's corpse. The slaves help her dress him in his finest clothes. The mothers put silver in his belt, and the men place a sword between his fingers. On his lap is a leather sack full of bread and cheese. The journey to Asgard takes nine days, and Njall will need the money and food to get there. They've also packed the pawns from the King's Table game for him. Nokki, Birger, and Egill carry Njall out of the village, followed by the rest of the inhabitants of Mimir's Stool, Danes and slaves alike.

They arrive at the death ship to the north of the village, where they lay Njall to rest on a pile of pine trees. Then, with four torches, they set the wood on fire. It doesn't take long before the whole pile is ablaze. It emits an incredible heat. Everyone takes a few steps back. Njall's body twitches in the flames. His legs writhe as the fire consumes his muscles. His stomach explodes with a pop. Sparks rise into the gray sky and are carried away by the wind. Njall is on his way to the underworld. Later, they will scatter his ashes in the grass among the stones.

That afternoon, the men gather at Naefr's house. Nokki fills their cups with dark beer. Naefr drinks as if he were Thor himself. He mutters that the gods must be angry with him, that the Norns are playing tricks on him. None of the men say a word, probably because they think he's right.

"My son is dead," he says over and over again.

Nokki wants to tell him that he has another son, that he, Nokki, could be as good a helmsman as Toke. But he says nothing.

"Fortune has abandoned me," Naefr laments.

"Your fortune will return, son," Gudrun says.

"I'll burn that slave's daughter alive." Naefr scowls.

The men nod and glare at Toke as if this is all his fault. Toke doesn't dare to contradict his grieving, drunken brother. He just stares at the flames in the fire trench, where the ashes are as gray as his soul.

Outside, the wind howls. When night falls and the full moon rises like a shield in the sky, a dark figure storms into

Naefr's house. The door falls shut with a dull bang. The men around the fire can't quite make out who it is. With its head hidden under a wide hood, it walks toward them, leaving a wet trail on the floor. Birger reaches for his hammer. Egill gets up from his stool and takes a step back. For a moment, Nokki thinks it's his brother back from the dead. Naefr reaches for his ax and whispers that the goddess Hel has come to Midgard.

Toke is the first one to recognize her: it's Signe. She slides back the hood. Her hair is soaking wet, her skin is wrinkled and pale as a dead fish, and her eyes are red from the salt water. Her whole body is dripping. Nokki knows that Signe is the best swimmer in the village, that she used to pick oysters off the seabed when she was young, and that she can stay underwater longer than anyone around. He, too, has heard the tales of her shedding her human skin on the full moon and transforming into a seal.

Nokki looks down at Signe's dark feet to check for webbed toes. She opens her cloak. Hanging from the belt around her wet dress is a sword. She pulls out the weapon and lays it carefully—as if it were a child—in Naefr's arms. Nokki recognizes the sword by the gold ring forged into the hilt and the word "Vengeance" carved into the iron blade.

Sten and Troels saw their sister throw the sword overboard and told Signe roughly where it had fallen into the water. She must have gone after it and searched the seabed for hours.

The weapon is off balance; Naefr feels that immediately. The tip is too heavy and the hilt is too light. But he caresses it as if it were a work of art forged by elves. Besides, all he needs is something to chop with. One well-aimed hack to leave a wound too deep to heal, a wound that will become infected and lead to the fever of death. Naefr will sharpen its blade until the iron sings. He will make the sword Vengeance worthy of its name. The fact that Signe found it is a good omen. Naefr feels new energy pulsing through his veins.

He embraces his brother. It's all settled. His fortune has returned.

Naefr stands up and points to Toke, Birger, Egill, and Nokki.

"We're going after Yrsa and that nun," he says.

"On which ship?" asks Nokki.

"Any sloop that floats and has oars!" Naefr declares. "We'll sleep for a few hours and leave with the tide."

He throws the rest of his beer into the fire. It hisses, like an offering to the gods.

20

FOAM SPLASHES ACROSS THE BOW, spraying Yrsa and Job with a salty mist as the karve cuts through the sea. What if the wind fails? What if it turns? What if they hit a sandbank? Or sail too far away from the shore and the current drags them out to the open sea? At least Yrsa is sure of one thing: they're not going to fall off the horizon.

At the helm, Job mutters one Our Father after another. If there's anything she's afraid of, it's the sea. On her last voyage, she was stowed away among the sacks and barrels and hardly dared to look overboard. But at least that time she could trust that the helmsman and rowers knew what they were doing. Now she's at the mercy of an impulsive Danish girl who has never sailed alone.

A wise monk at the monastery had drawn it out for her in the sand: the world is a wheel surrounded by water. Six-sevenths of the earth is land and the rest is water, he told her. Job used to have nightmares about the sea. In her dreams, she struggled to keep her head above water while the seaweed clung to her arms and invisible monsters took bites out of her body. There were fish with sharp teeth and spikes, spiderlike crabs, and creatures so slimy and hideous that they'd scare even the bravest men in the Bible. The beasts of the deep were always hungry, like the rats she saw fighting over a ham that Sister Mark had hung too low to the ground. The dry land belongs to the Lord, because that is the good part of the world, the monk assured her. But at sea, evil reigns.

Yrsa looks over her shoulder. The Great Dune is out of sight.

The men will probably come after them on their longship, the *Huginn*, a vessel propelled by forty rowers. The ship can reach tremendous speeds when the wind is in its favor. With the power of muscle and wind, it glides through the water like an osprey through the sky. The *Huginn* was made for trade and war. It could overtake them in no time. But the ship is currently bobbing in the shipyard without a mast. When they left, the slaves in the shipyard were just about finished scraping the moss and shells off the hull, but there are still many rusty nails and chipped planks that need to be replaced. They will need at least five more days to make the ship seaworthy again.

Yrsa wants to take over the tiller, but Job shakes her head. Her fingers are glued to the helm, so Yrsa sits down near the bow. There's a cramp in her bad foot. She can't stop thinking about her father: his head in the water, his screams. *I'm such a fool*, she thinks, *to save this nun's life at the cost of my own.* What would Nokki think of her now? Yrsa the Cripple, who helped the nun kill his younger brother, stole his sword, and ran off with the karve. The whole village must think she's a disgrace. What will Nokki do if he ever sees her again?

She looks back, but there's no one chasing them. She knows to follow the coastline, that somewhere to the south is Hedeby, the town that Gudrun and the village mothers visit at least once a year. It's also the place where Job's father's envoys are expected. They must be there by now, she thinks. Perhaps they can pay her as soon as they arrive. Otherwise, she'll travel to Ganda with the nun. One hundred pounds of silver, Charlemagne's great-great-granddaughter said—that's a fortune. Yrsa could buy half the world with that.

That afternoon, Job and Yrsa pass a fishing boat and spot an island looming like a dark shadow in the distance. The wind keeps blowing from the north. The boat glides through the water like a salmon to its spawning grounds. Every hour, Yrsa climbs the mast to make sure they're not being followed. But the sea behind them remains empty. The goddess Rán must be satisfied with their offering of the sword, Yrsa thinks.

Job can't stop babbling prayers and kissing the cross around her neck. Yrsa finds it annoying, but when you're fleeing an army of raging Danes, it's good to have as many gods on your side as possible. Meanwhile, Job clutches the tiller as if it's the Bible itself. Every once in a while, Yrsa corrects the course by muttering "port" or "starboard," and Job will either push the tiller away from her or pull it closer. Her eyes remain fixed on the bow. She hardly dares to look out to the sea.

Yrsa has traveled this route before. Despite her bad foot, Gudrun always insisted on taking her along with the women to the market in Hedeby. She made sure to point out all the major landmarks to her granddaughter: an island here, a headland there, a hill with a village on it.

The day seems to last an eternity. Yrsa's lips and throat are bone dry. The salt burns in her mouth and her stomach is as empty as a shell on the beach. They haven't eaten anything since the few clams at the old fisherman's hut. They see the hunger and thirst in each other's parched faces, but say nothing. Job just stands there with her hand on the tiller. Her whole body trembles with fatigue.

"Sit down," Yrsa says. "Let me take over for a while."

"No."

Yrsa moves toward her. "Come on, sit!"

Job releases the tiller and bursts into tears. "He hit me. He was on top of me!" she screams.

Job clings to Yrsa and presses her face into her cloak. She cries and shakes and screams.

"It's over now," Yrsa repeats a hundred times.

"When I close my eyes I see that grin on his face. I feel his weight on top of me. The pain. I can smell his breath, hear his panting," Job mutters. "I keep asking God to help me forget, but I can't."

"It's over now."

"It will never be over. It's my fault. I provoked him by praying at that stone every day."

"No, it's not your fault."

"I shouldn't have killed him," says Job.

"Njall should've had a harder head."

"Revenge is in the hands of God," she says. "Not of man."

Yrsa rolls her eyes and lets go of her. *Odin, give this nun your wisdom!*

"I must ask God for forgiveness, and for that, I need a priest. Only a priest can save me."

"I already saved you," Yrsa cries.

"You can't save me. You're a pagan," Job exclaims.

Odin the dog saunters over to Job and pushes his snout into her belly. She hugs the dog. The animal looks up at Yrsa with its one eye, as if he blames her for something.

"Don't look at me like that, Odin. You're just a stupid dog," Yrsa mutters.

The wind holds steady for the rest of the day. The sun sets, giving way to a big, bright moon. The clouds clear, and soon the stars come out, offering enough light to continue sailing. Yrsa stands at the bow and keeps her eye on the waves. Her father taught her how you can always tell where the sandbanks are by the shape of the waves. The wind dies down a bit, but it keeps blowing from the north. Yrsa can't help but feel that fortune is on her side.

"We're not alone. Fortune is with us."

"What? What do you mean?"

"Fortune is a spirit. She follows a person like a shadow and determines their luck. We call her the hamingja."

"A female spirit?"

"Yes, but she has a will of her own. If she has had enough of you, if you bore or annoy her, she will walk out on you and abandon you to your fate. She may never return."

Job doesn't answer, and keeps her eyes fixed on the sea.

"But if the hamingja likes you, if she sticks with you, she'll put the fear of the gods into your adversaries. Today, we had fortune on our side. We've been lucky."

"Lucky? I've had the worst day of my life, and you're talking about luck? Go away with your hamingja."

"Don't shout. She's listening. You'll scare her away. She's a sensitive one."

Suddenly, Job lets go of the tiller. She flinches and grabs hold of her cross.

"There," she stammers. "The Leviathan!"

Yrsa looks to the side. The dark sea churns in the moonlight. Under the surface of the water is a giant looming mass.

"Hands on the tiller!" Yrsa shouts. But Job isn't listening. She falls to her knees, clasps her hands in prayer, and wails. The dark mass shoots out of the waves right next to the ship, splashing water across the deck.

"God save us!" Job shrieks. "It's the boiling water of the Leviathan!"

Yrsa pushes her aside and takes the tiller.

"Those creatures won't harm us," Yrsa declares. "Why do you think we call the sea the whaling road? Look!"

Job trembles as she peers over the edge. A giant whale swims in front of the boat. Its tail slaps the water, sending spray up to the sail. Job screams, and Yrsa laughs. As many as twenty whales swim past the ship. They don't seem the least bit interested in the karve.

"Maybe the writers of that book of yours never went to sea," Yrsa says.

Job takes hold of the tiller again.

"I'm sailing here," Job snaps. "You go to the bow."

"Follow the whales," Yrsa says. "They avoid the sandbanks."

Mother Philip told Job that sometimes the monks go out to sea without any preparation whatsoever. They climb into a boat and trust that God, the Great Helmsman, will take them safely to their destination. And He does.

The land is nothing more than a dark streak in the distance.

"Look up!" Yrsa cries. "You see that bright star over there?"

Job looks up at the mass of stars.

"That bright star is Loki's torch. That way is north. As long as we keep that star behind us, we won't lose our way."

Job searches for the bright star but can't find it. And even if she does, how on earth is she supposed to keep it behind her?

"Heathen," Job murmurs quietly.

Horizontal wrinkles appear at the top of the sail. One of the sides of the sail flaps. Yrsa walks over to the ropes and tightens them. The sail's belly is full again.

"You came for me," Job says.

"What?"

"You broke an oath to the sea king. You left your father. You left everything behind. For me."

"No, not for you. For silver, remember?"

Job shakes her head. She doesn't believe her.

"You're right," says Yrsa. "I also did it because I didn't want to be the third wife of a man who brags about killing a huge polar bear, but didn't. And I hated Njall's guts. What he was doing to you, I couldn't, you know, I... well, it made me furious. As furious as Odin."

"You saved me, Yrsa daughter of Toke."

"Ah, come on, give me that tiller," Yrsa barks.

Job lets her take the tiller. Yrsa points to the bow.

"There's a long pole up front. Stick that into the water. As long as you can't feel the seabed, we'll be all right."

Job walks to the bow, picks up the pole, and sticks it into the water at the side of the ship. It goes all the way down. She pulls it out again.

"All good," she shouts.

"Keep doing that every few minutes. We don't want to get stuck in shallow water."

"Right," she shouts back.

"We'll make a Dane of you yet," Yrsa shouts, and she can't help smiling.

Job and Yrsa stay awake the whole night. They take turns at the tiller and the bow. They never get stuck in shallow water.

At dawn, the sky burns red. The gusts have died down considerably, and Yrsa mans the ropes by hand to catch as much wind as possible. She spots the mouth of the river that leads to Hedeby.

"We need to go in there," she says.

"How do we do that?"

"We pay rowers."

Along the mouth of the river is a beach lined with huts

made of driftwood and old nets. Men run up the beach and push a skiff into the surf. They jump into the little boat, and soon they're rowing toward them.

"Who are they?" Job asks.

Yrsa can barely suppress the agitation in her voice.

"Rowers," she replies. "They'll take us to Hedeby."

Yrsa loosens the ropes, and they slide through the rigging blocks. The sail starts flapping, and the karve bobs on the waves. When the skiff reaches them, a boy climbs aboard. His teeth practically fall out of his mouth when he sees that it's manned by two women. Odin barks himself hoarse, and Job holds him in her arms.

"Where's the crew?" he asks.

"Eaten. We threw their bones into the sea," Yrsa says.

The boy just stares at them with his jaw dropped.

"We're mermaids. Daughters of Rán. The men came at our singing. They shouldn't have done that."

Then the boy finds his voice again.

"You're joking," he says hesitantly.

"You're a quick one, aren't you?" Yrsa retorts. "What's your name, kid?"

"Orm, like my father."

"Can you and your mates row us into Hedeby, Orm son of Orm?"

"Sure," he says. "The tide is on our side."

Yrsa holds up a coin in the air: the dirham she got from Troels in exchange for climbing the tree. She had sewn it into her belt.

"Will this be enough?"

The boy turns and whistles. Three young men climb aboard. They're older than Orm and all look like him—all sons of Orm. They hoist two extra oars on board. One man stays behind in the skiff and rows back to the beach. Their bodies are worn from a life exposed to the elements. They're dressed in old leather, hemp, and furs stitched crudely together. On their heads are tattered wicker hats. They reek of manure and rotten crabs.

"The *Muninn*?" Orm asks as he deciphers the runes on the sail. "Isn't this the boat from Mimir's Stool?"

"It most certainly is," says Yrsa. "I'm the helmsman's daughter."

"Toke son of Thorsen?" asks Orm, who isn't as stupid as he looks. He gazes down at Yrsa's foot and then back up at her. "You're his daughter with the crooked foot."

Yrsa nods, but inside she wants to scream. This Orm fellow sure is nosy. Soon all Jutland will know that Yrsa daughter of Toke is in Hedeby.

"And who's that?" he asks, pointing at Job, who's still holding Odin. Her right eye is completely swollen shut, like a dark patch on her face.

"That's none of your business," Yrsa says.

The boy looks surprised.

"What brings you to Hedeby?" he asks.

"You see that wolfhound over there?"

Orm looks at Odin, who growls and shows his teeth.

"You know what he likes best? Nosy little boys."

Orm son of Orm shrugs sullenly and stands by the tiller.

Two other sons of Orm take a seat at the oars. The third one lowers the yard, bringing down the sail. Yrsa helps him pack it. Then the men row up the narrow mouth of the river. As the river widens, they hear loose ice floes scraping against the hull of the ship.

"Winter is almost over. Summer is coming," says Orm at the tiller, as if Yrsa doesn't know there are two seasons in a year.

"Hungry?" he asks, pulling some smoked herring, oatcakes, and a jug of beer out of his bag. Yrsa accepts the food and sits down beside Job against the wall of the stern.

"Can we trust these men?" whispers Job, eyeing them skittishly.

"Of course not," Yrsa says. "But they'll take us to Hedeby."

Yrsa wolfs down the herring, bones and all. She washes away the salty taste with a few slugs of beer. Job munches on an oatcake and hands a piece to the dog.

"What do we do when we get to town?" she asks.

"If your father's envoys aren't there, we'll have to continue to the west coast," Yrsa says. "From Hedeby, goods are transported to the coast by carts and sloops. It's not that far—a day's journey at most. At the coast, we can look for a ship to cross the Western Sea."

"Cross the sea again? Why don't we go to Francia by land?" asks Job.

"Don't be ridiculous," says Yrsa. "A Dane travels by sea. Only idiots travel by land. On land, everything looks alike. Have you ever walked a Roman road?"

"No, but with horses we can—"

"Horses? All these beads aren't enough to buy half of one. Besides, I've never sat on a horse in my life. Naefr was the only one who had any in his barn."

"We can continue on foot, like pilgrims," Job says.

"I'll never make it with my bad foot."

"Will they even let us on a ship with that foot of yours?"

Yrsa shrugs. "I'll just say that I broke it recently."

"And how will we pay for the crossing?"

Yrsa points to the nine beads on her necklace. She can use them to trade.

A little while later, Yrsa falls asleep.

Job recites her morning psalms by heart. She's exhausted, but afraid to close her eyes. She thinks of Ganda, of her beloved convent. She can picture the dark chapel before her and the dancing flames of the oil lamps. She can almost smell the incense. She doesn't even notice that she's quietly humming the "Kyrie eleison."

21

ON JOB'S LAST NIGHT IN GANDA, the bells rang. The sisters were startled awake. The stars were still twinkling in the sky, and the bats were out. It was hours before the call to morning prayer. Yet, the ringing was so loud that, for a moment, Job thought the monk was trying to rip the bell out of the bell tower. Mark made the sign of the cross and murmured a Hail Mary. Reverend Mother Philip lit a tallow candle. A rat scurried across the hall.

"Veils on," Mother Philip shouted. She pulled her dark habit over her petticoat and tied the white veil tightly around her head before walking out. Job did nothing. She stood up on her bed and stuck her bare head out of the hole in the wall. Outside, right in front of the monastery, where the farmers came to bring their harvest and where it was always buzzing with people and activity, stood a small army of the count's men. They seemed to be made of iron: they wore helmets and chainmail that covered their bodies from throat to ankle. They held the reins of their horses tightly. The animals snorted incessantly and trembled on their legs.

Soon, a few monks went out to greet them with torches. The light reflected in the warriors' helmets.

One of the monks pointed to the river and then to a spot somewhere downstream. Mother Philip stormed up the stairs and made as many as one hundred signs of the cross before reentering the dormitory. "The Vikings are coming. They heard that our palisade collapsed and that the count moved south with his troops, leaving our monastery undefended. They will be here in an hour or two."

Sister Mark kissed the bronze cross around her neck. The convent was normally enclosed by a wooden palisade, but on the south side, close to the gate, a section had been washed away in a recent flood. The heavy wooden beams were carried away by the Scheldt. All the pagans had to do was step through the muddy opening and climb the hill to reach the monastery.

"Those heathens will kidnap us all," John muttered.

Job rolled her eyes. As if a hundred-year-old dried fig like Sister John would ever be taken hostage. Job pulled on her habit, secured the white veil tightly around her head, placed her psalmbook in the pouch on her belt, buckled her clogs under her leather slippers, and followed the other sisters outside. Their footsteps clattered over the stones. The monks were already in the courtyard loading a cart with cups, bowls, and crucifixes used for worship. The gold and silver glistened in the moonlight.

Moments later, the exodus was in full swing. It was so dark that they could barely see the two fortified towers of

Ganda a mile downstream. No one dared to light a torch. They fled through the gate into the night and followed the road south. Everyone was in a hurry. No one looked back.

After half a mile, they passed a farm. Dogs barked and geese croaked. A man emerged from a reed hut with a torch and spear. He heard the word "Vikings" and was ordered to extinguish his torch. He whistled his family awake, and soon he and his wife and children were gathering their livestock and following the procession south. Job spotted the three monks from the writing chamber ahead of them, looking distraught.

Job liked those three friars. Every day, after the first meal of bread and cheese, Job had crossed the courtyard to the writing chamber. She'd find the three friars standing at their desks, always complaining about something. Sometimes the ink wasn't dark enough or there were hairs on the parchment, or it was so wrinkled that it looked like it came from the skin of an old donkey. In the winter, they complained about the cold and their frozen inkwells. The other day, when they discovered that a tomcat had snuck in and sprayed all over their pile of finished pages, they were as angry as God at the Egyptians. The Bible they had been working on for fourteen months was as good as ruined, they claimed. They'd never get the smell of cat pee out of it. And the book had been commissioned by the bishop. That meant that every time the bishop opened the sacred text to proclaim the word of God, he would inhale the faint but unmistakable aroma of piss. There wasn't enough incense in the church to hide the smell.

Job told the friars the smell was not that bad and she would clean every page. This calmed down the monks considerably. The girl had a solution for everything. Every day, she floated into their writing chamber like sunshine. One monk wrote the Latin scripture, another designed the capital letters, and the third decorated the pages with flowers and illustrations to bring the text to life. Job prepared the paints, using plants and mosses from the monastery garden, and mixed the colors. The sacred words of the New Testament always needed a little color. She admired the capital letter monk the most. His K had a snake wrapped around it and there was always a cat sleeping under the M; the O was the Blessed Virgin with the Savior in her arms. The old monk used to say that this Bible would be his last.

"And surely your finest," Job would say with a cheerful look, as if he were still a young man.

The friars passed all the finished sheets to Job. It was her job to clean them by wiping away the lead pencil lines and sanding away any imperfections. The men had become attached to the color girl who brought a bit of light and warmth to their long, dark, cold days in the writing chamber. The bishop's Bible with its 258 pages—each one written in ink and adorned with tiny paintings—was nearly finished and ready to be bound. The sheets were piled between two wooden boards to keep the parchment from curling. The entire bundle weighed fifteen pounds. No one would ever know who had made the Bible, but the monks didn't mind. Vanity was for fools. Job was proud of the work too, even if it did smell a bit like cat pee.

On the night of the exodus, Job ran to the three monks.

"Are you all right?" she asked them.

"They chased us out of our beds," complained one.

"We weren't allowed to enter the writing chamber," said the other.

"And the bishop's Bible?" asked Job.

"It's still back there," said the capital letter monk, his face white as a sheet. "My finest Bible."

Job stopped in her tracks. The Bible. Her Bible. Her colors. Her corrections. She had read every word, admired every letter he had drawn. That Bible shouldn't even be touched by pagans, let alone stolen. She had to save it. God was calling her to. If she truly trusted the Lord, if she was quick and didn't hesitate, she could run back to the writing chamber right now and save the Bible from the filthy hands of fire worshippers. Without a word to anyone, Job kicked off her clogs. She could run faster barefoot. The monks didn't stop her. She would get their Bible back. The girl had a solution for everything.

The psalmbook—the one containing 150 chants for the seven prayers of the day—bounced against her thigh in the leather pouch as she ran. Occasionally, she heard someone calling after her, but she didn't respond. She was on a mission—a mission for the Lord, for the capital letter monk, and for the bishop. She dashed through a flock of confused geese, dodged a herd of bellowing cattle, and passed countless crying children and hooded figures in the night. Soon, the dirt road was deserted. She ran through the open gate and raced up the hill, panting. The reed huts along the road suddenly looked a lot less sturdy now that they were empty. Skinny cats huddled in the dark corners watched her hurry by. There was an eerie silence in the air, as if the final judgment day had arrived. To the east, she could already see the purple light of dawn. When she reached the top of the hill, she stopped to catch her breath. Her feet were covered in cuts and scratches.

She walked through the gates of the monastery, crossed the courtyard, and hurried into the writing chamber. The three tall lecterns in the little room stood like pillars of knowledge, each one laden with beautiful blank sheets of parchment. She wondered whether they would ever be used to transmit the Word of the Lord.

She found the pages of the bishop's Bible on the table under the two heavy planks. There was no string to bind the loose pages together, and it was too dark to search for any. She took the bundle in her arms and several pages slipped to the ground. She laid them back on the table and groped around on the floor for the fallen sheets. She found five of them and jumped up to retrieve the rest. But then she felt another page under her foot. She wailed in frustration. She put the bundle down again, picked up the page, and set it on the pile. Then she lifted the bundle again and pressed it into her chest. The edges of the stiff animal skin cut into her chin.

She carried the unbound Bible out of the writing chamber. Not too fast—she didn't want to drop any more pages. The parchment was almost as heavy as the bronze candlestick on the altar. The muscles in her arms twinged with pain. All she had to do was walk down the hill, follow the road, and catch up with the refugees. She would find the monks and give them the Bible. They would take the pages from her, run their fingers across the beautiful text, and place them in the right order. The capital letter monk would smell it and say, "Yes, this is indeed our fragrant masterpiece."

Job walked out of the monastery gate again and strode down the hill. She didn't look at the empty streets or houses. In a moment, she would reach the open gate in the palisade.

Just then, she spotted silhouettes standing in the gray light of the early dawn. She was so startled that she almost fell. She pressed the parchment firmly against her chest. The Gospel of Mark was supposed to offer protection from pagans. Before her were men with round shields, spears, and helmets. Their hair was long and their arms were covered in tattoos.

One of them approached her. He was tall and broad and wore a wolf pelt around his shoulders that reeked of fish.

"Where is everyone?" he asked in Danish. She understood what he was saying. The count's watchman was a Dane with a cross crudely tattooed on his arm so everyone could see that he had been converted to Christianity. He used to accompany her on walks along the shipyards when she was eight years old, and taught her words and phrases from his own language. There was also a Danish miller who worked on the monastery grounds at the water mill, and she sometimes chatted with him in Danish. She was good at it.

Job tried not to look at him. "Never look a man in the eye," the Reverend Mother had urged her. "Always look straight ahead at the Lord."

"Did an elf steal your tongue, nun?" the Dane asked.

Job straightened her shoulders and glared at him. She was proud to be a nun. She didn't have to respond to this man. She clasped the 258 sheets of parchment to her chest like a shield—a shield as thick as her upper arm and as strong as the four evangelists combined. As long as she held the Bible to her chest, they couldn't harm her.

"They're far away by now. They left last night," she lied in broken Danish.

The man stepped in front of her and pulled a knife from his belt.

"Don't," Job stammered. She squeezed the bundle of sheets.

He grabbed the leather string around her neck and pulled Job toward him. She felt the cold blade against her skin.

"Hail Mary full of grace...," she murmured.

The man cut the leather rope and caught Job's gold cross in his hand. He weighed the gold in his palm and grinned.

"That's mine," murmured Job, but he didn't hear her. He tugged at her arm, and the Bible pages fell in the sand and quickly scattered across the road.

"Wait!" she cried. "It's a Bible. It's extremely precious."

"It's a bunch of painted animal hide."

"Painted with the Word of God!" Job exclaimed. She bent down to pick up the sheets, but the man pulled her upright again.

"Why don't you show us where the monks keep the silver," he barked, pushing Job in front of him.

The pagans trampled over the sheets of parchment as if they were dead leaves. The wind hurled one of the pages all the way down the dusty street.

The bishop would never get his Bible.

22

THREE WEEKS BEFORE Job met Yrsa, she found herself on the deck of a longship propelled by Danish oars. She couldn't see the riverbank, but she could see the tall reeds passing by. She didn't dare to look at the monster's neck on the high bow. They were sailing downstream on the Scheldt, headed for the sea. Job had never seen the ocean before. None of the sisters at the convent had. The very thought of it made her reach for her cross, but it was no longer there.

Yesterday had been just a normal day in the safety of the convent, and now here she was on the deck of a ship laden with stolen goods. Behind her was a tall barrel full of sacks of grain. At her feet were cups and bowls looted from her church, and up in the bow was the bloody carcass of Moses the pig.

But the bowls, cups, and sacks of grain weren't the real bounty. The real bounty was Job herself—Job and the fourteen other young people who had been kidnapped. They sat side by side in the middle of the ship with their ankles tied together so they couldn't jump overboard. There were ten girls—mostly daughters of fishermen or farmers—and four boys. Some were crying and wailing for their parents. Job was the only one from the convent.

Next to her sat a boy who kept shaking his head and muttering to himself. He couldn't believe what had happened to him. That morning he was driving his sheep to the river, and all of a sudden he was seized by two men and thrown onto a ship. In a matter of seconds, he'd gone from humble shepherd to captured slave, soon to be sold at a North Sea slave market. The names of those markets—Diepe, Walacria, Hedeby—sounded like the gates of hell.

It was all happening so fast, the boy moaned to himself.

"Stop whining, sheep boy," barked one of the Danes from his rowing bench. Job knew that she too would be sold as a slave. She had met former slaves before. Every once in a while, one would return from the North after many years of hard labor, a boy who had become a man, a seafarer. His family would welcome him home like a prodigal son.

But no woman had ever returned. *Ever.*

Despair pulsed through her veins. Her hands trembled. She was defenseless without the cross on her chest, her comfort and her confidence. She prayed a Hail Mary, and then another. And another. Until she could think clearly again.

She clutched the leather pouch on her belt that contained the book of psalms. She mustn't lose hope. These pagans were about as smart as the parchment-nibbling mice she used to chase out of the library. They were fire worshippers from the nests of Satan, ignorant fools who wouldn't know the warmth of the Lord if they burned their hairy behinds on it. They would do anything for silver, gold, and other things of earthly value. No, she would not give in to these tattooed barbarians. She had to have faith. The Lord was with her. The Holy Spirit was inside of her. She knew that God was testing her and that He would remain at her side.

She closed her eyes and imagined that she wasn't on a ship, but kneeling on the floor of the monastery church before the image of Christ the Savior, surrounded by candles. She was not alone. A bride of Christ was never alone.

As evening fell, the river became so wide that Job could no longer see the reeds or even the trees on the bank from the deck. That night, the Danes rowed their boats to the bank. The helmsmen called out to one another, and the rowers declared a race to see who could reach the shore first, as if it were all a game. The men pulled their vessels onto the beach. In the distance, Job saw the sea sparkling in the moonlight. The longship had reached the mouth of the river in just one day.

As soon as the ships hit the sand, people from a neighboring village came to the beach with bread, cheese, barrels of beer, and birds they'd caught on the shore. They had rough fingers, deep wrinkles, and rotten teeth. The Danes haggled over the price of their wares. The prisoners were all dehydrated, and each one was given a scoop of beer from a barrel to drink. It tasted horrible, but Job drank every last drop.

The ten ships on the beach were a remarkable sight. The men removed the monster heads from the bow, fastened them to the decks of their ships with ropes, and covered the faces with cloth. They didn't want to frighten the elves as they sailed toward home. The slaves—at least a hundred of them—were huddled together on the wet sand and guarded by a couple of the younger Danes. One of the blond ones was joking around with his friend. Up close, they didn't look so tough. The blond boy held a spear on his shoulders as if it were an ordinary stick.

All of a sudden, the young shepherd sitting beside Job sprang to his feet and took off running like a wild man into the dunes. For a moment, no one ran after him—the boys were afraid someone else might try to run away and they'd get a beating from their captain, the man with the snake tattoo on his arms.

"Go after him," the captain shouted. "Or do you want me to leave you behind on this beach?"

The two boys chased after the fugitive. Job watched until they were out of sight. The captain spat in the sand as if the whole situation had left him with a bad taste in his mouth. The prisoners kept their heads down, afraid to catch the heathen's gaze and incur his wrath.

"They'll find the kid," said the helmsman to the captain. He always seemed to be laughing, that helmsman, as if life were one big joke, as if they were on some kind of pleasure trip and hadn't just robbed a hundred young men and women of their freedom. There were dark lines tattooed on the helmsman's eyelids, and on his neck was the image of a raven with a crooked beak and flat head, as if it had flown into a wall. The capital letter monk drew much more beautiful ravens than that.

Job saw the captain looking in her direction. She quickly averted her gaze. *Don't see me*, she thought. *Please, don't see me.*

But he saw her.

"You there," he shouted. "Stand up."

Her entire body was shaking; it felt as if her lungs were about to collapse. She wanted to pray Hail Marys, but the words didn't come. Instinctively, she placed her hand on her chest, but her golden cross wasn't there.

"You there, nun," the helmsman roared. "On your feet!"

Job stood up slowly. The man eyed her carefully and scratched at the green snake on his arms.

"I'm of noble blood," she muttered.

"What?" he asked.

"I said, I'm of noble blood," she repeated, this time looking him straight in the eye. A woman of nobility is not afraid of some smelly Viking.

"I have a soft spot for noble girls," the helmsman grinned, pushing away the dark hood of her habit. He was surprised to find yet another hood underneath, a white one without a speck of dirt on it. It was tied tightly around her head so that only her face was showing, and not a hair was visible.

"My father is the Count of Flanders," Job said. "My mother is Judith, daughter of the king in Aachen. My grandfather is Charles the Bald, son of Louis the Pious, grandson of Charlemagne, ruler of the world from Rome in the south, the Pyrenees in the west, the Elbe in the east, and all the way to the sea in the north. And who are you, heathen?"

The captain stared at her and the helmsman laughed.

Job was so small that the top of her head barely reached the bottom of the helmsman's beard.

"This little nun here talks like she's a giant from Jotunnheim," the helmsman chuckled, and he kept right on laughing, as if her kidnapping were some kind of game.

"She's barely five apples tall," said the captain. "How can she be a descendant of the emperor? That Charlemagne was a pretty tall man, wasn't he?"

"Maybe that was all talk to frighten our ancestors," the helmsman replied.

"She's bluffing," the captain said. "If she is the king's granddaughter, why isn't she covered in gold and silver?"

"Because she's a nun," the helmsman concluded.

"So what? Those abbeys are full of gold and silver," the captain declared.

"My father bought me a place in the convent," Job said. "I took my vows."

"Vows?" the helmsman asked. "Is that the same thing as an oath? Something you swear?"

"We don't swear," said Job. "Swearing an oath is a mortal sin."

"So what's a vow then?"

"A vow is a promise to God. I took a temporary vow. When I'm sixteen, I'll take an eternal one."

The captain and his mate weren't following. But they knew that monks and nuns generally came from well-to-do families, and this girl wouldn't have been in a convent if her Christian father hadn't paid for her to be there. On top of that, she was haughty; she had fierce eyes, candle-straight posture, and spoke in such a way that, even in Danish, suggested that she might very well be of the highest nobility.

"So your grandfather is the king?" the helmsman demanded.

"Charles the Bald, King of West Francia," said Job. "So I advise you to take me back to Ganda at once, before my father, my grandfather, and all their armies come after you and chop you to pieces."

"Let them come," the captain laughed.

"Let's take the nun hostage," the helmsman said. "We'll demand silver in exchange for her freedom."

"If you bring me back quickly and unharmed, you heathen, I'm certain you will be rewarded," Job said.

"A reward," scoffed the captain. Then he grabbed her by the collar and pulled her into his chest. Job could smell the sour beer on his breath. It almost made her gag.

"I wouldn't touch her, Naefr," the helmsman said. "If you ask me, that girl is worth her weight in silver."

"She doesn't weigh much," the captain snarled.

Then they heard shouting. The two boys had returned with the fugitive. His head was covered in blood, and he could barely stand on his feet.

"We still want to sell the kid, you know," the captain called out to the two boys. "This is all your fault."

The boys forced the poor shepherd to sit. Neither one said a word.

"How about I leave you on this island, Sporr? That'll teach you a lesson," the captain said.

The two boys' jaws dropped at the captain's words.

"You can't be serious, Father," the blond one said.

"Shut up, Nokki," the captain barked.

"He doesn't mean it, Sporr." The helmsman laughed, pointing to the fire on the beach. "Come, tonight we feast on roasted pig."

The helmsman took the boys with him. The captain was clearly annoyed. He pulled a girl from the group up by her hair. She screamed. Then he dragged her into the dunes. Job didn't dare to look. She shivered. That man was more terrifying than the sea itself. She couldn't help but feel guilty because the girl had been taken in her place. She prayed for forgiveness for the lies she had told the pagans about herself.

Job had never lied so much in her life.

23

JOB WAKES UP WITH A SCREAM. She grabs Yrsa's arm.

"I dreamed of Njall," Job says. "How he beat me, how he—"

"It's over now," Yrsa whispers into Job's ear.

At both sides of the river there is only wilderness. Yrsa puts her arm around Job's shoulder. They listen to the splash of the oars and the chirping of the birds. They feel the warmth of the sun on their cheeks. Job gazes at their two shadows on the wooden deck.

"With a bit of luck, we'll find your father's men and you'll be on your way home tomorrow," Yrsa says.

"Why don't you come back with me?" Job asks. There is still fear in her voice.

"What? To your convent? Your flooded land? No, no, no, I'm staying in the North."

Job leans her head against Yrsa's chest. She holds on to her. On the deck, they are only one shadow now.

"We have arrived!" shouts Orm.

From the river, Hedeby is a wondrous sight. The houses with their mossy roofs look like sea creatures that crawled out of the river to bask in the sun. Outside the town are huts and tents for travelers and merchants. Wisps of smoke swirl up from the rooftops, forming a grayish smog that hangs over the city. The sun is high in the sky. It must be afternoon by now. The closer they get to the shore, the stronger the smell of the water. The river reeks of fish waste and human excrement.

The rowers tie the boat to a dock that juts out into the river on stilts. A man approaches them. He introduces himself as the dock master and says that mooring costs one piece of silver per day.

"One piece of silver a day? You must be joking," Yrsa says.

She glares at him as if he were a beetle asking her permission to crawl out from under his rock.

"It's not a joke, miss, that's the rate," the man says in surprise.

"Does this dock belong to you, then?" Yrsa demands.

The man stares at her wide-eyed for a moment, then stutters, "No, but that's the rate in Hedeby. Just ask the boys in the boat."

"I'm not asking them anything," Yrsa says.

The dock master looks bewildered. Then he asks, "Why are you being so difficult? One piece of silver. That's the price. It's a fine place to dock."

"I understand that even dock masters have to make a living," Yrsa says. "I'll leave my boat here for a few days, and then I'll give you one of my beads."

The man looks at the orange beads on her necklace.

"One bead a day," the man says.

"One of these beads is worth at least three pieces of silver. Or should I tell my father in Mimir's Stool that the dock master of Hedeby chased me off?"

Only then does the man look at the ship and notice the raven carved into the bow.

"One coral bead for three days then," the man says.

"Agreed," Yrsa says. "I'll pay you in three days."

Yrsa steps off the dock, and Job follows her. She doesn't have time to wait for the man's answer.

Yrsa and Job walk down the main street that runs parallel to the river. The whole town stinks of the animal hides being scraped on the banks. The rooftops are dripping in the sun. People shout and carts creak. An old woman carries a bundle of wood on her back; a young girl herds three black pigs with a stick. The street is made of logs packed down with sand and dirt. Yrsa's bad foot hurts. She shouldn't have left her walking rod on the sands of Mimir's Stool.

Yrsa feels small and vulnerable in the crowded city. She misses Gudrun, who knows all the artisans by name. She used to take Yrsa with her on her rounds to the workshops and inns. There are Norwegians, Swedes, Franks, Frisians, and Saxons here. Odin the dog trots alongside Job as if he has never done anything else in his life. No one notices Job's strange appearance. The residents of Hedeby walk past her without a second look.

"I want to see a priest," says Job.

"Good idea," Yrsa thinks aloud. "A priest will know whether your father's emissaries have arrived."

"Only a priest can grant me forgiveness and tell me how to atone for my sins," Job says flatly.

Yrsa stops at a comb maker's stand. Displayed on a small table are all kinds of combs for hair and beards, as well as bracelets, skates, flutes, spoons, whistles, and small knives. Everything is made from animal bones and deer antlers. Yrsa asks the man hunched over his work table if he knows where they can find a priest. The man points toward an alley leading uphill. The cathedral is up there, he says.

"A cathedral!" Job exclaims. "I didn't see one from the water."

The thought of it brings tears to her eyes. Job practically flutters into the alley. Yrsa can barely keep up with her.

"A cathedral," Job repeats. She looks up in search of a tower rising above the houses built of clay, wood, and straw. Twice she stumbles over her own feet. Then she stops and says, "No, this can't possibly be it."

Yrsa, Job, and Odin stand in front of a wooden structure with a cross on the roof. The waves of the sea have been carved into the wooden gutter around the top of the structure.

Is this it? Job cannot believe her eyes. Where is the bell tower that points to the heavens? Where is the high roof supported by formidable columns? Where are the stained glass windows that let in the sun and spray colors on the sacred cathedral floor? Where are the statues of God and the winged angels? And why are there no gargoyles?

"This place isn't even big enough to be called a chapel," Job groans.

Job pushes open the door. A candle illuminates the altar.

It's the only source of light in the dark, windowless room. Above the altar is a soapstone statue of Jesus. He doesn't look as mournful as the one at the monastery. This Jesus is wide awake. There are holes in his hands, but he doesn't seem bothered by them. His arms are open wide, as if he's just returned from a sea voyage and wants to hug his wife. There's no crown of thorns on his head. Instead, he's wearing the crown of a king. At his feet lies a dead snake, and on his belt hangs a sun stone—a round stone with a pin in the middle that helps Danes find their way home at sea. His beard is full, almost cheerful.

Job throws herself on the floor. Mumbling, she crawls toward Jesus's feet. The sand on the boards crunches under her clothes. She raises her clasped fists and presses her forehead to the floor as if she is not worthy of even looking at the statue. She mutters something about her sin, her great sin, her immeasurable sin.

A man enters. He makes the sign of the cross and bows down on one knee.

"Are you a monk?" Yrsa asks.

"Speak softly," says the man. "You are in the house of God."

"But you are a monk?"

"I am the bishop of Hedeby, appointed by the pope in Rome," the man whispers with his nose in the air. He reeks of manure.

"Rome," Yrsa repeats skeptically. She doesn't believe a word of it. "Rome is on the other side of the world."

"Indeed it is," the man mutters. "I have a letter from the pope himself. With his seal."

He eyes the amulet of Frigg on her chest with contempt.

"So you have come to chase away our gods?" Yrsa demands.

"I am a missionary," the man hisses. "I am here to share the light of Christ with the wicked."

"And how is that going for you?" Yrsa asks with a cheeky grin on her face.

"And who, might I ask, are you?" he demands.

Yrsa ignores the question and says, "My friend and I would like to know if any Frankish messengers have arrived in recent weeks—envoys from Ganda. If they are here, surely they must have visited you, a bishop appointed by Rome."

"There have been no envoys," he whispers.

Job gets up and says, "Father, I want to confess."

The bishop approaches her, lays a filthy hand on her head, and says, "Of course, my daughter."

Yrsa walks outside. She leans against the church wall and lowers herself to the ground. The dog walks up to her.

"We're a long way from home, Odin," she says. "And we're not rich yet."

The beast yawns. He tries to scratch himself, but his paw gets tangled in his long, sticky mass of fur, and he falls over. He scrambles to his feet and takes a walk around the block with his nose to the wind as if nothing happened.

There's no way that dog is Odin in disguise, Yrsa thinks.

* * *

Meanwhile, Job tells her story to the bishop. The bishop forgives her for the lies she told the pagans. He forgives her for the death of Njall, who was nothing but a godless savage. Together, they pray twelve Our Fathers as penance. During the fifth Our Father, Yrsa sticks her head into the church.

"How much longer?" she hollers.

"To the Lord one day is like a thousand years, and a thousand years like one day," the bishop replies enigmatically.

"Okay, but we need to hurry," Yrsa says.

The bishop gets up and shoos Yrsa out of the church. Then he returns to Job and lays his fat hand on her white veil again.

"Where were we?" he asks.

Time creeps by. Yrsa sits with her back against the church wall, goes off to buy some nuts, and comes back. She dozes off a bit. The sun is past its highest point in the sky when Job finally emerges. On her forehead is a black cross drawn in charcoal. Yrsa gives her a handful of nuts to chew.

"What did you tell that dung beetle?"

"Everything. The bishop told me to pray five hundred Our Fathers."

"I can't even count that high."

"I'll teach you to count to a million if you want. My mother taught me all about numbers."

"I can't wait," Yrsa says.

"And he said I have to convert you. If I want to save myself, I must save your soul. Then my mortal sin will be forgiven."

"What?"

"In short, you must be baptized."

Job beams. The black cross on her forehead has restored her strength. She's already walking out of the alley toward the main street. The dog follows her.

"Come on! What are you waiting for?" Job calls over her shoulder.

Yrsa scrambles to her feet and struggles to keep up.

"What do you mean? You want to hold me underwater until I drown?"

"You won't drown," Job says.

Why on earth did the weavers under the world tree have to tie her fate to this fanatic nun who marches into cathedrals and tells her whole life story to unknown bishops?

"You're out of your mind if you think I'm going to become a Christian," Yrsa says. "And didn't you hear the bishop? No envoys have come from Francia. There's no ransom here."

Job says nothing.

Suddenly, Yrsa remembers a trader who used to buy Gudrun's furs. He would take the pelts to the west coast in his sloop. Most goods are transported this way because the area is so swampy. Upon arrival, they are transferred to a knarr and taken to Frisia.

"I know a pelt trader who can take us to the west of Jutland," Yrsa says. "Once we reach the coast, we can find a boat to take us to Frisia or Ganda."

They emerge on the busy main street. Yrsa pauses to get her bearings. Where did that fur trader live again?

Job walks farther down the hill toward the jetties, away from the hustle and bustle of the main street.

"Where are you going?" Yrsa asks. "We've already wasted so much time."

But Job doesn't answer. She just stands by the riverbank. Yrsa follows her incredulously. The river stinks even more than it did that morning.

"What is it?" Yrsa demands.

"There's something else I have to tell you."

"Come on, we need to hurry," Yrsa says impatiently.

But Job is in no hurry. She peers at the forest across the calm water. There's not a breath of wind. The bare branches are perfectly still. The sun warms her face.

"The bishop has forgiven me my lies," says Job. "Now I have to tell you the truth too."

Yrsa is only half listening. She needs to go back to the necklace maker she just saw on the main street to trade her beads. She wonders how many pieces of silver he'll pay for nine of them.

"My father is the Count of Ganda," says Job, "but my mother is not the countess. She was the count's lover. Or she used to be. She had a child. Me. And when I was ten years old, I went into the convent with her."

Yrsa is still thinking about the necklace maker. Could she get three pieces of silver per bead? She'll ask for at least twenty for all of them.

"So I'm an illegitimate child of the count," Job says flatly, "and not the only one." She gazes at the shore with her arms tucked into her sleeves. Ropes tap against the masts and tired waves wash against the muddy shore. Only then do Job's words sink in.

"Wait, what are you saying?" Yrsa cries. "You're the granddaughter of Charles the Bald, aren't you?"

"Actually, I'm not."

"What?"

"I have no royal blood."

Yrsa stares at her.

"And my hundred pounds of silver?"

"My father will reward you with coin. Enough for a horse."

"A horse? What am I supposed to do with a horse?"

"Or you could buy something else with it. It was just an example."

"But didn't Gudrun make you write that letter? You filled three sheets of parchment!"

"None of you can read Latin. I wrote that I had been kidnapped by heathens, that you were demanding a ransom, and that I understood my father could not pay it. I pressed them not to worry. God was testing me, just as He tested Job in the Bible, to see if I would give up my faith in the North. I wrote that I trusted God and I was sure He would bring me home again."

Yrsa's jaw drops in amazement. This information catches her off guard. As if she hadn't already been stupid enough to fall in love with a boy who didn't love her back, now she was double stupid for running off with a lying nun. And triple stupid for thinking that she could collect all that silver just like that. And quadruple stupid for swearing an oath to a nobleman only to break it one day later.

"And there's one more thing," Job says.

Yrsa looks up, confused. "Another thing?"

"I will never, ever, give up my faith. I will convert you."

Yrsa can't believe her ears. It's all too much. She has turned her back on her whole clan to save the life of this Bible-blabbering church mouse—this ungrateful, lying, veiled fanatic. Yrsa grabs the nun by her collar and slams her against the ground. The girl weighs practically nothing.

Odin growls.

"You know, I should've let Njall chop your head off in that barn," Yrsa roars.

Job reaches for her wooden cross, but Yrsa snatches it from her fingers and rips the book of psalms from the bag around her belt.

Odin gnashes his teeth.

"No," Job moans, scrambling to her feet. Yrsa runs to the dock over the river. Job chases after her.

"Don't, please!" she screams, but Yrsa is already at the end of the dock, where an old man is fishing. She throws the cross and psalmbook into the water.

"Hey," the old man snaps. "You're scaring away the fish."

Job shrieks, "Look what you've done!"

"I'm doing you a favor," Yrsa cries. "I'm helping that god of yours put you to the test."

A second later Job throws herself into the water. The fisherman winces. "So much for the day's catch," he grumbles.

Job's habit bulges in the water, and for a moment, it helps her float. She reaches for her psalmbook and the worthless wooden cross. Then her head disappears in the dirty soup. The fisherman looks puzzled, and Odin whimpers in panic.

"She'll surface any second now and walk on water," Yrsa snarls. "Her god is helping her."

The fisherman nods in bewilderment. Now that would be a sight to behold—someone walking on the river. The nun resurfaces, gasping for air, her arms flailing. Odin throws himself off the dock. Yrsa can't believe it: Odin is trying to save her! But instead of dragging her to safety, the dog just clings to her, and they disappear under the dark water together.

"Get out of there!" Yrsa screams. "Come on, I'm not jumping in there after you."

The dog manages to keep his head above water, but Job can't.

"I don't think that woman can walk on water," says the fisherman.

Yrsa pulls the woolen cloak over her head, kicks off her shoes, unfastens the silver pins in her dress, and shakes off her petticoat. Suddenly, the fisherman has lost all interest in his line.

Yrsa lowers herself into the water, gasping from the cold. She immediately grabs the nun by the habit as she thrashes and chokes in the water. Yrsa pulls her by the collar to shore. Odin paddles after them, and once they're on the bank he shakes the muck out of his fur. Job's habit is covered in filth.

Yrsa walks back up the dock and wipes herself clean.

"May I?" she asks, taking the bucket of clean water from the fisherman.

The fisherman looks up at the naked young woman in front of him and stutters. Yrsa doesn't wait for an answer and rinses her hair with the water in the small bucket. Then she pours the rest over her body.

"Thank you," she says, and pulls her petticoat back over her head. The linen fabric clings to her wet body. The fisherman can't stop gawking at her. It looks like his jaw is about to fall off, Yrsa thinks.

She points at the water. "Why don't you just keep an eye on the fish," she says. "I think you've got a bite."

Job plops down on the bank like a pile of mud. She's covered in slime and ooze. But there, in her lap, are her cross and the book of psalms.

"Godless wench," growls Job.

"What am I supposed to do now?" Yrsa demands. "There's nothing for me in Ganda."

Job shrugs.

"I should sell you myself. Here. As a slave. That's the only thing I can do. You must be worth a pound of silver."

"As much as your mother," Job snarls back.

"You shouldn't have lied to me," Yrsa snaps.

"I lied because I was afraid of being raped. I thought your people would at least show a little respect for a granddaughter of the king, a great-great-granddaughter of Charlemagne. Well, I thought wrong, didn't I?" Job cries. Fingers trembling, she reattaches the cross to the leather cord around her neck.

Yrsa extends a hand to help her to her feet. Job slaps it away. She wants nothing more to do with her.

Yrsa sighs and crosses her arms to get warm. What a mess they've gotten themselves into!

Suddenly, she hears a voice behind her. "Yrsa? Is that you?"

Yrsa turns around. Her heart skips a beat. There, standing in front of her, is Harald son of Karl, the slave master. Yrsa recognizes his bald head and the wispy long hair clinging desperately to the back of his skull. He's wearing a bright red tunic embroidered with flowers and a collar trimmed with gold thread. His belt is in the form of the serpent Jormundgandr. The snake bites its tail as if Harald's belly were as big as Midgard itself. Harald hands a coin to Orm, who stands beside him. Orm thanks him with a grin and a bow of the head. Yrsa curses under her breath. She should have known that Orm was an informant of his.

"Orm told me you were here. Didn't you want to stop by to see your uncle?" Harald asks indignantly.

"Of course I did, Uncle Harald," Yrsa replies.

"What's that?" he asks.

"Her name is Job," Yrsa says. "She's a strange one. Just now, she decided to go for a little swim with her habit on."

"A habit? So she's a nun?" asks the colossal man standing behind Harald. He looks like a giant escaped from Jotunnheim, with a massive bullish head and runes tattooed on his chest. His beard is woven into three long braids, and there are tin rings in his ears.

"This is my primary slave," Harald says. "I've had him since he was twelve, and he just kept growing. They call him the Colossus of Hedeby."

The Colossus makes the sign of the cross and kisses the tin cross around his neck.

So he's a Christian too.

"Peace be with you, sister," the man says.

"And also with you," Job replies. She stands up straight and lets the muck slide off her body. She smells like a cesspit, but she looks at Colossus with renewed confidence.

"What are you doing out with a nun, Yrsa?" Harald demands.

Yrsa hesitates for a moment. Despite all her threats, she'd rather not tell her uncle that Job is a slave and she'd be more than happy to sell her to him. But how else is she going to get herself out of this situation? What's she going to tell him? *Frigg, give me your advice*, she thinks.

But Frigg says nothing.

"I went to Mimir's Stool to convert the pagans," Job lies. "I'm a missionary."

For a second, Harald looks puzzled. He knows there are missionaries in the North, but this is the first time he's ever seen one who's a woman.

"And did you manage to convert those savages from Mimir's Stool?" Harald scoffs.

"No, I failed," Job sighs.

Harald laughs, and Colossus sadly makes another sign of the cross behind him.

"Yrsa was the only one I managed to convert," says Job.

"What?!" Harald cries. He can't believe his ears.

"It's true, she converted me," Yrsa stutters. "That's why we left together. We're headed west."

"Toke son of Thorsen's daughter has converted to Christianity?" asks Harald incredulously.

"Praise the Lord," says Colossus behind him.

"Praise the Lord," Job repeats.

"Praise the Lord," murmurs Yrsa, as if she's got a rotten clam in her mouth.

Then Harald asks, "But if you've converted, Yrsa, why are you still wearing Frigg on your chest?"

"I asked her to throw that idol into the river," Job explains. "Then she got angry and threw me into the water."

"How dare she!" murmurs Colossus indignantly.

Yrsa is speechless. What is the nun going to think of next?

"Believe me, Yrsa. You must do as I say and throw away that idol," says Job.

"What?"

"You heard her, throw it away," Colossus repeats.

Harald glares over his shoulder at his slave, who takes a step back and lowers his eyes in apology.

Yrsa should've let the nun drown. It's true what they say—nuns will fill your ears with nonsense until you forget your own gods.

"Show me that you've truly converted, sister," Job commands.

Yrsa wants to scream. She removes the cord from her neck. She unties the knot and slides off the beads. Then she removes the bronze medallion. Her eyes sting with tears. She has worn it for as long as she can remember. The wise Frigg has always guided her path and offered her protection.

"Do it," Job says.

Yrsa hurls the medallion into the water.

Harald looks pained and says, "Thor's lightning! You really have become a Christian."

"Hallelujah," says Job.

"Praise the Lord," says Colossus.

"Praise the Lord," Yrsa murmurs, almost too softly to hear.

"I think you'll miss our gods, Yrsa," says Harald. "Come and warm yourself by my fire. I want to show you my finest possession—my horse, Son of Sleipnir."

"A horse?" asks Job excitedly.

"A stallion of the gods," Harald corrects her. "Are you coming, Yrsa?"

Yrsa has no choice but to accept that they're not leaving Hedeby tonight. Still, all is not lost. Harald doesn't seem to know that she fled her village with a hostage. Naefr and Toke must be on their way. They'll have left Mimir's Stool by now, probably in a smaller boat, but the earliest they could be here is tomorrow around noon. That means they still have time.

"I'm coming, Uncle Harald," she replies.

24

THE HORSE IN HARALD'S STABLE is a descendant of Sleipnir, Odin's steed. Legend has it that long ago, a stonemason went to the gods and claimed he could build a wall around the Valhöll in three seasons. As payment he asked for the sun, the moon, and Freya's hand in marriage. Loki, the god who gave the rainbow its colors, thought Odin should accept the stonemason's proposal. In all likelihood, the stonemason wouldn't finish in so short a time, and with any luck, the gods would have half a wall for free.

But the stonemason's horse turned out to be as strong as a mountain. The animal could pull a sled full of rocks like it was nothing. The mason made quick progress, and it soon became clear to the gods that he would finish the wall in three seasons. According to Freya, there was only one god to blame for their terrible predicament: Loki. He had persuaded Odin to accept the stonemason's proposal. Odin was determined to prove the goddess of love right, and threatened to feed Loki to the wolves if he didn't come up with a solution.

On the last day of summer, Loki transformed himself into a mare. As soon as the stonemason's stallion laid eyes on the mare, his heart was on fire. He chomped at his bit and galloped after the mare, foaming at the mouth. And that's how Loki made sure that the last piece of wall was never finished. In the end, the sun and moon remained in the sky, and Freya didn't have to throw herself into the arms of the stonemason.

After that, Loki disappeared for a few months. The mare was pregnant, and gave birth to an eight-legged stallion. Odin named the horse Sleipnir.

"It's a beautiful animal," Job says.

"I don't trust horses," Yrsa murmurs. When she was eight years old, the stable slave who cared for Naefr's horse got kicked in his chest. She still remembers the boy lying in the hay with the imprint of a hoof on his breast—the blood on his lips, his short breaths, the panic in his eyes. It took days for him to die. Not even the elves could save him.

"Yes, he's a fiery steed, all right." Harald beams. "As savage as Odin himself. You have to earn his respect. He has to accept you." The stallion takes a few steps back at the sound of his master's voice and flattens his ears.

That animal is scared, Job thinks. Her mother's old stable master taught her how to observe horses. He told her what it means when their muscles tense, how they scrape with their hooves and lower their ears. Job kneels before the horse, takes some of the nuts that Yrsa gave her, and places them on the ground in front of him. The horse steps forward and licks up the nuts. His name is engraved in runes on his teeth. An old scar curls across his nose. From a whipping, Job suspects.

"Your god never had a horse like this," Harald snarls.

"No, my God rode a donkey. That was enough for him," Job says sternly.

"This beast is worth a fortune," Harald boasts.

Again, the horse startles at his master's voice. On his flanks, Job sees the wounds from spurs digging into his sides. The only time the horse leaves the dark stable is when Harald rides him. And when Harald rides, he uses a whip and spurs to make him obey.

Son of Sleipnir takes two steps toward Job. She straightens up. She raises her arm slowly so as not to startle him. Then she strokes his neck with her fingers.

"You're not going to bite me, are you?" Job whispers. "You're not a savage."

Night falls in Hedeby. Still, the streets are full of shouting and the creaking of carts. The town is one big market, a maze of alleyways that never sleeps.

"If you hadn't had to stop and make that confession, we'd be out of town by now and on our way to Francia," Yrsa hisses.

"You're a pagan," Job snarls back. "You don't know the first thing about guilt and penance."

Job brushes some dried mud off her habit. She reeks of manure.

There are more slaves in Harald's house than Yrsa can count. They're all young women, and they come and go with bowed heads. Their hair is cut short, their faces are glum, and when

Colossus calls for Job to be washed, they flinch like snails in their shells.

"No need for that," Job insists. "It's not washing day."

But two skittish girls lead Job into the kitchen, where they pull her habit and petticoat over her head. Job wants to protest, but as soon as the girls bring a bucket of warm water and soap, she lets them scrub her down. It is the first time she's ever been washed by others, and she can't help but enjoy it. It must be a sin, but she'll ask God for forgiveness later.

"The master usually sells his slaves at the beginning of the summer," Colossus explains to Yrsa. She nods and realizes that her mother must have been one of them once.

In the great hall, Yrsa looks around in awe. Candelabras dangle from the ceiling, a woven tapestry of a boar hangs on the wall, and a stained glass mirror stands on a table. Yrsa is surprised to see such a clear reflection of herself. It's different from the one she's always seen in the murky silver bowl back home in Mimir's Stool, the one that always made her face look like the top of a jellyfish. She keeps her eyes on the mirror as she weaves her hair into a tight braid, wipes some dirt from her cheeks, and slides her tongue over her broken teeth.

Harald's wife approaches them. Her name is Astrid and she's holding the hand of her son, Hefnir. He's a timid boy of about eleven. As soon as he sits down, a cat jumps into his lap. He's focused on a sheet of parchment covered in thin, curly characters. His eyes scan the page from right to left.

Toke once told her that people in the far south write from right to left.

"Yrsa?"

Yrsa turns around, and there stands Job dressed in an elegant Danish robe made of green fabric. It's held up by two simple iron pins, like every Danish woman's dress.

"That dress looks nice on you," Yrsa says.

Job smiles as if she has a toothache. She tugs at the short, close-fitting sleeves and can't seem to get used to her exposed neck and head. Her hair has been washed. It's slightly longer now, and the bald spot is barely visible.

"My habit is soaking in a bucket," she says.

The slaves are on their knees, roasting meat in a stone oven on the floor. They serve the meat in painted earthen bowls to their master and visitors. They also offer them cups of grape wine. Job can tell by the acrid smell of vinegar that the wine is spoiled.

"Ripened to perfection," Harald says after taking a sip.

Job can't help but think of the monks who move heaven and earth to keep their barrels of wine well preserved. These fire worshippers have no idea.

"It's hard to believe the two of you sailed that boat all the way up here," Harald exclaims, his tone almost questioning.

"The wind was in our favor," Yrsa says. "Rán—I mean, God—looked kindly on us."

She makes a cursory sign of the cross, but does it all wrong. Job rolls her eyes, but Harald doesn't seem to notice.

"Your father told me that even with that crooked foot of

yours you're worth more than his two sons combined. He says you're very handy with a spear."

His words annoy Yrsa. Handy with a spear! She doesn't need a pat on the back from her father, let alone from Harald the slave master.

"I heard, dear Uncle, that it was you who sold my mother, Cara the Frisian, to Toke," Yrsa says.

Harald nearly chokes on his meat.

"Frisia...," he says ponderingly. "Then I must have bought her in Dorestad."

"Dorestad," Yrsa repeats. "So Cara's family still lives there?"

"No idea," Harald replies, "but your family is here, in Denmark."

"Of course, Uncle," Yrsa murmurs.

"It was in this very hall that Toke first laid eyes on your mother. She was the most beautiful slave I ever had," Harald says.

Yrsa takes a piece of bread and chews on it spitefully.

Young Hefnir looks up from his plate and asks, "Why do we have so many slaves in Denmark, Father?"

Harald groans and casts an annoyed glance at Astrid, as if it is her fault that their son asks such silly questions.

"How do you think we build all our ships and make all those sails, my boy? With slaves! Even in the south, in Mikligard, they're jealous of our mighty workforce."

"What is Mikligard?" asks Job.

"The big city, Constantinople," says Hefnir, delighted to show off his knowledge.

"How do you get there?"

"By the Baltic Sea. The Swedes sail down the big rivers in the south," says Hefnir.

Job nods, but she doesn't want to know how far east the sea extends.

"Without slave traders, Denmark would collapse," Harald concludes. "That's the truth."

"So let it collapse," Yrsa murmurs.

Harald is surprised to hear his niece say something like that under his roof. But the rules of Danish hospitality—guests and fish stay fresh for one night—oblige him to provide the girls with shelter.

"I've heard rumors about you, Yrsa. Is it true what they say, that you're a seeress?" Harald asks slyly. "And that you predicted the death of Kveldulf the Norwegian?"

The question catches Yrsa off guard.

"Yes, news travels fast, you know, like a ship on the wind." Harald grins.

Astrid and Hefnir look at Yrsa with renewed interest. The slaves warming themselves around the stone oven also eye them curiously. Harald's grin is as wide as the claws of a giant crab. He points to his son with his cup of wine.

"If I toss some nightshade into the fire, could you tell me his fate too?"

"No, don't ask her to do that!" Astrid cries.

"The kid's fate is already set, woman," Harald barks. "There's nothing he can do to change it anyway. But I need to know if he will become a slave master like me, or if he will remain the weak little mama's boy he is now. If so, I may have to pass my business down to one of my bastard children."

"Hefnir is your son. He will carry on the business," Astrid says fiercely.

"Tell me my son's fate," Harald insists. "And I will arrange for a sloop to take you to the west coast tomorrow."

Yrsa sighs. There's no reason to go west now that she knows there's no silver waiting for her in Ganda. But still, she needs to get out of Hedeby before Naefr arrives.

"Fine," Yrsa says. For a moment, she catches Job's gaze. She looks into the nun's tiny, dark eyes. This girl has brought her nothing but misery. Yet somehow, Yrsa can't be angry with her anymore. Job was cheated, just like Cara. Of course she lied. She was just trying to survive. Just like Cara.

"Nun," Yrsa says, "slap me back to my senses, okay?"

Yrsa sits down in front of the fireplace in the middle of the house. The warmth of the fire causes her to sweat, stinging her eyes. One of the slaves brings a bowl of dried herbs. The only one that Yrsa recognizes is nightshade. She wonders whether this mixture will work as fast as the one Gudrun used. Harald tosses the herbs into the fire. They burn into a cloud of smoke. Astrid takes a step back. Yrsa inhales the hot smoke and staggers, but Job holds her by the belt to keep her from falling forward.

The boy comes closer. Yrsa clamps her fingers around his wrists and immediately sinks into his body. She sees Hefnir as a small boy. He can't take his eyes off a dark man with a cloth around his head. The man writes from right to left in beautiful cursive letters. Hefnir imitates him effortlessly, and the man explains the meaning of the curlicues.

Another wave, and Yrsa sinks further. She sees a corpse. It's Harald, with an embroidered sheet draped over his body. Hefnir pinches his father's nose to make sure he'll never call him a weakling or a mama's boy again. The boy walks behind the slow funeral procession, but his eyes are on the ships in the morning sun, sailing out with the tide. He doesn't want to stay in this city of fog, slaves, and dead fathers.

Then another wave hits, and Yrsa sinks even deeper. The pressure weighs on her lungs. Hefnir is a young man now, and he stands before the walls of a huge stone church. The towers are so high they almost touch the clouds. He's walking through a city with stone streets worn down with the tracks of carts, past a market full of strange fruits and spices. This must be Mikligard. In a shop by the river, he inspects a few bales of silk. He touches them one by one. Yrsa feels the soft, gray fabric on her fingertips. A woman lifts a bale of silk from the counter. Her shoulders are crooked. She hobbles to the back room with a pair of scissors. Yrsa wants to follow her. All she can see is her back. Suddenly, the woman turns around, and—

The slap on her cheek knocks it all away: the silk, Mikligard, Hefnir, the silk seller. Yrsa snorts and gasps for breath. Her heart feels lodged in her throat. Her ears are ringing.

"Are you all right? Can you breathe?" cries Job, who is struggling to keep Yrsa upright.

"The silk seller," Yrsa groans.

"What did you see?" Astrid asks, her voice trembling.

Yrsa's lungs swell with air. She tries to calm her breath.

"Tell us, what did you see?" demands Harald impatiently. "Will my son become a slave master?"

"No," she says. "He is going to Mikligard. He's going to be a silk merchant."

Harald can't believe his ears. "That can't be," he exclaims.

His son smiles.

"Wipe that smirk off your face before I disinherit you!" Harald barks.

Then Yrsa vomits on the floor. Harald and Astrid recoil in disgust. The weight of her fatigue rests on her shoulders like a hundred pelts. For a moment, her thoughts return to that crooked silk seller in Mikligard.

Then she falls into a deep, imperturbable sleep.

25

WHEN YRSA WAKES, her head is pounding. Her lips are dry as sand. Colossus is standing over her. She's startled to see him. Only after a moment does she realize where she is.

"Astrid wants to speak with you," Colossus says.

"Where's Job?" she asks. Her throat is so dry that it hurts to swallow.

"She's sleeping in the stable, miss, with the horse."

Yrsa struggles to her feet. It's as if there are weights hanging from her arms and legs. She staggers outside, hoping the crisp morning air will do her good. But out on the street, all she smells are wood fires, animal dung, and river sludge. She makes her way to the stable. Inside, she hears Job before she sees her. The nun still wears the green dress and talks to Son of Sleipnir as she gently brushes his hide. The horse rears its head as Yrsa approaches and whinnies loudly.

"Hush now," Job murmurs, and the horse calms down.

"The horse has accepted me," Job says.

"Now that's a surprise," Yrsa groans. "Did you convert the beast too?"

Odin scrabbles out of the wet straw, shakes his mass of fur, and barks. Job strokes his head, and he licks her fingers.

"Who can touch us now?" she says with a grin. "We've got Odin and Son of Sleipnir on our side." She kisses the cross on her chest and says, "I was only joking, Lord. Forgive me."

"I feel sick. Those herbs really took a toll on me," Yrsa says as she rinses her face with water from the horse's trough.

Job's habit is hanging over a wooden beam. She walks over to wring it out again.

"It's still wet. We can't leave until it's dry," she says as if it's just an ordinary day, and she's getting ready for her daily walk.

"If Naefr finds you here, he'll feed you to the gulls," Yrsa says. She leans on the trough with both hands and hopes she doesn't have a fever.

"I'm not leaving without my habit."

"That rape was nothing compared to what Naefr will do to you."

"Thank you for reminding me of that," Job snaps. She presses her cheek into the horse's neck, as if the animal is the only being in the world who can comfort her. The stable door creaks open. The horse steps back and snorts restlessly. Astrid enters the stable, followed by Colossus.

"I demand to know what else you saw," Astrid says.

Yrsa pauses to think for a moment. Her head throbs with pain. She has trouble remembering the details of the vision. It feels like a distant dream.

"Come on, hurry up, girl!" the woman barks.

"Your husband is dying," Yrsa says.

Astrid stares at her, bewildered. Colossus makes the sign of the cross.

"I saw Hefnir standing by his corpse," Yrsa continues. "He doesn't have much time left. Your son was no taller than he is now."

Astrid struggles to suppress a smile.

For a moment, everyone is silent.

"Harald was going to find some men to take us to the west coast," Job says.

"He hasn't had time yet," Astrid says. "There's a skiff from Mimir's Stool rowing up the river. Colossus saw the raven on their sail. They moored outside of town so they wouldn't have to pay the dock master. Harald went down to greet them."

Job's face turns as white as a communion wafer. Yrsa's fingers move to the cord around her neck, but her amulet of Frigg is no longer there.

"They've come to kill her," Yrsa says.

"We have to get to the docks," says Job uncertainly. "To our ship. We need to find rowers and—"

"You can't go until the tide goes out," Astrid interrupts. "And there's no point. The men from Mimir's Stool will catch up with you in no time."

Then Harald's wife turns to Colossus.

"Go to my husband," Astrid says. "Try to stall them a bit. Tell them the girls are still asleep."

Colossus turns and heads out the door.

"Follow the road south to the monastery of Hammaburg. It's a two-day walk," Astrid says hurriedly. "Farewell, Yrsa daughter of Toke." The woman gives her a hug and walks out of the stable.

"A two-day walk," Yrsa sighs as soon as the door closes behind her. "Can't that woman see I've got a bad foot?"

She sits down on a stool and holds her head in her hands as if it's about to roll off her neck at any moment.

"I can't go on," Yrsa groans. "Even if I find a stick to help me walk quicker. They'll catch up with us in no time."

"We're going," Job says decisively.

"You go. Get out of here," Yrsa moans.

"Absolutely not. A woman would have to be crazy to travel alone," Job says.

"You'll survive. Now get out of here!" Yrsa cries.

"Not without you," Job yells back.

"They're coming for you! Don't you understand that?" Yrsa shouts.

"Keep your voice down. You're upsetting the horse," says Job.

Give me your wisdom, Frigg, Yrsa thinks. Could they hide in the town and slip away after nightfall? Could they navigate the swamps in a sloop by themselves? No way, they'd never make it. Her head throbs and her legs are limp with fear. She feels as if she'll never be able to lift herself off this stool, as if she'll be stuck in this stable forever. There's no way out.

Suddenly, the horse whinnies.

Job is fastening a leather saddle on the horse's back.

"What are you doing?" Yrsa asks.

"We're going on horseback," says Job as she attaches the reins.

"There's no way I'm getting on the back of that beast!" Yrsa exclaims. "Besides, that horse only listens to Harald!"

"Harald is a brute. He has no idea how to handle this gentle giant." Job scratches the horse's neck and whispers something into his ear, as if he can understand what she's saying. Then she leads the horse by the reins to the stable door. She doesn't even have to pull. The horse walks beside her like a tame piglet. Yrsa leans back and pulls her feet in. The saddle smells of beechwood and old leather. It has four silver stripes on each side, eight in all, one for each leg of Odin's horse.

Job climbs onto the horse's back and perches on the saddle with her two legs to the side. She takes the reins. Yrsa can't believe it. The scrawny nun towers over her as if she and the animal are one.

"That's not a woman's saddle. If you fall backward, you'll break your neck!"

"I'm not about to straddle this creature like a man."

"Then how am I supposed to sit behind you?"

Job doesn't have an answer to that.

"Think of Thor," Yrsa says. "He transformed himself into a woman to get his hammer back. If you want us to get out of here on that horse, we'll both have to ride like men."

"Don't be silly. Take us to the south gate," Job says, and she remains seated with her legs to one side. She makes clicking sounds with her tongue.

The descendant of Odin's stallion walks through the open door, his hooves clacking softly on the ground.

Job pushes her hair back and tucks the cross under her

dress. Yrsa can't help but notice how beautiful she looks with her clear face and short hair. If she didn't know better, she'd think Job was a Danish girl.

Yrsa walks alongside Son of Sleipnir. They follow the flow of people into the bustle of the city. Yrsa can see the river between the houses. She hears the screeching of gulls, the squeaking of cart wheels, and the tapping of ropes against the masts on the water. The air smells of rotten fish and drying animal hides. A woman pushes a cart in front of her with a pile of herring on it.

"Is this the way to the south gate?" Yrsa asks.

"Follow me," says the woman as she leans in and pushes the cart with both arms.

Yrsa follows her. She grips the saddle strap as if she walks the streets of Hedeby with a descendant of Odin's horse every day. Job sits on the stallion like a noblewoman of ancient blood. His hooves clatter on the tree trunks under the sand. Job grips the reins and Odin the dog trots along behind them. The fishmonger stops to rest her arms.

"Is that Son of Sleipnir?" the woman asks.

"Harald asked us to take him outside the city to graze," says Job.

"Good idea," the fishmonger says.

"Can I help you?" Yrsa asks.

The woman looks at her in surprise.

Yrsa lifts the handles of the cart and heaves it forward. Together, they head toward the south gate. Yrsa can feel the pressure of the heavy cart on her bad foot. She bows her head to avoid being recognized and peeks over the pile of herring toward their exit. There, standing at the gate, she sees Birger, that rotten clam of a boy who got a bees' nest dropped on his head on midsummer's day. Her heart skips a beat. He's wearing a helmet and carrying a sword on his belt. Next to him is Egill, with his foxlike eyes. His hair has grown over the missing piece of his ear. They haven't seen her yet, but Egill has noticed the horse and the young woman sitting on it. For a moment, the dress and hair confuse him, and he stares at her as if he's trying to place her face.

Job sees them as well. She stops the horse in front of a man selling biscuits and tells him that she's Harald's guest and she'll pay him later. The man hands her four biscuits.

"Stop," the fishmonger says, but Yrsa doesn't stop the cart. She wants to get as close as possible to Birger and Egill. Stubbornly, she pushes the cart in their direction with her head down so the boys won't recognize her. Her misshapen foot remains hidden behind the cart wheel. Then she feels the fishmonger's hand on her shoulder.

"That's far enough," she says, and Yrsa lowers the cart. The woman takes three herrings, shoves a stick through their open mouths, and hands them to Yrsa.

"For your trouble," she says. Suddenly, Yrsa is standing there, holding three speared herrings in her hand. She uses the fish to hide her face as she spies on Egill and Birger. They're barely twenty steps ahead of her, but they haven't seen her yet. They're too busy gawking at Job on the horse.

It's now or never, Yrsa decides. Birger looks up in surprise as she takes off running. He immediately recognizes her by her gait. It even makes him chuckle for a moment, especially when he sees her clutching three herrings on a stick. She's only ten steps away from him when he realizes she's actually charging at him. He reaches for the longsword hanging from his belt. It's an expensive Frankish weapon forged from nine pieces of iron with a wood and leather hilt. Carved into the freshly sharpened blade is the name Bone Cracker, with one of the runes scratched out due to a spelling error.

Birger extracts Bone Cracker from its linen-lined scabbard. He raises the longsword high above his head with both hands. From there, he can swing the sharp edge down on Yrsa's shoulder with tremendous force. The blade will slice through her muscles, flesh, and bones like butter. If he had only taken two steps back, he might have very well hacked her to pieces.

But the Norns, those cranky weavers under the world tree, aren't done with Yrsa yet, and they must've been feeling particularly sadistic when they wove Birger's fate. The boy's had so much bad luck tied into his navel that it's almost unfair. As Birger lifts the Frankish sword above his head in the crowded street, Yrsa rams her shoulder into his diaphragm. The shock is so severe that Bone Cracker tumbles out of his hands and thuds to the ground, along with the three herrings on a stick. Birger falls on his back with Yrsa on top of him. The smack against the hard road knocks all the air out of his lungs.

A saddle maker who witnessed the scene from his stall drops five nails from his mouth. A blacksmith striking a horseshoe pauses between blows, and a woman braiding a basket looks up curiously from her work. They wouldn't miss a good street fight for the world.

Yrsa pushes herself upright and lifts Birger's sword off the ground. Egill charges at her with an ax and shield. Odin growls and lunges for Egill's ax arm. The skinny boy spots the dog just in time and blocks him with his shield. For weeks afterward, the people of Hedeby will wonder what kind of creature flew across the street that day. Was it a sheep? A wolf? Or something in between? In any case, Odin lands in the basket weaver's stall, sending the poor woman flying—crutch and all—into a heap of tattered reeds and wickerwork.

Yrsa swings the sword above her head with all the strength and speed she can muster. Then she drops it down on Egill's shield. The mighty blow leaves a dent in the outer ring. The iron folds. The wood splits. But Egill catches the blow with ease. Kveldulf taught him how to respond to such a predictable attack. He thrusts his shield against Yrsa's chest. She feels the iron edge of the shield ram into her throat, and the pain ripples through her head. Then he delivers a hard kick to her bad foot. Her ankle snaps, and she falls. Egill stands on her sword hand and places his ax on her throat.

"Drop it, cripple."

Egill grins. He has always been the craftiest of the three. She lets the sword slip from her grip. It falls to the ground.

"Where's my horse?" cries Harald, who comes running up out of nowhere. But Job and the stallion are nowhere in sight. *She's run off*, Yrsa thinks. Perhaps the nun has saved herself, and they're already galloping toward Hammaburg. Behind Harald, Yrsa's father appears, and she knows that all is lost. Suddenly, she's overwhelmed with exhaustion. She just lies there in a puddle and lets the muddy wetness soak through her clothes. Her foot is throbbing. What was she thinking? That she could escape her fate? That she could outwit the Norns?

"My horse!" shouts Harald to everyone in the street. "A piece of silver for whoever finds Son of Sleipnir!"

That gets the bystanders' attention. Everyone begins looking around, scouring the street. Some children dash toward the river to see if the horse is there.

Toke leans on the fishmonger's cart. He has rowed all day and night with Naefr, Birger, Nokki, and Egill. The skiff is a clumsy vessel, and they only had four rowers. They could have taken shifts, but Toke refused to sleep. He rowed all night long. He was stronger than the boys. He let Egill and Birger lead the way when they docked, but he quickly went after them to make sure the two hotheads didn't decide to avenge Njall and harm his daughter. But now, at the sight of Yrsa with an ax to her throat, he feels as queasy as a monk at sea.

"That's one tough girl," the fishmonger says. "She knocked that one flat on his back."

It almost makes Toke smile.

"She's my daughter," he says, remembering Cara with her bright, proud eyes. His heart breaks as he thinks back to that night when Gudrun decided to throw the deformed child into the sea. He sees Cara standing before him again, knife in hand, her eyes full of hatred. She growled at him like a wolf.

"Get away from my child," she snapped. It was the last thing she ever said to him.

"Why are you just standing there?" Harald hisses. "Go fetch your daughter."

Toke sighs and shouts, "Stay down, Yrsa."

"She's not going anywhere!" Egill shouts back.

"The horse!" someone cries in the street.

Harald whips around. The horse comes trotting up from an alley between two houses. The slave master is shocked to see the nun straddling his horse like a man. Her feet don't even reach the stirrups. Harald marches up to the animal and spreads his arms wide.

"Halt, Son of Sleipnir! Listen to your master!" he shouts, but his voice barely rises above the noise in the street.

Job makes the horse swerve. The animal's hoof crushes Harald's right foot. He screams, curses, and falls over like a scarecrow in a gust of wind. Toke leaps forward to yank the nun out of the saddle. He grabs her dress. Just one firm tug, and she'll be on the ground. But Toke should've been keeping his eyes on the horse. Son of Sleipnir clamps his teeth into Toke's long red hair and pulls hard. The sharp pain brings tears to his eyes. He lets go of Job and ducks away from the raging stallion's teeth. He stumbles back onto the cart of herrings. The fishmonger screams as it tips over, and Toke finds himself on the ground covered in dead fish.

"My poor little fishies!" the woman cries, as if they were her children.

There's shouting from all directions. Son of Sleipnir roars, snorts, and tries to move forward, but now the blacksmith is running into the street. He reaches for the reins. The saddle maker approaches the horse as well and tries to knock Job out of the saddle. Even a swine herder and a washerwoman join the fight to capture the horse and rider.

"Odin!" Job shouts, and the stallion rears up on his hind legs. The blacksmith gets whacked in the head with a hoof. The saddle maker and washerwoman duck out of the way and plop down in the mud. The swine herder starts screaming. Then Job digs her knees into the horse's flanks, and they charge toward Egill.

Egill just stares at Job with his mouth open—such a tiny person on such a massive horse. Then, he lifts his ax away from Yrsa's throat. He grips the long handle with both hands, ready to split the horse's head open.

"Bring it on," he mutters to himself.

He hears the dog growling behind him. Egill is as quick as an osprey. He turns, lets the handle of the ax slide down through his fingers, and takes a step toward Odin. The dog keeps his head low to the ground and snarls.

"Back off, Odin," Job screams, and Egill is shocked to see the dog obey. Egill turns to Yrsa, but she's no longer lying on the ground. She's standing beside him wielding Birger's Bone Cracker in both hands. She swings it down with a wild cry and hears a bone snap as the blunt edge hits Egill in the arm. The boy cries out in agony. The sword is living up to its name.

Job slows down the horse. She slides down the saddle a bit and extends her arm. Yrsa hobbles toward her, hooks her arm in the nun's, and swings herself onto Son of Sleipnir's back. She takes her position in the saddle behind Job. She can hardly believe it. She clamps her legs around the horse's torso.

"Forward, Son of Sleipnir!" Job cries. Yrsa wraps her arms around Job. She presses her head into the nun's back and watches the people whooshing by, calling out to her. The horse trots through the south gate with Odin barking wildly at his heels and gnashing his teeth at any bystander who tries to stop them.

Just outside the city, Yrsa spots their final obstacle. Nokki is running up the hill with a spear in hand. Naefr still stands by the river, shouting, "Kill the wench!" For a moment, Yrsa locks eyes with her boy from the dunes. He's only twenty, thirty steps away. If he throws the spear now, there's no way he can miss. It will pierce her right in the back. Yrsa squeezes her eyes shut, bracing herself for the blow. Here, at the south gate of Hedeby, she will finally meet her fate.

But the spear never comes. Son of Sleipnir gallops down a muddy path between the tents and barracks, his hooves splashing in the sludge. Pigs dash out of the way. People scream.

A few moments later, the tents are behind them. The road continues along the river to the south. There's no one chasing them anymore, only Odin struggling to keep up. His tongue hangs from his mouth like a wet rag.

Yrsa is terrified of falling off the beast. She bounces in the saddle and clings to Job.

The road rises over the Danevirke, a long wall of sand designed to protect Jutland from the Frankish kings.

As they head into the forest, the horse slows to a trot. The wooded path is one long mud puddle. All around them, the trees are dripping. The last ice has melted. Winter is gone.

26

IT'S AS IF THE MAIN STREET of Hedeby has been swept up in a whirlwind. The basket weaver's stall has collapsed, herring are strewn all over the street, and people are helping one another to their feet. Harald lies in the saddle maker's cottage. The comb maker, the basket weaver, and the fishmonger are all gathered around him. No one is sure how to help. Harald's screams are louder than all the seagulls in Mimir's Stool combined.

Egill plops down in the middle of the street with his broken arm in his lap. He curses the gods of Asgard. Birger walks hunched over, as if he's thrown out his back. Nokki helps him to a bench.

"Sit down, man," he says.

He also helps Egill to his feet. Both boys are as pale as the inside of an oyster.

"That crippled bitch," shouts Egill. "I'll chop her to pieces!"

Nokki is too tired to think. They rowed all day and night in that stupid boat. He can't feel his arms and legs anymore.

Colossus and the blacksmith carry Harald out on a plank.

"My horse, my horse of the gods," he groans.

Naefr swings his sword at his son. "Why didn't you throw your spear?" he shouts.

Nokki takes a few steps back, afraid that his skull is about to be bashed in. It is Toke who answers, "Quiet, Naefr. They were already too far away."

Naefr whips around, and as he does, the sharp edge of his sword slices into Toke's side.

"I wasn't asking you!" shouts Naefr.

Toke looks at his half-brother in shock.

If the helmsman had been wearing his chainmail, the sword wouldn't have touched him. But Naefr's men left their heavy iron shirts in the boat. This morning, no one thought they would need them. After all, they are only here to pick up a couple of runaway girls.

Toke curses Odin when he sees the wound in his side. Blood is already soaking through his shirt.

Naefr's rage subsides when he realizes he has wounded his brother. He returns the sword to its scabbard and takes Toke's arm over his shoulder. He helps him sit down.

"You sharpened that thing pretty well," Toke says as if he's only cut his finger. But his vision is becoming spotty as blood gushes from the wound. He presses his shirt into his abdomen.

Nokki runs over to help. He rips open Toke's shirt and presses a cloth against the wound. The cut is as wide as a fist.

"We need to get to Harald's," Naefr cries. "He has a surgeon."

"He has his work cut out for him today," Nokki says, and Toke smiles despite the pain.

A large crowd has gathered in front of the slave master's house. Everyone steps aside to let Nokki, Naefr, and Toke through when they see the blood on Toke's shirt. Harald is lying on a table in the main hall. Next to him are Astrid, Hefnir, and the Saxon healer, Ernulf.

Nokki helps Toke onto a chair.

"It'll be all right, boy," says Toke. "It's just a little flesh wound."

Nokki nods, unconvinced.

"I saw three swans land on the river this morning," Toke adds. "That was a good omen."

Astrid recognizes Toke. She puts a hand on her amulet, a silver-plated bear claw.

"Ernulf will attend to your wound in a moment."

Surgeon Ernulf doesn't know what to do with Harald's right foot. There's not a bone in it that hasn't been crushed. It's swollen to three times its normal size and is black with bruises.

"The best we can do is amputate," the surgeon whispers.

"No, not my foot!" Harald shouts. "Not my foot."

"Listen to the surgeon," says Astrid.

Harald slaps her across the face.

"Don't interfere! Bring me some ice!" Harald roars. "It's just a fracture."

Surgeon Ernulf shakes his head. It's much worse than a

fracture. He looks at Astrid, and it's clear: the broken foot may cost her husband his life.

"Put his foot on ice as he demands," Astrid says. The surgeon looks puzzled. Astrid's face is as hard as stone. Her muscles are tense, the corners of her mouth rigid. She takes hold of her son's hand and squeezes it.

"You'll pull through," Naefr says.

"The girl is headed for Dorestad," Harald groans. "Where her mother was from."

"Dorestad?" Naefr asks.

"I want my horse back," growls Harald.

Toke's face is white as bone.

"That's a nasty wound you've got there," Ernulf says. "I'll wash it and sew it up. Then I'll rub it with honey and cover it in cobwebs."

"Thanks," says Toke. "I don't want my intestines falling out when I sneeze."

"We'll get them," Naefr says that night. Egill's wrist is wrapped in a splint. Lucky for him, the surgeon knew how to straighten the bone. Afterward, he hammered a nail into an old lime tree outside the city and told Egill that by the time the nail disappears into the bark, his fracture will be healed.

Next to Egill sits Birger, still hunched over in pain. Ever since he got that bees' nest stuck on his head, he's felt pretty low about himself, but today his self-confidence has been completely destroyed. Yrsa got him again. Why didn't he draw his sword faster? He shudders at the thought of that giant horse rearing its head, its hooves pounding like hammers down the wooden street. And that nun, that girl barely bigger than a cricket, sitting on his back like Odin's corpse collector. Birger just wants to go home, back to Mimir's Stool. All he wants to do is wrap his arms around that giant stone on the beach.

"What do you want to do, Father?" Nokki asks.

"We're going after them," says Naefr.

"On horseback?" asks Nokki.

"No, are you crazy? We're going by sea. We'll take the whaling road."

"Maybe we should just let them go?" says Toke, his lips trembling with cold and fever. A black bloodstain has formed on the bandage around his abdomen. He drinks mead to dull the pain.

"Let them go?" Naefr asks incredulously. "Weren't you the one who wanted to take that nun hostage in the first place? You said she was worth a fortune."

Toke doesn't answer.

"And that cripple of yours murdered my son," says Naefr. "I'll slit her throat, you understand? If it's the last thing I do in this mortal world. Odin as my witness!"

"I won't survive this wound," says Toke.

"Sure you will, you idiot."

"Don't call me an idiot. We're brothers. We've sailed halfway around the world together. We swore allegiance to each other on the tip of a spear. Now you've cut me in half. You broke your oath. Odin witnessed that too."

Naefr clutches the golden hammer around his neck and rubs the snake tattoo on his arm.

"You're not going to die," he says.

"I think Odin has already sent his corpse collectors," says Toke. "They're trotting over the rainbow bridge as we speak. They're coming for me."

"Enough of that talk!" roars Naefr. "It's just a scratch."

"My daughter foresaw my death on a dock by a river."

"She also said we would get a hundred pounds of silver and that winter would last for weeks," Naefr says. "That girl just says whatever pops into her head."

"I hope you're right," says Toke. He staggers away from the table and lies down on the bench that Astrid prepared for him. The furs under his head feel soft. His left hand grips the hilt of his sword. *Just hold on*, he thinks. *Hold on.*

"So what now, Father?" Nokki asks.

Naefr slaps him hard across the face. The force of the blow knocks Nokki off his stool. His head spins.

"Next time, you throw the spear!"

"I will, Father," Nokki says.

"Swear to me."

"Next time, I'll throw the spear."

"No, swear to me that you will avenge your brother," Naefr roars. The flames from the fire flicker in his eyes. "This is your chance to make a name for yourself."

Naefr draws Vengeance.

"Swear it on the tip of your brother's sword," he commands.

Egill and Birger watch with their jaws dropped. Nokki hesitates.

"Or do you want me to take you to the Valhöll in a cage?

Hang you in Odin's banquet hall so your ancestors can hurl boar bones at you? At the boy who was too much of a coward to throw a spear at the girl who killed his brother? Swear it!"

Nokki looks at the sword pointed at him. He feels Egill's and Birger's eyes burning into his skin.

"You will have another chance," Naefr says.

"Chance? Sporr had no chance in that storm," Nokki murmurs.

"What did you say?"

Nokki doesn't answer. He doesn't dare to look his father in the eye. He has never killed anyone before. Now he has to kill the fiercest girl in the village—the girl who can weave a sail like no other, whose cheeks blushed red every time she saw him, who kissed him until his lips were numb. Why couldn't he just love her?

Birger shifts uncomfortably on his stool. Egill chuckles stupidly with his broken arm wrapped tight in branches and linen. Nokki touches the tip of the sword and whispers, "Odin!"

"Odin!" Naefr shouts.

With that, Nokki has taken an oath on the sword Vengeance, before Odin. He has no choice but to kill Yrsa daughter of Toke, and the nun along with her.

27

YRSA IS IN AWE of the wide Roman road upon which they have been traveling for three days now. She almost cannot believe the road was made entirely by humans. It's a straight line through the landscape, lined with stones and mud trenches and beaten down with the hoofprints of cattle. Yrsa has never seen such a straight road.

Job keeps her eyes forward, as does Son of Sleipnir. She holds the reins tightly, gently pressing her knees into the horse's sides to steer him in the right direction. The animal follows her every move.

The first night they slept in a forest half a mile from the road. The trees rustled around them, their naked branches creaking in the wind.

"The elves are whispering," Yrsa said.

"It's just the wind," said Job as she stamped her feet to get warm.

"They're here," Yrsa murmured. She placed a few crumbs by the stones and under the oldest trees. "They'll protect us tonight."

"Well, if the elves are talking, pray tell me, Yrsa, what are they talking about?"

"Why, about us, probably. About our tale. Our saga. Did we not escape from Hedeby when no escape was possible? Did we not ride on the back of the Son of Sleipnir? And were we not protected by Odin himself, who took the shape of a fierce, bloodthirsty hound?"

"Pagan nonsense," said Job, but she couldn't help smiling.

"Our names will be whispered in Danish houses around the fire for many winters to come."

"I thought Danish sagas were always about gods and men."

"True. Perhaps we are just side characters in the great saga of Naefr, who will not rest until he has ripped out our guts. Sagas end in blood and grime. We cannot escape our fates, sister," Yrsa said gloomily.

"Well, tonight we have the elves to protect us," said Job. She got up, walked over to the rock next to the tree, and put her last bread crumbs on it.

"What are you doing?"

"I want you to feel safe too," Job said.

"Because you already feel safe, protected by Jesus?" Yrsa asked.

"And by you," she said. Job gave her that smile again—the nice one.

Job and Yrsa huddled together with their backs against the tree and their arms in their cloaks. Odin settled down at their feet and curled up. They held each other's hands and held them fast. Only when they had both fallen asleep did their hands drop.

At first light, they were on their way. Around noon, they passed the monastery of Hammaburg.

"We should avoid the monastery," Yrsa said. "The Danes have spies there."

"What do you mean, spies?"

"Merchants who travel between Hammaburg and Hedeby and keep the Danes informed of what's happening and who's been passing through."

So they continued without stopping to eat.

The second night they found shelter in a farmhouse. It was home to a couple with three children, a dozen chickens, and three goats. The whole place smelled like a barn. In a field behind the house was a row of simple crosses marking the graves of their dead children. By the fire, Yrsa fell asleep immediately, and Job had to wake her up to eat. They were offered a bit of sandy bread and some dry cakes. The couple and their children were deeply impressed by Job's presence. They had never seen a nun before. Of course, Job didn't really look like a nun in her green Danish dress, but with all her prayers and psalms she quickly had them convinced.

"I am happy to be among good believers," Job said.

When Job uttered a prayer before dinner, asking the Lord to bless not only the food but also the family, their dozen chickens, and their three goats, the couple became ecstatic.

"Thank God," cried the husband.

"Thank God," repeated the wife.

Job made the sign of the cross and the couple and their children followed suit. Yrsa didn't move. After the prayer, the children snatched up the black bread. The man frowned at Yrsa.

"She didn't make the sign of the cross," the man said.

Yrsa was already chewing on a piece of black bread.

"I'm a pagan," Yrsa said with her mouth full.

The man's eyes grew wide. He picked up the bread knife.

"Get away from my table, devil girl," he bellowed.

With her cheeks bulging with bread, Yrsa looked up in surprise.

The man grabbed Yrsa by the collar and dragged her over to the chickens and goats, who began clucking and bleating around her. He kicked open the door and threw Yrsa into the yard. Then, he pointed the bread knife at Job.

"How dare you bring a pagan into our house?"

"I intend to convert her," Job said, but the man wouldn't hear of it.

He grabbed Job by the collar and threw her into the yard as well. The man looked at the two young women lying in a heap among his leeks and seemed unsure what to do next. He was still clutching the bread knife. It wasn't until Odin stepped in front of the girls and gnashed his teeth that the man stepped back.

"That dog is the devil," the man said as he picked up a cross and wielded it in front of Odin.

Job took hold of Odin, afraid the man would hurt him.

"I'd rather sleep under a tree," Yrsa said as she made her

way back over to Son of Sleipnir, who was nibbling on the last bales of rotten winter hay in a stall.

On the morning of the third day, Yrsa had a dream about her father.

His wound was still sore, but Toke was feeling better. Much better. He downed an extra slog of milk and ate some bread with hard cheese. In the faint morning light, he walked down the hill to the river. The dock was deserted. The water sloshed wearily against the bank. Fishhooks tinkled languidly in the breeze. Off in the distance, in the merchants' camp outside of town, two ships were preparing to set sail.

He sat down on a mooring post—just as the giant Mimir had ·perched himself on the old stone in Mimir's Stool— and took in the view. He watched the sun rise behind the morning fog. Two terns dove through the air. Those birds are good omens, he thought. He heard men pushing a ship off the dock and plunging their oars into the water. Only then did he recognize the vessel. It was the *Huginn*. Why was the longship leaving without him? Without a helmsman?

Then he saw a rat on the bank eating a giant carp from the inside out—a sign of doom. Was his time up then? Would he ever see Little Sten and Troels again? Or his newborn daughter and his beautiful wife? Was this the moment when the Norns cut off his thread of life?

He groped around for the hilt of his sword, but it wasn't there. It was back at Harald's house. He hadn't thought to drag the heavy thing with him on his walk to the river. But he needed his sword, for he was about to meet his ancestors in Valhöll.

Then he saw the *Huginn* rowing away. The sun glistened on the water. He had to get up from that mooring pole, go back to Harald's house, and get his weapon. But he couldn't get up. His legs were too heavy. He slowly collapsed on the pole. He could still hear the tinkling of fishhooks and the sloshing of the river.

Suddenly, the dream ends. Yrsa wakes up, surprised to find herself lying under a tree with a dog at her feet.

On the evening of the fourth day, Yrsa and Job come to a wide river. The only way to cross is a small ferry that is already full of pilgrims on their way to Breem. There is no room on the raft for two girls, a dog, and a massive horse. They have no choice but to wait at an inn near the water's edge. Yrsa and Job share a bit of bread and cheese and warm themselves by the fire. They sleep in the stable with the dog and horse out of fear that someone might try to steal Son of Sleipnir.

The next morning, they see the ferry making its way back across the water.

"It's taking forever," Yrsa sighs.

"They'll let us on, right?" asks Job.

Yrsa shrugs. Suddenly, she says, "Back in Hedeby, when I was holding Hefnir's wrists, I saw him in Mikligard. He was buying bales of silk from a woman. I could only see the back of her head, but she had a crooked foot."

Job looks at her, surprised.

"You mean . . . no, surely it wasn't you. You're not the only woman in the world with a limp."

"No, of course not," Yrsa says. "I can't imagine ever traveling that far, all the way to Mikligard!"

They're both silent for a moment.

"You know, my father taught me and my brother Troels to sail," Yrsa says. "My brother didn't want me in the boat with my crooked foot. He was afraid we would capsize. My father was so strong. When I was a child, he told me that he was the one who moved Mimir's stone to the beach. I believed him. I thought he was indestructible. But he's not."

Yrsa gazes out at the river, at the fishing lines in the water.

"I saw his death in a dream," she whispers.

"A dream?"

Yrsa looks up sadly at Job.

"It was just a dream," the nun says gravely.

But Yrsa's gloom lingers like the fog before the sunrise. No, this wasn't just a dream.

Job puts her arms around Yrsa. It takes a moment for Yrsa to lay her head on Job's shoulder. But finally, she does. Then she cries. She shakes, she wails with grief. She sobs as wildly as Frigg when she lost her beautiful son Baldr.

"Remember Yngvarr's final story?" whispers Job. "He told us what would happen after the end of the world, when everything is dead: Odin and Thor, the gods, the people, the animals, and even the plants. The world will be plunged into darkness after Fenrir the wolf eats the sun. But, Yngvarr said, it won't remain dark for long. A new sun—the daughter of the old sun—will appear. The sons of Odin and Thor will survive the great battle of Ragnarok and warm themselves at the fire trench in the Valhöll. And on Midgard, a woman named Líf—'life'—will emerge from the forest. At the beach, she will meet a man by the name of Lífthrasier, or 'lover of life.' Together, they will begin again. Nothing ends."

Yrsa wipes the tears and snot from her face. She blows the misery out of her body. She wants to stop crying, but she can't. It doesn't matter. Frigg kept crying too.

The horse grazes along the side of the road. The dog gnaws at the fleas in his fur, and after what seems like an eternity, the ferry finally reaches the shore.

"This must be the slowest ferry in the world," Yrsa grumbles.

Only then does Job let go of her.

28

ON THE AFTERNOON of the seventh day, Yrsa and Job spot a streak of blue on the horizon—the Rhine. There are islands in the middle and houses along the southern bank. Tufts of green have sprouted in the fields, and the land is waiting for Freyr, the god of fertility, to set the world in bloom. The houses are separated by crooked fences, and sloops rest on the muddy banks. This is Dorestad, where Yrsa's mother came from. This must be where Cara grew up.

Yrsa and Job steer the horse up the dirt path that connects the houses along the river.

They stop at the first barn on the path, a tannery. Out front, children scrape animal hides clean while the women cut and stitch pieces of leather. There's a table laden with belts, saddles, and hats for sale. The whole place smells like a carcass.

"Please, my lady, feel free to inspect my wares," says a burly older man. The leather merchant introduces himself as Hrotbert. He's dressed in a simple leather coat. If he's rich, he certainly doesn't show it. There are no rings on his fingers, and the only gold on his body is the cross around his neck. Job introduces herself, and when Hrotbert realizes she's a nun, he bows his head.

"You are most welcome here, sister," he says.

"We are looking for the family of Cara the Frisian," Yrsa says, explaining that her mother was sold to the Danes seventeen years ago. Hrotbert has never heard of Cara or her family.

"She came from here. From Dorestad," Yrsa says.

"Fathers from the hinterland show up here every week to sell their daughters," says Hrotbert. "The poor men hope to get a sheep or a couple of goats and a few pounds of millet or wheat so the rest of the family can survive. Everyone knows that the Danes come here to buy slaves."

"So it's possible that Cara was from the hinterland?" asks Job.

Hrotbert nods.

"No, Harald said she was from Dorestad," says Yrsa.

Without so much as a goodbye, she walks to the next house: a farm with a yard full of honking geese. She knocks on the door. Job waits on the path with Odin and Son of Sleipnir.

Yrsa goes to each house along the bank and asks everyone she encounters if they knew Cara. She explains over and over again that her mother was exceptional—tall, lean, beautiful, the kind of beauty one doesn't easily forget, with sharp features and black hair. But no one can help her. No one remembers a young woman named Cara.

But Yrsa is not discouraged. She continues from farm

to farm and knocks on the door of every workshop and fisherman's cottage she can find, always asking the same question. They form quite the procession along the Rhine: two young women, a giant stallion, and a hairball on legs. The sun is low in the sky when Yrsa finally sits down. She massages her misshapen foot. Pain throbs in her ankle.

"I can't walk anymore," she says.

"Let me help you on the horse."

Yrsa nods, defeated. Job holds her steady as she places her good foot in the stirrup and pulls herself up.

"I want a roof to sleep under tonight," Yrsa says.

"And tomorrow?" asks Job.

"Tomorrow we leave for Ganda."

They find shelter at a guesthouse run by horse breeders, three women known as the Hildis sisters. Berhildis is the oldest of the three. She is tall, smells like manure, and talks in a booming voice. Every word she says sounds like an order. On her command, Job and Yrsa march down to a stream to bathe. The cold water makes them gasp for air, but once they're in up to their necks, it actually feels quite pleasant.

"I still haven't managed to convert you," says Job.

"Good luck with that," Yrsa says, washing her hair with egg yolk.

"I'll do it in Ganda. After a few days in my convent, you'll understand. You will believe."

"Perhaps."

"You will be safe there," says Job in her angelic Bible voice. "Our walls are a meter thick. We have our own meadows and fields, our own fruit trees, our own garden. It's paradise. Once you get there, you won't ever want to leave."

"Don't start telling me that you want to make me a nun now too."

"Why not? You said so yourself—the only thing that matters is your hugr. Everything on the outside, your hamr, can be shed. You can become whoever you want. That's what you told me."

"I'll become whatever the Norns have decided," Yrsa says, and she dips underwater to rinse the yolk out of her hair.

Job walks out of the water, and Yrsa watches her from behind. She's like a blade of grass, she thinks, with those thin wrists and skinny legs. Job quietly puts on her linen undergarment and twists back her hair. Then she pulls her dress over her head. *She's really quite pretty when she's not wearing that awful habit*, Yrsa thinks.

It takes Yrsa three tries to pull herself up on the bank with her crooked foot. She wraps herself in her woolen cloak to get warm. The rough, hard fabric itches against her skin. Yrsa looks down at her reflection in the water. A limping forest troll from the North, that's what she is. That's why Nokki didn't want her.

Meanwhile, Job carefully hangs the wooden cross around her neck.

"Why can't it be the other way around?" Yrsa asks.

"What do you mean?"

"Why can't you become a pagan?"

Job looks at her speechlessly for a moment. Then she says indignantly, "That's ridiculous. I would lose my calling!"

"Not necessarily. If I became a nun, I'd still have my gods and elves."

"But your gods and elves are just made-up stories. God is real. God is alive!"

Yrsa shakes her head. There's just no reasoning with her.

"Don't you understand?" Job says. "My calling is everything. My calling is my life."

That evening, more guests show up at the Hildis sisters' house. They are three pilgrims: two youths with giant crosses on their chests, accompanied by an older man with tattoos on his hands and jewels in his ears. He tells them that he has traveled halfway around the world, that he has visited the holy lands, that he has been to Jerusalem and Mikligard and seen the Church of Holy Wisdom, the largest church in the world. He says that he was enslaved for many years, but his knowledge of languages and customs allowed him to earn his freedom. Job clings to his every word. She can't get enough of his stories.

Yrsa sits by the fire pit, warming her feet in the ashes. She feels like she has been cold for days. They've slept sitting up with Odin at their feet every night since they left Hedeby.

"Why don't you wear a cross around your neck?" asks one of the young pilgrims.

Yrsa doesn't answer, but the question makes her nervous.

"Have you been baptized?"

"Not yet," she murmurs.

"If you don't want to be baptized, Francia is no place for you," says the young pilgrim. "Being unbaptized is punishable by death."

"Quiet," says the old pilgrim.

"I'm not going to sleep under the same roof as a fire worshipper," the young pilgrim grumbles.

"These women are under my protection," Berhildis declares. "If you don't like it, go sleep with the animals."

The boy mutters something under his breath, but says nothing more.

Job doesn't understand why Yrsa has to be so stubborn. If she continues to refuse to be baptized, she's going to get them both in trouble. Job kneels before the small altar in the room. It's nothing more than a stone with a bowl of bread, a cup, and a bronze cross on top. She flips through her psalmbook, but has no idea where she left off. This has never happened to her before. She looks back at Yrsa. Her head is slumped on her chest. She's fallen asleep sitting up. The fire illuminates her face. Her lips are moving.

Yrsa dreams that she's on a horse, trotting through a dark valley. It's the road to Niflheim, the underworld. The path before her is endless, and she can barely see her hand in front of her face. The only light is an occasional beam of moonlight. But the horse knows the way. She hears the river before she sees it. Its raging waters roar. She crosses a bridge made of gold and suddenly finds herself at the gates of the realm of the dead, the Nágrind. The fence before her stretches to the left and right, disappearing into the mist. She's not alone. She stands in a line of shadows waiting to be greeted by Hel, the goddess of the underworld. The goddess's head is hidden under a giant hood, but Yrsa knows what lies behind it: a face that is one-half flawless and the other half rotting flesh. Hel is both alive and dead.

"What do you seek here, living girl?" asks Hel. Her voice is as soft as silk.

"I have come to get my mother. She died just after I was born. She was still young."

"You cannot retrieve your mother," Hel says.

"Then I challenge you to a game of King's Table. If I win, I get to take my mother back. If you win, you may do with me what you will."

The goddess comes closer. For a moment, Yrsa sees the rotting half of her face. White maggots squirm in the hole of her cheek.

"Go back to the world of the living, girl," Hel says.

"You don't have to do anything. If you let me in, I'll find her in no time. I know what she looks like. I am a seeress."

"Leave the dead alone, and they will leave you alone too," the goddess says. "I make exceptions for no one, not even the gods."

"You almost did for Baldr."

"Yes, but Baldr was mine," she says.

"My mother, Cara, was never mine."

"If Frigg could not retrieve her beloved Baldr, then you, seeress of Mimir's Stool, will never get your mother back. If I allow that, then I'll have all the gods, dwarves, and giants lining up at my gates. They'll all want someone back. And I'll never hear the end of it."

"Then I'll wait here, like a phantom in the fog. No one will miss me in my own world."

"Are you sure about that?" Hel asks.

The goddess turns her head so Yrsa can see the other half—the gentle, living side of her face.

"Go back to your own world," Hel whispers. "And take your spear, for Odin's raven is coming with shields and swords. On its prow is the head of Jormundgandr."

Yrsa jolts awake with a shout. The pilgrims choke on their ale; Job looks up from her book of psalms. She immediately sees the terror in Yrsa's eyes.

"The goddess Hel just spoke to me," Yrsa says excitedly.

The pilgrims make signs of the cross.

"Idolatry!" hisses the young pilgrim.

"It was a warning," Yrsa continues. "I'm sure of it."

The three sisters and the pilgrims look at her, confused.

"The raven. The *Huginn*. The Danes are coming."

The pilgrims look startled.

"They're on a rampage!" Yrsa cries, springing to her feet.

"Calm down," says Berhildis. "The Danes haven't raided our village in years. They come here to trade. They exchange their cloaks and silver for our pottery and slaves. They buy my horses."

The old pilgrim nods. "Dreams are deceptions, girl."

"No, they're not! We have to get out of here!" Yrsa snaps. She takes her cloak and pulls it over her head.

"Surely we're not going to raise the alarm just because you had a nightmare," says Berhildis.

"I saw the sea monster on the head of their bow," Yrsa

adds. One of the young pilgrims starts murmuring Hail Marys, but Berhildis shrugs.

"Yrsa daughter of Toke is a seeress," says Job. "In Jutland, no one questions her prophecies."

At that, Berhildis is startled. Despite the silver cross on her chest, she spits in the fire like a pagan to ward off evil.

"Come on, Job, we're leaving," Yrsa says as she heads for the door.

"No, you're staying right here," says Berhildis. "I'll drum the alarm."

29

THE TWO LONGSHIPS arrive just before dawn. The oars glide through the water, as quiet as carp. The warriors on board are silent. The captains have instructed the men to wrap their swords and spears in their cloaks so they won't clatter. The vessels slice through the water one after another, their sea monsters' heads a sign of the rampage to come. Each ship carries at least fifty men.

On the *Huginn* are warriors bound by oath to Captain Naefr. They're all from Mimir's Stool and its hinterland. On the other ship are men recruited in Hedeby, paid by the captain in silver. Most of them are sons of fish peddlers, fur traders, and blacksmiths. They've never been on a raid. Some of them even know Dorestad. They've drunk in the inns, at least the ones that allow pagans. They know the tanner, the jeweler, the potter, the coin makers, and the infamous Hildis sisters who breed the best horses in Frisia.

Nokki has been to Dorestad too, and the fact that his father plans to plunder a place where they used to do business doesn't sit well with him. But he has also heard the men complain about the Frisian villagers, who are always haggling for a deal. Word has it they'll cheat you out of everything you have. They don't wear their gold and silver around their necks or arms like normal people do. No, they toss it in a sack and hide it in a pit. They wear dirty clothes and pretend to survive on turnips and spoiled eel. Those hypocrites! Nokki has often heard the men say they'd like to teach the people of Dorestad a lesson. And today they will. Naefr will find their gold and silver and distribute it among his men. He'll take the town with his dead son's sword. This time, he's not just after riches—he wants revenge.

The two girls were on their way to Dorestad. Harald son of Karl was very sure of that. After the raid, there will be no more trading with Dorestad, but Naefr doesn't care. He will take his furs, cloaks, and amber elsewhere. There are plenty of other markets around!

The ships slow down and avoid the docks, so as not to wake the village dogs. Silently, the Danes climb overboard and lower themselves into the shallow water. Then men on the ships hand them their swords, shields, and spears. Downstream, a goose honks. Upstream, a dog begins to bark. But the rest of the market town, which stretches over a mile along the river, is still asleep. The doors and shutters remain closed. There's not a single breath of smoke rising from the roofs. Not a torch in sight. The moon is but a tiny sliver in the sky, and the night is as dark as a rabbit hole.

In the pitch blackness, the warriors wade through the shallow water and climb through the tall reeds. They slip on the high, muddy banks. Occasionally, there's a splash followed by a curse on Thor as someone falls in the water. The men help one another up the bank. They head for the horse farm, sloshing in their leather shoes. They want to be the first to take prisoners and find out where the gold, silver, and coins are hidden.

Nokki and Birger enter the house of the Hildis sisters. Two cats scurry away, and as Nokki's eyes adjust to the darkness, he sees that the house is empty. He walks into the stables, where several horses look up in surprise. The colts neigh and whinny at the sight of the intruders.

Nokki and Birger walk outside and see their warriors coming out of a barn. They have already searched the first houses, where they hoped to find the jeweler, blacksmith, and priest, but they too were deserted. All the houses are abandoned, and the valuables are nowhere to be found. Some warriors hold the amulets around their necks. They ask Thor, Odin, and Tyr where the people have gone, but the gods are silent.

As the sun rises, they notice something shimmering on the hill.

The Danes curse and spit on the ground to ward off evil. They thought this raid was going to be a breeze, a surprise attack at dawn. The villagers would panic. Some stupid farmer might charge at them with a pitchfork or a club or a rusty knife. Perhaps a few boys would throw spears at them. But nothing more than that!

But there are no riches here for the taking, as Naefr had promised. He said that the merchants would have silver, that the church would be full of gold, that the tanner would have saddles, and the jeweler would have plenty of precious amber that turns translucent in the sun. He said there would be loads of women for the taking, that they could have their way with them, sell them in Hedeby, or even take them as wives.

The raid was only supposed to last an hour, two at most. After that, the two ships would row back up the river and out to sea, full of fresh loot. The men could already imagine it as they rowed in last night.

But now, all they see are the knives, swords, and spears glistening in the morning sun.

The people of Dorestad stand at the top of the hill, behind a row of shields. Five horsemen tower above them, and one horse is taller than the rest. Is that Son of Sleipnir?

Nokki tries to guess how many there are. Four hundred, he suspects, about a fifth of the inhabitants of Dorestad. The others have fled. A courier has probably been sent to the nearest Frankish garrison. But that's miles away, and it will probably take a day or two for backup to arrive.

"So what!" shouts Naefr. "You're not afraid of a bunch of old men, women, and children, are you?"

Their opponents may be well armed with spears and swords, but they're no match for an army of experienced Danish seamen. Naefr shouts his orders.

"We attack, we take the richest bastards on that hill, and we torture them until they tell us where they've buried the loot," he roars.

"What an original plan," Nokki mutters.

Egill shoots him a dirty look. With his good arm, the boy is dragging a stallion he found in the Hildis sisters' stables. Naefr ordered him to take it.

"Make the wall!" shouts Naefr.

"Make the wall," Nokki repeats. "Three men deep."

The men of Mimir's Stool have known the command since childhood. They line up in three rows. Those in the front row hook their shields together to form an impenetrable line.

Nokki knows they will win this battle. But at what price? The people of Dorestad are defending their homes, their property, everything they have. They're ready to fight with every sharp object they can find. They, too, line up, forming a shieldlike wall.

The hundred Danish warriors strike their shields with their swords. The sound thunders over Dorestad. The dogs bark and the geese honk in response. There will be no running; rather, the Danes will slowly march uphill to the enemy. When they reach them, they will smash their shields against their opponents' and thrust their spears and axes from above and below, striking whatever they can. The Frisians' wall will crumble. The survivors will flee. Then the Danes will draw their longswords to slay the final resistance. But for now, the Frisians hold the higher position, and the hill is wet and slippery.

"We will not be deterred by a bunch of peasants!" cries Naefr. The men they recruited in Hedeby have lined up in the back row. They have no intention of risking their lives today. If things go wrong, they'll run back to their ship. But the Frisians on the hill are afraid too, Nokki knows that. They're not fighters.

Nokki sweats under his helmet. The leather cheek pads stick to his skin. The sun creeps over the hill and blinds the Danes. He looks at the men beside him. They won't even be able to see the spears, stones, and arrows being thrown at them. Naefr's helmet flashes in the sun.

"Wait! Demand the women first, Father," says Nokki. "Negotiate!"

For a moment, Naefr wants to lash out at his son and shout that he doesn't need his advice. But then he realizes the boy is right. It's a smart move. He should negotiate.

Naefr swings himself onto the horse Egill found for him and urges him forward. The stallion slowly plods up the hill. When Naefr is fifty paces from the Frisian line, he tugs on the reins. The animal comes to a halt.

"There's no need for blood!" Naefr roars. "We don't even have to take slaves. Twenty pounds of silver for my men is enough."

The Danes grumble from behind their shields. Only twenty pounds? They rowed all the way to Frisia for that?

"Twenty pounds and not a drop of blood!" shouts Naefr. "Think about it."

The Danes continue to grumble. They ask one another how much twenty divided by a hundred is. Odin only knows, someone says.

"Twenty pounds of silver," Naefr continues. "And the crippled girl and her slave, who killed my son Njall by smashing his brains in with a stone while he slept.

"Odin will give me my revenge!" cries Naefr, and the warriors of Mimir's Stool shout, "Odin! Odin!"

"Is it true?" asks Hrotbert. "Did you kill Naefr's son?"

Yrsa realizes that the people of Dorestad would much rather hand them over and pay twenty pounds of silver than fight the Danes.

"Was it an honor killing?" Berhildis asks in her booming voice. She has one spear in her hand and a second spear tied to her back.

"Yes, I killed Njall," says Job. "After he raped me."

Berhildis makes the sign of the cross.

"Surely, the rape was her own fault," she hears a Frisian say.

"Is she really a nun?" asks another. "Where's her habit?"

"She's just some runaway slave," says another.

"I was taken hostage," Job replies.

"And I want that horse too!" shouts Naefr fifty paces away. "That stallion is Son of Sleipnir. Those women stole him from Harald son of Karl."

For the Frisians, it's one surprise after the other. Everyone knows Son of Sleipnir.

Hrotbert turns to Yrsa. "Is what he says true?"

"Give those women to us, and we'll spare your lives. Pay us the silver, and we'll leave you alone!" cries Naefr.

Berhildis brings her horse alongside Son of Sleipnir and grabs the reins.

"Don't," says Job.

"I'll sell that horse back to Harald," says Berhildis.

"I warned you they were coming!" Yrsa cries, stepping in front of the horse.

"You didn't say anything about an honor killing," says Berhildis.

"Please, don't hand us over to them. Give us a chance," says Yrsa.

"Give them the slave girl and the cripple!" cries a Frisian woman.

Another rider steps forward to block Son of Sleipnir so Job can't get away.

The stallion is nervous. His ears go flat. He snorts and grunts.

"Quiet," says Job. "Quiet, boy." She lies down on the horse's neck and strokes his shoulder. The horse settles and his head hangs low.

"That animal listens to her," Berhildis says. "That girl is a rider. She's not a slave. She is of noble blood. Anyone can see that."

"Give me a weapon," Yrsa demands. "A spear and a shield."

"What are you going to do with a spear, girl?" scoffs Hrotbert.

"I'm going to challenge that piece of boar shit to a duel," says Yrsa.

"You don't stand a chance," a man says, laughing.

"God is with you, isn't he, nun?" Yrsa asks.

Job looks Yrsa in the eyes.

"The Lord is with me and with you!" Job shouts.

"Declare a duel!" Yrsa cries. "And let that god of yours decide!"

"No, we should hand them over," says Hrotbert, but Berhildis hands Yrsa a spear.

The weapon is perfectly balanced. The iron tip is as heavy as the long wooden shaft. It's a magnificent spear.

"Let them duel. God will decide," says Berhildis.

The Frisians and Hrotbert look up at the horsewoman.

"God will decide," Hrotbert finally repeats. He hands his shield to Yrsa. It's made of beechwood, but feels heavy.

The Frisians' wall of shields opens. Yrsa steps forward with Son of Sleipnir beside her. Job is perched on the saddle like a man, with one leg on either side. The wall closes behind them with clattering, pushing, and shouting. Three hundred paces away are the Danes. Naefr has gone back to his men on his horse.

Yrsa hooks arms with Job. She puts her good foot in the stirrup and pushes with her bad one. But Job is in the way, and the shield hinders her movement. She can't quite swing her leg over the horse's back, and she almost pulls Job off the horse.

"Careful!" Job says.

Yrsa lets go of Job's arm and flops down in the grass on her back.

The Danes roar with laughter from behind their shields.

Yrsa leans on the spear and pulls herself to her feet. She looks down and realizes that the iron edge of the shield has sliced open her left arm.

"Don't bother!" shouts Naefr from his horse.

"Hand me the spear and pull yourself up," says Job.

Yrsa lets the shield fall from her arm. It will only get in the way. She hands Job the spear. Job clamps the weapon under her arm, and Yrsa hoists herself into the saddle.

"You'd be better off riding a donkey!" cries one of the Danes, and the men bowl over with laughter. But Yrsa is in the saddle now. She clings to Job. The horse slowly trudges forward.

"Not too close," Yrsa says.

Job clicks her tongue, and the horse stops immediately.

"I am Yrsa, daughter of Cara the Frisian and granddaughter of Gudrun the Torch. I am the völva of Mimir's Stool."

"You? A völva?" cries Naefr, and the men laugh. The captain's helmet and chainmail sparkle in the morning light.

"I can reverse your fortune in an instant, Naefr son of Nokkvi," Yrsa bluffs. "Surely, you don't think you can stand up to the völva who has seen your death. You couldn't even kill me when I was an infant."

At that, the Danes stop laughing. They look at each other for encouragement, but no one is smiling anymore. "Come here, you daughter of doom!" cries Naefr.

"The Norns call you the trash of Midgard!" cries Yrsa.

"Come here," he roars.

"Why don't you come here so I can smell your fear when you shit your pants, you worthless captain! Or don't you dare to fight me?"

Naefr draws the sword Vengeance. He's still two hundred paces away, but Yrsa can hear the blade scraping along the sides of the scabbard.

Job makes herself small on the horse's shoulders. Yrsa clamps her legs around the animal's torso. She hears Job praying: "Hail Mary full of grace..."

"Odin!" shouts Naefr, pounding his stirrups against the horse's flanks. The animal whinnies in pain and gallops forward.

Yrsa raises the spear and shouts, "Frigg!"

Then the horses storm at each other. Their hooves send chunks of dirt flying into the air. Son of Sleipnir is a colossal beast. Naefr's horse is smaller but strong. Naefr raises the unwieldy weapon in his right hand; the blade glistens in the sunlight. Yrsa keeps her arms free. When Naefr is thirty feet away, she'll throw the weapon. She has never thrown a spear from a galloping horse before. She has never thrown a spear at anyone before. She's speared plenty of animals, but they're easy enough to hit as they run away. They don't know the spear is coming. But a man on a horse knows what he's in for. A spear is slower than an arrow. Naefr will catch or repel it with ease and then—with a swing of the sword—split her head like a block of wood in the shipyard. Then he'll torture the nun until she begs him to kill her. *He has already won,* Yrsa thinks for a moment. *We're already dead. This is the end.* The Norns are waiting with their scissors, ready to cut her thread of life.

Job leans forward on the horse's neck so Yrsa can throw the spear. Naefr is just about thirty feet away. She can see the snake tattoo on his arm and the sweat on his forehead.

"Get away from his sword arm!" cries Yrsa. Job jerks on the reins, digging her knees into the horse's shoulders, and Son of Sleipnir swerves to the right. For a moment,

Naefr is confused. He was holding his sword on the right, but suddenly his horse is charging to the left. He straightens up in his stirrups and tries to hit Yrsa from the other side. But the sword is too unwieldy and his arms are too slow. Yrsa holds her spear in both hands. She stretches out and slams it down with all her strength, striking Naefr in the left thigh. The iron links of his chainmail break on impact, and the tip of the spear barrels into his flesh until it hits bone.

Yrsa clings to the spear for a moment without realizing that it's pulling her off the horse. Then it jerks out of her hands and she crashes into the grass on her right shoulder. She feels the shock ripple through her bones. She springs to her feet immediately, but lands on her bad foot, causing her to fall over. She scrambles up again, but she no longer has a weapon. She feels as naked as she is on washing day.

Naefr's horse comes to a halt. It snorts. Naefr curses at the gods as he tries to pull the spear out of his flesh, but the weapon is wedged in deep. His muscles are already clenched around the iron and refuse to let go. *A wound in the thigh won't kill me*, Naefr thinks. He leaves the spear in place and turns his gaze to Yrsa. There's nowhere for her to run. She's just a few yards away from him. He's got her trapped like prey.

Naefr kicks his heels into the horse's flanks. The animal jumps, startled, and trots forward. The girl doesn't stand a chance. He'll slam Vengeance into her shoulder, and with any luck, the blow won't kill her immediately. He wants to prolong her suffering. Her howling will scare the Frisians, and he'll demand more silver and gold. Maybe this is going to be a good day after all. He raises his sword, ready to seal Yrsa's fate. He doesn't notice the huge horse approaching on his right.

Then Son of Sleipnir hits him head-on.

His horse falls to the side from the tremendous blow, and Son of Sleipnir leaps high over the fallen animal's flailing legs. Cries of shock and disbelief rise from both the Frisian and Danish lines. The men of Dorestad will later say they felt the ground tremble as the two horses collided at full gallop.

Naefr is thrown from the saddle, and his helmet rolls off in the muddy grass. Yrsa's spear in his thigh breaks off, and the tip cuts through him like a butcher knife. Naefr tries to get up. His whole body is trembling. His face is as white as cooked fish. His chainmail is dark with blood. He leans on his sword and hoists himself upright.

"You're going to die, cripple!" he shouts, taking a few steps. The torturous pain of his wound can be heard in his voice.

Yrsa remains standing, with her shoulders straight and her chin up, just as Cara the Frisian once did.

"Defeated by two girls!" shouts Yrsa. "Tell them that in the Valhöll, you pathetic excuse for a warrior. Your ancestors will be ashamed. Odin will laugh himself silly."

Naefr continues to limp in her direction.

"I have seen your death, Naefr son of Nokkvi," Yrsa bluffs. "You will die here, today, on this hill."

Naefr leans on his one good leg, but every step is pure agony. He grinds his teeth. Yrsa doesn't move. Not a sound can be heard from the Frisian or Danish line. Everyone holds their breath. Naefr's blood leaves a red streak on the green landscape, but the man doesn't fall. His anger keeps him on his feet. When he reaches Yrsa, he stops. He's completely out of breath.

"You're mine," he grunts.

"I'm not leaving," Yrsa says. "I will stand here on this spot and watch you die, you coward. Your son was a rapist who got what he deserved. You will fall at my feet with the sword of your foolish son in your hand. That's what the Norns have told me."

In truth, the Norns haven't told Yrsa anything at all. She's lying through her teeth. "Help me, Frigg and Thor and all the elves who've accepted my offerings. Help me now!"

Naefr roars, raises the sword over his head, and lunges forward. With his last strength and all the rage inside of him, he swings the clumsy weapon in a deadly blow. But Yrsa steps aside and Naefr falls past her, thrust forward by his own momentum. He hits the ground like a ship on a sandbar and lies there, motionless.

Yrsa turns to the wall of Danes. She sees their bedraggled, uncertain faces peeking out from behind their shields and spears. No one moves.

"I am the völva who saw Naefr's death!" she shouts. "And Kveldulf's. There is no honor or silver to be had here, only doom. Go home before I curse you, before I call on the Norns to cut your threads of life, before I ask the gods to punish you with fever, cramps, and oozing ulcers. Leave before I ask them to send a monstrous winter that will never end."

She plucks Naefr's helmet from the grass and sees Son of Sleipnir trotting toward her. Job holds out her arm. Yrsa grabs hold of it, and this time she swings herself into the saddle in one fell swoop.

Yrsa, Job, and the Frisians watch as Nokki and the Danes lift their captain's corpse from the ground and carry it away. Egill picks up the sword Vengeance from the grass. Yrsa watches them until they are out of sight. Everything hurts—her back, her shoulders, her arms. It feels as if she has pulled every muscle in her body. But the worst pain is in her hugr. She realizes that she has always loved Nokki, even when he had no hair on his chin. "Let him love me back," she'd asked the elves as she made her offerings.

The Danes kick over fences, shatter earthen pots, set fire to a house, and steal three skinny pigs on their way out. But that's it. They return to their ships and row back out to sea. The children of Dorestad run after them along the shore. They shout, whistle, pull down their pants, and turn their butts to the ships.

"God has granted us this victory," Berhildis declares. "A victory over the pagans. The king of West Francia will certainly hear of how God sent two Christian girls to save us."

"Two Christian girls?" chuckles Yrsa.

"We are going to baptize you," says Hrotbert. "We can't possibly tell the king that we were saved by a pagan. God sent you to us."

Yrsa locks eyes with Job. She knows what the nun is thinking. According to the bishop of Hedeby, Job will never be completely absolved of her mortal sin until Yrsa is converted. Only then will Job be allowed to enter the kingdom of heaven. And it's true, the nun did save her life. She came for Naefr on a horse like a hooded valkyrie of death. So Yrsa agrees.

The next day, a monk baptizes Yrsa behind the church in the icy waters of the Rhine. He declares that there is only one God in heaven and on earth, and she repeats after him. Yrsa, her head still heavy from last night's honey wine, renounces her gods and declares that she believes in Christ the Risen Savior, who is all-knowing and infinitely good. Then the monk clamps his hand around the back of her neck and pushes her into the Rhine. She remains underwater for five counts. When the monk pulls her out of the river, she is a Christian—a cold, wet, shivering Christian. Job helps her out of the river. Her wet shirt clings to her body.

The monk gives her back her leather necklace with the beads on it, only now instead of the amulet of Frigg, a silver cross hangs from it. Apparently, the blacksmith of Dorestad took the liberty of melting down the pins from her dress and hammering them into a rudimentary cross. The monk also gives her a staff. It is pine wood, neatly polished with a small iron cross on top.

"Now you're like me," says Job. She is proud, but not because she helped defeat a heathen army or because she converted this fierce Danish woman to Christianity. She is proud of Yrsa. Her companion has let God into her heart. Now they will be more than friends. They will be sisters.

30

J

OB CAN'T GET BACK to Ganda fast enough; she walks ahead of Son of Sleipnir while the horse trudges down the Roman road as if he has all the time in the world, stopping to nibble on every thistle along the path.

"Come on, boy," Job says to the horse. "We're almost home."

On her command, Son of Sleipnir briefly breaks into a trot, making Yrsa bounce in the saddle. She'll never get used to traveling on horseback. Her rear end is covered in blisters and her back is stiff. Odin the dog occasionally looks at Yrsa with his one eye, as if he's trying to figure out where on earth they're going. Around them, the world is in bloom. Trees burst with delicate blossoms as if preparing for a feast. Birds sing in the trees, and an early swallow soars through the sky—all good omens.

They stop at a wide river, and Job plops down on the bank. She scoops up some water in her hands and drinks.

"This is the Scheldt," Job says, as if she can tell by the taste of the water.

Yrsa has never seen so many waterfowl in one place. Ducks, geese, swans, and herons skim the surface of the river. Job finds a ferryman with a sloop big enough to carry them and the horse across. They pay him with a coin and continue following the old Roman road on the other side of the river. Occasionally they pass a village—usually just a few houses and an old linden tree—and the locals come out to stare at them. Most people wear crosses around their necks, but they're not true believers. There are still ribbons hanging in old linden trees, offerings scattered among the roots, and nails hammered into trunks.

Job asks the villagers how far it is to Ganda. They don't know; they just point south. She explains that she is a nun from the Convent of Our Lady of Ganda and is on her way home. The people cast strange looks at her Danish dress and uncovered head, but then they bow politely and make the sign of the cross. Some try to hide the bird skull or wolf tooth around their neck. Others glance at the old lime tree in embarrassment.

Later that day, Job and Yrsa come across a peddler selling hammers, scissors, and pliers. When he tells them that the monks and nuns returned to the monastery a few weeks after the raid, Job bursts into tears. That must mean that all her sisters are alive and well.

By the evening of the fifth day after leaving Dorestad, Job is trembling with excitement. They sleep in the stable at an inn.

"Tomorrow I'll be home," Job says.

Yrsa leans against the stable wall with a blanket over her legs. "This will be our last night together, then."

"Do you want to predict my future?" Job asks.

"No, I don't. I don't want to see how you will meet your end."

"But I want to know what will happen to me in the monastery."

"I don't have any nightshade or wolf cherry with me."

"You can see without it. Just try. Look inside me, Yrsa. Please."

Reluctantly, Yrsa takes hold of Job's wrists. She feels her heart racing, the blood rushing through her veins. Yrsa is so tired that her eyelids droop shut. It takes a long time before she finally feels herself sinking into Job's insides.

She lands in a monastery on a hill surrounded by swampland. Pilgrims enter and kneel before Job. Everyone wants to see her, to touch her habit, to steal a bit of her power. A bishop in expensive clothes kisses her hand. She eats with the sisters. She walks through a vineyard.

Then a wave comes. Job is the Reverend Mother. Her oval face, wrapped in a white veil, has grown old. Her fingers are like skinny twigs covered in rings. It's winter. She's wearing her habit. She pulls her old Danish cloak of hard, rough wool over her head with great difficulty. The garment is threadbare. It's full of holes and the collar is frayed. The sisters shake their heads as she walks out the door. They whisper, "Why is she putting that dirty rag on again?"

Old Job, with her crooked back, walks on the arm of a

young sister until she reaches the river she calls the Scheldt. She's out of breath. Mist hangs over the water. The young sister admonishes Job as young people admonish their elders: the Reverend Mother mustn't stand out here for too long. She should save her strength and be careful not to catch cold. Old Job crosses her arms and pulls the cloak tight around her body.

Yrsa opens her eyes and inhales the smell of manure and animal breath in the stable. Job stares at her questioningly, her eyes wide.

"You will grow old in the monastery of Ganda," Yrsa says after a moment. "Pilgrims will travel from near and far to touch you."

"The pilgrims come to see me?" repeats Job incredulously.

"They think you will bring them prosperity. They're convinced that you're very special."

"Really?" she asks. Her voice is almost inaudible, as if she's afraid that speaking too loudly might undo the vision.

"That's what I saw."

"And were you there too?"

"No, I wasn't there."

Job nods. Indeed, that's to be expected. But she mustn't be sad. She touches her cross and says, "I have Jesus. I will never be alone."

And like every night since they left Mimir's Stool, Job and Yrsa fall asleep, shoulder to shoulder.

* * *

Six days after their departure from Dorestad, Job finally sees her convent on the hill. Her eyes fill with tears.

"You're home," Yrsa says as she slides off the horse. Job wipes away her tears, puts a foot in the stirrup, and hoists herself up. She takes hold of the reins and sits sidesaddle as a woman should, with her legs to one side. She's so excited that the horse becomes restless.

"Let's go," she says. Yrsa walks in front of Son of Sleipnir, and the massive horse clambers across the road and through the gates in the palisade. They trod up the path to the top of the hill.

Job greets Oda, the blacksmith's wife, as if she just saw her yesterday. Oda lets out a cry. She drops her basket of washed sheets and makes thirteen signs of the cross. She, like everyone else in Ganda, has heard of Job, the novice taken by the Danes. They had prayed for her soul, because everyone in Ganda assumed she had been killed up there in the wild north, and that she was in heaven at Christ's side.

A little farther on, the goose-herder named Mary recognizes Job as well. The woman falls to her knees and cries, "Praise the Lord!"

A farmer pushing a cart of winter cabbage, parsnips, and red beets up the hill hears the commotion behind him and looks back. Men and women emerge from their homes and workshops and follow the girl on the horse. They point at her, touch her, tell one another who she is, and kiss the crosses around their necks. The farmer pushing the cart hears people saying "Sister Job," and he remembers that he too had prayed for her soul. But there she is, riding in on a stallion. He realizes that he must be witnessing something extraordinary—a miracle. The farmer has often heard the monks talk about miracles on Sundays. They talk about water turning into wine and sick children being healed, all thanks to the Lord in heaven. And now, right here in front of his vegetable cart, one is taking place. A lost sister has returned.

The farmer lets his tears flow. He can't stop crying. Children run toward the convent. They want to be the first to tell the monks and nuns that the lost sister is back. The girls storm into the nuns' quarters and the boys pound on the monks' gate, shouting, asking if they can ring the church bells.

Job's own mother, the Reverend Mother Philip, is the first to step out into the square. The bells are already clanging. Four boys hang like monkeys from the ropes. Mother Philip is noticeably irritated by their unruly behavior, but then her eyes fall on Job. Who is that girl on the horse, she wonders. It cannot be her kidnapped daughter. The girl in that saddle has shoulder-length hair hanging loose around her shoulders—her daughter would never let her hair grow that long—and she is wearing a green dress that exposes her tanned calves. And look at her face! Chin held high, nose to the wind, eyes as sharp as knives. No, this isn't Job. Her daughter is as humble as the apostles.

Then Sister Mark cries out behind her, "Good heavens, it's Job!" And Sister John, who is almost as old as Sarah, the wife of Abraham, and whose eyes are so worn she can barely read her book of psalms, recognizes Job too. "The girl is back," she murmurs.

Mother Philip can't believe her eyes until the horse—what a beast!—is standing right in front of her nose and the girl slides off his back and says, "Hello, Mother."

Philip used to reprimand Job for calling her "mother." After all, Philip is the abbess, the Reverend Mother to all the women, and Job is no more or less than the other sisters. Philip is a mother to all in her community. But in this moment, it doesn't occur to her to correct her daughter. She's speechless. She doesn't even realize that she's weeping. All she can say through her sobs is "What are you wearing, dear child?"

Then Job pulls her mother into her arms.

Philip wipes away her tears and shouts for an animal to be slaughtered. It doesn't matter what. She knows it's inappropriate, of course. Fresh meat is for fall and winter. But there must be a goose, a swan, or an old pig around here somewhere. Anything that can be roasted, that will form a crispy crust and thick drops of delicious fat, will do.

The monks, surprised by all the shouting, emerge from the writing chamber. The men squint in the sunlight and pass around a dirty rag to wipe the paint and ink off their fingers. They can't believe it—their color girl is back! They, too, weep their eyes red and pass one another the rag again, this time to blow their noses and dry their tears.

Then Mother Philip notices the Danish girl standing with the horse and dog. Everything about her is different. Her purple dress is torn and covered in stains. Still, anyone can see that it's an expensive garment, trimmed with gold thread.

Her long red hair is shamelessly tied in a loose ponytail, and her right foot is crooked. She holds a staff and carries a spear on her back, and a silver cross hangs from her neck.

"This is Yrsa daughter of Toke. Without her, I wouldn't be standing here before you today," says Job. "She has been baptized. I made her a Christian."

"Praise the Lord," crows old Sister John, and she presses her toothless lips to Yrsa's mouth. The other sisters follow her example. Job told Yrsa that nuns, like monks, greet each other with a kiss on the mouth. But Yrsa is startled to discover she wasn't kidding.

"We're home," Job says, her face dripping with tears of joy.

The church bells keep ringing. Men and women from the shipyard hurry up the hill. They want to see the nun who returned from the edge of the earth, the nun who was stronger than the pagans. Everyone wants to see Job and touch her for a moment, even if it is only the hem of her dress.

The nuns lead the way to the chapel. The Lord must be thanked.

Job remembers the first time she entered the chapel. The building was dark and the candlelight danced like lace on the thick stone walls. The wooden crucifix was beautiful and the head of Christ was so lifelike, the way it rested on his right shoulder with the thorns piercing his skin. Job stood under the cross and wanted nothing more than to catch the Lord in her arms. She was eleven years old at the time.

And just like that first time, Job kisses the floor tiles under the wooden crucifix. One of the sisters chants the "Kyrie eleison," and Job and ten other sisters answer. Their voices go up and down like a skiff on a calm sea. Yrsa can almost hum the tune.

That afternoon, Job and Yrsa exchange their Danish dresses for habits. Their arms disappear into the wide sleeves. Job's hair is trimmed. All the nuns gather in the kitchen as if they still can't believe their lost sister is back.

"Now you," Job says as she ties a white veil around her head.

"What, wear a cap? Cut my hair? No way!" Yrsa protests. "I'm already wearing a habit."

"The cap won't fit around your head with all that thick hair."

"If you cut my hair, I'll become a slave!"

"No, not at all. You'll become one of us," Job says enthusiastically.

"You didn't say I would have to cut my hair!"

The sisters take a step back and stare at Yrsa as if she's some kind of sea monster. Job looks at her mother.

"No one will ever harm you here. I promise you that," Philip affirms.

Yrsa is exhausted from the journey. She longs for Mimir's Stool, where she was protected by the elves. She could always rely on them. But now here she is, surrounded by Job and all these nuns with golden crosses around their necks.

"Here you'll be safe from the world," Job whispers.

"Outside, storms will rage, wars will be fought, and civilizations will perish, but inside these walls you are safe. The Lord will protect you."

Yrsa looks around for a sign. A chickadee lands in the doorway of the kitchen and pecks around at some grains under a stool. Yrsa is the only one to notice the brave little bird. Could it be a good omen? Or is it not an omen at all, just a hungry little bird? Yrsa wonders if she has lost the ability to spot omens altogether now that she has been baptized. Job's father, the count, will give her coin. That's what Job said. It will be enough for a horse, enough to go back...or to Sweden, perhaps. She can find a ship that will row down the rivers of the Baltic, all the way to Mikligard, that marvel of a city with this woman merchant who looked so much like her. For now, she has to be patient and not attract attention. So first the haircut, then the silver, and then the voyage.

"Well then," Yrsa says finally, and Sister Mark chops off her long hair. The red strands fall to the floor. The sisters mutter among themselves—so much hair!

Then Job shaves a circle on the crown of Yrsa's head and helps her into the white cap. Yrsa can't help feeling sad. She always thought her thick, reddish-brown hair was her best feature. Nokki had taken a lock with him when he left with the men that early summer's day so long ago. Now, Yrsa feels plain. When she looks up, she notices tears in Job's eyes.

"You look so beautiful," Job says.

31

YRSA SLEEPS ON A WICKER MAT in the kitchen by the dying fire. The first night she is eaten alive by mosquitoes. Sister Mark makes her a poultice of lavender and catnip to rub on her neck, cheeks, and wrists to keep the buzzing pests away.

In the morning, she wakes up to the sound of church bells calling them to morning prayer. She unrolls her woolen robe, which she uses as a pillow, shakes the ants and spiders out of her mat, and follows the sisters to the chapel. They walk silently down the corridor on the balls of their feet. Yrsa is still sleepy, but the sisters are already bursting with energy. The pages of their psalmbooks crinkle. They carry oil lamps so they can read the text. Sometimes they mumble their prayers, but mostly they sing together as one climbing, high-pitched voice, and for a moment the chanting lingers over Yrsa like a seagull in the wind. Then it falls silent again, and the sisters all inhale at the same time and continue.

Yrsa floats on their voices. The chapel connects the sisters to those who came before them as Mimir's stone connected her to her ancestors. In a way, it brings her peace.

* * *

After morning prayer, Yrsa follows the sisters to the dining hall. At home in Mimir's Stool, people make sounds to let everyone know they are enjoying the food. The men are especially loud. They smack their lips, slurp, and burp to express their appreciation for the smoked salmon, goat kidneys, or herring stew. But in the convent, everyone eats in silence. No one says a word. Yrsa can't even hear the sisters chewing their goat cheese. They gesture to one another with their fingers when they want more salt, goat's milk, or a piece of bread. Only Yrsa makes noise when she eats, and some of the nuns look up at her, disturbed. They furrow their brows to make it clear that they find her table manners appalling. After a while, Yrsa hardly dares to chew, let alone slurp the goat cheese from her spoon. She slips a few pieces of bread into her sleeve to eat later in the barn with the horse and the dog.

Odin steers clear of the nuns' dark, wide robes. Their strong, purposeful gait—they never slouch—unsettles the dog. In Mimir's Stool, Odin was used to nipping anyone who bothered him in the calves, but here he's learned to stay out of the nuns' way, or else!

The monks use Son of Sleipnir to pull the stones and wood for the final repairs to the palisade, just as his forefather once helped build the wall around Valhöll.

A week after they arrive, Job and Yrsa climb the ladder to the bell tower, the highest point in Ganda. From the narrow tower, they have a sprawling view of the landscape, which is covered in a spiderweb of waterways. The entire region is a tangle of small rivers that connect to the great River Scheldt, which flows north. Along the banks are two dark, imposing towers. She can see the spears and helmets of the guards on the battlements. They're watching for boats on the river. To the north, narrow streams sparkle in the sunlight, and some of the meadows and trees have been overtaken by the water.

"This is the Pagus Flandrensis," Job says proudly. "The flooded land. If you walk out there, you'll come home with wet feet. The streams are constantly overflowing their banks, and only barley and oats can survive."

Yrsa swats away a mosquito.

"The flowers in Ganda are the prettiest in the world," Job adds.

Yrsa smiles. It is true. The swampy meadows and riverbanks are lined with patches of color.

"It's more colorful than Loki's rainbow," Job declares triumphantly.

Yrsa nods. She can see for miles from up here, but she can't see the sea.

Job kisses the gold crucifix on her chest. "I think you're really going to like it here."

Yrsa scratches at the white veil wrapped tightly around her head and can't help but feel annoyed by Job's enthusiasm.

"When is the count coming to Ganda?" she asks.

The question immediately puts a damper on Job's cheerful mood. "Why do you ask?"

Yrsa doesn't respond. Why did she bring Job here in the first place? Because she had no other choice, she thinks.

Now the journey is over, and she's standing here with a cross around her neck, hardly any hair left on her head, and no idea what to do. Should she stay or go?

"You think you saved me," Job says, exasperated. "But it's the other way around. I saved you. From your family, your fate, and all your silly idols."

At that, Job turns and climbs down the ladder in the bell tower.

Over the next few weeks, visitors come to meet Job—monks and nuns from other abbeys, noblemen and warriors. Even the bishop, who—according to the nuns—gets news from God every day, wants to meet Job. He wants to hear the story of her abduction and time with the pagans for himself. He asks two young monks with ink-stained fingers to write down her entire account. Their pens scratch the parchment as Job tells the bishop about the Bible she tried to save, the storm at sea, the ferocious wolfhound that protected her in the barn, the horse that helped her escape, the boy who violated her, and how she beat him to death on the beach.

"With a rock," the bishop adds. "Just like David and Goliath. It was the hand of God that threw the stone."

The two monks write it all down.

Job also tells the bishop about Yrsa daughter of Toke, and how she helped her escape.

"That heathen girl was sent by God," says the bishop with certainty, and he asks to speak to Yrsa as well.

Yrsa wants nothing to do with the bishop, whose gold cross and ring she's supposed to kiss. When she makes the sign of the cross incorrectly, the man snarls, "Again." When she confesses that she still doesn't know the Lord's Prayer by heart, the bishop recites the prayer line by line for her and demands that she repeat after him. If she says a word incorrectly, he slaps her fingers with his gilded staff. Finally, he asks Yrsa to tell him more about Job and the miracles she witnessed with the nun.

"Fortune walked at her side," Yrsa says.

"Fortune does not walk," the bishop snaps. "It was God, and God alone. You renounced your idols, didn't you? Odin and all that? Or do you still pray to them?"

"No, we don't pray at all," says Yrsa. "We make offerings. We ask them for advice and look for signs."

The young monks chuckle and shake their heads at her pagan nonsense. They tap their pens in their inkwells and continue scratching them across the parchment. Finally, the bishop follows Job and Yrsa to the barn to see the horse and the dog. He blesses the animals.

"Now, they too are children of the Lord," he declares.

After the bishop's visit, all anyone can talk about is Sister Job. Her story has spread like wildfire across the region, to the far corners of West Francia, the kingdom of Charles the Bald, and even to East Francia, ruled by his brother, Louis the German. As summer begins, rumors circulate that the sick have been miraculously cured after touching Sister Job's habit. They say that God has chosen Job to be his tool. Even old Sister John is convinced that she will live to see Job become the next reverend mother.

* * *

By the time the count returns to Ganda with his men later that summer, Yrsa has been at the convent for more than two months. The barley and oats have yet to be harvested, but the cherries have all been picked. Two giant Norwegians with large, dark green crosses tattooed on the backs of their hands arrive in chainmail to inform Mother Philip that the count wishes to see his daughter and the Danish girl.

They greet Yrsa and Job with less-than-cordial growls and walk ahead of them down the hill. They march along the muddy banks of the Scheldt and cross creaky, narrow bridges over its many tributaries. They pass the shipyard, where the pounding and hammering remind Yrsa of Mimir's Stool. The slow grating of a saw on wood takes her by surprise. For a moment, she stops to watch the two men trying to saw a log into planks. She shakes her head. *That's not how you do it—you're supposed to chop it into planks with an ax. How clumsy can you be?* she thinks.

"Are you coming?" Job calls.

Yrsa has fallen behind and, holding her new staff, hurries to catch up with Job. She slips in the mud on her bad foot and falls on her side. Job helps her up. The Norwegians don't stop to help. One grins at the sight of Yrsa's muddy habit. The other sighs in exasperation. They wait by a sloop that will take the two sisters across.

"My father found those men in Walacria. They converted to Christianity, and now they live here with their families," Job explains.

Yrsa rubs her throbbing ankle and wonders whether the two Norwegians really converted. She suspects they still have the hammer of Thor hidden somewhere under their chainmail.

"Where is Walacria?" Yrsa asks, trying to wipe the wet clay off her robes.

Job points north. "It's about a day's walk," she says. "But you have to cross a wide, sandy plain that's only passable at low tide."

"Have you ever been to Walacria?"

"No, and I have no interest in going there. That place is full of heathens. It's not safe."

"And the count just lets them carry on with their pagan activities?" Yrsa asks.

Job shrugs and says, "It's a market city close to the sea. He just goes there to sell cloth and grain, and recruit mercenaries for the king."

"How much silver will the count give me, do you think?"

"I don't know," says Job gruffly.

"Are you coming, or do you have to bless the river before we go?" one of the Norwegians hollers from the sloop.

"We're coming!" Job shouts.

A moment later, the two men are pushing the sloop across the river with long poles.

The count's tower is the westernmost of the two towers on the banks of the Scheldt. It's made of solid oak. Yrsa follows Job up the muddy wooden staircase. The second floor is a dark room with a hollowed-out stone in the middle of the floor that's used as a fireplace. The walls are decorated with tattered, faded carpets, and in one corner is a chest buried under a pile of parchment scrolls that have been eaten away by mice. A chainmail coat and shirt are slung over a chair.

The chainmail reminds Job of the first time she met her father. She was about ten years old and dressed in her most expensive clothes to show that she was of noble blood. She went with her mother on horseback to Compiègne, a city in northern Francia where King Charles the Bald has his palace. Job couldn't wait to see the famous camels of Compiègne that the king had received as a gift. She stood among the local children for an hour, ogling the strange creatures. After that, she met her father for the first time: a sullen man with a helmet full of dents.

"His name is Baudouin," her mother told her. "But they call him 'the Iron Arm' because he's so strong and tough." Her mother pushed Job forward, and she wrapped her arms around the man's belly. He reeked of sweat and iron. Job's dress got caught in one of the rings of his chainmail. She managed to wriggle it free, but it tore a hole in the fabric.

"What are you doing here?" the count asked her mother. "I send you money for the child, don't I?"

"I heard that you're looking for a new abbess for the women's convent in Ganda," Job's mother said. "Why don't you appoint me?"

"Do you really want to enter the convent?" the count asked incredulously.

"Yes, I do, and I will take our daughter with me," Job's mother replied.

"I want to become a bride of Christ," Job said confidently. "There's nothing else I want in this life."

Not much more was said. What Job remembers most is that hole in her dress, and how the garment lost its luster.

Job greets her father with a bow, and Yrsa follows her example. The count studies the young women before him. He's wearing a tunic with a bear woven into the fabric and a large, bronze cross around his neck.

"The people around here don't like this old tower," the count says. "They think it's still haunted by the ghosts of the Romans."

Yrsa instinctively reaches for her amulet, only to find the cross hanging around her neck. She immediately lets go.

"The Danes don't dare to attack my towers," says the count. "They know it would cost them too many men."

"Praise the Lord," says Job, and Yrsa mutters the words after her.

"I got your letter last winter," says the count.

"A lot has happened since then. Naefr is dead," Job says. "Yrsa and I defeated him."

The two Norwegians chuckle. They don't believe a word she says. One of them even bursts out laughing.

"I have his helmet in my cell at the convent," says Yrsa. "It makes an excellent chamber pot. If you ever learn some manners, maybe I'll let you borrow it sometime."

At that, the Norwegians fall silent.

The count remains calm. He has already heard about

what happened in Dorestad. He sips a cup of wine and says, "I met Naefr in Walacria a few summers ago. He came to demand silver. In exchange, he promised not to sail down the Scheldt that summer and attack Ganda."

"And you paid him?" Job asks indignantly.

"Yes, I paid the stupid heathen," the count replies irritably.

"He was my uncle," says Yrsa, with a hint of pride in her voice. Her hatred for Naefr is as deep as the sea, but if he's a stupid heathen, then she is too. The count ignores Yrsa's remark and looks at her as if she has no right to speak, as if he is having a conversation with Job and Job alone. As if Yrsa is worth nothing more than the mud smeared across her habit.

"Daughter, I am glad to see you back unharmed," the count continues.

"Thank you, Father," says Job.

"It's time you took your eternal vows. You're sixteen now."

"Of course, Father. I'll do it in the harvest month. Mother has already decided."

"The news of your miraculous return hasn't only reached the king in Compiègne, it's also reached the pope in Rome," says the count.

"Rome," Job repeats, with disbelief.

"The bishop wrote him a letter with the whole story. You are living proof that we will win the battle against the infidels. The pope will beatify you. And after your death—may God bless you with many more years—you will undoubtedly become St. Elftrudis."

"Elftrudis?" Yrsa asks.

"That's my baptismal name," says Job.

Yrsa laughs.

"Wipe that smirk off your face," snarls the count.

Yrsa is startled. She catches Job's gaze. *Show a little respect*, her eyes say.

"St. Elftrudis," the count continues. "That's what they'll call you one day—the patron saint of hostages. People will pray to you when they've lost all hope. Your name will give them hope again. St. Elftrudis will be forever bound to Ganda."

Job can't believe her ears.

"Rome," she says again.

"We will prosper," says the count. "The pilgrims will come with gold and silver to see you, to receive your blessing. Our monastery will be revived. We will place a statue in your honor."

"Yes," she whispers. "Yrsa predicted this."

The count looks up, his brows furrowed in confusion. Job makes a sign of the cross. She is embarrassed before God and her father of what she believes.

"Yrsa is a seeress," says Job. "She can see people's fates."

"But she's not a pagan anymore, is she?" says the count nervously. He might be able to scare off the Danes with his towers, but he's still not comfortable having a seeress in his living room.

Job takes Yrsa by the hand and grins from ear to ear. "Not anymore. She's been converted. She's staying with us. She's going to become a nun."

"A nun? Really? Can she read and write Latin? Does she know the New Testament?"

Job is startled by the aggressive tone in her father's voice. She doesn't dare respond.

"In his letter to the pope, the bishop wrote that the Lord sent you a pagan, a horse, and a dog. All good things from the Lord come in threes," the count says.

Job makes the sign of the cross.

Then he turns to Yrsa. "That means you are an instrument of God."

"Praise the Lord," Job says immediately.

"Praise the Lord," Yrsa repeats. "Your daughter assured me that I would receive a reward for returning her safely."

The room falls silent. Job turns her eyes submissively to the floor, as if she's embarrassed by what Yrsa just said.

"Silver," Yrsa clarifies.

"Everyone wants silver from me," the count sighs. "My father-in-law, the Danes, the monasteries. Do you think I can just sift silver out of the Scheldt?"

One of the Norwegians chuckles at the joke.

"I am grateful to you, Yrsa daughter of Toke," the count says finally. "And thanks to my daughter, you have found true faith. You have also enjoyed the sisters' hospitality for quite some time now. I will do for you what I did for Elftrudis and her mother. I will give you a place in my convent so that you may become a novice. And, when you are ready, a nun."

"Oh, thank you, Father," Job exclaims. "Thank you."

Yrsa stares at the count. She wants to say that she has come for silver, beads, or coins, not a place in the convent.

But Job looks at her with tears streaming down her cheeks. She's overflowing with joy. Her eyes beg Yrsa to accept the offer.

Finally, Yrsa says, "Thank you, Lord Count."

Yrsa is in a foul mood as they walk back to the convent.

"What's wrong?"

"'Do you think I can just sift silver from the Scheldt?' What a mussel-brain!"

"Think about what my father is offering you."

"Oh, I'm thinking about it. I'm thinking that I'll never get away from here!"

"Please don't say that."

The chapel bells are ringing for noon prayers.

"Go to mass, sister."

"But, Yrsa—"

"Go. Leave me alone," Yrsa says.

Job walks off, joining the other sisters as they disappear into the chapel. Yrsa walks through the market stalls and sits down against the stone well. Her staff drops, but she doesn't pick it up. She is trapped. That's what she is. And it's all her doing.

"You're the young Danish woman, right?"

Yrsa looks up. The man who addresses her is a trader. She has seen him around Ganda, buying fancy cloth and other goods. He hands her the staff. Job has warned her not to leave the staff lying about.

"What do you want?"

"I can't help seeing that you're out of place here."

"Is it that obvious?"

"I'm assembling a shipment of Flemish cloth, Frankish swords, and wine. I plan on taking it to Sweden."

"Sweden?" Yrsa repeats.

"Yes, leaving in a month from the port of Walacria."

Yrsa nods. Walacria. A day's walk, Job had said.

"It takes a few weeks to cross the sea, weather permitting. And I'm still looking for rowers. And of course, Danish rowers are the best."

"Have you noticed that I'm a woman and I have this clubfoot?"

"Well, your foot doesn't bother me. And you wouldn't be the first Danish woman to row across the sea."

Yrsa observes him. He sounds calm and earnest. He has long hair and wears earrings. She wonders if she can trust him.

"Sweden," she muses.

32

THE HARVEST MONTH has finally come. Job and Yrsa walk along the creeks, picking wild strawberries and other berries. The greenness of the landscape is starting to fade, and the flowers are nearly gone. Summer is almost over, but it's still a beautiful day, as if the gods rolled out the sun on their cart just for them. Swarms of mosquitoes hang over the water.

Yrsa leaves offerings under the willow trees along the banks. Job is afraid someone will see her and tell somebody. She prays for Yrsa every night in the chapel, asking God to help her give up her pagan ways.

They come to a deserted river bend and take off their clothes to bathe.

"You missed prayer again," says Job.

"I know," Yrsa says as she lathers herself with soap.

"The sisters are starting to grumble about it. You're baptized now, and you dress like one of us, yet you don't pray."

Yrsa shrugs and hands Job the soap.

"The Reverend Mother says you're not doing your best to learn Latin. You still have a lot to learn before you can become a novice. And you've been here for four months already."

"I've seen the way the Reverend Mother looks at me, how she turns up her nose in my presence, as if I stink of my gods."

"You mean your idols."

"I think she's afraid I might turn you into a pagan and you'll lose your calling."

Job bursts into laughter. "That's ridiculous. My mother isn't worried about that at all. I'm going to take my eternal vows next week. Then I'll be a full-fledged nun. My mother knows my calling is the most important thing in the world to me."

"She doesn't want us spending time together. She's always giving me silly chores to do and sending me off to places where I won't run into you. My presence annoys her."

"That's not true," Job says with conviction. "But you shouldn't talk about your old gods."

"But the sisters are always asking me about them. Did you know that your days of the week are actually named after my old gods? Friday is the day of Frigg. Thursday is the day of Thor. Wednesday—"

"Enough!" says Job.

"And admit it," Yrsa continues, "you like taking a bath every week on washing day too, like we did in Denmark."

"I'm going to stop. It's a bad habit." At that, Yrsa throws herself on Job's shoulders and pushes her underwater for five counts, as long as the monk in Dorestad held her underwater for her silly baptism. Then she lets go and Job splashes to the surface, gasping for air.

"Why are you being so childish!" Job cries once she's caught her breath.

"Because you're always so difficult," Yrsa snaps, but she already feels sorry for what she did. She lays her hand on Job's bare shoulder. Job pushes her hand away, climbs up the bank, and pulls the linen petticoat over her wet body. Then she pats down her short hair. She doesn't have much hair left.

"Your tonsure is three times as wide as mine," Yrsa says, rubbing the bald spot on the top of her head.

"Well, I also believe in God three times as much as I did before," Job retorts.

"It makes you look like a monk. It's ugly. And your pimples are back."

"The Lord sees my beauty," Job growls.

"I'm sure Odin saw it too when you rode Son of Sleipnir through Hedeby and pulled me into the saddle. Even I saw it."

For a moment, Job is utterly confused.

"Everyone here believes in God. Why can't you?" demands Job.

"If the people of Ganda don't believe in Thor, why do they all want to get married on a Thursday?"

For a moment, Job is speechless. Then she shouts, "There will come a day, Yrsa daughter of Toke, when the days of the week will be named after the apostles and the angels. Petersday, Lukesday, Michaelsday, and so on. Otherwise, we'll never be rid of those silly idols."

Yrsa steps out of the water. She dresses in silence, as does Job. Once Yrsa has fastened her white veil under her chin,

Job leans in and tucks a loose strand of Yrsa's hair back into her cap. She takes a step back and nods in approval.

"I talked to Jalke, the Frisian trader, the other day," Yrsa says. "He's leaving Walacria for Sweden in a few days. He was looking for another rower."

Job gazes at her in astonishment.

"Jalke the Frisian?"

"I agreed to be one of his rowers."

"What? But you can't do that!"

Yrsa looks away. "I think the Reverend Mother has given up on me anyway," she says.

"That's not true," Job insists. "You just need to try a little harder."

"You have everything you want here," Yrsa says. "You're happy in Ganda. You will be honored. Your name will become a legend. After you're gone, believers will come to the monastery to pray on the church floor where you prayed, to touch the things you touched. The counts and bishops will do everything they can to keep your memory alive and attract more pilgrims. Even your bones will bring them silver. The legend of Job will bring wealth to the entire region."

Job knows it is true. Her miraculous story will help spread Christianity throughout the land. Bells will be rung for her from Ganda to Rome, spreading the Word of God, and eventually the memory of the old gods—even if the days of the week are named after them—will be stamped out like a bush fire.

"Please, don't leave," Job whispers.

"Come on, you'll be late for vespers."

Job follows her. Please don't let her go, she prays to Mary. There must be a thousand reasons to persuade Yrsa to stay, but Job can't think of one. She follows Yrsa through the convent garden where they grow herbs, vegetables, and vines. The garden is Yrsa's favorite place. She could sit there for hours.

"Aren't you going to miss me?" asks Job.

"You know, Job, for a moment I really thought I could shed my hamr like Signe does on the full moon when she transforms into a seal. Or like Thor, when he transformed himself into a bride. It's true that we all have different beings inside of us. But in me there is no nun."

"And in me there is no pagan."

"No," Yrsa replies with a sad smile. "In you there is no pagan. And it's true, I will miss the garden."

The garden will still be here tomorrow, Job thinks. The birds will still chirp. The bees will still buzz, and the cat will still sleep in her usual spot in the afternoon sun. The apples will still hang from their branches, a little heavier than the day before. The barrel that catches the rainwater will be a little fuller, and the roses in the hedge will be a little higher. The herbs will still be here, and so will the plants and mosses that Job uses to mix her colors for the monks. But Yrsa will be gone, and the garden will never be the same. Her friend will be on her way to Sweden.

"You can come along if you want. I'm sure Jalke will be prepared to take on a passenger if we pay him," Yrsa says.

"No, no, no, you've seen my future. It is here," Job almost shouts.

"Of course, I wasn't thinking," Yrsa says, embarrassed.

"Surely, you understand that I could never give up my calling for you," Job says. "My calling is my life. Without it, I have no reason to live."

Job's face is pale. Her lips tremble. Her dark eyes glisten. For a moment, she imagines herself taking the whaling road again, sticking a pole into the water to ascertain that they are not in shallow waters. The wind in her hair. The sail flapping.

"I know. You belong here," Yrsa says.

She scans the river. A vague sense of doom ripples through her mind. A few nights ago, she saw the old sea serpent Jormundgandr in a dream. It was a warning. She knows that the people of Mimir's Stool, all those uncles, aunts, and cousins of hers, aren't just going to let her go.

"So you're leaving!" Job shouts. "And what are you going to do when you get to Sweden?"

"Once I reach the Baltic Sea, I can sail down the big rivers to the south."

"To the city where Harald's son will go?"

"Mikligard." Yrsa smiles. "Perhaps."

"To get there, you'll have to cross the Inhospitable Sea."

"It can't be that bad."

"There's a reason they call it that, you know, because of all the storms. You're crazy. You won't survive."

"It's not without danger," Yrsa admits. "I can only hope that fortune stays with me."

"How much fortune can a person have?" asks Job. "You told me yourself that your fortune, your hamingja, is a fickle creature that can abandon you at any moment."

Yrsa's hand reaches for the cross around her neck.

"What are you doing?" Job asks.

Yrsa turns the cross over. On the back is a rudimentary carving of a hammer. Job is taken aback.

"You're incorrigible, you know that!"

"How did we survive all of this?"

"Because God was with us."

"Because fortune was on our side."

"Nonsense!"

"Because you were my fortune," says Yrsa. "You *are* my fortune, Job. You are my hamingja."

The sun disappears behind the clouds. A shadow falls over the garden. The cat wakes up and stretches.

"Let me go," Yrsa says, and she takes Job into her arms.

Job can smell the sea on Yrsa's neck—the breeze, the salt water, the splashing of the waves.

Yrsa feels Job's entire body tremble. They hold each other until the cat rubs against their legs to let them know he's hungry.

Job and Yrsa walk silently out of the convent garden and cross the courtyard. Job prays a Hail Mary. Why doesn't Mary help her? Why can't she persuade Yrsa to stay?

Then she notices that Yrsa has stopped following her. She's standing in the middle of the courtyard.

"What's wrong?" Job asks.

Yrsa points to an owl nailed against a door. Its wings are flapping. The animal is still alive. Job makes a sign of the cross.

"That's what my mother does to keep the devil away," Job says.

"It's a bad omen," Yrsa says.

"Are you out there?" they hear Mother Philip say. She walks out the back door of the convent. "Well, aren't you coming in?" she asks.

The Reverend Mother is nervous. Her hand shakes like the hand of the god Tyr when he reached into the mouth of the giant wolf Fenrir.

"What's the matter, Mother?" Job asks.

"Don't call me that."

The hooded head of Sister Mark appears in the doorway. She searches for Yrsa's eyes and points to the river with her chin. Only now does Yrsa see the ship. It's long and narrow, designed for speed. A ship for trade and war. The prow is tall and thin like a knife that can cut through waves. Yrsa doesn't have to read the runes on the side of the ship to know that it's the *Huginn*.

Job doesn't recognize the ship and continues inside. Yrsa meekly follows her. Mother Philip pulls the door closed behind her and turns the iron key in the lock. *This is it then. What did you think, Yrsa daughter of Toke? That you could escape the fate knotted in your navel?* She can already hear the

Norns cackling with laughter in their den under the tree. They've got their scissors ready. Today is the day they will cut her thread of life.

Job walks through the kitchen into the dining room. She's surprised to see her father, the count, sitting at the table. Then she recognizes the other guests and drops her basket of berries.

"Yrsa!" Job screams.

But Yrsa isn't startled to see the old woman—the gold in her white hair, the warrior's knife on her belt, the bishop's ring on a silver chain around her neck.

Gudrun has come for her.

33

GUDRUN SEES THE TWO NUNS walk in and wonders where Yrsa is. You can usually hear her coming, the old woman thinks, by the way she leans on her left foot, always a thump-step-thump. And she always has something swinging from her belt as she walks. But the nuns who enter are as quiet as mice. Gudrun recognizes their former hostage. What a tiny thing she is.

"What do you want, Grandmother?" she hears one of the nuns say.

Only then does Gudrun recognize her. For a moment, she's shocked to see her granddaughter dressed in dark robes with a tight white veil over her head. Then she bursts out laughing.

"Is that my granddaughter? Well, look at you!" she cackles.

"What's going on?" asks Job.

"They've come for her," says the count. He's wearing his iron chainmail and has his sword on his belt. His Norwegian bodyguards stand behind him.

"No, they can't," Job says immediately. "Father, this is

hallowed ground. Yrsa has been baptized. She's going to become a nun. You can't let these pagans take her."

"She is not a nun," barks the Reverend Mother. "A tonsure on her head doesn't make her a novice. She refuses to give up the name Yrsa because her earthly mother gave it to her. She doesn't want to take the name of a saint. She only comes to prayers twice a day and just murmurs along with the psalms. Last week, I saw her place a cup of milk at the foot of an old oak tree. Don't deny it, girl!"

"Oaks are thirsty trees," Yrsa retorts.

"That's true," says Gudrun, still reeling from her fit of laughter.

"Yrsa belongs in a different world, daughter," says Mother Philip. "She belongs in the wild, with the fire worshippers."

The smile disappears from Gudrun's face. How dare this woman call her a fire worshipper? She worships the gods of Asgard, imperfect as they are. Gudrun shoots the Reverend Mother a dirty look, as if she would like nothing more than to smash her brains in with an ax.

"I have a good life here, Grandmother," Yrsa says, but her tone isn't very convincing.

"I have arranged a marriage for you," says Gudrun. For a moment, Yrsa is speechless. Has Gudrun brought the jeweler's son from Odin's Hill? A young man steps out of the shadows. It's not the jeweler's son. He strokes his goatee and flashes a smile that could melt all the ice in the North.

Job groans. "Nokki..."

"He's the one you wanted, isn't he?" asks Gudrun. "More than anyone else on Midgard?"

Yrsa looks at Nokki and no one else. Doesn't he want revenge for the deaths of his brother and father? Surely blood demands blood?

"Nokki won't harm you," Gudrun says.

But Yrsa doesn't believe her.

"That girl must die!" someone shouts. It's Egill, who has just marched in with Birger at his side and is standing before the count's men.

Gudrun rolls her eyes. "I told you to stay on the ship."

"Nokki swore an oath to his father!" Egill shouts.

"That oath can wait!" shouts Gudrun. "And you shut up."

Yrsa searches Nokki's eyes. He doesn't look bitter or resentful. He mostly seems sad.

"The bride price has already been arranged. Nokki will marry you," says Gudrun.

Yrsa can't believe her ears. "And what about Rikiwulf?"

"Ah, the sea king has women enough. He understands, as long as you still agree to be his personal seeress."

"I'll marry you if you still want me," says Nokki.

"Of course she does!" Gudrun exclaims.

All Yrsa can do is stare at him.

"Did an elf steal your tongue, Yrsa daughter of Toke?" Gudrun demands.

"She doesn't love him!" Job cries. "She loves this convent and the women here. And we love her."

The sisters huddle together in a corner of the dining room. They bow their heads as if God himself were standing in the room.

"You're coming with us," Gudrun says. "We'll row up the

Scheldt and wait for Lord Rikiwulf in Walacria. The whole fleet is gathering there. From Walacria, we will sail to the mouth of the Seine. From there, it's two more days of rowing to Paris."

"Paris?" Yrsa repeats in astonishment. "What are we going to do in Paris?"

"The monasteries in Paris are so full of silver that they're practically sinking into the ground." Gudrun grins. "We're going to help them with that."

The nuns all shriek and begin murmuring the Lord's Prayer.

"Count Baudouin here isn't going to tell anyone about our plans," says Gudrun. "He's been very well compensated for his silence."

Job's father nods in resignation, the traitor.

"You tried to escape your fate, Yrsa," Gudrun says with a hint of understanding in her voice. "Your flight and battle in Dorestad are a saga in themselves. You've been very brave. But fate will always catch up with you in the end."

"The saga of Yrsa daughter of Toke." Egill chuckles. "That's ridiculous. Sagas are only about men."

"Shut up, Egill," says Gudrun.

"Egill, how's that arm of yours, by the way?" asks Yrsa.

His eyes fill with rage.

"And can you sleep on both ears yet?"

He reaches for the sword in his belt.

Gudrun smacks Egill on the head and sends him outside. Nokki grins, and Yrsa feels herself blushing.

"We're waiting for Rikiwulf's fleet in Walacria," Gudrun says. "What do you think, granddaughter?"

"Summer is almost over," Yrsa says. "Is it wise to sail south now? It will be winter when we return. The storms will come. We might not make it home."

"That makes this the ideal time to go. The Franks are off their guard," says Gudrun. "Our spies have informed us that there's only one small garrison in the city, and that Charles the Bald has headed south with his men to fight a battle against some cousin of his."

"But you can go to Paris without me, can't you?"

"You're the best seeress Denmark has ever known. Why, I wouldn't be surprised if one day Odin comes to you disguised as a traveler and asks you to predict his fate. If there's a storm coming, you can tell us. If the abbot refuses to tell us where the silver is, you can grab his wrists and force him to reveal his secrets."

"So now you need me? The child you wanted to sacrifice to the gods?"

"The gods didn't let you freeze to death," says Gudrun.

"My *mother* didn't let me freeze to death!" Yrsa snaps.

"Surely, you know better than any of us," says Gudrun softly, "that you don't belong between these stone walls? That you, Yrsa daughter of Toke of Mimir's Stool, were not made for this boring swampland among these graying women? You are a maiden of the sea, your forefathers are seafarers, and your children will be too."

Yrsa says nothing. She knows Gudrun is right.

"We'll arrive in Paris with so many ships that the monks will have no choice but to give us their silver in exchange for their lives. We might not even have to fight for it."

"Lord have mercy!" cries Job.

"Lord have mercy!" repeats old Sister John, and all the nuns reach for their crosses.

The count takes Job by the shoulders and says, "The fate of that Danish girl lies with her own people, just as yours lies here in the convent."

"Stop it, Father," says Job. "There's no such thing as fate. It's a pagan invention. And if you've sold your soul for a bit of silver, you're no better than them."

The count punches Job in the face. Blood sprays from her nose. She falls to the ground. Behind her, the eleven sisters let out a collective scream.

Yrsa takes a step forward, but Gudrun grabs her by the arm.

"We're done here," she says.

Yrsa looks at the count in horror. Sister Mark helps Job to her feet. Job sees Yrsa's clenched fists, and they give her courage. She wriggles free from Mark's grip and, with blood dripping from her chin, turns to her father. "Is this how you want them to remember you? Count Baudouin, the man who struck St. Elftrudis in the face?"

The count stares at her, speechless.

"To the chapel, Job!" cries Mother Philip. "Go pray and ask the Lord to forgive you for your pride."

The Reverend Mother grabs Job by her veil and shoves her out of the room. The nuns follow in a flurry of rustling habits.

Gudrun steps in front of Yrsa and says, "Now, take off those rags."

Gudrun points to the chest on the table. Nokki opens it. Inside is a cloak trimmed with fur and a silk dress embroidered with gold thread. The dress has been dyed blue, a color so expensive and rare that some believe it to be a color of the gods.

"Rikiwulf wants his seeress to impress," says Gudrun.

Yrsa lets the silk of the blue dress slip between her fingers and smiles. She has never felt anything so soft in her life.

34

THAT EVENING, after the final prayers, Job walks down to the banks of the Scheldt, where the *Huginn* was docked that morning. Now the ship is following the river to the sea. She remembers the dream Yrsa had: that Job would grow old and keep going to the river, that she would continue to wear her old, threadbare Danish cloak over her habit. She had heard that the ship would sail to the market town of Walacria on the island of Walcheren. Yrsa would arrive there tomorrow, and they would wait for the fleet of ships from the North.

Walacria. It's not even that far, only a day's walk from Ganda. All she has to do is cross the Heath Sea at low tide to reach the island. She feels her heart racing.

Job walks across the convent courtyard. There's still light coming from the monks' quarters as they get ready for bed. She pushes open the door to the chapel, where she was sitting with the sisters only an hour ago. There's no one left in the chapel but Christ on the cross and the lingering smell of incense.

She kneels on the stones and gazes up at the crucifix she'd been so enamored with when she first came here. The monastery on the hill seemed so perfect to her back then. Separate spaces for the monks and nuns, each with a chapel and a church dedicated to Mary, plus an orchard, a vineyard, and land for the cows and sheep to graze. It's heaven on earth. She had everything here that she would ever need. Before the convent, life had been uncertain, even chaotic, staying in homes of uncles or cousins. She'd followed her mother, who was always lamenting that the count didn't want to marry her or see his daughter. Even as a little girl, Job knew that nobody really wanted her.

When Job was ten, her mother told her that they would be safe in the convent. All she had to do was follow her sisters' lead and heed their words. A massive storm swept across the country during the first year she lived here. She remembers how the wind whistled through the holes in the masonry, how the rain pounded on the roof, how the cows in the valley bellowed as they were swept away by the flooded river. She remained calm and continued to pray with the other sisters as she protected the flame of the oil lamp. Inside the convent walls, she was safe from the storm, and she felt wanted. Her homecoming had been the best moment of her life. How happy she was to run her hands along the walls again, to see the faces of the nuns she had lived with for years, to breathe in the smell of incense in the chapel.

But now, more than four months later, she misses the journey that brought her here. She misses the horse's muscles beneath her legs. She misses the churning sea under the boat, the splashing of the waves, and the salt on her lips. She misses the evenings when she and Yrsa would fall asleep leaning against each other under a tree. She misses the horizon that was a little different every day. And above all, she misses Yrsa. That tall, redheaded girl who laughed at the Leviathan, who shouted that she would make a Dane out of her, and who held her hand while she was falling asleep in the wilderness. The feeling of loss is as deep as the sea. Suddenly, the thought of spending the rest of her life within the safety of these walls is unbearable.

She bends down and presses her forehead against the cold tiles. Ever so quietly, she whispers that come harvesttime, she will not take her vows after all. That she is sorry. Then she gets up, kisses the feet of Christ on the cross, and walks out of the chapel.

Job clutches the cross between her fingers. The moon is full, and there's not a cloud in the sky. It's the kind of night when men turn into wolves, women into seals, people into gods, men into women, and women into men. She walks to the washroom, where the monks' robes are hanging to dry. She looks for the smallest one and pushes her arms through the sleeves. She pulls the white veil off her head and pats down her short hair. Her tonsure is as wide as a monk's. Then she walks to the stable. Odin the dog prances up to her as soon as she opens the gate.

"How do you like me as a monk?" she asks in a deep voice.

Odin licks her fingers. Son of Sleipnir turns around

in his stall at the sound of her voice. He can't wait to go out for a ride. She lets the dog and horse out of the stable, and together they walk down the hill: a tiny monk, a giant stallion, and a big, hairy dog. Job feels her ears tingle in the crisp night air. The whole world is asleep.

They slip through the gate in the palisade. For a moment, she looks back at the convent walls and the tower glowing in the moonlight. Fear washes over her. Suddenly, she feels so weak that she bends her knees. She recites a Hail Mary to calm herself and thinks of Yrsa. The thought that she is on her way to Yrsa gives her strength.

Job climbs on the horse, straddles her legs over the saddle like a man, and clicks her tongue. Son of Sleipnir plods steadily up the road. Once they hear something rustling in the bushes, but Odin lets out a mean growl, and whatever it is falls quiet. They follow the path north through the marsh.

A few hours later, Job feels the sun rising behind her. When there's enough light, she lets the horse break into a trot. By the time the sun is high in the sky, she is already far from home.

Later that morning, she encounters a group of laborers along the road with carts carrying wood and stone. She recognizes the man in charge, Diederik, a mason from Ganda.

"Brother," says Diederik, who greets her with a slight bow.

"Where are you heading, mason?" Job asks.

"To the coast. We're building a tower for the count. He wants to keep the Vikings out of our flooded land."

"About time. So you'll be traveling to the edge of the Heath Sea?"

"Sure, we're not far off," says Diederik, who cannot keep his eyes off the horse. "What a magnificent animal," he declares.

Diederik wants to know all about Son of Sleipnir, so she tells him the story of the stonemason who brought the horse's ancestor to Odin's palace, and how it dragged half a mountain of rock to build the walls of the Valhöll. He laps it up as if it were rice pudding.

Then Diederik kisses the cross on his chest so that the Lord in heaven will see that he doesn't really believe in such stories, even though he enjoys them all the same.

That afternoon, they arrive at the edge of the Heath Sea. The plain of wet sand, gullies, and heath-covered salt marshes stretches for miles. The island of Walcheren is a dark speck on the distant horizon. It's low tide, but it will still take hours to cover the distance. A heron hovers over the plain. Job wonders if it might be a good omen.

"I have to go to Walacria," says Job.

"You have to get there before the tide rolls in. If I were you, I'd wait until tomorrow," Diederik says.

"Tomorrow is too late," Job mutters, pushing her horse toward the Heath Sea.

"Be careful with that horse of yours," says Diederik. "If he sinks in the quicksand, you'll have a tough time getting him out. It'll cost you a lot of time, and you might not make it to the other side."

Job's courage starts to waver.

"Should I leave him behind?" she asks, more to herself than the man.

Diederik says he's willing to buy the horse from her. He could use a strong horse like Son of Sleipnir for hauling wood and stones. Job stares at the vast plain of sand before her.

"Fifteen pieces of silver?" she asks.

"That's a bargain," Diederik says, already reaching into his pouch.

"I'll only sell him if you promise to take care of him like a son and never forget that he is the son of Sleipnir and a descendant of the gods."

Diederik promises and asks if Job will bless him and his men.

Job hesitates. "I haven't taken my eternal vows yet."

"Doesn't matter. A temporary vow is good enough for us."

He kneels on the road, and the other workers follow suit.

Job prays the Lord's Prayer and then, with the confidence of a monk, makes the sign of the cross. She asks that the Lord bless them in the name of the Father, the Son, and the Holy Spirit, that He give them His peace and protect them from all idols. The men make the sign of the cross and say, "Peace be with you, brother." Then they head on with their oxen and their carts.

Diederik watches in amazement as the young friar whispers words into the horse's ear, how he lays his head against the animal's neck and runs his fingers through its mane. When the monk finally turns away from the horse, his face is red and swollen, as if he's standing before a blacksmith's furnace.

"You must hurry, brother, or it will be too dangerous to cross," Diederik says.

"This horse is very dear to me," says Job as she wipes the snot from her nose. Then, she hurries out into the wet sand, followed by the dog. Son of Sleipnir whinnies and tramples restlessly. He wants to follow his master, but Diederik holds him back by the reins.

"Don't dawdle along the way!" Diederik shouts. "And stay on the hard sand!"

Job and Odin race across the sandy plain. They leap over gullies and make sure to keep their feet on solid ground. Job feels the hard ripples in the sand under her bare feet. Sometimes they have to scramble over loose, marshy patches and hurry around the heather bushes. She sinks in up to her knees at least three times and has to climb out of the mud. Shorebirds squawk in all directions, rooting their beaks in the tide pools. She hears the sound of the approaching tide in the distance. By the time the water splashes around her ankles, the island's dunes are in sight. She almost has to swim the last hundred yards, but finally, she reaches the shore. Odin shakes out his wet fur, completely exhausted.

They rest on a dune until the entire plain is engulfed by the sea. An hour or so later, they continue on. The road through the dunes becomes increasingly crowded.

By the time they pass the first houses of Walacria, it's nearly dark. The streets are filled with noise and shouting.

The hustle and bustle reminds Job of Hedeby. People greet her with a short bow and call her "brother." The houses look like the ones in Denmark: long, whitewashed buildings with straw roofs. She hears the men speaking Norwegian and Danish among themselves. Yrsa once told Job that all Viking expeditions stop in Walacria to stock up on supplies before sailing farther west across the Narrow Sea. They trade or use silver to buy bread, fish, and meat. Many try to get their hands on a Frankish sword. It's like a Danish island in Francia.

Job asks a few passersby if they know Jalke the Frisian, and they point to the river where his knarr is moored. On the deck of the freighter, Job finds the man named Jalke. He is young, barely twenty, and has cheerful eyes.

"What can I do for you, brother?" asks Jalke kindly.

"I heard that a woman asked to join you as a rower."

"Yes, that Danish girl, but she never showed up. It's too bad. I haven't found anyone else."

"She was on a Danish ship," says Job.

"Then she's probably on the island," says Jalke. "A whole Danish fleet has gathered here—at least a thousand men. The people around here can't wait for them to leave. You never know what could happen when that many savages get together. Their camp is up that way. You can see their fires from here."

Job gazes at the fires along the creek banks. It's a clear night, and the water glistens in the moonlight.

"Do you still need a rower?" asks Job.

Jalke is taken aback.

"I can row," says Job, and Jalke laughs.

"No, brother, there's no way you can row with those twiggy arms of yours."

"But I can," says Job. "And I assure you that it never hurts to have a monk on your ship."

"Listen, friend," he says. "I'm transporting a shipload of linen to Sweden. We'll be traveling for weeks."

"I understand that," says Job.

"What are you going to do in Sweden? There are no monasteries up there. Only pagans."

"That's precisely why I want to go. I must convert those pagans to God."

"Aren't you a little young to be a missionary? And aren't you afraid I'll sell you as a slave to the Swedes?"

"If you do, the Lord will curse you to the thousandth generation."

Jalke makes five signs of the cross.

"Very well, then. I do need a rower. And God's help wouldn't hurt."

He holds out his hand, and she shakes it.

"My name is Brother Job," she says.

"Welcome aboard the *Nineveh*, Brother Job," he says.

Job smiles. Nineveh is a name from the Bible.

"How far is the walk to the Danes' camp?"

35

THE SHADOWS of Danish and Norwegian warriors passing by are projected onto the side of the small tent. There are at least fifty fires burning, scattered across the sandy, creek-lined plain. Yrsa counts the masts of twenty longships. But to lay siege to a city like Paris, they need at least a hundred ships, each with a spare sail. Yrsa tries to calculate just how much sheep's wool would be needed for such a fleet, how many months of work it would take for each ship and sail, and how many slaves would be needed to do all that work. The numbers get bigger and bigger until they fall apart in her head. The only person she knows who can handle those kinds of calculations is Job.

The warriors shout and laugh around their campfires. Yrsa thinks back to the silence in the chapel, the murmur of voices, the singing.

"Why the long face?" Nokki asks.

Yrsa looks up at him, at the boy she wanted for so long. She strokes back her short hair.

"What about your oath?" she asks. "Are you going to kill me after Paris?"

"No," he says.

"And what if Gudrun asks you to? After Paris, she won't need me anymore."

"Please stop asking such stupid questions," Nokki sighs.

"Just remember: I'm the dangerous one," she says.

"That you are."

They're both silent for a moment.

"Remember, back then in the dunes," Yrsa says suddenly. "I was so sure that our fates were tied together."

He kisses her, but she no longer blushes.

"They are," Nokki says. He sets down a hunk of black bread and a wooden bowl containing two roasted goat ribs with a crispy outer crust.

"Walcheren goat. Eat it. It will be a while before we taste fresh meat again," he says. "Once we're at sea, it'll be nothing but stale biscuits and dried fish."

Suddenly, Nokki jumps to his feet with a yelp. There, standing in front of the tent, is a giant wolf. Nokki reaches for his ax in the sand.

"Odin!" Yrsa shouts in surprise.

The dog stumbles into the tent, tramples between them, and pushes his cold snout into her neck. Then he smells the bowl of meat, and before anyone can stop him he sinks his teeth into the goat ribs.

"Get out of here, you beast," Nokki roars as he tries to extract the meat from his maw. Odin clamps down hard on the ribs with his teeth and growls. His one red eye looks menacing. Nokki lets go.

"How did that fleabag get here?" he asks.

"How dare you call the Alvader a fleabag," Yrsa says with a smile, stepping out of the tent.

Odin lies down and crushes the ribs between his teeth.

Yrsa glances around, and sure enough, there is Job. She emerges from the darkness in a monk's habit, her bare head glistening in the firelight. The men outside all stare at her in amazement.

"Bless us, young brother!" shouts one, laughing.

"Got any of that holy wine with you, little man?" scoffs another.

Job ignores the men and freezes at the sight of Yrsa.

"Odin found you," she says.

"Shouldn't you be at evening prayers, brother?" asks Yrsa. Nokki comes out of the tent and lays his hands on Yrsa's shoulders.

"Is that . . . ?" he asks.

"Yes," Yrsa replies.

Job is speechless at the sight of Nokki's hands on Yrsa's shoulders. Job can't help but admire her blue dress; it looks so beautiful on her. It's held up with ornamental silver pins, and on her chest hangs a gold hammer of Thor on a string of orange beads. Her short hair is combed back to hide the tonsure, and her eyelids are tattooed with a black line illuminating her bright eyes. She is leaning on a handsomely sculpted wooden staff, the staff of a völva. She looks so Danish, so distinguished, so beautiful. The longer Job looks at Yrsa, the quicker her confidence melts away.

"Did an elf steal your tongue, nun?" Yrsa asks.

Job can't help but think that all is lost. That she fled the convent for nothing. That she's lost Yrsa for good. Her friend has returned to her boy from the dunes.

"Well?" whispers Yrsa.

Job snaps back to reality. She feels her heart pounding in her throat. Then, she just spits it out: "The day before yesterday you asked if I wanted to go with you to Mikligard."

Yrsa is stunned.

"Mikligard?" repeats Nokki in amazement.

"You remember, Yrsa? What you said about the hugr and the hamr? Well, I've shed my outer skin. I want to go to Mikligard with you. We can leave tonight with the tide."

Yrsa stares at her in shock. Then she shakes Nokki's hands off her shoulders, takes a step toward Job, and whispers, "You're not safe here."

"I persuaded Jalke the Frisian to hire me as a rower."

Yrsa can't believe it. This girl is dumber than a crab.

"No. I have seen your fate, Job. I have seen how the pilgrims will come to Ganda to kiss the hem of your habit. How they will hope that you'll look into their eyes, if only for a moment. How even the bishops will ask you to lay a hand on their heads. You'll grow old in that convent, and after you die, you'll become a saint. The convent is your destiny. You don't get to choose. The Norns do."

"Pagan nonsense!"

"But I've seen it!" Yrsa cries. "I'm a seeress!"

"The best in Denmark, according to Grandma," says Nokki.

"Stay out of this, Nokki," Yrsa snaps.

She wants to grab Job by the shoulders and shake her. She has to go back to Ganda where she belongs. She won't last an hour here in Walacria—the sharks will eat her alive. When Gudrun finds out she's here, she won't hesitate for a moment to avenge the deaths of her son and grandson. She'll rip the ax from her belt and hack Job to pieces before Yrsa can count to ten.

"Yes, you are a seeress," says Job. "But your predictions don't always come out of nowhere. I've been thinking on the way here. Take that fisherman's daughter, for instance. You might not have realized it, but you probably saw the signs of an approaching thunderstorm, like flowers closing their leaves or insects being carried off by the wind."

Yrsa thinks back to the day of her vision. Was it true? Had she seen flowers closing their leaves?

"And the story of your mother running away in the snow? You might have overheard someone talking about it as a child without understanding what it meant. The village women must've gossiped about it for years while you were asleep."

"You don't know that."

"And that Naefr and Toke wanted to toss you into the sea because of your crooked foot—deep down, you must have always suspected that. And anyone could see that Kveldulf the Norwegian wouldn't survive the winter. He was always out of breath."

"I saw more than that."

"But you can only guess other people's fates, Yrsa. You are no more chosen by your gods than I am by mine."

Yrsa doesn't know what to say. She hears the men

shouting and laughing across the dark, sandy plain. A fight breaks out around one of the fires, but no one seems to care. Yrsa still can't believe that Job has left her beloved convent.

"We can go south together," says Job.

"It's too dangerous," says Yrsa.

"We'll sail down the rivers..."

"There are rapids, waterfalls—"

"We'll cross the Inhospitable Sea..."

"But there are storms, pirates—"

"...and we'll see the Great City."

"You'll never get there alive," Yrsa concludes.

For a moment, they're silent. They're both out of breath, as if they've already made the journey.

"If I was the fortune that walked beside you, then you are mine," says Job.

"What about your calling?"

Job hesitates. She thinks of the calling she has felt since she was eleven years old. She will miss the convent. And the sisters. And the daily prayers together. And the chapel.

"You love Jesus more than life itself," Yrsa insists.

"Yes," says Job. "But I love you even more."

Yrsa stares at Job. The ridiculous things she says! She glances at Nokki. She expects him to be taken aback as well, but he just stands there grinning like a giant oaf. He seems to find the whole thing amusing.

Then the dog emerges from the tent and pushes his greasy snout into Yrsa's opulent dress. Loud laughter breaks out around one of the fires.

"Look out," says Nokki. "Here comes Gudrun."

Job glances over her shoulder and immediately spots the old woman. She's wearing expensive armor made of iron plates that overlap like the scales of a fish. Hanging on her chest is the necklace with the bishop's ring. The flames flicker in her shiny armor, as if there's a fire burning in her chest. Gudrun the Torch looks like a valkyrie.

The men in the camp stand up and greet her one by one.

Job's hands begin to tremble. Suddenly, she looks like a child in a forest full of trolls. She can't hear Gudrun's soft, crackly voice, but all the men around the fire seem to be hanging on every word the woman says.

"Get out of here. That old squid's going to kill you," Yrsa says.

Job doesn't budge. "I'm not going back to the convent."

Yrsa is getting desperate. Any moment now, Gudrun will see them and stab Job to death! She pulls Job toward her and searches for words—sharp, stinging words. "What are you, stupid? Did you think I would follow you, nun? I'm a Dane. I'm going to Paris. I'm going to be rich."

Job shakes her head. She doesn't believe her.

"And I'm going to marry Nokki," Yrsa declares.

Job stops shaking her head.

"Go away," Yrsa hisses. "The gods despise you."

Yrsa sees Egill and Birger appear behind Gudrun. They look in her direction.

"I'm not going back," Job sputters.

Yrsa knocks her on the chest with the staff. Once. Twice. Job flinches from the sudden pain.

"Go back to where you came from, brother!" Yrsa shouts.

At that, Job turns around and runs.

Yrsa watches her go. She sees her silhouette race along the river toward the market town. For a moment, her shadow is illuminated against the white smoke of a campfire, and then she disappears into the darkness.

36

"**W**HAT A STRANGE, ugly girl that nun is," Nokki says.

"Her god thinks she's beautiful," Yrsa says.

Nokki hands her a piece of bread. "Gudrun wants me to make a child with you."

"And what do you want?" asks Yrsa.

"What Gudrun wants, Gudrun gets. That's what my father always said."

"You're afraid of her."

"My father was afraid of her too. The man didn't dare to fart without asking his mother's permission first."

Yrsa grins, but suddenly, a thought strikes her—a connection between Naefr and the night Cara left the village that had eluded her until now. *What Gudrun wants, Gudrun gets.* Then Nokki brushes her cheek, and the connection is gone before she can pin it down.

"I'm not sure I really want to marry you," Yrsa says.

Nokki flashes her that ice-melting grin.

Her voice is cold, but Nokki seems undeterred.

"You loved me last winter in the dunes, didn't you?" he asks.

Nokki kisses her. His lips are soft and warm. There was a time when they were all she wanted in the world, but that feels like forever ago.

"See, nothing has changed between us," he whispers.

"One time, I dreamed that you asked me to fetch Fenrir the wolf's tail for you as a sign of my love," Yrsa says. "I immediately went out in search of the rainbow bridge. As soon as I stepped onto the bridge, my foot was no longer crooked. I had two perfectly straight ankles. I could run. *Run!* I ran all the way to Asgard, where I met Heimdal, the watchman on the other end of the bridge. His ears are so sharp that he can hear the wool growing on the backs of sheep. I asked him if he could hear whether the wolf was sleeping. Heimdal replied that the great wolf always slept when the sun was high in the sky. I thanked him and turned to leave, but then he asked what I, a girl from Midgard, was seeking in the world of the gods. I said that I came for love, and what was more important than love? Heimdal said that eventually I would pay a price. He showed me the way to Lake Amsvartnir. When I got there, I swam to the island in the lake where Fenrir had been chained for ages. The next day, when the sun was high, I snuck up behind him with my ax and chopped off the tip of his tail. Fenrir let out a howl loud enough to wake all of Asgard. I ran away. I could feel his spit on the back of my neck, but I managed to dive into the lake just in time. Then I ran all the way back to Midgard."

Nokki smiles. "What a dream!"

"But when I gave you that piece of the tail, you didn't recognize me. You were still the same, but I wasn't. I had grown old, as old as Gudrun. The journey had cost me a lifetime. That was the price I had to pay."

Nokki's hand reaches for the hammer and wolf fang hanging from his necklace. He knows that dreams always mean something.

"Well, I'm here now," he says. "You have everything you want."

Yrsa takes a bite of the bread. She chews it slowly and searches for words. Then she says, "I won't give my life away to someone who doesn't love me."

Nokki looks pained, as if he's just lost a game of dice.

"What are you going to do, Yrsa? You can't go against Gudrun's will."

Yrsa is quiet for a moment. Up ahead, at a campfire where they're still serving food, Gudrun is standing with Birger and Egill at her side.

"What an idiot!" says Yrsa. "Did you hear what Job said? That she convinced that Frisian trader to take her on as a rower? As soon as he finds out she's a woman, he's going to throw her overboard."

"Not if she's a good rower." Nokki laughs.

Yrsa walks back to the tent. Odin is lying belly up in the sand. He opens his one eye as she crouches down beside him.

"Clams for brains, that girl," Yrsa mutters, and Odin yawns.

"You know," says Nokki. "That morning in Dorestad, when you charged at us on that stallion, at our wall of shields... you were incredible. You would've sent all the trolls in Jutland running."

Yrsa doesn't answer. She remembers Dorestad and now she feels empty, like a shell on the beach. Why did Job come after her? Surrounded by her own people, Yrsa hasn't thought about her since she left. But now, she's chased Sister Job off. Suddenly, she realizes that Job left the convent to come for her, just like she came for her in Hedeby, in Dorestad, and even on that wretched sandbank in Mimir's Stool. Yrsa looks in the direction of the town. She has one thought only: to go find Job. Paris can go to hell.

"There are my grandchildren," Gudrun crows.

She stands in front of their tent. There's a youthfulness to her appearance, so it must be true what the women have been saying. Gudrun ate a golden apple from Asgard and cannot die. Every step she takes, every movement she makes, is that of a woman in the prime of her life. Even her white hair has darkened again. The armor doesn't even seem heavy to her. Egill and Birger follow her around like bodyguards. They eye Yrsa and the wolfhound at her feet suspiciously.

"How did that beast get here?" Egill demands.

"He's called Odin for a reason," says Yrsa. "The Alvader goes wherever he wants."

Egill and Birger look nervous, but Gudrun laughs.

"Rikiwulf's ships are close. They'll be here in a day or two."

"Nokki, darling?" Yrsa asks sweetly. "Will you get us some more ribs?"

Nokki shoots her a puzzled look, but then he picks up

the bowl and heads over to the campfire where they're still roasting goat meat on iron skewers.

"How are you, granddaughter?" asks Gudrun.

Suddenly, it dawns on her, that connection she was trying to figure out in her mind.

"It was you who wanted me dead," Yrsa says.

"What?"

"When I was born. It was you who said I should be killed. Not Toke. Not Naefr. Your sons didn't dare to scratch their own behinds without your permission. It was you. It's your fault my mother fled in the snow."

"Don't be silly," Gudrun laughs. "That's ridiculous."

Yrsa drops her staff and grabs her grandmother's wrists. Her nails dig deep into Gudrun's leathery skin.

"What are you doing?" Gudrun asks, startled. She tries to pull away, but Yrsa is stronger.

"Help me!" Gudrun shouts to Birger and Egill.

"Odin!" Yrsa roars, and the dog rises from the sand like Fenrir the wolf. He arches his back and eyes Egill, his old nemesis. Egill reaches for the hilt of his sword and the dog growls, gnashing his wolflike teeth. Birger takes two steps back, a safe distance from the girl who once dropped a bees' nest on his head and pounded him to a pulp in the streets of Hedeby.

"Let me go," Gudrun shrieks.

Egill doesn't dare to draw his sword at the one-eyed wolfhound before him. Yrsa pushes herself against her grandmother so that the armor cuts into her skin.

"Rikiwulf will never reach Paris. His ship will be lost in a storm," Yrsa says.

"Silence!"

"The Franks know you're coming. They, too, have spies on the shores of the Western Sea. The count is playing both sides. What were you thinking? That he wouldn't tell his father-in-law the king that you're coming? They'll be waiting for you. They're putting feathers into their arrows and sharpening their spears as we speak."

"I said silence!" Gudrun roars.

"The retreat to Denmark will take weeks. The goddess Rán will be furious. She'll send headwinds and storms at you. And you, Gudrun the Torch, will never see Mimir's Stool again."

Gudrun steps on Yrsa's good ankle. Pain shoots through her lower leg. She lets go of her grandmother's wrists and falls into the sand. Gudrun's hands clasp the bishop's ring on her necklace. Egill and Birger are frozen in place. Yrsa was bluffing; she has no idea what will happen to them. She tries to lean on her good foot but keels over in pain.

"You're lying, you insolent child!" shouts Gudrun. "You're just saying whatever pops into your head! Paris will be ours."

"I have seen your death, Gudrun," Yrsa mutters. "Here in Walacria."

Gudrun pulls the sax from its sheath. The razor-sharp warrior's blade sparkles in the moonlight.

Yrsa tries to pull herself up, but Birger seizes his chance. He charges at her and kicks her, first in the gut, then in the chest. He raises his spear and aims the tip into her neck. "Enough of your doom, Yrsa daughter of Toke," he shouts with false confidence.

But Odin sinks his jagged teeth into Birger's right calf. The boy screams and falls to the ground. Then the dog drags him through the sand like prey. Egill grabs a torch and hurls it at the animal. Odin's thick fur catches fire. The animal howls, releases Birger's bloody leg, and nips at the flames in his fur. Egill grabs his spear, ready to strike the burning dog. Odin rolls in the sand, writhing in pain.

"We'll take Paris without you," Gudrun snarls, lunging at Yrsa with the long knife. There's no escape.

Then Nokki wraps his strong arms around Gudrun's chest and shoulders.

"Run, Yrsa!" he shouts.

Gudrun is furious, but she can't free herself from Nokki's iron grip. Yrsa clambers to her feet and bears down on her good foot. Pain shoots up her thigh. Her ankle seems broken. She limps forward. Every step is torture. It's low tide, and the riverbed a few yards ahead of her has turned to mud.

Yrsa looks over her shoulder and sees Egill charging at Nokki and pushing him to the ground. Birger lies groaning beside the tent, and Odin is nowhere to be found.

Gudrun the Torch, with the light of fifty campfires burning behind her, is making her way toward her.

Yrsa leaps from the bank. She plops down in the mire and sinks up to her knees in the sticky, salty sludge. Her only chance is to reach the other side and disappear into the night. She claws her way through the sticky mud. It's slow going, but she doesn't dare look back.

At last, she reaches the running water. She throws herself

into the river, which is barely two meters wide at low tide. She plunges in headfirst. The strong, fast current drags her a couple of yards downstream. She comes to a shallow stretch and struggles to her feet. The water is up to her chest. She sees a red glow coming toward her.

She rubs her eyes, which are burning with salt. The glow is from the torch burning in Gudrun's hand. She must have followed her along the bank. Yrsa's grandmother is ankle deep in mud, panting with exhaustion. She pushes the torch into the sand. The flames dance in her shiny breastplate, in the jewels around her neck, and on the smooth, sharp blade of her knife.

Yrsa stands in the middle of the fast-flowing river. To reach her, Gudrun has to step into the water as well. "You cursed girl!" cries Gudrun, unsure of what to do next.

"Come on, you old bitch!" Yrsa roars. "Come do what you wanted to do sixteen years ago!"

Gudrun grasps the knife with both hands, holds it tip-down, and hurls herself at her granddaughter with a scream. Yrsa tries to move aside, but her grandmother's knees hit her in the chest. The razor-sharp weapon cuts through her woolen cloak and rips open her right shoulder. The salt water burns in the wound like fire. Yrsa's back hits the bottom of the river.

Gudrun tries to strike her a second time but fails. She's overtaken by the rushing water and slips in the slimy sand. The heavy armor weighs her down, making it hard for her to stand. When she finally finds her footing, she's panting with exhaustion. She wipes the salt from her eyes and looks around.

The river is empty. Yrsa is gone.

Gudrun turns around, brandishing the long knife, but there's no sign of Yrsa. She keeps spinning around, left to right. She looks down into the murky water and scans the dark banks. Everything around her is flowing, churning. Her granddaughter is nowhere to be found. Gudrun feels her feet sink deeper and deeper into the mud, but all she can think about is her cursed flint of a granddaughter. Has Yrsa been swept downstream? Did she drown? Or can she turn herself into a seal, like her stepmother? She taps her bishop's ring for a moment.

Then she hears water splashing behind her. There she is. *Yrsa.* Gudrun grins. This time, she will strike the girl with her sax. The tip of her knife will cut through wool, flesh, muscle, and bone. But as Gudrun tries to turn, she stumbles. Her feet are caught in the mire. A moment later, she feels Yrsa's weight on her back. Gudrun falls again, forward this time, hitting the water headfirst. Yrsa climbs on top of her and pushes her down as deep as she can. Only then does she let go. She regains her footing in the muddy riverbed, expecting Gudrun to burst out of the dark water in a rage. But Gudrun's clothes are soaked, and the heavy armor and silver chain around her neck weigh her down. She surfaces for a moment in the swirling current a few feet away, shouts something unintelligible, swings her sax, and goes under again. She won't let go of the knife, for she too wants a seat in Odin's Hall.

Just when Yrsa thinks she might have to swim after her grandmother and save her from drowning, someone strikes her in the head. Dizzy, she looks around and sees Egill charging at her through the water with his sword high above his head.

Only then does Yrsa notice that the sword Egill is holding is the one he forged for Njall. The unwieldy weapon she sacrificed to the goddess of the sea. The same one that Naefr held in his hand as he charged at her on horseback in Dorestad. Vengeance has found her after all, and this time it will crack her head open. *What a laugh this must be for the Norns*, Yrsa thinks, *seeing me finally defeated by this clumsy excuse for a sword.*

Suddenly, Nokki appears behind Egill, ax in hand. He smashes the side of the ax into Egill's temple, and the boy falls forward without a whimper. Nokki grabs his cloak so he won't be swept downstream.

"Get out of here!" Nokki roars.

Yrsa wriggles her feet out of the mire, letting the muck swallow her shoes, and crawls up the riverbank barefoot. Her fingers claw in the mud. Her head pounds. She struggles forward. Her shoulder burns. She crawls through the heath and looks back. Nokki is dragging the unconscious Egill to the bank. The sword Vengeance slowly sinks into the mud.

Gudrun has disappeared without a trace, swept away by the tide.

Only when the fires of the camp seem far enough away, and she's sure no one is coming after her, does Yrsa stop crawling. She lies on her back in the sand and slowly catches her breath. When she tries to get up, she falls down again with a scream. Her good ankle is purple and swollen. Blood still flows from her shoulder. *What now, Frigg*, she thinks. *What now?* She scans her surroundings, looking for a sign. But nothing comes.

"Get up," she mutters to herself, but she stays down. She can't go on. She thinks back to that day on Heath Ridge. How, that day too, she found herself lying in the sand among the scraggly heather bushes and dead crabs. How she thought her fate was unfolding before her eyes. She can hear the seagulls screeching overhead as she gazes up at the stars, like sparks from the world of fire. This is it. She won't rise again.

Until she hears Job's voice calling out to her.

"Stand up!"

37

JALKE THE FRISIAN CAN'T SLEEP. He watches over his cargo by the light of an oil lamp. Job sits down on the bank.

"Did you find the young Danish woman?" he asks.

Job nods.

"So, are you still going to Sweden?"

Job shrugs. He's the saddest monk that Jalke has ever seen.

"Are you in love with her beautiful eyes, brother?"

Job doesn't answer. There's a lump the size of a boulder in her throat. She grips the cross between her fingers, but she's too tired for Hail Marys.

"You know, brother, you can decide later. Go get some sleep with the men."

He points to a hay barn where three men are lying. Job is asleep before she even feels the hay on her cheek.

She's awakened before sunrise by one of the rowers. It's still dark, but a new day is dawning. Jalke brings her bread and a cup of milk.

"Your dog is back," he says.

Odin tramples over to greet her. She hugs the animal so hard he falls over while licking her hands. He smells like burnt hair. His entire back is scorched, as if he rolled through a campfire. Job gets up, pees in a ditch behind the barn, and heads for the ship. The dog remains faithfully at her side.

"So, what'll it be, brother? Are you coming with us or not?" asks Jalke.

Job doesn't know. She now realizes what a crazy idea it was—to try to sail all the way to Sweden disguised as a man.

Yrsa saw her future. She belongs with her sisters in Ganda.

She shakes her head. No, she can't go with Jalke.

Then Odin jumps on deck. He trots past the rowers to the bow and sticks his nose into the wind, as if he can't wait to hit the open sea. Job can only think one thing: it's a good omen. She prays a Hail Mary with the cross between her fingers and climbs aboard.

The ship leaves at first light. Jalke the Helmsman keeps an eye on the bow and makes sure the freighter stays in the middle of the river with the current. He knows where the sandbars are. The ship is fully loaded, and if it were to get stuck in the sand, he and his four rowers would have a hard time getting it out. He keeps one eye on the river and the other on his new recruit, making sure the little monk is keeping up with the others. The vessel glides silently down the river. The birds on the banks don't even look up when they hear the rhythmic splashing of the oars.

The cargo is stored in the belly of the ship, and the food for the journey is kept between the men in sealed barrels. They know they're carrying precious goods: fine linens, dyed in the most beautiful colors. Each pile is carefully wrapped in leather. The entire load is covered in an old Danish sail that has been rubbed with tree tar, animal fat, and fish oil. A faint image of a deer is still visible on it. The sail is covered in patches, and the weave is frayed at the edges. If Yrsa were here, she'd want to repair it properly, Job thinks. She'd say it was nothing, just a few weeks of sewing, braiding, and tying knots. *When I'm done with it, there won't be so much as a loose thread*, she'd exclaim. *Those knots will hold up in any storm.*

For a moment, Job can't breathe. Her arms tremble at the thought that she might never see Yrsa again.

Job thinks about the world she's leaving behind—her sisters in the convent, the monks in their writing chamber, her father the count, who rang the bells a little longer this summer so everyone would know that his lost daughter had returned. What is she doing rowing out to sea?

She looks to Odin for courage. The animal is lying comfortably with his head on a lump in the cargo, as if it's his personal duty to protect it. Job concentrates on rowing. On the oar in her hands. The movements of her arms. The splashes in the water. It reminds her of the day she and Yrsa fled Mimir's Stool, and how afraid she was of falling over the horizon.

"Pull in!" cries Jalke, and Job pulls her oar out of the water. They glide past a sandbar in the middle of the river.

"Row," Jalke orders, and they lower their oars back into the water. The boat glides forward again.

With every stroke, she feels the cross beat against her chest, the wind on her cheeks. She smiles at the thought of sailing the open seas again, of being on the move.

"Pull in!" shouts Jalke again.

The freighter slows down. On the shore are three Danish warriors checking cargo. Jalke raises his hand to greet them, and they drift slowly past the men. The Danes scan the cargo and the rowers on deck.

"What are you carrying?" one of them asks.

"Cloth!" cries Jalke the Frisian.

"Where to?"

"Birka, Sweden," replies Jalke.

"Have you seen a Danish girl around here? Walking with a limp?"

Job feels her heart pounding. She stares at Jalke, who's standing at the tiller.

"No, haven't seen her," he says.

One of the Danes seems to be considering whether they should board the ship and lift the old sail to have a look at the cargo underneath, but just then Odin stands up. The wind tugs at his thick coat. He glares at the three men with his one eye.

"Good sailing, Frisian," the Dane finally says, and Jalke thanks him with a nod of the head. They drop their oars back into the water. Odin looks out across the flat landscape of creeks, dunes, and brush. Then he lies back down and lays his head on the exact same lump of cargo.

Job studies the bulbous shape under the old sail. Has it moved since they left? Could that be Yrsa under the canvas? Could she be hiding among the expensive sheets? Is she just waiting for them to reach open water so she can come out, stretch her arms and legs, and gaze out at the horizon as if it belongs to her and her alone? Would she then turn to Job and smile, and take her into her arms?

"Brother," Jalke shouts. "Keep up!"

Job turns red, looks forward, and mutters an apology. If Yrsa were on board, Jalke would know. He sleeps with his cargo to make sure nothing gets stolen.

They've almost reached the sea, but Job doesn't look at the waves. She keeps her eyes on the helmsman and the land, on the river as it churns and widens, the water foaming beneath them.

She feels the pull of open water and the sea breeze blowing against her neck. Her cheeks tingle. The smell of salt fills her nose, her lungs, her head. She's no longer afraid of sea monsters. The first time she sailed with Yrsa, she felt so small, so worthless, so lost. She held on to the tiller for dear life while Yrsa caught the wind with the sail.

"It's not the monsters we should be worried about!" Yrsa had shouted at her.

"Pull in," the helmsman roars. The rowers lift their oars out of the water. Job's arms shake with fatigue. She's been rowing for hours. Her wet shirt sticks to her back. The freighter rocks up and down on the surf. Past the stern, the waves roll toward the beach, and the dunes and creeks of Flanders beyond.

"The sail!" cries the helmsman.

The two rowers at the bow stand up. They untie the knots around the sail. The ship bobs up and down.

"Keep it perpendicular to the waves!" Jalke commands. Job and the other oarsman put their oars in the water so the ship won't drift. Job feels the water splashing on her cheeks. She tastes the salt on her lips.

The two men hoist the yard and tie it to the bow and stern with a rope. The sail beats and flaps. The men push the ropes through the rigging blocks and pull. The sail tightens and catches the wind. The *Nineveh* slices through the waves.

Job lays her arms on top of the oar and rests her head. She thinks of Yrsa. Memories wash over her like waves on the beach. She looks over at Odin, who is still lying with his head on the same lump in the cargo.

Again Job wonders if it's moved. Is that Yrsa's shoulder? Has she changed position? Is she lying there under that cloth? Job bites down on her lip until she tastes blood in her mouth. *Don't be stupid*, she thinks. *This is the life you want. You've made your choice, and you can do it on your own. You're a pilgrim on your way to Mikligard. There's no way Yrsa is hiding under that dirty old sail.*

Odin stands up to scratch. His hind paw gets caught in his matted fur, and he falls against the cargo.

The lump definitely moves. The rowers all laugh. Odin glares at the men with his one eye. Job's eyes begin to burn.

"You all right there, Brother Job?" asks Jalke.

"It's just the wind," she says, but it's so much more than that. Tears stream down her face. She misses Yrsa so much she can't stop shaking.

"Will you bless the ship, brother?" Jalke asks. "For a safe voyage."

Job wipes the tears away. Her fellow rowers stand up. They cross their hands and bow their heads. Job makes the sign of the cross, and the men follow suit. Job asks the Lord to grant them a safe passage, to protect them from storms, monsters, and pirates, and to bring them safely to Sweden. "Amen," she whispers, and they all repeat it.

The men sit back down. Odin lays his snout back on the lump in the cloth. What if it's just a barrel of water or a package of dried meat or fish for the journey? What if Yrsa isn't there after all? What if Job never sees her again? If there's no one under that sail, then she'll have to take comfort in the sea.

Suddenly, she hears honking overhead. It's a flock of geese flying up from the south. All the men gaze up at the giant birds floating on the wind as they skim over the ship. They're flying so low that Job can hear the flapping of their wings.

"There's a lot of them," says one of the rowers.

Job counts nine. It's an omen. A great omen. She can hardly suppress a smile. Soon, she will stand up, loosen the knots, and lift the cloth. Soon. All of a sudden, she's sure it's Yrsa under that sail. It has to be. This is the gods' way of telling her.

GLOSSARY

ÁLFAR: elves, supernatural beings in Scandinavian mythology.

ASGARD: the world of the gods.

BALDR: the unlucky son of Odin and Frigg.

BIRKA: a town on the island of Björkö, Sweden; now an archaeological site.

BREEM: Bremen, Germany.

DIEPE (OLD DANISH FOR "DEEP"): Dieppe, in northern France.

DORESTAD: the town of Wijk bij Duurstede, the Netherlands.

FENRIR: the giant wolf chained in Asgard.

FRIGG: the goddess who gives advice; Friday is named after her.

FRISIA: Friesland, part of the present-day Netherlands.

GANDA (CELTIC FOR "ESTUARY"): Ghent, Belgium.

HAMINGJA: the fortune that can abandon a person at any moment.

HAMMABURG: Hamburg, Germany.

HAMR: one's outward appearance; the human shell.

HAVN (OLD DANISH FOR "PORT"): present-day Le Havre, France.

HEATH SEA: known today as the Western Scheldt. In the ninth century, a wide estuary of gullies, mud flats, and salt marshes that was fordable at low tide.

HEDEBY (OLD DANISH FOR "MOORLAND SETTLEMENT"): in German, this city was called Haithabu. The other name for the site was Schleswig, the wic, or the trading port on the Schlejfjord. The city of Schleswig still exists today as the relocated trading town; once part of Denmark, it's now part of Germany.

HEL: the goddess of the underworld.

HUGR: the absolute essence of a person; who one really is; one's insides. Hugr is not unlike the concepts of the soul and the mind.

INHOSPITABLE SEA: the Black Sea.

JÓL: a pagan winter feast observed by Nordic peoples (sometimes spelled Jul). Its traditions were mixed with Christmas when Denmark was Christianized in the eleventh century.

JORMUNDGANDR: the giant snake that holds the human world together.

JOTUNNHEIM: the world of giants.

JUTLAND: the northern European peninsula that forms the continental portion of Denmark.

KARVE: a light cargo ship.

KNARR: a cargo ship with a wide, deep hull that was shorter than a longship and could be operated by smaller crews.

LOKI: the jealous god, and the father/mother of Jormundgandr, Sleipnir, and Fenrir.

MIDGARD: the human world.

MIKLIGARD: the city of Istanbul, which was known as Constantinople until 1928. In the ninth century it was the largest city in the Western world and the capital of the Eastern Roman Empire.

MIMIR: the reverie; the wise giant.

MUSPELHEIM: the world of fire.

NARROW SEA: the English Channel, the strait between Britain and France.

NIFLHEIM: the world of the dead.

NORNS: deities in Norse mythology who shape the course of human destinies.

ODIN: the father of the gods; also known as Wodan or Wotan. Wednesday is named after him.

ODINSVÉ (LITERALLY "SANCTUARY OF ODIN"): Odense, Denmark.

PAGUS FLANDRENSIS (LITERALLY "THE FLOODED AREA"): the "Flanders area," part of present-day West and East Flanders in Belgium.

RAGNAROK: the fate/fall of the gods.

RÁN: the goddess of the sea, wife of the giant Aegir.

SLEIPNIR: Odin's eight-legged stallion.

THOR: the god of protection; Thursday is named after him.

TYR: the god of war; Tuesday is named after him.

VALHÖLL: the hall of Odin in Asgard; the term "valhalla" is from the nineteenth century.

VALKYRIE: the grim corpse collectors of Odin; during the German Romantic period they became known as *Walkuren.*

VIKING VOYAGE: originally a journey along the vici (Latin for "markets"); the term "viking" is probably derived from this word.

VÖLVA: a seeress.

WALACRIA: Domburg, the Netherlands.

WESTERN SEA: the Danish term for the North Sea, which stretches from the west of Denmark to the tip of Brittany (France).

YGGDRASIL: the world tree connecting the nine worlds; a yew or vine tree. In Old Danish, it is called "the evergreen tree."

ACKNOWLEDGMENTS

Writing this book was a fascinating journey into the world of the ninth century. Archaeologists Dries Tys (Belgium) and Adam Bak (Denmark) pointed me in the right direction, and I am indebted to Neil Price, author of *Children of Ash and Elm*, for helping me understand the Viking mind. Some of the definitions in the glossary are his. My editors, Belle Kuijken (Belgium) and Irene Vázquez (U.S.), were wonderfully demanding; translator Kristen Gehrman made my sentences sing in English. Thanks go as well to Tyler Darnell for his insightful notes and to Flanders Literature for promoting my novels. Wende Wilbers and Arthur Levine, my publishers, put my stories into the world. Finally, I thank my wife and reader, Virginie Oltmans, and my children, who inspire me and from whom I learn every day.

SOME NOTES ON THIS BOOK'S PRODUCTION

The art for the jacket was created digitally by Matt Roeser in Adobe Photoshop using various stock elements. He was inspired by the strength of the two main female characters and wanted the jacket to feel like an old image that could have been painted in blood. The endpaper map was drawn by Irene Van Ryckeghem. The text and display were set by Westchester Publishing Services, in Danbury, CT, in Broadsheet, Baskerville, and Bell. The book was printed on 78 gsm Yunshidai Ivory uncoated woodfree FSC™-certified paper and bound in China.

Production supervised by Freesia Blizard
Book interiors designed by Christine Kettner
Editor: Irene Vázquez
Managing editor: Trent Duffy